Solitary Cove

Written by: Cathy Walker

To Fabienne
all the Best

Cathy Walker

Review

Solitary Cove is a Winner! If you love fast-paced romantic suspense novels peopled with characters you'll cheer for, SOLITARY COVE is the book for you. A seaside village in Nova Scotia, a movie hero with a daughter he barely knows, and a woman on the run from danger equal the perfect formula for a terrific read. Cathy Walker has a winner on her hands!

USA Today Bestselling Author Barbara Bretton

***

Chapter One

N icole's old life had ended with a bullet. Her new one started with the throw of a dart. Keeping it as simple as that, as simple as black and white, kept her from thinking too much about the gray areas. Or the pain. Unfortunately, it didn't keep the nightmares at bay.

Still feeling weak from last night's nightmare, Nicole gave a sigh, sipped her tea, and raised her face to the warm touch of the sun. Morning from the deck of her lighthouse was amazing. The Atlantic Ocean glowed with the sun's gold and orange hues, while the gentle breeze rippled the water in lazy waves.

She turned to look at her new home. A small, rectangular house that boasted gently arched windows of leaded glass and a lighthouse tower that connected directly to the house rather than being a separate tower. Melding together, the keeper's house and tower symbolized the union of man and light that had saved many storm-bound ships over the decades. Colors of white and cherry-red accented both house and tower, while an ancient Fresno light that had once signaled to the mariners of long ago sat atop the tower.

The peace of the place calmed her. Solitary Cove. Her husband's shocking murder four months ago, and his killer's threat, had set Nicole on a course, and though she was sorry for the circumstances, she couldn't regret finding such a beautiful place to live.

A worried whine reminded her that she wasn't alone and she tore her gaze from the ocean. Her dog, Sumo, lay at her feet, massive head resting on his paws as his liquid brown eyes stared adoringly at her. Laughing, Nicole leaned over and rubbed the rottweiler behind his ears. After Jeff's death, she'd made a trip to the humane society and picked up the fiercest looking dog she could find. Sumo. It turned out he wasn't fierce at all, just a big suck. Although when she'd researched the breed, she'd found that rottie's had territorial tendencies that could cause them to become very protective of what or who they considered theirs.

She hoped that was true, but in the meantime, he was a great companion. Unfortunately, even Sumo's attention couldn't make up for the loss of her husband, or the guilt she felt. The guilt that ate at her day and night and was probably the cause of her nightmares. She assumed that's what a therapist would tell her anyway.

Sinking into a deck chair, Nicole rested her hand on Sumo's head. "Damn, what do I have to feel guilty about?"

Sumo stared at her with his unblinking gaze.

"I know, I know. He died trying to save me. He died because of me, and I'll never be able to forget that." Her words ended with a strangled sigh.

She sipped her tea and forced herself to breathe deeply. The police had been helpful after Jeff's death, even making a point of sending a patrol car past her house on a regular basis. Unfortunately, they hadn't been able to find out much about the threatening letters that started showing up in her mailbox. Letters from her husband's murderer demanding she give back what belonged to him.

She'd feared for her life. Threats, combined with nightmares of the killer's hot breath on her neck when he'd jammed the gun into her side and demanded his due or she was next, were enough to make Nicole flee. She'd put the house on the market and sorted through her belongings, but hadn't felt strong enough to go through Jeff's stuff, so she'd packed it all in boxes. She sold all the furniture, closed her bank account, and paid the bills.

Finally, she was ready.

Having always had a yearning for the east coast, she did

something foreign to her character, something that Jeff would have scoffed at as an immature, useless act. She threw a dart at a map, with the intent that wherever the dart landed, was where she would head.

The dart headed straight and true to Solitary Cove, a small town on the northeastern coast of Nova Scotia. This was her home now, due to the blindly thrown dart. Home, as long as her stalker didn't find her.

***

Ian Calder watched his date wriggle her shapely rear down the dimly lit garden path to the taxi. With a snap of her shawl and a backward glance of disgust, she folded her long legs into the cab and slammed the door. Ian grimaced, but wasn't surprised at her hasty and heated departure. Once again, he'd managed to disappoint. It was embarrassing that he had no interest in sex anymore. Well, he was interested, but a certain part of his anatomy had a mind of its own.

He sighed and went back inside his glass mansion resting on the sandy dunes of Malibu Beach. Staring out the patio doors at the breathtaking view of the Pacific, he considered his life of luxury; rich beyond most people's belief and everywhere he went women gravitated to him. What more could a sane person want? Ian decided he mustn't be very sane, because he wasn't happy. His date that night had been the last in a line of empty headed, money grasping starlets, looking for entry into the after parties. He labeled them the three B's: Beautiful. Brainless. Bimbo. Until now, he'd been fine with the concept. A service for a service.

He threw a pillow across the living room and sent a pile of scripts scattering from the table to the floor. Damn, he'd almost forgotten about their existence. His agent, Gibney, was waiting for Ian to choose between the three of them.

Pick whichever one you want, just pick something.

Gibney was of the firm belief that taking a break between

movies was hazardous to a career, not to mention his bank account, and it had been six months since Ian had completed his last film. An action film of course, because that's what he did best.

As if thought produced action, the shattering ring of the phone cut through the empty house. Not feeling social, but seeing Gibney's number on the call display, Ian sighed and answered the phone.

"Hey, Gibney."

"Hey, Ian. How's it going, my main man?"

"Don't bother with the flattery. I know why you're calling."

"Ian, I'm hurt. I'm calling because I care about you. Of course, I'm also wondering if you've decided on a script yet. It's been over a month since I sent them to you."

Ian sighed. "Yeah, I know." He'd read the scripts and felt no stirring of his acting juices when he'd read the first two, *Blast Away* and *Stars, Stripes, and Guns*. That had left, *Weekend in New England*, a tale of bittersweet love and longing about a famous rock star who meets and falls in love with a woman in a small New England town. When obligations call him back to the big city and the pressures of being famous, the woman refuses to uproot the life she loves and move to the city.

Ian had read the entire script in two hours, and when he'd finished, his eyes were misty. Powerful stuff for sure, although he had doubts that any woman would refuse to give up jeans and obscurity for pearls and the big city. He also had doubts about playing the part. He didn't have a romantic bone in his entire body—never had. At the best of times, he was grumpy and slightly self-centered.

"Ian. You still there?"

"Yeah." In an impulsive act he'd likely regret, he stated. "I've decided to do *Weekend in New England*."

Gibney's laughter echoed over the phone. "You're kidding. I only sent that one as a joke. Come on, Ian. It's too late to play games. Which one is it?"

"I told you. *Weekend in New England*."

"Ian, they're filming that in some place called Solitary Cove, a piss ant town located on the coast in Canada somewhere. You know, to keep costs down. You'd hate it there."

"Sounds like my kind of place. Send the contract over. I'll be waiting."

"You're serious, aren't you?"

"Gibney, I'm too old to keep bouncing off walls, chasing down bad guys, and roaring around in speeding cars."

In a voice rift with uncertainty and a hint of fear, Gibney cajoled, "Come on, Ian, think about Sean Connery and Harrison Ford. Great actors, both of them older than you, but they keep churning out the action films and turning the women to jelly."

"Sean and Harrison are...well, Sean and Harrison. Who am I to think I can compete with them? Besides, it's time to expand my acting horizons and this script will test my abilities. It's just what I'm looking for."

"Just what you're looking for? Ian, are you feeling all right?"

A simple enough question, but one not easily answered. People looked at him as a hero, an icon of masculine strength and fortitude. How did he tell someone that he was lonely? His daughter was married and didn't need him. He owned no pets because he'd never gotten around to replacing his dog, Jasper. After the German shepherd had drowned, Ian decided that owning pets was too painful. Work was the only thing left in his life. Impatience and loneliness mingled together in Ian's gut and he spoke sharper than intended.

"Just get things rolling, would you."

The sound of whispering voices came over the phone. Ian recognized Gibney's wife's voice. "Say hi to Jan for me."

There was a moment of shuffling and then Jan spoke. "Say hi to me yourself. Are you serious? You're going to do the romance?"

"I am."

"Good for you. I think you'll do a wonderful job."

Ian snorted.

"Really. You have depths that you don't even realize. I know

Gibney doesn't agree with me, and that's a reason you should have me as your agent, not him. I believe in you."

Before Ian could respond to Jan's attempt at winning him into her line-up of stars, Gibney was back on the phone. "Don't listen to her."

"You mean you don't think I can do it."

"No. Yes. I mean, don't let her sweet talk you away from me. I believe in you, big guy. I know you can do anything you set your mind to, but I want you to realize what you're letting yourself in for. It's a small town, which means no five star hotels, no hot tubs, no top of the line restaurants, no starlets chasing you all over."

"Good. That settles it."

"Oh. I see."

"No. You don't see." Ian didn't want to get any more personal, so he decided it was time to end the conversation. "Just make the call or whatever you have to do to get me in the movie."

"Are you absolutely sure? For God's sake, Ian, you're only fifty-one. You've spent thirty years building your screen image. I can't believe you'd want to throw it all in a thoughtless move that might ruin your career."

Only fifty-one. Spoken with the guile of youth. Sure, he was fifty-one, but he looked forty-one. Maybe younger. Ian knew he wasn't classically handsome, but people told him that he had charisma, and an aura that attracted and overpowered. He flexed his chest muscles to make sure he still could. Yep! Nothing wrong with him. Until he looked lower. Down to the culprit that was causing him all this grief and self-doubt.

"You rotten little bugger. After all I've done for you, this is how you repay me," he muttered at the offending organ.

"What. Did you say something, Ian?"

"No. Please, Gibney, just do as I ask."

"Please. *Please.* Now I know there's something wrong. Are you feeling all right? I mean, you haven't started taking drugs have you?"

"I'm feeling fine, and, no, I'm not on drugs."

"Okay. If your mind's set on this, then I'll make the arrangements.

"Good. Talk to you later." Elation and dread weighed heavy in Ian's chest, and he hoped he hadn't misplaced his trust in the loyalty of a fickle public. He also hoped he could spend two or three months in some small town in the middle of nowhere without going crazy.

Chapter Two

I n town to run a few errands, Nicole stood on the dock's edge and reveled in the salty breeze that blew in from the Atlantic Ocean. Like a lover's hand, the breeze played with her mahogany hair, displaying the silken strands in a dance of nature. She inhaled. Briny scents from the fish market mingled with aromatic scents from the local candle store, and her nostrils quivered. Scents that defined the day. One of the best things about Solitary Cove. Monday's scent was cinnamon from the bakery, Friday was candyfloss from the local candy store preparing for the weekend tourists, Saturday morning was fish as the fishermen brought in their catch and set them up for sale.

For the first time in a while, Nicole believed she could have her life back. The atmosphere of this small town imbued a person with hope and helped wash away the ever-constant sense of fear. She loved the general store, quaint bed and breakfast on the edge of town, and the lack of rush hour traffic. Heck, she even loved the noisy seagulls that haunted the coastal village. The waves slapping the shore and beating against the dock hypnotized her, and she felt her shoulders relax for the first time since she'd awakened from her nightmare a short while ago.

With a smile, she snapped her fingers to recall a wandering Sumo and strolled over to *Wishes*, the local New Age store. Small and cozy, the storefront faced the main street while the back boasted a bay window and a door that opened to the docks. Knowing Sumo would be welcome, Nicole opened the back door for him and entered the quirky store. Everything from fresh flowers to tarot cards, chocolates, candles, herbs, crystals, delicate faerie figurines, and books filled the store. If Josephine, the owner, didn't have it, she ordered it. And if a customer needed something more spiritual, she guided them in her own subtle manner.

Nicole felt safe with Josephine. And she hadn't felt safe in a while.

"Good morning, you two." Josephine's face lit with a welcoming smile as she reached under the counter to retrieve a dog treat. Sumo sat expectantly and grabbed the treat from the air with expertise that showed familiarity with the routine. "I'll be right with you as soon as I serve these customers."

Nicole envied the ease with which Josephine dealt with her customers. Her breezy air and caring attitude helped people relax; even the ones who entered her store warily or inclined to find fault. Ringing up a sale and patting the young woman's hand, Josephine exuded comfort and reassurance. The same qualities that had drawn Nicole to her when first they met. The day Nicole moved her things in, she'd found the store owner stocking the fridge for her.

Even with the difference in their ages, they had hit it off. Nicole envied the confidence of the older woman and enjoyed spending time in her company on a regular basis.

"You love doing this, don't you?" Nicole smiled at Josephine, who closed the door behind her latest customer with a sigh.

"Of course I do. I wouldn't do it otherwise. Besides," she ran a hand lovingly over the smooth but worn wooden countertop, "I spent a lifetime searching before I came to this town. I felt a sense of belonging as soon as I drove my decrepit car down the main street. Well.part way down the street before it died on me. I took that as a sign that this was as far as I was going. This is where I belong." She laughed. "Not to mention the years I spent eating bologna sandwiches and Kraft dinners saving up for this place, and then there's the hours of sanding, varnishing, painting, and decorating involved." She rolled her eyes.

"Don't even get me started on that."

Nicole laughed. "For some reason, I thought you'd been born here."

"Gosh, no, I found Solitary Cove quite by accident. The place, and the people here, saved me."

"Saved you?"

"From oblivion. A lifetime spent in a job I hated, wondering what more there was to life."

"Oh." Nicole's throat tightened. Her problem wasn't quite so simple.

"So, what brings you two wanderers to my humble store?"

"I need something to read, and you know there's nowhere else in town with your eclectic taste in books."

Josephine's laugh lit up her usually plain, somewhat plump features. "That's one way to put it. Others in town have said worse."

Nicole noticed the shadow that briefly crossed Josephine's face and she sympathized with her friend. "You wouldn't be talking about a curmudgeonly old coot we both know, would you?"

With a snuffling snort, Josephine flicked her wrist. "I'm sure I have no idea who you're talking about."

"Well, the person that 'you have no idea who I'm talking about,' just walked over to the cemetery." The front window gave a great view of the local cemetery across the street where, currently, the object of their conversation hobbled over to a gravestone and laid down a bouquet of red roses.

Josephine's face softened, and a sad smile curved her lips. "Yes. His yearly visit to his wife's grave. Anyway," she slapped a palm on the counter. "No sense mooning over what's not to be. I have stock to unpack and customers to serve."

"Josephine." Nicole reached out a hand.

"No. It's fine. I'm fine. Really. Now, why don't you take that mutt of yours and go say hi to Jacob. I'm sure he'd love to see you both."

Nicole knew that was Josephine's roundabout way of making sure Jacob was okay, without going over there herself and intruding on a private moment. After all, it might be awkward consoling a man you had an interest in, over his dead wife's grave.

"Sure. We'll go over." She snapped her fingers. "Come on, Sumo."

***

Josephine watched them go and wished she was going instead. Bah! With an effort, she looked away from the man she had come to love and turned her attention to her store. She did love it here. Her life was complete. Almost. A true believer in destiny, Josephine knew she and Jacob belonged together. The cards told her that simply enough. Why was he so thick headed that he couldn't see that? She sighed. She'd helped so many people, why in blazes couldn't she help herself? Oh, well, no time to dwell. She had customers. At that moment, there were four or five people perusing the store, and they all looked to be holding their own. Her glance roamed over each of them as she played her guessing game.

The couple in the corner looked to be fairly well off, probably from inland somewhere, as they seemed so much in awe of the ocean view out the store's bay window. Married for sure, as they each wore a wedding ring. To each other? Maybe. These days it was hard to tell.

Her gaze wandered to the tall man in the corner. He looked uptight. Must be the tarot cards on display or maybe the mini pentagram pendants hanging on the counter. He was curious, but had the looks of a strict religious upbringing. He probably believed that evil walked in this store. She smiled and tagged him for a minister of sorts.

The next man was easy. He was that big name movie actor. Almost handsome and formidable at the same time, his aura powerful but unsettled. Definitely a soul in search of himself. Look out, because when he found himself, there'd be no holding him back. He was hiding in a corner, probably afraid of being recognized. He'd relax soon enough in the quiet surroundings of Solitary Cove.

The last customer was the hardest to figure out, and Josephine wasn't sure she wanted to try. His energy choked her. He was average build, average looks, average coloring; there was nothing about him to make her cringe. Yet, she did. At that moment, something on the street distracted him. It was too early for much to be going on, and Josephine tried to get a look at what drew his attention. All she could see were Jacob and Nicole entering the cemetery.

The stranger turned to her and their eyes connected. Black eyes stared through Josephine as if she didn't exist. Suddenly, there was nothing average about him. He became the culmination of all her nightmares. With a jerk, he tore his gaze from hers, ducked his head, and ran from the store.

"Strange guy."

Josephine jumped at the deep voice so close to her ear. It was the actor. "Yes, he gave me the willies." A shiver punctuated her words.

"Is he a local?"

"No. Thank goodness."

"Not to worry then, he's probably just passing through." The actor held up some candles. "I'll take these."

Josephine frowned. "Are you sure?" He had chosen her most powerful love candles. Packed with dried roses and rose incense, they would ensure a powerful evening of romance and love.

"Yes, I'm sure. Shouldn't I be?"

Josephine had read the man's energy and love wasn't in the picture. She sensed that it hadn't been for a long time. There was no Mrs. Big Actor, and if he lit those candles around the wrong person.well, she didn't want to be the one responsible for what might happen.

"It's just that those aren't our most popular candles. Here, let me show you a couple of others better suited for your needs."

Josephine took a couple of steps forward, and then realized the actor hadn't moved. She turned to meet the full force of his rather arrogant, albeit confused glare.

"I'd like these. Thank you."

His tone was final. His voice demanding. Josephine had no choice but to give in. She was in business to make money, after all. She rang up the sale and wrapped the candles, all the while trying to understand her conflicting feelings for the actor. She sensed arrogance balanced by a lack of confidence. No, that couldn't be right. She shook her head and sighed, garnering a strange look from the actor.

"Sorry, my mind tends to wander and the next thing you know, I'm talking to myself. Happens all the time. Folks around here get used to me, but I tend to worry tourists somewhat."

Satisfied with the explanation, the actor thanked her and left the store. Josephine watched him stride up the street to the *Wyllow Wood Inn*.

Must be nice to have money. Accommodations at the *Wyllow Wood* were far beyond her budget, but then she wasn't a big name actor. What was his name anyway? Darned if she could remember.

***

Ian left the store, his mind intent on running through his lines from the movie script until the beeping horn of a passing car jarred him from his memorization work. It seemed that everything made him jump these days. When had he become so stressed? Used to people following him around and constant commotion, the peacefulness of this place seemed eerie. The extreme difference jarred him, and it had only been two days.

Once he'd signed his contract and found out the shooting schedule, he had decided to show up in town a week before the crew. He needed to unwind and have time to realign his acting techniques and shift his thinking so he could act a romantic role rather than action.

A church bell sounded in the distance, drawing Ian from his reverie. The deep bellow of a foghorn drifted lazily over the rolling waves of the ocean, and the bustle of early day activity echoed through the main street. Ian enjoyed perusing the shops with their unique window displays. Simple and obviously put together by the store owners themselves, the unpretentious displays attracted him in a way the elaborate designs in Hollywood stores never had. He took a moment to wonder how the townspeople would react when the movie crew came into town and did their usual makeover. Chaos would rule and nothing would look the same.

He stepped onto the cobbled stone walkway that wound to the front door of the *Wyllow Wood Inn*. Built in 1822, the inn retained its original exterior, which was a beautiful, graceful combination of fieldstone and accents of wood. Rising from a grassy knoll, the main building reached four stories high and then gave way to finely etched gables and delicately designed gingerbread latticework.

Across from the inn, the morning sun rose above the cemetery gates, etching shadows in the ancient stone and reflecting colors of rose and silver. The rod iron gates stood open to receive visitors to the hallowed grounds, and Ian's gaze followed the pebbled pathway to the only two occupants of the cemetery. The man kneeling by the gravestone was only about ten years older than he was, but the harshness of life etched in the man's face made him look older.

Even from where he stood, Ian saw the pain that flitted briefly across the wrinkled face. Sparse wisps of gray hair brushed across a furrowed brow, and his lips were set in a harsh line of grief. Once handsome, the man wore the age of time like a banner. The ocean and sun had leant a hand in forming his features as well. That was obvious in the leathery tanned skin and squinting eyes of a fisherman forced to spend his days in the glaring sun and water.

The woman leaned down to speak to the man, and her

words created a transformation that Ian wouldn't have believed if he hadn't of seen it with his own eyes. The man smiled. It grew slowly from a twitch of his lips to a full-blown smile and then softened his eyes into a twinkle of subtle joy.

The woman at his side captured Ian's attention. Dressed in jeans and a copper shaded tee shirt, she was beauty itself in the form of a slender woman with fawn colored eyes and mahogany hair. Ian's breath caught in his chest. Did she have any idea that the sun shone in her hair and created rich shades of brown and gold? She leaned forward and a strand of her hair brushed against smiling lips meant for kissing. Ian's heart skipped a beat when her fingers gently moved the hair aside and then settled on the man's shoulder in a gesture of comfort.

Were they a couple? No, the man kneeling by the grave was too old for her. Which also meant that Ian was too old for her.

Come on, get real. You're here to film a movie, nothing more, nothing less.

Tearing his gaze from the couple in the cemetery, Ian tucked the bag of candles under his arm and entered the doors of the *Wyllow Wood Inn*, deciding he'd try to spend some time reading, a pursuit in which he didn't usually have time to indulge.

Chapter Three

Another beautiful day. Nicole turned off her laptop and stretched her stiff muscles, all the while wondering how Jacob was doing. He'd seemed calm enough yesterday morning at the cemetery, but she had a feeling that the man harbored deep emotions that he never allowed to the surface. She decided to call later to make sure he was okay.

Leaning forward in her lounger, she poured herself some ice tea and wondered if she should spend more time writing or go for a walk. Surprisingly enough, she'd been able to knock off two chapters in one afternoon. She attributed the spurt of creativity to the relaxing atmosphere of her surroundings.

Rocky cliffs riddled with caves and barely-there pathways gradually dipped toward the cold Atlantic ocean, while the lighthouse, a beacon of times gone past and memories faded yet not forgotten, rose up from a smooth rock ledge bordered by the ocean to the east and a thick forest in all other directions. Built with the dual purpose of home as well as lantern to guide ships, the lighthouse had withstood many a blustery storm and forceful hurricane.

That's what Jacob had told Nicole when he'd rented her the place. Nicole smiled at the memory of how he'd tried to talk her out of renting the lighthouse. It's too remote for a woman alone. But Nicole's first sight of the building perched so lonely on the cliff's rocky edge had hooked her.

As she gazed in awe at the simple, yet regal structure, Nicole had known that nothing and no one could stop her from spending time in the remote lighthouse. She didn't understand why, but she knew that this place would help her to recover from the horrid events of the past.

She shivered.

Sumo's whine attracted Nicole's attention, and she looked around to see what had prompted the complaint. A flutter of movement down the cliff trail drew her attention. It was nothing more than a glimpse of white material and a brief reflection of dark hair in the sunlight. Strange, the locals knew the trail wasn't safe after rain, and it had poured last night.

A sliver of fear tugged at Nicole's heart. It was either a tourist unaware of the dangers of the slippery trail, or.no, that didn't even bear the respect of a thought. She'd covered her tracks well. No one knew where she was. She'd rented the lighthouse partially for the safety it offered. The forest was distant enough to offer a pleasant view, yet offered plenty of open area so she could be aware of approaching visitors. If anyone stepped on the sparse grass and moss that struggled to remain alive on the rock, the ensuing crunching sound would provide a warning.

Curious, and a smidgen worried, she rose from her chair and crept to the cliff's edge with Sumo by her side. Heart pounding, she peered over the edge and saw...nothing. No one. Yet she could have sworn she'd seen someone. Sumo had as well. Maybe the person had only come so far, realized the hazardous condition of the pathway and turned back. She gazed over the landscape below to make sure she'd missed nothing, but saw only the winding trail that led from the cliff top down to the shore. She didn't think there was a place for anyone to hide, but she'd never actually explored the trail herself, so she could have been wrong.

Sumo settled down. He lay beside her with his head resting on his paws. Well, that settled it, if Sumo wasn't worried, she could relax. But he'd been whining at something.

"Hellooooo." A voice echoed from the driveway around front of the building.

Nicole jumped. Sumo barked and bolted toward the approaching intruder. In his haste to perform his duty of guard dog, Sumo ran smack into Nicole's legs. The resulting view would have been funny to someone who didn't find themselves caught in the mass of arms, legs, and paws. Nicole toppled onto the hard surface of smooth rock with Sumo directly on top of her, a paw on either side of her head. In a final gesture of humiliation, Nicole found her face swathed with a rough, wet, pink tongue. Apologies given, Sumo jumped up and raced to the person who was the cause of confusion.

With a groan of frustration, Nicole rolled to her knees and slowly stood, all the while checking for broken bones. After all, one hundred and ten pounds of dog had just landed directly on her. Wiping her hands on her jeans and making sure everything was in place, she turned to face her visitor. She sighed with relief; it was only Josephine.

"Hi, Nicole, sorry I startled you. Are you all right?"

"I'm fine. No thanks to that hairy beast."

Sumo was making a fool of himself by groveling with his belly and all four legs extended to the sky above. Josephine smiled and scratched his belly until moans of delight caused both women to laugh. Looking abashed, but satisfied at the attention he'd received, Sumo rolled back on his feet and returned to Nicole's side, his guard dog duties fulfilled.

Josephine motioned to the laptop and chair on the deck. "Did I interrupt your writing?"

"Not really." Nicole frowned. "Were you just on the cliff pathway?"

"No way. It's not safe after a storm."

"That's what I thought. But I could have sworn I saw someone."

Josephine shrugged. "Might have been the wind. It blows in strong from the ocean at times and whips up the cliffs and through the trees."

"Could have been." Nicole pursed her lips and sent a questioning look at Josephine. "I know we haven't known each other long, but can I ask you a personal question?"

"Of course. Although there's nothing says I have to answer."

Josephine chuckled.

"I'm just curious as to why you're single." Nicole wondered if she'd overstepped the bounds, but what the heck, she might as well finish her thought. "It's just that I think you and Jacob would make a great couple." A heartbeat of silence followed her question, and Nicole held her breath.

It started as a twinkle in her eyes and grew into a resounding echo of laughter. "You and me both, Nicole."

"Really? Then why don't you ask him out or something? I'm sure he's too shy to do the asking."

"Too shy, or too curmudgeonly." Josephine laughed and then quieted. "I don't know, I guess the slow pace and peace of Solitary Cove takes over, and I put off doing anything until another day. Besides." She shifted in her chair. "I don't think he'd be interested in me, but that's okay. I don't need any more than what I have. The peace of Solitary Cove and the sense of belonging to a family that is there for you no matter what. I love watching the fishing boats chug out of the bay every morning, knowing they'll return each afternoon. I feel safe walking the streets because everyone looks out for everyone else. It's a haven of comfort, and I don't need any more than that." She turned a sly gaze toward Nicole.

"What about you, how come you're still single?" Josephine's question was innocent. She had no idea the pain such simple words resurrected deep within Nicole, but it must have shown on her face, because the older woman quickly apologized.

"I'm sorry. Please forget I asked."

"It's all right. I did love someone once, or I thought I did, but I don't think I can talk about it yet. Maybe one day." She smiled and asked, "So, what's the real reason you came to see me?"

Josephine's face brightened. "I came to see if you'd come to the fireworks with me tonight."

"I'd love to, thanks for asking."

"Great. I'll close the store at eight, we can go from there."

"Sure, sounds good."

Josephine gave a cheery wave and strode across the smooth rock outcropping to the nearby road. Nicole marveled at the woman's spryness, then sighed as she remembered Josephine's question. She found herself aching with a sense of loss and loneliness and wondered what life had in store for her. She was only thirty-six and still attractive. Was there a man out there waiting to fall in love with her? Maybe she'd meet someone soon.

"Whoa. Where did that come from?" Nicole said aloud. When had she even started wanting to meet another man? Jeff's death was too raw and the stalker was still out there somewhere. It was too dangerous to take the chance of having anyone in her life.

Chapter Four

I t seemed as if everyone in town had shown up for the fireworks. Since it was one of the main events of the year, they probably had. Nicole waved at a few familiar faces, and oohed and aahed along with the crowd. It felt good that the people of the town accepted her. And it hadn't taken much time, almost as if they'd decided to trust her until she gave them a reason to do otherwise.

Another round of fireworks exploded in the dark night sky. Vivid colors of orange and yellow formed a starburst, while red spider-like tendrils burst and all the colors melded into a blinding display of light. Nicole took the opportunity to search the crowd for Jacob. She hoped to see him and make sure he was okay after the visit to the grave that morning. She didn't find him. Instead, her gaze locked with that of a man standing on the edge of the crowd.

Sounds of revelry and firecrackers stopped, her legs turned to rubber, and she had trouble taking a breath. The firelight dimmed, yet etched in her mind were familiar features of a good looking, but not traditionally handsome man. Tanned and trim, he possessed strong cheekbones and a no-nonsense expression. His hair was short, gray, slightly wavy at the ends, and the lines etched into his face belied an age more advanced than hers. Dressed in black jeans and a black shirt, it was hard to see his body with such a fleeting glimpse, yet he had looked fit.

In that moment, Nicole's world shifted.

She didn't understand the urge, but her befuddled mind told her to wait for the next burst of fireworks to get another look at him. She didn't have long to wait; the familiar whistling of fireworks warned of another shot of light into darkness. Eagerly, Nicole looked to where the man had been. The park lit up, but he wasn't there. Frantic, she searched the crowd, but couldn't see anyone even remotely resembling the man she'd seen. *Damn!*

Disappointed, she chided herself for acting like an adolescent. The man was too old for her anyway and definitely not her type. She could just chalk it up to the excitement of the crowd, as well as the feeling of finally belonging somewhere. Yes, that was all it was, nothing more. Yet, she still found herself searching.

Josephine's excited voice distracted her from her scrutiny of the thinning crowd. "Did you see him? That's the actor I told you was in my store earlier. I'm not sure why he's in town before all the other movie people, but there must be a reason, don't you think?"

Nicole had trouble clicking her brain back to normal. "What? Sorry, I was thinking about something else."

Josephine rolled her eyes. "The movie star, Ian Calder, he was standing right over there. How could you not have seen him?"

Nicole stood in a state of shock. That's where she had seen the man before, he was the famous actor. Jeff had enjoyed his action-packed movies, while she usually preferred romances or comedies. She couldn't have been drawn to him in the way she thought, because he had to be at least fifteen years older than her. It must have been a trick of the light. From what she understood, they'd be here filming for a couple of months, so she'd have plenty of opportunity to see him in the revealing light of day. Then she'd get a more true view of what he really looked like. He was probably quite unattractive along with being too old.

"Maybe what I said is coming true." Nicole came to full awareness. "What."

"You know, at *Wishes* before the fireworks. Don't you remember?" Josephine laughed. "I'd say your age is catching up with you, if you forget things so easily." Her eyes twinkled as she teased.

"Why, you brat," Nicole laughed. "I'm not nearly as old as you, so watch what you say."

They laughed in easy camaraderie and Nicole felt the strands of friendship winding strengthening.

"Do you really not remember what I said?"

"Of course I remember. I was just pulling your leg." She'd met Josephine at *Wishes* as planned, but a couple of customers intent on staying past closing gave Nicole time to browse. She'd spent a few minutes looking over some of Josie's new stock. Books on meditation, beautiful crystal pendants, herbal teas, and candles were the main items. Josephine hovered around, pointing out a couple of items of interest to Nicole. Then, in a sudden gesture, Josie had grasped her arm and squeezed tightly.

"What the..."

"Quiet. I sense something, but I can't quite grasp the message."

Nicole had been about to protest, but the intent look on Josephine's face stilled her questions. It was weird, but she'd remained quiet while Josie closed her eyes and concentrated.

"Ahh, it seems that you will meet a star in the midst of fire. The star will enchant and confuse you until you become one. But beware the darkness that hovers on the edge of light. Danger from your past will haunt your present, but the star will guide the way."

With those words, Josephine had retained her usual state of cheery enthusiasm. As if nothing untoward had happened, she rang up the red candles that Nicole had only considered buying.

"You made the right choice. These candles are exactly what you'll need."

Now, the words spoken a few hours ago came back to cause Nicole a flurry of doubt. She remembered the vivid colors of firelight highlighting Ian Calder. A star in the midst of fire. Those were Josephine's words. Nicole had assumed the she meant a star in the sky. Truth be told, she hadn't given a lot of consideration to what Josie had said. She'd never believed anything she couldn't see, touch, or smell. Someone telling the future was just...well, just not possible. But she couldn't get Ian's face out of her mind, and she'd have a restless night thinking about the physical reaction she'd had to just the fleeting glimpse of him across the park.

Josephine had also said something about a danger from her past would haunt her present. It must have been coincidence, but she shivered anyway.

"Nicole, are you all right?" Josephine asked.

"I'm fine." Nicole tried to control the shaking of her voice. "Say, how about we grab an ice cream cone from the deli before I head back to the lighthouse?"

"I don't know." Josephine patted her stomach. "I need to watch my girlish figure." She giggled. "But maybe if you twist my arm." Josephine extended her arm for Nicole, who promptly twisted it in a gesture of persuasion. Arm in arm, the two of them strolled across the street to join the growing line of ice cream lovers.

***

The bitch. How dare she have fun? It hadn't taken her long to get over her husband's murder, sashaying her shapely ass down the main street as if she didn't have a care in the world. He'd seen the look she gave that actor, too.

He shifted on the hard surface of the park bench and cursed the fates that had brought him to this stupid town in the middle of nowhere. When his original plan of scaring Jeff into a confession by killing his wife had ended up with Jeff dead, he realized he could easily use the same plan against her. Jeff must have told her where the diamonds were, and now that he'd found her, he'd get them back. But he needed a plan.

He'd be patient, but not too patient.

He sneered at the bitch's amateurish attempts to evade him. The fact that she had gone to the bother proved that she was as guilty as her back stabbing husband. Well, she'd get hers, and he'd get the diamonds. Sounded like a deal to him. A sweet deal as he remembered the lush rise of the bitch's tits and her tight ass that she wriggled with slutty intent. Maybe it was a good thing Jeff had stepped in the way of the bullet. The wife would be more fun to torment.

***

Ian slid his key card in the door, waited for the green light and entered his cabin. His eyes roamed over the room in an ingrained habit of making sure there was no one waiting for him; a naked woman offering herself to him; a maid looking for an autograph; a well-intentioned fan swearing that they needed to meet him or they couldn't go on living. Everything looked in place, and he breathed a sigh of relief.

For a small town inn, this place rivaled any five star hotel he'd stayed in. *Wyllow Wood Inn* stood upon a small hill on the edge of town and consisted of various self-sufficient cabins as well as the rooms at the Inn. He had purposely chosen the most remote cabin. Nestled in surrounding pines, the dark blue, single story structure was within sight and sound of the crashing surf of the ocean. Daylight presented a vista of lush gardens, sandy beach, and occasional wildlife, punctuated with the cry of gulls over the ocean. Night time fell into silence and filled the expansive sky with sparkling stars.

His gaze wandered to the sea and surf while his mind pondered his reaction to the woman he'd seen again. Their eyes had locked for nothing more than a split second, yet during that time, his emotions had taken a plunge into forgotten depths. The flashes of fireworks had highlighted her face and made her eyes look as if fire sparked from them. The sparks touched him and the ensuing warmth liquefied his limbs until he wanted to do nothing more than take her in his arms and feed upon the heat.

Whoa, where had that poetic thought come from? Definitely not his usual manner of thinking about women. Most amazing of all was the fact that he'd felt a familiar, yet long gone twinge. A stirring of life given up for dead. Jeez, could it be true or was it wishful thinking? He needed to touch the woman and find out.

That had been his intention until an overzealous tourist, and his self-proclaimed biggest fan, had yanked on his arm until he agreed to meet her family. He spent the next few minutes signing autographs and listening to well-intentioned platitudes of adulation. By the time he was able to excuse himself, the fireworks had finished. Hoping to find the woman, he'd searched the crowd leaving the park, but been unable to find her.

The ringing of the phone startled him, and he debated whether to answer or not. It could be anyone on the other end. His presence in town had become common knowledge. Most people would make the conclusion that he was staying at the *Wyllow Wood Inn*. He didn't feel like talking to a reporter looking for a story, or one of those dedicated fans he seemed to garner.

The ringing stopped and silence filled the room. Pervasive silence lingered and settled over Ian. It took him a moment to recognize the emotion he was feeling, but when he did, it surprised him. He was lonely. He snorted. Lonely, that didn't make sense. He was rich and famous and could have any woman he wanted with the snap of his fingers. Well, maybe that wouldn't mean much these days, but he shouldn't be lonely. He had friends, but when he tried to conjure up the name of someone he would feel comfortable calling at this time of night just to talk, no one came to mind. Okay, he had his daughter. When had he talked to her last? He couldn't even remember.

Ian sat on the edge of the bed and buried his head in his hands. What game was life playing with him now? Why did he suddenly feel so restless? Everything had been fine for so long, but now he found no satisfaction in any aspect of his life. It didn't make any sense.

The phone rang again. Ian practically jumped off the bed. Damn! He'd talk to anyone now just to keep himself from wallowing in his own despair.

He snatched the phone from its cradle. "Hello."

"Dad?"

"Vanessa." Surprised to hear her voice considering he'd just been thinking about her, Ian stumbled over his words. "How did you find out where I was staying?"

Idiot. He admonished himself for sounding accusatory. "I mean..."

"It's okay." Vanessa's voice held a thread of censure and hurt. "Gibney told me."

"Good, good, I'm glad he did." Ian's tongue felt like a useless piece of raw meat. Vanessa never called him—small talk was not their thing. It was more for Christmas holidays and the occasional Thanksgiving with periods of sparse communication through mutual acquaintances or distant family members. Ian frowned. They'd drifted apart over the years and now found themselves faced with the awkwardness of a normal phone conversation.

"So, Dad, how are you?" Vanessa inquired with false brightness.

"I'm fine. You?" What else could he say? He knew little enough about her life that he couldn't even contribute to the conversation.

"Oh, you know, I'm all right. Better than some, not as good as others."

The laugh that drifted over the phone was a nervous one, and Ian wondered what that cryptic remark was supposed to mean. He had his own problems and didn't have time to decipher Vanessa's.

"I see." He saw all right. Vanessa was the spoiled wife of a rich investor. Her husband gave her everything she could ever desire, and she didn't have to work. What problems could she have?

"I hear you're starring in a romance. That's quite a change from your usual action films."

"I thought it was time for a change. Not as young as I used to be, you know."

"You're okay, aren't you? I mean, you're not sick or anything?"

"No, I'm fine. It's just time for this old guy to let some of the young bloods into the action."

"Hmmm, I have one or two female friends who would disagree with you on that one."

"Really?"

"Yeah, Dad. Some of them think you're quite gorgeous."

"Really."

"Dad, you sound like the proverbial broken record."

Sorry, I just don't see myself as much of an attraction to the ladies these days."

Silence and then softly spoken words. "You'll always look great to me, Dad."

Fingers of uncertainty crept slowly around Ian's heart. "Vanessa."

Before he could ask her real reason for calling, Vanessa whispered in haste. "Dad, Bob's home. I gotta go. It was nice talking to you. Bye."

As quickly as that, she was gone. Ian sat with an annoying, buzzing phone to his ear.

"What the hell?" he muttered as he replaced the receiver and debated calling her back. But if she'd wanted to talk to him, she wouldn't have hung up. Women! Go figure. It was probably hormones or something. But even as the chauvinistic thought flitted through his mind, he knew there was more behind the phone call. Not used to this kind of situation, he didn't know what to do. Probably best to give her a day or so and then call back to make sure everything was fine. Yeah, that sounded like a plan.

Still feeling lonely, Ian sighed, undressed, and crawled into his bed only to spend the night dreaming of flashing eyes in sparking firelight.

**

It was happening again. Terror mounted as whipcord-like branches thrashed her face and impeded her flight from the shadowy figure chasing her through the ghostly forest. The mugginess of the summer day faded, and within the creeping shadows, the scent of decomposing wood and decaying leaves assaulted Nicole's nostrils.

She stopped for a breath, the sound of pursuit ravaging her senses. Her ragged breath would give away her position, so she had to keep moving. Her imagination played havoc with her senses as she imagined the figure throwing her from the cliff top and leaving her bleeding on the rocky shoreline below. Silently, she screamed her fear. She tried to run faster, but the forest was so thick that her progress resembled a stumbling parody of awkwardness. Then, suddenly, she was in the clear. The forest broke open to the brightness of the moonlit sky. The pathway winding its way around the rocky cliff shone clear in the night like a ribbon of safety.

Feeling that safety within reach, she ran for the pathway, but a figure stepped from the darkness of the forest and grasped her arm in a steely grip of inhuman strength.

"No," Nicole screamed, to no avail. Pain exploded in her chest as a knife thrust into her heart. Death came quickly. Nicole had only a split second to recognize the face leering at her as she fell from the ragged cliff. Her dead husband.

Before hitting the rocky shore, Nicole awoke. Covered in sweat and shivering with fear and unwanted emotions, she threw the covers off and stumbled to the bathroom in time to deposit the remains of her pasta dinner in the toilet. She hugged the cold porcelain bowl until there was nothing left to upchuck. Then she cried.

A cold, wet nose nudged itself under her arm and a rough tongue licked the tears from her face. In an assertive movement, her dog, Sumo, pushed between Nicole and the toilet and deposited his butt in her lap—all one hundred-plus pounds of butt. Nicole laughed. She wrapped her arms around the rottweiler and hugged until the pervasiveness of her dream disappeared.

"God, Sumo, you're my savior. What would I do without you?"

He whined and swept his tongue over her cheek, wriggling his rear end in an attempt to wag a non-existent tail.

"Ow. Okay, bud, as much as I love you, you weigh too much, so get off." She punctuated her words with a half-hearted shove. Half-hearted because there was no chance of getting him off unless he decided he was getting off. Thank goodness, he was in an obedient mood, because he moved off her lap.

"Come on, I could use some tea." Nicole trailed a hand across Sumo's back as the two of them headed for the kitchen. During the mindless effort of preparing her tea, her thoughts easily wandered to the past and her marriage. Funny how she didn't miss Jeff. Well, not so funny, she thought, as the familiar feeling of guilt weighed heavy in her stomach. He had been her husband. She should miss him.

Nicole sat at the kitchen table, and in an attempt to quell her guilt, tried to remember only the good times. Like when they'd bought a dining room table for forty dollars at a yard sale and stripped it down to reveal the beauty of dark cherry wood. The delicate pair of oriental figures they had discovered in the dusty corner of some flea market. They had paid five dollars for the male and female figures and found out they were worth five hundred dollars, but the value hadn't mattered, not as much as the closeness she and Jeff had shared on their weekend treasure hunting jaunts.

That had been the beginning of their marriage. As time passed, they'd spent less time together. Jeff would argue that he couldn't pay the bills if he wasn't working and would ask when she was going to start contributing to the household income. That had been a bitter argument. Nicole considered the fact that she answered the phones, did the monthly accounts, handled all inquiries and walk-ins, negotiated sales, and helped in all aspects of setting up the art gallery and maintaining it, as well as the usual cooking, cleaning, and laundry, to be her contribution to the income. In her spare time she'd found time to write, something Jeff had considered a waste of time.

Everything she did was to further his career, but he hadn't seen that, he had considered it his due. The tortured artist who demanded time alone to work while someone else handled the business. Well, dammit, he had never understood how much work was involved in running the gallery; he expected more. When they argued, Jeff would lock himself in his studio to create. As time passed and the arguments increased, Nicole had spent many hours alone.

Nicole felt shame for her bitter thoughts. Jeff had loved her dearly, so what if he had been demanding and meticulous? She needed to remember that he had given his life for her.

With a weary sigh, she put her teacup in the sink and went back up to bed with Sumo following. The distant swish of waves rolling in to the shore lulled her into a light sleep. She didn't know how long she'd been asleep when Sumo's insistent whining and the touch of his cold nose on her face woke her.

"Hey, guy, what's up?" she mumbled. Her words only caused Sumo's whining to become more aggressive. He ran to the bedroom door and scratched.

A crash from downstairs echoed within the lighthouse. Nicole woke instantly and Sumo clawed at the door, barking frantically to get out. Before he could do any damage to the wooden door, Nicole pulled it open and let the beast free. Her heart pounded in fear. She prayed that the crash was a result of the blowing wind outside and not a dangerous intruder who would hurt her or her dog.

Not for a second did she think it could be the stalker. She

was sure she'd covered her tracks too well. Pulling on her robe, she listened to Sumo sniffing around downstairs. He obviously hadn't found anyone, or he'd be barking a streak by now. Mix Sumo's deep, reverberating bark with his intimidating looks and only an idiot would still be hanging around. Taking a deep breath Nicole thanked whatever instinct it was that made her buy a rottweiler, then crept down the winding, narrow staircase. Tentatively, she reached out and flipped the light switch.

Everything looked normal. The overhead light fixture reflected off scarred pine cupboards and made the butter yellow kitchen glow. The floor had been re-done recently with peel and stick tiles and depicted buttercups against a creamy background. Knickknacks lined the small window shelf above the sink. Nicole had only taken a cursory look at the small figures, but most of them seemed to be of water nymphs and faeries. She had no idea who they belonged to, or whose idea it was to decorate with such fey creatures.

With Sumo by her side, Nicole turned the lights on one by one and took a quick look around the rest of the living area, which consisted of a living room, small den, and a single bathroom, all on the lower floor. Her bedroom was the only room on the second floor, with the winding stairs leading up to the lighthouse tower.

Brightly colored scatter rugs lay in no particular order on the wide planked floors, and each room lay claim to various pieces of well-used antiques that had seen better times. A bookcase shaped to look like a boat, craftily converted lobster traps that now served as end tables, mirrors set in a porthole metal frame, and much more. Nicole's favorite was the writing desk. Trimmed in brass and possessing ornately carved legs and mahogany ball feet, the desk also boasted five drawers down the right and left sides.

She ran her hands lovingly over the desk and decided that she could see nothing that would have made the crashing sound. It must have been the wind or something else outside. Sumo was used to living in a busy town, whereas here the sounds where different. He just needed to settle down. Satisfied that nothing was amiss, Nicole started to turn out the lights she'd turned on in haste. Just then, her eyes detected a glint of something by one of the windows.

The living room windows propped open on a hinged stick. Nicole moved closer and reached out to touch the glinting object. It looked as if one of the window frames that attached to a hinge had rotted enough for the hinge to break off. That hinge now lay on the rug under the window and the stick that had propped the window sat bent on the window ledge.

It looked as if the hinge had broken while the window was propped up, which would release the stick and cause the window to bang shut. Her heart pounded fiercely. She was sure she had shut the windows before going to bed. So, if the window had banged shut that would mean someone had gained entrance to the lighthouse through the window. The intruder was no longer here, or Sumo wouldn't be sitting quietly at her feet. But someone had been here, and Nicole no longer felt safe.

Should she call the police? No one but Jacob knew her story, though, and she wanted to keep it that way. If she called Corporal Moody at the Royal Canadian Mounted Police office, she'd have to explain her suspicions and back it up by explaining about her husband's murder and the stalker. Within no time, the entire town would know everything about her.

Nicole reasoned that there was no way the stalker could have found her here. If someone had actually been in the lighthouse, it had probably been local kids looking for a place to party and didn't realize she'd rented the place. That made sense.

She looked at Sumo and decided he was as good a guard as any policeman. For insurance though, she'd keep a heavy stick by her bed.

***

Stupid window. He stamped through the forest to the

nearby path that led to town. Branches slapped his face, but he didn't care. He welcomed the pain. He'd been in the house with her, and he'd been so quiet that dog hadn't even known he was there. Ha. Useless mangy mutt. Things had gone great until the damn window slammed shut. What crappy luck.

He groped the inner pocket of his jean jacket. Fumbling, his fingers touched upon the photograph he'd stolen. The bitch would never notice it missing from the photo album. In the meantime, he could look at the photo of her in a bikini, flaunting herself for his eyes alone. He moved his hand from the photo to his groin and rubbed lightly. At least he'd have a small measure of satisfaction until he held the real thing within his grasp. A tight feeling convulsed his groin, and he moaned in anticipation.

Chapter Five

A sphere of glowing energy, the sun arced upward from the horizon and shone its brilliance on the ocean. Like diamonds of the clearest, brightest cut, the water reflected its beauty and almost blinded Nicole, who sat on the deck at the cliff's edge. She brought her hands to cover her eyes against the sudden arrival of morning sun.

It felt good. After last night's confusion, she hadn't been able to sleep. Instead, she'd paced and fretted all night, eventually sitting with coffee in hand to greet the coming of the new day. She was usually up early anyway, as she found morning the time of day that she did her best writing. Jeff had always been a late riser. Funny how little they'd actually had in common, yet their relationship had worked most of the time. Jeff had sometimes been a difficult man to live with, and Nicole often found herself compromising in order to keep peace.

Nicole stopped her thoughts before going too far in that direction. She didn't want to make the mistake of idolizing her husband because he was dead, yet she felt guilty for any negative thoughts winding their way into her mind. Jeff hadn't been perfect, but according to him, most of their problems had been her fault. No matter how hard she'd tried to be quiet in the mornings, she always managed to wake him. She could understand his frustration. The fact that her paperwork always seemed to be on his way was due to her lack of organization skills, a character trait she'd worked hard at improving. Her lack of fashion sense had never bothered her until Jeff pointed out that minor fault, with comments meant to be tactful and helpful. Besides, he'd been right, she was a couple of pounds too heavy to wear some of the sleek fashions she'd attempted.

Oh, well, that was the past. Breathing deeply, she inhaled the tangy salt of the ocean and gave full appreciation to the freshness of the air and the muffled silence of the early morning. A time when nocturnal animals disappeared and animals of the day had yet to stir. It helped calm her nerves.

Thinking about last night, she considered her decision not to inform the authorities about her late night visitor, or visitors. What if it hadn't been local kids? She sighed. It was a moot point now, because her decision had been made, and there was no sense second-guessing herself.

"Come on, Sumo." She jumped from the chair and strode to the kitchen with her empty mug. "Let's go shopping. I feel the urge to indulge myself."

With a happy whine of agreement, Sumo leaped to his feet with butt wriggling and tongue hanging out. Feeling the momentary depression lift, Nicole laughed at Sumo's carefree antics and gave thanks for being in such a beautiful place with her loyal canine companion.

***

Ian had a restless night. He'd been here four days and the urge that had driven him here a week early still reigned strong within his blood. That urge had prompted him to walk the streets from one side of town to the other, check out each unique store in the small town, even stop to talk to strangers in hopes that they'd hold the answer to what drove him.

Stiffly making his way to the bathroom to relieve his full bladder, he chuckled in remembrance of the stunned looks of the people he'd stopped for no other reason than to talk with them. Usually, he was the one pestered while trying to enjoy a quiet day of shopping and relaxation. Some small part of him experienced a sweet twinge of revenge at giving back a little of what he'd put up with for so many years. Although, he doubted anyone he'd stopped had been too upset. After all, he was famous. They were probably glad he'd saved them the trouble of intruding on his time. He'd intruded on theirs instead.

Ian splashed cold water on his face and took the opportunity to give himself a once over in the harsh light of the bathroom fluorescent light. His face boasted a few days of stubble, but that only enhanced the masculine image he portrayed. After all, he was a great action star. He had to live up to his image. He had wrinkles, sure, but they gave his face character and helped hide the faint scar that ran down his cheek to the corner of his mouth. His silver-gray hair presented a stark contrast to his vivid blue eyes. Eyes that could render bad guys powerless. On screen, anyway. Ian had spent a lot of time perfecting the hypnotic Don't mess with me stare that had helped make him famous. He practiced it on himself in the mirror and found that he hadn't lost his touch.

"Enough," he muttered. "You're still a handsome son of a bitch." To anyone listening, his words might have sounded arrogant, but they were an attempt to reassure and build the confidence that had taken such a battering lately with his little problem. All he wanted was...was... Damn, he'd almost pinpointed his exasperating need.

The elusiveness of what had brought him to Solitary Cove frustrated him. He needed to relax. What he really needed was a massage, a day at the beach with a good book, and a quiet dinner in his room where no one could bother him. The *Wyllow Wood* staff could supply the massage and dinner, but where could he buy a book worth reading?

He tried to remember if he'd come across a bookstore in his journeys, but all he could remember was the shop where he'd bought the red candles. If memory served him correctly, there had been some interesting books, as well as some incense. What the heck, if he was going to relax, he may as well go the whole way. Incense. Candles. Whatever it took.

The store was easy enough to find again. Of course, he had to sign about ten autographs and dash the hopes of a young woman hoping for a night of unbridled sex with a superstar. Jeez, she didn't even know him, yet she was so willing to jump into bed. For all she knew, he could be some psycho who liked beating up women.

Stepping around a scary looking, but docile dog on the front step of *Wishes*, Ian pondered the fact that not long ago, he would have taken the woman up on her offer. What had changed? Beside the fact that he couldn't rise to the occasion, he also felt no desire to waste his time on empty pursuits.

His hand was on the door of the shop when the mini-enlightenment hit him. When had he decided that having sex with beautiful, willing women was an empty pursuit? Wow. Talk about a complete turnaround of ethics. A fleeting vision of mahogany hair and rich hazel eyes flashed in his mind. Yeah, a night of unbridled passion with the woman from the fireworks wouldn't be out of the question.

Whew! There was nothing wrong with him after all. Except for the fact that even if the desire was there, the ability wasn't.

"Goddamn!" Ian yanked open the door in anger and frustration, only to become the object of an intense stare of disapproval from the woman who ran the shop.

"You may be famous, but I would appreciate you keeping your profanity outside, thank you." The woman spoke quietly, as if wanting to keep any confrontation from the few customers who roamed the store.

Ian fumbled for words. He wasn't used to someone chastising him for swearing. "Sorry, I just." He threw his hands up. "I'll behave myself, I promise."

"I'm sure you will." The bookshop owner smiled. The generous gesture lit the woman's eyes in a way that pervaded Ian's dark mood. He grinned.

"Oh? And how can you be so sure?"

"Because if you don't, I'll box your ears."

Ian laughed. "That's something my grandmother would have threatened, and I know you're not that much older than me."

"Flatterer," the woman mumbled and blushed. "Tell me, Mr. Calder, what are you looking for today? Have you burned your candles already?"

"Please, call me Ian." He extended his hand and found it grasped in a soft feminine hand.

"Thank you, and I'm Josephine."

"Josephine, that's an unusual name."

"I've been told I'm rather an unusual person."

They laughed, and Ian silently agreed with the verdict. About sixty-five with short, blond hair and pretty features, the woman had aged well, but her clothes—what was she thinking? Long and flowing described everything she wore, right from her purple silk pants to her cream-colored shirt. At her waist, she wore a chinked belt of smoke-colored metal inlaid with chunky turquoise stones. On her feet, she wore a comfortable looking pair of slippers that matched her pants, except for the fact that shimmering stars and glimmering moons decorated them.

Ian smiled. "Actually, I'm here to browse through your books. I'm looking for something to read down on the beach. Nothing too heavy, like the meaning of life or anything, just some light reading."

"Hmmm, I think I have just the thing. Take a right in the second aisle, go to the end of the row and straight-ahead on the fifth shelf from the floor, you'll see a book titled, *Your Reason for Living*. I'm sure you'll find what you're looking for to fill the need."

"No, I said I didn't want to read about the meaning of life."

"I know what you said. I also know what you need." She smiled sweetly, innocently, making him feel like a schoolboy. "Trust me, you'll like what you find."

"Yes, I'm sure I will. Thanks." Ian frowned as he turned to follow the woman's directions. He could have sworn the woman had flashed a smug look his direction.

He shrugged and decided his imagination was probably

playing tricks on him. Stocked full of lava lamps with blobs of luminous material roiling aimlessly, the second aisle ran from the front to back of the store and ended directly beside the windows that looked over the harbor. In the distance, the sun rose above the horizon of the water and shot a shaft of golden light into the shop window directly up the length of the aisle. The light poured in through the window, and Ian stopped to let his eyes adjust.

A figure passed in front of the window, blocking the sun and enabling Ian a moment of relief. The person's shadow stretched across the floor and touched Ian's feet while the sun offered Ian the outline of a rather shapely feminine form browsing the book section in the general area that Josephine had sent him. Other than that, she was a mystery. It didn't matter, he was off women.

Once he reached the bookcase, the sun angled away from his eyes, and he quickly found the book that Josephine had suggested sitting on the top above the now crouching woman. No problem, it would only take him a second to reach over her. He stepped forward, his knees only inches from the woman's back, reached out and grasped the book he was after. The book was just clearing the edge of the shelf and he was almost home safe when smack, a very hard head banged him in the chin.

Chaos reigned.

The woman stepped on his toe, he dropped the book from his hand, and as he reached down to grab the falling book he banged his forehead on the woman's shoulder.

"Ow." Was that his voice or hers?

"Sorry." That was definitely a feminine voice.

"No, it's all my fault. I shouldn't have been reaching over the top of you."

Polite words, proper apologies given, everything was fine until he looked into her eyes. His groin tightened as golden-brown eyes flecked with jade green connected with his. There was no looking away. Sound fell into the distance, and Ian became painfully aware of a pulse throbbing between their bodies. Inexplicably drawn, he leaned toward the woman. Her eyes widened in surprise and confusion, but he couldn't stop himself, he needed to be closer, he needed to feel the heat that radiated from her body. Gold, brown, and green swirled together in her eyes, a whirlpool of imagination and timeless emotion. Ian felt the power of a connection that went beyond the physical. He swallowed. He wanted to take her in his arms and hold her until their two bodies melded into one.

He reached out and brushed his fingertips across her cheek. She shied away, and then leaned closer while her eyes took on a dreamlike quality. Ian became aroused. Jesus, he felt like a kid again, but not the way he'd felt with Josephine. His groin ached for fulfillment, and his heart beat with anticipation. He tilted his head and focused on the lips in front of him. He needed to kiss her. He ached to kiss her.

The heat of her hand came to rest on his chest ever so gently, slightly hesitant. It burned him, yet made him crave more. Closer they came. Butterflies flitted deep in his stomach. He felt giddy with the energy that sparked around them.

"Did you find what you were looking for?"

Like glass thrown smashing to the ground, Josephine's voice sliced into the moment. Ian jolted to awareness, and the woman he'd been about to kiss blushed crimson and stepped away from him.

Ian tried to speak, but cotton might just as well have filled his mouth. He cleared his throat and tried again. "Ahem. Yes, I did. Thanks for your help." He looked to the blushing woman who stood beside him avoiding his gaze.

Josephine broke the awkward silence. "Okay, then, if there's anything else I can help you with, just let me know." She turned to the still silent woman beside him. "Nicole, I think I found just what you were asking about. Over here are a couple of books on the history of the lighthouse and families that have lived there." Josephine hooked her arm through Nicole's and practically dragged her up the aisle.

Still dazed, Ian stared open-mouthed as Josephine, acting

like a chaperone at a Sweet Sixteen dance, pulled the woman away from him. Coldness replaced the aching heat and he fought an overwhelming loneliness.

"Come on, man. Pull yourself together. What the hell has come over you?" he mumbled, in an attempt to gain sanity. But he knew, as surely as the sun rose in the east, the woman had affected him. The intensity of that brief moment scared him, and he still trembled with the aftershock of what they had shared.

His gaze followed the women as they moved from one part of the store to another. Nicole, what a pretty name. She moved with the innocent grace of one unaware of her beauty. He listened to the sound of her voice drift across the store, and he imagined what it would feel like to kiss her.

"I'll be damned. It is him, George. Didn't I tell you it was that actor fellow?"

The nasal sound of a woman's voice jolted Ian from his fantasies at the same time as a hand on his arm jerked him around to face a purple-haired, camera toting, pen wielding senior and her polyester clad husband. He moaned. The star-struck couple didn't even notice, as they were too busy firing questions at him and prodding him into prime positions for picture taking.

"My word, you look better on screen than in person. Must be all the make-up. George, don't you think he looks better on screen?" The woman pulled his arm so he stood beside her, all the while motioning for her husband to snap and shoot.

"I don't know, Martha, they say the screen adds ten pounds and I don't think that sits well with him. Truth be told, I think he looks better in person, not quite so pudgy, you know."

The old biddy pushed Ian to stand beside her husband while she snapped happily away. "George, don't slouch, you could look as good as him if you'd stand straight."

"Women," the old man whispered conspiratorially. "Never satisfied. But being a big star and all, you probably can't relate to the problems of the little guy." The old man winked and punched Ian in the arm.

"Now, George, don't go bruising the man up. I keep telling you how you don't know your own strength."

Ian stifled a laugh. He'd hardly felt the punch, but he rubbed his arm as if it hurt, just to make the old guy feel good. A soft laugh reached his ears, and he noticed that the odd couple was drawing a bit of a crowd. The laugh had come from Nicole. The heat of her gaze touched him. It seemed as if she was enjoying his discomfiture.

Ian grinned, just to show he could take a joke as well as the next guy, and her laughter changed from humorous to a gentle hint of an intimate smile. Her gaze warmed Ian, and suddenly the strange couple accosting him no longer existed, the store no longer existed, nothing mattered except getting close to her.

Somewhat rudely, he pushed the couple aside. They never noticed a thing as they continued their rowdy banter and wandered out of the store as if Ian had never captured their attention. They had their photographs, so he no longer mattered. Ian had grown used to that part of his life, but it left him feeling used and unimportant.

That didn't matter now, though. What did matter was the woman who drew him so intensely. She stood as if waiting for him, her hair soft and gleaming in the shimmering shaft of sunlight. She was casually dressed in snug fitting, faded jeans, and a jade colored tee shirt that formed to her curves wickedly. She waited for him. She was his. His mouth watered in anticipation.

"Come on, Nicole, I have one more thing to show you." The damn shopkeeper interrupted. Again. With a wave of her hand, Josephine dismissed Ian, drew Nicole to another room, and closed the door. A sign on the door quite boldly pronounced it was off limits to customers.

Ian clenched his fists in frustration. Okay, he'd wait until Nicole came out, and then he'd ask her out to dinner. They could get to know each other, and then who knows where the evening might lead. He felt a need, and since that woman had been the cause, it seemed only right that she be the one to fulfill it.

**

Nicole only half listened to Josephine drone on about the lighthouse, she was too busy remembering the almost-kiss. When she'd stood up, right in the arms of that actor, she'd been confused by the overwhelming emotions pelting her. A longing for something she couldn't identify overcame her, and she felt as if she'd suddenly found something that had been missing in her life.

His gaze had burned into her. Challenging, questioning. And when he'd leaned forward as if to kiss her, her heart had beat fiercely. Such an intimate act from a stranger had surprised her, and she'd pulled back in protest.

"Damn."

"Nicole, are you okay?" Josephine put down the book she'd been leafing through and turned her full attention to Nicole.

"Sorry. I'm fine."

"Are you sure?" Josephine hesitated. "I make a great listener, you know, and I saw what was happening out there."

Nicole snorted. "Nothing was happening except some famous actor used to getting what he wants, when he wants, made a pass at me."

"Is that what you think?"

"It's what I know." Nicole had to protect herself from hurting, and the actor certainly offered nothing more than a one-night stand. She also knew that the powerful emotions sparking between the two of them placed Ian in a dangerous position. Until Nicole was sure Jeff's murderer wouldn't find her, anyone that got too close to her wasn't safe. As far as Nicole was concerned, she felt nothing but gratitude for Josephine's well-timed interruption.

Josephine stared at Nicole, so she attempted to lighten the

mood. "Hey, how many women can say they've been kissed by Ian Calder? Maybe you should have let him kiss me before you interrupted us."

"Hmmm, that is a thought, but the time's not right. You both have issues to work through." Josephine placed her hand on Nicole's arm and said, "Know that no matter what, I am here for you. If you need anything, day or night, just call. Okay?"

Nicole sobered. The urge to confide was strong. It was only the knowledge that anyone close to her was in danger that stopped her. Avoiding Josephine's eyes, she replied, "I will. Thanks."

Josephine handed Nicole a couple of books and pointed her to the back door. "You're not ready for each other yet, so I suggest you leave that way."

Nicole wrinkled her brow. Not ready for each other yet. Nicole knew why she should avoid the actor, but Josephine was just being weirdly cryptic. Wanting to return to the store, but knowing that would be a mistake for many reasons, she left through the back door. Sunlight shone over the docks, and Nicole inhaled the salty ocean air and reveled in the beehive of activity from the nearby fish market. She called for Sumo and while she waited for the canine, her traitorous mind tingled with the memory of Ian's lips as they drew near. Her pulse quickened, and she felt an empty ache for the kiss that had never been.

***

Ian paced the smooth wooden floor while his imagination ran rampant with thoughts of seduction and passion. What was taking the two of them so long? He couldn't wait to talk to Nicole and get her alone to experiment with his renewed capability, so to speak. Could his problem really be over that easily? She'd definitely seemed amenable to his advances, and though they hadn't spoken a word between them, there'd been a primal understanding of each other's need.

Ian preferred his sex with no talking, because the women he dated usually blew the mood when they opened their mouths...to talk, that is. But he had a feeling that Nicole was different from his usual three B type. It didn't matter. If she was the one to re-awaken his sexual prowess, then so be it.

A slamming door jolted him from his jumbled progression of thoughts. Josephine stepped from the office and smiled. "Oh, you're still here. Was there anything else I could help you with?"

"No, I'm fine." Ian glanced behind her.

Josephine shrugged and turned to talk with a woman who had wandered over to the cappuccino machine. Tall, slender, and sleekly dressed in silk designer pants and a matching blouse, the woman regally brushed a strand of blond hair back into place and let her blue-eyed gaze wander over Ian and then dismiss him with a twitch of her nose. The finely tuned drawl of some southern state colored the woman's voice as she talked with Josephine.

Ignoring the conversation, Ian's frustration mounted as the office door remained stubbornly empty. Where was she? Time stretched as Ian became aware of the sound of the clock ticking, a dog barking outside, the lap of water against sturdy wooden docks. The sounds assaulting him made him grit his teeth. Silently, he swore and paced the floor outside the office, an action that earned him another imperious glance from the woman with Josephine.

"I must say." The woman delicately sipped her cappuccino. "I'm not at all pleased about these movie people over-running our town. I had to wait in line to get seated for brunch because that rabble of a crew had taken over the *Horizon Cafe*."

Josephine merely smiled and offered the woman a tray of shortbread. Ian wondered if he should stick his head in the office and ask if Nicole had a moment to talk with him. A narrowing of Josephine's eyes and a shake of her head quelled that thought, and he resigned himself to waiting for Nicole to come out. She must be making a phone call or something. He just wished she'd hurry up, so he wouldn't have to listen to any more complaining from that blasted woman who droned on with one complaint after another.

"The next thing I knew, I was getting a phone call saying my BMW wouldn't be repaired for a couple of days because the garage guy, what's his name, is closing to spend time as an extra in the movie. Those people, all they do is come into town and disrupt the locals. I tell you if there's any talk of filming another movie here, I'll lodge my complaint with the town council."

Josephine rolled her eyes at Ian who chuckled. It was a familiar tune wherever they filmed. Some people were all for it, then you had the ones who couldn't be made happy no matter what you did to compensate them for the disruption.

"As a local merchant, I'd encourage another movie filming here. My business has already increased and eased the pressure of what's usually a slow time for me. Not only that, but I'm getting reimbursed for time that filming blocks the foot traffic to *Wishes*."

Josephine's words provoked a stare that would have frozen the harbor in mid-summer.

"I see." With a deliberate snap, the woman set her cup on the table. "I don't think I'll be buying anything today. Goodbye." The woman's heels clicked on the wooden floor, and the door banged shut behind her. Ian and Josephine looked at each other and laughed.

"Believe it or not, she's not even a local. She and her husband only come here a couple of weeks a year, but treat us as if the whole town is here for their pleasure."

"I'm sure there are plenty of locals who feel the same way, though. I see it all the time."

"You do?"

"Okay, maybe I'm too busy signing autographs, but the behind the scenes guys have a hard time. You know, the set coordinator, location manager, regular crew members—they get the hassle from the people. I just get the glory." His eyes flicked toward the office door, wondering what was taking Nicole so long.

"If you're looking for Nicole, she went out the back way."

Ian's heart thumped, all talk of the hassle of filming forgotten. "Oh."

"I'm sorry, I don't think she knew you were waiting for her."

"How could she not know?" Ian frowned at the delay in his planned seduction, and he felt an unwarranted, acute fear that he may never see her again. "Where can I find her?"

"I can't give out that kind of information. As famous as you are, you're still a stranger, and we protect our own around here."

"Protect? You think I'm a threat to her?"

"I'm not thinking anything, just following certain practices." Josephine smiled coyly. "No matter, she's gone now, but I'll let her know you want to talk to her. Where are you staying? Maybe she can get a hold of you?"

Ian was stunned. He was used to women chasing him. Now, he was doing the chasing, and he couldn't even find out where she lived. Bitter disappointment roiled in his stomach, and he felt a twinge of empathy for some of the obsessed fans that would do anything to find him. He wanted Nicole, and he couldn't have her. At least, not right away. But anything worth having was worth fighting for.

With a determined smile, Ian looked Josephine directly in the eyes and said, "Tell her I'm staying at the *Wyllow Wood Inn*, and if she doesn't come looking for me, I'll come looking for her." With those words, he stomped out of the store and stood on the front walk where he found himself shaking with the roller coaster of emotions he'd experienced. His unusual rudeness surprised him, but he chuckled at the freedom he felt at expressing himself when he was usually so careful of his public image.

A prickling sensation on the back of his neck prompted him to turn and look, hoping it wasn't another out of control fan wanting some part of him. The street was quiet. The morning rush had slowed, and lunch had not quite started. A few tourists wound their way from one store to another, with only an occasional glance his direction from someone wondering if they should approach him or not. A horn honked, scaring a stray dog into leaving the middle of the street. A couple of kids raced each other to the ice cream store at the far end of town, and the outdoor cafe seated a young couple underneath a brightly colored umbrella. Nothing menacing, yet he felt threatened.

A flicker from the store window across the street alerted him, and he looked toward the bakeshop. Beneath a green and white awning, a man's face peered through the window. Ian managed to catch only a glimpse, but the weasel face was familiar. Oh, yes, the strange man who had dashed out of *Wishes* the other day. He must be a local if he was still hanging around.

The man's intense scrutiny made Ian shiver. Giving in to the sudden need to get as far away as possible, he set a hurried pace for his hotel. It didn't take long to reach *Wyllow Wood* and check for messages at the front desk. Assured there were none, he wound his way down the narrow path to his private cottage. Rounding the bend in the tree lined pathway, he found himself facing the last person he would have expected to see in the small middle of nowhere town.

"Vanessa?"

"Hi Dad." The young woman rose to greet him. Normally in a chignon or braid, her unrestrained blond hair fell loosely about her fine features. No doubt about it, Vanessa had her mother's good looks. Ian experienced a momentary pang for a once great relationship gone sour, actually two relationships gone sour, the one with his ex-wife, as well as his daughter.

She looked so young standing on the veranda waiting for him. When he reached the top stair, he didn't know whether to hug her or not. Vanessa put an end to the question when she reached out and gave him a brief hug. An awkward hug. Ian hugged her and stepped back to look into her face.

"You look like you've been crying. Are you all right?" Vanessa brushed a hand across her sky blue eyes and explained, "Oh, I've been driving for awhile, I'm just tired is all."

"The airport's not that far away."

"I didn't fly, I drove."

"What? Why would you do that?" His daughter and her husband, Bob, lived in New York, which would have made for about a twenty-hour drive. Ian suddenly noticed the luggage that sat unobtrusively in the corner of the deck. Louis Vuitton it wasn't. In fact, it looked like the same luggage he'd bought for her when she went off to college.

"Oh, I just felt like a relaxing drive."

"I see. Do you have somewhere to stay?"

"No."

Was it his imagination or was her voice shaking? Something wasn't right, but knowing his daughter, she wouldn't tell him until she was ready. She'd probably had a fight with Bob and was trying to teach him a lesson. Vanessa was like her mother in that respect, she liked to manipulate and play games. With a sigh, he picked up her luggage and led the way into the cottage.

Gruffly he declared, "You may as well stay here with me, there are three bedrooms and a kitchen in this place."

"Are you sure? I could find somewhere else."

Ian was tempted to tell her to go ahead. The two of them had never done well in close proximity for any length of time, but something prompted him to keep her close.

"Yes, sweetheart, I'm sure." He grinned. "I'll stay out of your way, if you stay out of mine, all right?"

"Sure, Dad."

"Good. You can take this room. I've got the one up in the loft." He led her to a cozy bedroom with an amazing view of the ocean. He'd decided against that particular room for himself because he'd found it too feminine with its purple pansy bedspread and delicate antique dressing table with finely arched mirror. A warm breeze drifted in the window, and lavender sheers blew gently on the summer wind. Yes, it was definitely a woman's room.

Ian threw the luggage onto the bed and left Vanessa to her unpacking. Her husband, Bob, had confided in Ian that Vanessa had bouts of jealousy and reacted badly to suggestions and well-intended advice. Bob's job demanded late evenings wining and dining potential investors and clients, while Vanessa sat home and stewed that he was cheating on her. She had too much time on her hands, but as far as Ian was concerned, running away when things didn't go the way she wanted, was not acceptable. That's what her mother had done years before. Bob needed to stop giving her everything she wanted and encourage her to find a hobby or some interests of her own. Ian sighed. They'd probably argued over something ridiculous like who to invite to one of their dinner parties.

In the meantime, shooting started in a few days, so Vanessa would need to keep herself occupied. He'd be too busy putting in twelve to fourteen hour days. Heck, by that time she'd probably miss Bob enough to hop in her car and drive back home. Meanwhile, he'd spend some time with her; she was his daughter after all.

With that settled, Ian's thoughts turned to Nicole. Funny how someone he'd never even spoken a single word to could wind herself into his mind so intensely. His groin tightened as he remembered their almost-kiss in the store earlier today. He meant what he'd said to Josephine —if Nicole didn't come looking for him, he'd go looking for her.

She had until tomorrow.

Chapter Six

Josephine watched Jacob saunter up the docks to her store. He hesitated at her back steps, his face mirroring reluctance as if the task before him was one he would rather avoid. With a shake of her head and a muttered, "Narrow-minded boob," Josephine opened the back door and motioned him in before he scurried back to the docks.

"I'm getting there in my own good time, woman."

"I know, Jacob, but the store opens in ten minutes so I don't have time for your tender sensibilities."

They entered the dimly lit store and the screen door banged shut behind them. Jacob mumbled about how a man around the place could fix that problem and then planted himself in the middle of the room with his eyes glued to the hardwood floor, as if the store's contents might somehow curse him.

Josephine laughed. It was a gentle laugh threaded with frustration. She was used to his attitude, but she'd never admit that it hurt. "Come on, Jacob, there's nothing here to hurt you. It's just a store with candles, books, cards, and jewelry."

"Yep." He shuffled his shoes on the floor. "I know. It's just." He lifted his eyes and scanned the store so warmly lit with the morning sun arching over the horizon and shining through the windows. "It's all weird stuff."

Josephine snorted. Jacob blushed.

"Just tell me what's so urgent you had to drag me in here."

"I'd like to drag you somewhere all right," she mumbled.

"Pardon."

"Nothing, Jacob." She paused and questioned, "Are you

keeping an eye on Nicole?"

Jacob frowned. "I talk to her now and again."

"That's not enough, Jacob." Josephine wondered how to make him realize that danger lurked, without telling him how she knew. He was too much a man of the sea, a *Don't believe it unless you see it* kind of a person. Salt of the earth, sure, but his imagination, or lack thereof, limited his view of life.

Josephine was used to dealing with instincts and a belief in a world beyond this one, whereas, Jacob focused on the day-to-day chores of catching enough fish to pay the bills and keep his trawler in serviceable condition. If she told him that her spirit guide had appeared in her dreams and warned her about an evil lurking in the shadows, the shadows surrounding Nicole, he'd walk away and never speak to her again.

She respected his beliefs. She'd like to see him understand the abundant energy that flowed within and without the human body, as well as the powers and abilities of the mind.

"What, woman? What are you driving at? And be quick about it, I have a ship and crew waiting to set sail."

"Jacob, look me in the eyes. Have I ever lied to you, steered you wrong, done anything to anyone that you felt was wrong?"

Jacob looked her hard in the face, as if trying to fathom what was on her mind. "Well, no, I can honestly say you deal fairly with people. Humph, you've even helped a one or two of them out with stuff from this store of yours." He waved his hand dismissively about the store.

"Then please believe me when I say that Nicole is in some kind of danger. Call it women's intuition or whatever, but something is going to happen, and it's not going to be good for Nicole."

Jacob came to alertness. "Danger? What have you heard? Did someone threaten her?"

"No, nothing like that. It's just a feeling."

Jacob narrowed his gaze. "A feeling, aye? Can't get too alarmed about a feeling."

"Oh, really," Josephine snapped indignantly. "I seem to remember a day last spring that had been forecast as being beautiful and sunny, but instead of setting sail you kept the Miss Gale docked for the day."

"That's different."

"No, it is not. Everyone laughed at you when you said a storm was coming, but they stopped laughing when it hit and wreaked havoc with the ships that sailed that morning. How did you know about the storm, Jacob? No one else did."

"I just knew," he mumbled. "I've been sailing these waters my whole life, and I can sense when things aren't right."

Josephine smacked her forehead with her palm. "The saints preserve me from idiots!" She turned to Jacob and demanded, "Then why can't you understand that I've been dealing with people my whole life, and I know when something's not right with someone? It's no different than you and the waters you've always sailed."

Jacob looked pained, but he was a fair and logical man. "Well, when you put it that-a-way, there may be something to what you're saying. Tell me more."

"I can't. All I know is that there's some kind of danger, and I think that we both need to keep a close eye on Nicole until I figure it out."

"Wait a minute, if there's some kind of danger involved and you go poking about, you might put yourself in danger."

"How sweet of you to worry," she teased. "I'll be fine, Jacob. Just keep an eye on Nicole for the next while."

"Humph! Okay." His gaze fell on a nearby assortment of scarves and jewelry. He pointed to a rather vivid peach scarf and said, "I'll take that. It'll give me an excuse to go visit her, but it will have to be tomorrow, because I'm tied up for the rest of the day." He took another quick look around. "Maybe I'll take some of those candles as well. You know, in case I lose power on the ship sometime, they can be my back up."

"Of course." Josephine smiled inwardly at Jacob's sweet attempt at peacemaking. He'd insulted her store, now he wanted to say he was sorry. She knew she shouldn't, but she teased,

"You made a good choice, these candles are rose-scented."

"Jeez, woman, I don't care about the scent. Just give them to me." He snatched the package, threw some money on the counter and turned to leave. He hesitated. "Don't worry, we won't let anything happen to Nicole. She's one of us now, right?"

Tears threatened, and Josephine had to fight to keep them from falling. It wouldn't do to scare Jacob away now that he was finally in her store. "Right, Jacob." Stubborn and narrow-minded he may be, but he was also sweet, giving, and not too bad looking —if you liked a sea-faring, crusty kind of a man.

***

Darkness swathed the countryside in a heavy cloak, and Nicole had trouble catching her breath. Through the clinging branches of the forest she ran, pursued by a shadow whose face she had yet to see. Whispered threats of death drifted in and out of the misty fog, as the shadow laughed at her fear. She came to the edge of a cliff, and the rocky terrain below gave her nowhere to flee, so she turned to face her pursuer.

From the underbrush, a figure emerged. He stepped into the intermittent moonlight and Nicole saw his face—the face of her dead husband. Quicker than she could imagine, he reached out and slapped her.

"How dare you talk about me to your friends." It was Jeff's voice, but not. Nicole struggled to wake from the nightmare, but a slap from the ghostly Jeff kept her there.

Nicole cringed and begged Jeff not to hurt her. "Please, I only told Jennifer that we argued about buying a new car. Nothing more. Really."

Another slap resounded through the misty air to mingle with the crashing of waves on the shore far below. Nicole lost her balance as her foot slipped on a loose rock. She grasped for Jeff's arm, but it was too late, and the last thing she saw was disbelief register on his face when he realized that she would fall to her death.

The crashing waves came closer and Nicole screamed, but not so loud that she couldn't hear Jeff pleading for forgiveness. The wind whipped the words from his mouth, but Nicole thought she heard him tell her to fly with the hawks. The hawks? She had no time to ponder the words, because the rocks were coming closer, and she needed to wake up before she hit bottom.

She awoke with a start and in a cold sweat. At the same time, the alarm blared with the morning's wake up song. Trying to calm herself, Nicole listened to the Barry Manilow tune and appreciated the irony of the words about yesterday being a dream, facing the morning, crying on a breeze, and pain calling. Substitute Jeff's name for Mandy, and you pretty much had Nicole's night in a nutshell. With a shaky sigh, she swung her feet over the edge of the bed and tested the reliability of her legs. They seemed all right, and she was able to make it to the bathroom with no mishap.

Standing in the shower, she angled herself to allow the hot water to hammer down on the back of her neck and shoulders. The steam fogged the window and created a dreamlike haze in the small bathroom, but Nicole kept the water on hot. She needed the relief it brought. Her dreams about her relationship with Jeff worried her, and she was finding it hard to differentiate the dreams from the reality of the bonds they had shared.

Jeff had been a difficult man to live with, and, yes, he'd struck her a couple of times, but most of the time things had been fine between them. No relationship was perfect, there was always compromise and she'd considered her acceptance of Jeff's short temper, her compromise.

Funny, now that she was free from his influence, she could see certain circumstances in a different light. Over the last months, she'd taken care of herself and found that she liked the responsibility. She received enjoyment from something as simple as paying the electricity, balancing the checkbook, or even deciding to sleep in late if she wanted. Chores that had once seemed arduous, had taken on a new light. Jeff's expectations had placed pressure on her to do things and do them right or else. Now, she could simply enjoy.

Jeff had wanted her constant attention, yet wasn't willing to let her do anything for herself. Once she'd mentioned taking a night course at the local high school, but Jeff had vetoed that idea, so she'd suggested a correspondence course, another idea Jeff had been against.

"I want your only responsibility to be me." He'd taken her in his arms and said, "I guess I just love you too much, and I'm not ready to share you yet. Maybe in another couple of years you can look into something. Unless we have children, of course, then you'll stay home to take care of them."

At the time, Nicole had been flattered at such devotion, so she'd squelched her feeling that she was being stifled and manipulated. Now, she saw that Jeff tried to control her in every situation. Even when it came to kids, he kept prodding her to stay on birth control, because he wasn't ready to share her yet. So, their life had gone on quietly and unfulfilled—at least for Nicole. Jeff had buried himself in his paintings and left her to her own devices. But he always expected her to be waiting for him when he finally emerged from his studio. A studio that had been off limits to her while he'd been alive.

Dry from her shower, Nicole pulled on a black lace bra, matching thong, a pair of jeans, and a bright peach colored tee shirt that complimented her mahogany hair and hazel eyes. Buttoning up her jeans, she remembered her astonishment the first time she found the nerve to step into Jeff's studio after his death. Paintings lined the walls and littered the floors. Beautiful paintings. Nicole had no idea the depth of Jeff's talent, and she felt guilty for ignoring something so obvious while he'd been alive. So no relationship was perfect; blame needed dealing on both sides.

Wildlife and nature had been the most prevalent of paintings, and Nicole had had no trouble selling most of them once she'd set her heart on the task. There were too many to keep for herself, so she'd picked eight of her favorites, boxed them, and stored them until she found a permanent life without fear of the stalker.

She shivered. The present intruded, and Nicole decided to treat herself to brunch. Just then, Sumo lifted his head and whined. Not worried, because the whine was subdued and not territorial, Nicole stepped over to the window. Since her room was located up the winding staircase on the third floor, she could look over the landscape for miles.

The beauty of the panorama spread out below her and into the distance. She appreciated the rhythm of the undulating ocean waves and the sheer power of the rocky cliffs. Just then, a wind blew from across the ocean, bringing with it the tangy taste of salt, as well as the threat of an impending storm. Nicole shivered as the cool wind brushed across her face, and she hastened to pull the window shut.

Grabbing a light jacket in case the day did turn to stormy weather, Nicole hastened downstairs and out the door with Sumo on her heels. He went everywhere with her, and Nicole was grateful that the people in town accepted him so readily. Being a rottweiler, Sumo tended to send people to the other side of the street with no more than a toss of his massive head, but if people only knew how affectionate he was, they'd feel embarrassment at their unwarranted fear. Although, Nicole wouldn't want to see what her faithful canine would do to anyone who threatened her, his protective tendencies could erupt into a lethal killing machine. Just then, he looked up at her with tongue hanging from the side of his mouth. Nicole laughed and wrapped her arms around him in a quick hug.

"I love you, Sumo. Now, let's go eat, I'm hungry."

With a responsive bark, Sumo bounded off around the lighthouse to the cliff, as if he knew exactly what Nicole had said. Nicole followed, only to see Sumo vigorously sniffing the ground, looking for signs of a rabbit, no doubt. He loved chasing the fleet creatures. Walking the circle around the building, she headed to the woodland trail that led to the main trail into town. The drive to town was ten minutes on the winding road that led away from the coast and back again, but Nicole preferred to hike the path from the lighthouse. A more direct route, it took no longer than the drive and offered picturesque scenery of rolling ocean waves, craggy cliff tops, majestic white pines, and an assortment of spruce and fir trees.

Today, Nicole walked the path without thought to her surroundings. Instead, she pondered her growing sense of self-worth and the re-awakening of her emotions. And she felt only the slightest twinge of guilt for yesterday's encounter with the actor, Ian. Even now, the memory of the almost-kiss filled her with a longing for something she didn't even know was missing in her life until she'd looked into steely blue-gray eyes. She'd been lost in their depths, but not in a bad way. Not the way it had been with Jeff, when her wants and needs had come second to everything he had wanted. The swirling sense of becoming one with another human being had given her a feeling of unity and completeness, instead of the self-destructive love she'd shared with Jeff.

Why had it taken his death for her to wake up to her own talents and possibilities? It scared her to think what would have happened if Jeff had lived, and she'd buried herself in his wants and needs for the rest of her life. She would have ceased to exist, except as an extension of him. Yet here she was, months since Jeff's death and the sky hadn't fallen in while she had the beginning of a great new writing career. Nicole was beginning to realize how Jeff had manipulated her into believing she couldn't get by without him.

She shivered. That train of thought was morbid and fruitless. Things had happened the way they had, her life was what it was, and she would make sure never to let another man overwhelm her to the extent that she became a non-entity again. Thoughts of yesterday pushed their way into her mind and the power the man had wielded over her with a look. She decided it would be a good idea to avoid him for the endurance of filming, for her sake as well as his. She didn't need another man getting in the way of a bullet meant for her.

Chapter Seven

Brunch at *Horizon Cafe* was worthy of the finest restaurant anywhere. Nicole sipped her mimosa and tried to focus on the fast moving conversation. Upon arriving, all the tables had been full, and Nicole had agreed to share with a woman already seated. Vanessa, a guest at the *Wyllow Wood Inn* was in town for a few days.

There were a lot of transients. Just in town for a while. Nicole gave a silent snort. Josephine had stopped her outside the cafe and told her Ian's message: If she doesn't come looking for me, I'll come looking for her.

Who did he think he was anyway? Just because he was rich, famous, and handsome, he didn't have the right to give ultimatums. He was probably used to getting any woman he wanted. He was probably used to getting anything he wanted. He had the manners of a spoiled child. Anger built, and Nicole stabbed a spear of asparagus imagining it to be Ian, or maybe it was Jeff. That thought stopped Nicole cold. Was she confusing the motivation of the two men?

"Nicole?" Vanessa's voice interrupted Nicole's thoughts.

"Sorry, I was busy enjoying the food." To prove her point she popped a cheddar stuffed mushroom in her mouth.

"I was just saying how I love the color of your hair. What do you use?"

"Use? I'm not sure what you mean."

"Hair color. What do you use?"

Nicole laughed. "I don't color my hair. To tell you the truth, I like my hair color."

"Really?" Vanessa looked confused. "I thought everyone

over thirty-five colored their hair."

Nicole stopped her fork halfway to her mouth, hollandaise sauce dripping from her poached eggs. Vanessa must have realized the insult, and her face colored red. The two of them looked at each other and then, as if on cue, they broke out laughing.

Nicole had been alone and dealing with so many emotions for the last while that it felt great to share laughter with another woman. It was a release, and she found the laughter soon turning to tears. It was then she noticed that the same thing was happening to Vanessa, except that the tears had turned to sobs.

Nicole put her hand on Vanessa's arm. "Hey, are you okay?"

Vanessa sniffled and brushed her hair away from her face and the falling tears. That small motion exposed a bruise that looked suspiciously like a handprint.

Nicole gasped and drew her hand back as if she'd been the one struck. "Vanessa, what happened to your face?"

Self-consciously, Vanessa pulled her hair forward to cover the bruise. "Oh, nothing," she said, her eyes darting around the room.

Nicole's heart thudded unsteadily in her chest. She recognized that type of bruise. Her throat constricted, and she had to force the words out. "Vanessa, I know what happened. I'm here if you want to talk about it. Sometimes it helps."

"I don't know." Vanessa pushed her eggs around her plate with her fork. "It's okay, really. It doesn't happen very often, and I've usually done something to tick him off. His job is stressful, and I shouldn't nag him when he comes home."

Her fingers brushed lightly over her bruised cheek. When she spoke, her voice was a mere whisper. "This time was really bad, though." Her eyes darted around as if making sure no one was looking, and then she raised her blouse to expose a wicked looking purple and yellow bruise on her ribs. "He hit me, and when I stumbled over the coffee table to the floor, he kicked me. I think I may have cracked a rib or two."

"Jesus, Vanessa. Have you been to a doctor?" Nicole asked.

"No." A sob shook Vanessa's shoulders. "I left. I was so afraid, I grabbed some clothes and left."

"He let you just walk out?" Nicole was surprised. Men like that usually didn't let the object of their abuse leave so easily.

"Well...no, he locked me in the spare room until I settled down. As if I was the one who needed settling." Vanessa laughed a bitter, ironic laugh. "I packed the luggage I used in college with a few extra clothes I kept in the closet—my other clothes and luggage were in our bedroom—and then I climbed out the window."

"You climbed out the window? I don't think I would have had the nerve."

"I had no choice. I was afraid of what he'd do if I stayed." She rubbed her ribs gently and said, "I couldn't stand it anymore. There was no one to talk to and things kept getting worse. Every time I tried to talk to my dad, he sided with Bob. He'd tell me that I was lucky to have a man who gave me everything I wanted, and I should stop acting like my mother. She left us, you know. She was bored with her life and wanted a change, and she and my dad...well, he had an affair." Her eyes flew to Nicole, and she blushed. "It doesn't matter. They just didn't get along."

Nicole gave Vanessa a reassuring pat on the arm, tears of pity welling in her eyes, and she asked, "Did you tell your dad that Bob was hitting you?"

Vanessa sniffled and wiped her nose with a napkin. "No, I didn't come right out and tell him. I was too embarrassed. I'd been so adamant about marrying Bob, and I didn't want to admit I'd made a mistake."

"What did you tell him?" Nicole prodded.

"I told him how Bob was staying out late a lot and that I thought he was seeing other women. I told him how there was nothing to do all day long, and that Bob expected me to be home when he got there, no matter what."

Nicole's heart thudded deep in her chest. What a familiar

story, except Jeff had only slapped her a few times, he'd never gotten as physical as Bob. Did it matter? None of it was acceptable, it was only a matter of varying degrees.

"Vanessa." Nicole kept her voice soft and gentle; she didn't want to sound as if she were criticizing Vanessa. "Your mom left your dad because she was bored, and you told your dad you weren't happy because you had nothing to do all day.

Vanessa frowned. She must have realized the significance of Nicole's question, and she flushed. "Oh. I sounded like a bored housewife. I sounded like Mom. But that shouldn't matter. He's my father. He's supposed to know when I need help." Vanessa sniffled and managed to look lost and forlorn.

Nicole gave her a hug. "You didn't tell me, why Solitary Cove? Do you know someone here?"

"Yes, I came to see my father." She snorted. "A lot of good that did me. He wasn't exactly thrilled to see me. I'm sure I cramp his style."

"I doubt that. I'm sure he's glad to see you. Vanessa, we may have only just met, but I want you to think of me as a friend."

"Thanks. I haven't had a friend in a while. Bob scared them all away."

"He found some reason for you to stop seeing all your friends, didn't he?" Nicole asked.

Still sniffing, but seemingly under control, Vanessa nodded. "Yeah. He said my best friend, Betty, had come on to him at the Christmas party, and he wasn't comfortable around her anymore. Another one supposedly had a drug charge against her in the past. Bob said it would be detrimental to his career if he associated with such a person, so I wasn't allowed to see her anymore."

"Did you ever talk to either one of them to find out their side of the story?"

"No. Bob wouldn't let me. Pretty stupid of me, huh?"

Nicole squeezed Vanessa's hand. "No, not stupid. You were trying to keep peace in your marriage, and there's nothing wrong with that."

Narrowing her eyes, Vanessa looked at Nicole. "How do you know so much about this?"

"How do you think?"

"Oh, I'm sorry."

The smile they shared formed a brief, unspoken bond until the waitress cheerily interrupted their moment."Is there anything else I can get for you?"

"I think I'd like some more cappuccino, please," Nicole said.

"Me, too. With extra whip cream and chocolate shavings on top." Vanessa laughed. "One of the last things Bob told me was that I was getting fat. So that's for you, jerk." She made a rude sign with her finger.

Nicole stared in surprise. "He said you were getting fat. You're kidding, right?"

"No. It was right before he slapped me the second time. He said that if he was fooling around, it was my fault for letting myself go to pot." Vanessa picked at her napkin with her fingers.

Nicole was furious at the obvious manipulations. Vanessa was beautiful, with her hair reflecting like gold threads in the subdued light, sky blue eyes full of caring and vulnerability, and a body that would drive most men to drooling.

"Vanessa, look at me." She waited until she had the other woman's full attention before continuing. "You are an absolutely gorgeous woman. Bob is an asshole. End of story."

Vanessa laughed and seemed to relax. "Oh, Nicole, I just had a thought. Why don't you come to dinner tonight? I have to warn you, though, my dad will be there. I'm trying to get someone to act as a buffer because we don't have a lot in common, and I can never think of anything to talk about."

"I don't know. Maybe you and your dad should spend time talking. You've only told him half the story. Maybe it's time to tell him everything."

Vanessa pleaded, "I will, but I'm not ready. I don't know how to talk to him. Please come. He's got some business meeting this afternoon, so I'm all right then, but I need you tonight."

Her heart went out to the younger woman. Maybe she could be of some help. She could gently steer the conversation where it needed to go, act as mediator, maybe even get Vanessa and her father on the right track to a better relationship. The thought of helping someone get over an abusive spouse made her feel good, so Nicole said yes. No sooner had the words left her mouth than Vanessa moaned.

"Oh, no. Speak of the devil. Here comes Dad now. Is my bruise covered?" She fumbled with her hair trying to hide the evidence of Bob's hand hitting her face.

"You're fine, Vanessa." Nicole turned to greet Vanessa's father and found herself staring directly into familiar blue eyes. "Oh. My. God." The breathless words formed an almost silent curse.

His eyes narrowed. Barely sparing a glance at Vanessa, Ian spoke. "You."

"You two know each other? Nicole, you didn't tell me you knew him." Vanessa looked questioningly between the two of them.

Nicole's voice croaked. "I didn't know he was your father."

Ian's fierce stare made Nicole uncomfortable, but Vanessa didn't seem to notice the tension building. Nicole shifted under his gaze and couldn't believe she'd agreed to have dinner with Vanessa and Ian Calder. The man she'd vowed to avoid. The man who made her limbs feel like they were melting into mush. The man who, at that moment, was making her body shiver with anticipation with nothing more than a look. Damn! How could she get out of dinner?

"Vanessa, about dinner tonight."

"Yes, don't worry about bringing anything. Dad's cooking, and he's got everything organized."

"You're having dinner with us?

Nicole flushed as the slightest hint of a smile curved Ian's lips, and he crossed his arms across his chest. Damn him. It was a simple enough question, but his tone carried a challenge.

He knew she had accepted dinner without knowing who she'd be having dinner with. Now, he expected her to cancel. Typical man, they thought they knew everything. Vanessa looked at her with confusion, and a flicker of uncertainty crossed her face.

Nicole was lost. Her original reason for accepting dinner still existed. Vanessa needed her help. There had been no one for her to turn to, so she wanted to be there for Vanessa. Lifting her chin, she pulled all her self-confidence to the surface and replied, "Yes, I'm having dinner with you and Vanessa."

Ian's smile grew into a grin. What worried Nicole was the predatory look that darkened his eyes. "Good, I'm glad to see Vanessa making friends so easily. She doesn't have many at home." He looked at his daughter and said, "You're like your mother. She was always a bit of a loner."

Tears formed in Vanessa's eyes, but Ian had no idea his daughter was on the verge of falling apart. Nicole fumed at the man's insensitivity, but reminded herself that he didn't know the whole story. She still felt like hitting him over the head with a plate. Not just any plate, but one of the heavy stoneware ones decorating the walls. A glint of angry intention must have shown in her eyes, because Ian took a step back. Then he laughed.

God, he's arrogant, Nicole thought as she watched him look at his watch and then take notice of an approaching fan.

"Sorry, ladies, I have to go." Without even a backward glance, he was gone.

Against her will, Nicole noticed how he filled out his jeans and quickly looked to make sure Vanessa hadn't seen her checking out her father's butt. She hadn't.

The screeching voice of the approaching fan intruded. "He left. I could have sworn he saw me coming. Do you girls know where he's gone? Do you know him?" The sixty-something woman shoved a pen and paper at the two of them. "Can you get me his autograph? I'll pay you."

Vanessa waved her hand in dismissal. "Sorry, we don't

know him. We just happened to be in the right place at the right time."

The woman's features caved in with a look of extreme disappointment. "Oh." Tears filled her eyes. "I wanted to meet him so badly, you know. He reminds me so much of my dear departed Wilbur and I thought." she ran a hand through her overprocessed hair. "You know, I'm not too old, and I've been told I look like Catherine Zeta-Jones, an older version of course. Are you sure you don't know him?" Nicole had the worst urge to laugh, and considered sending her after Ian thinking it would serve him right, but one look at the hopeful desperation that filled the woman's eyes, and she felt a stab of pity. Meeting her hero would only leave the woman frustrated, and her dreams dead. The woman could hold onto her dreams as long as she could hope to one day meet him and he'd fall at her feet claiming undying love.

"Sorry." Nicole shrugged her shoulders and watched the dejected woman leave the cafe, looking as if she'd just had the worst day of her life.

"Wow. I guess that happens to your dad a lot."

"You have no idea. People feel as if he owes them something just because he's famous, so he never gets any privacy. They hound him everywhere he goes."

"I don't think I'd want to live like that, even if I could be rich and famous."

"Me neither. He handles it pretty well, you know. He tries to be polite, usually to the detriment of his own time and privacy, but some of these people are so...I don't know."

"Desperate?" Nicole supplied.

"Yeah. Desperate, as if touching him or meeting him will change them somehow. It's sad, but Dad always shows them respect. He hardly ever bites anyone's head off." Vanessa laughed, and Nicole joined her.

"You sound proud of him."

"I think I am. I had never thought about how his life is affected by his fame." Vanessa looked shamefaced. "It's no wonder we drifted apart."

"I'd say. Look on the bright side, today you've taken the first step to understanding him, next you can start to build a relationship."

"You have such a positive outlook on everything. I wish I could be more like you."

"No, you don't because there's nothing wrong with you."

"You're right. And you know what, to make myself feel better, I'm going shopping. I'll see you tonight. And, Nicole, thanks for everything. I feel like things are going to be all right." Vanessa surprised Nicole by throwing her arms around her and hugging her.

Nicole left the café and looked for Sumo, who seemed to have wandered off the front porch. She saw him in the park stretched out under the shade of a huge maple tree and soaking up the attention of two children who had braved the big, scary looking beast. Smiling, she whistled for him to come, which he did reluctantly.

Picking up milk and bread at Marlin's Grocery Bin, she headed home for an afternoon of writing. All the way back, her emotions ran from confused denial to intense desire. Man, oh, man, what had she gotten herself into? More importantly, what was she going to wear to dinner with a famous, attractive man? Okay, she was having dinner with Vanessa, Ian would just happen to be there. Same thing.

Winding her way through the forest to the lighthouse, she ignored the whisper of the wind in the trees, and barely acknowledged the inquiring bunny that flicked his ears her direction then disappeared into the safety of the forest. Mainly, she argued with herself whether or not to cancel dinner. The urge to get close to Ian scared her. She'd never felt this kind of excitement before and the curiosity to explore the powerful magnetism between them was strong.

But was it safe?

It should be, she thought, answering her own question. Six months had passed with no hint that the stalker had found out her new identity, that should mean she was safe. Ian's steely gray eyes flashed in her mind, and her heart fluttered. He was not exactly handsome in the traditional sense, but he was so...she was so...she was so attracted to him. That was it, he was your average looking kind of guy, but he exuded such character and magnetism, especially in his movie roles. For years, he had played characters that embodied the masculine hero, and he played the part well.

Nicole shook her head to clear her thoughts. Was she getting his on-screen persona confused with who he really was? She didn't even know him; she'd never even spoken two words to him until today. How could she be so attracted to him? Maybe she should cancel dinner.

Damn it, no. She wouldn't cancel dinner. She had to take a chance sometime, and what better way to get her feet wet, so to speak, than with a rich and famous actor. She'd go to dinner and damn the consequences. Actually, the consequences could prove to be very interesting. After all, she hadn't even kissed a man in a very long time. It would be a romantic interlude, a brief, hopefully torrid affair, and then they could both get on with their lives.

Nicole giggled. She wondered what the great actor Ian Calder would think if he knew she'd planned their entire relationship already. The lighthouse came into sight and Nicole heaved a shuddering sigh of release. She sensed that a new world was about to open up for her.

Chapter Eight

Ian tried to concentrate on Jeb Braxton comments, but his mind wandered to golden-brown eyes. He recalled the gentle curve of Nicole's lips when she smiled and the way her delicate features had lit up when she had first seen him in the cafe. And how, just as quickly, she had schooled her face into a mask of indifference.

No matter. The avid, never-ending attention of female fans had worn thin and Ian had stopped taking advantage of the blatant offers a long time ago. He relished the thought of a relationship that wasn't a sure thing. He looked forward to the flirtation, the getting to know you stage, the first kiss, and the anticipation of never knowing for sure whether the game would end with the joining of two bodies in a primitive act of passion.

"Ian."

Ian snapped from his daydream to find the director staring at him. Jeb had arranged the pre-filming meeting in his suite at the *Wyllow Wood Inn*, and expected all the actors to be there for instructions. Dressed in loose fitting jeans and food-stained white tee shirt Jeb pushed his glasses up his nose and ran a hand through his thinning blond hair.

"Sorry, Jeb. What did you say?"

"Don't play stupid with me, Ian. I know you heard me, and pretending you didn't doesn't change the facts, as much as you would like it if it did."

"Really, I wasn't listening. What did you say?"

Jeb's piercing gaze calculated the truth of Ian's denial. Having decided the validity of his statement, he repeated his words. "I said Melissa had to back out of the film, that's why she's not here today."

A creeping suspicion caused Ian's heart to beat that much faster. There had only been three actresses considered for the part of the leading lady, if Melissa had pulled out, that left only two possibilities. Lord, let it be Amanda. Please don't let it be Candace.

"Candace will be taking her place." Jeb raised his hand to stop Ian objections. "Look, I know you two don't get along, but let's be professional here, okay. Besides Melissa, she's the best one for the part."

Ian leaned forward, his face close to Jeb's. Everyone watched, as if waiting for him to explode. Well, he wasn't going to disappoint them.

"Professional. You want professional? I suppose you consider breaking into my room and waiting naked in my bed, professional. I suppose telling my wife we were having an affair, which was a lie, professional. Or maybe professional would be spreading lies about me to the rag mags when she didn't get what she wanted. Oh, yeah. She's professional all right."

"Come on, Ian. You wanted to divorce your wife anyway, Candace only sped up the process, and most men would give their eye teeth to find her waiting naked in their bed." Seeing the fierce look on Ian's face, Jeb tried again. "Okay, I know she can be a bitch, and she likes things her way, but she's an amazing actress and this film needs her. I need her. Please try to get along with her. Be the better person."

Ian took a deep breath and considered his options. He didn't have any. He'd signed a contract. With a sigh of resignation, he sank into the nearest chair. "Damn it, Jeb, you had better keep her away from me unless we're filming."

"I will, I promise. Now that we've settled that, let's get on to the shooting schedule."

They spent the next couple of hours figuring out who needed to be where and when. The schedule was in hard copy anyway, so Ian didn't bother listening too closely. His gaze wandered over the other actors, and he cursed the fates that had brought Candace back into his life. She was a bitch, and she was responsible for turning his world upside down, for a time anyway. Although, to be honest, he'd let people believe Michelle had left him because of Candace, when the truth was that she had grown bored with their marriage, and the supposed affair had only been an excuse for her to leave. His ego had dictated the dishonesty, and sometimes he believed it himself. He found it easier to blame Candace rather than his own shortcomings. But she still had no right to break into his room and then spread lies about him to anyone who'd listen. Damn. Suddenly the film had lost some of its appeal.

Aware that people were leaving and saying good-bye, Ian realized the meeting had ended. Too bad life wasn't like a script —what you didn't like, you simply re-wrote.

"Hey, Ian, how about we go grab something to eat. I'm kinda hungry."

Ian looked to Keirnan, the young actor who played his son in the film. In his early twenties, with long dark hair, deep cobalt eyes, and a tan that highlighted his handsome features, Keirnan epitomized the sulky, sultry youth that was taking over the movies these days. He was in demand because he was a good actor, and he was gorgeous. Or so Ian had heard from the girls and women who hounded Keirnan constantly. Even in his best years, Ian hadn't fostered the magnitude of fans that flocked to Keirnan. Frankly, he wasn't sure he would want to. He snorted, another surprisingly new enlightenment into his own character.

Ian smiled. "Sorry, but I've got to make dinner for my daughter and a guest."

"Oh, okay, no problem."

Thoughts of Nicole made the blood rush to his head. He had forgotten about her for a couple of minutes in lieu of Jeb's disturbing announcement, but as he left the hotel room, his attention returned to thoughts of preparation for the evening.

***

Nicole threw another dress into the growing heap on her bed. Nothing looked right. In fact, she would lay dollars to donuts that she'd gained weight over the last few months, and now all her clothes made her look fat. Pursing her lips and standing with hands on hips, she considered the remaining clothes she had yet to try. Then it struck her.

"What are you doing?" With a disgusted snort, she grabbed the nearest piece of clothing and proceeded to dress. "You're supposed to be staying away from men, remember." She yanked the silken rust-colored dress over her head and settled it about her hips. "You have no interest at all in him, even if he is rich, famous, and good looking."

Pirouetting in front of the mirror, she ran her hands over the form fitting, oriental style dress and wondered if it was too short. "Besides, he's too old for you." Stepping into seldom worn high heels, she vainly appreciated the way her calves suddenly developed shape. "Maybe it's too dressy for dinner." But she liked the way the slit ran up the back of the dress and the contrast of the virginal mandarin collar as it opened up into the heart shape that bared skin and hinted at cleavage.

"For goodness sake, enough." Nicole grabbed the matching shawl, stomped down the stairs in an unladylike manner, whistled for Sumo, and mumbled all the way to her car how the evening was a big mistake.

That thought increased threefold as she pulled her Wave in behind Vanessa's rented car. She knew it was Vanessa's because she'd seen her driving it yesterday, and she could safely assume that the black Jaguar sitting so obtrusively beside it was Ian's.

"Must be nice." Stepping from the car, she tugged at her dress thinking it was definitely too short. In an attempt to calm her nerves, she took a moment to appreciate the small cottage perched on the edge of the shoreline. The A-frame wooden structure was painted powder blue and accented with royal blue window shutters. Also royal blue were the gingerbread designs that decorated the posts of the wraparound deck.

"We're actually eating in tonight." A deep masculine voice teased, breaking Nicole from her reverie.

Ian stood at the top of the stairs, his figure outlined in the cottage door. Nicole's heart beat faster, and she could have sworn her knees were knocking together. Yep, she should have worn pants. Her own voice suddenly betrayed her, but she forced the words out. "I'm sorry, what did you say?"

Ian laughed. "I said we're eating inside. You've been standing out here for five minutes, so I thought I'd let you know dinner's inside." His gray eyes sparked with humor, and the dimming light of dusk reflected blue in their depths.

"Great start, idiot," Nicole mumbled to herself.

Just then, Sumo trotted from the woods where he'd gone to have a pee, chase a rabbit, or something. Moving like a shadow on silent paws, Sumo ran across the lawn, up the stairs, and launched the full weight of his body at Ian who had been blissfully unaware of the dog. Suddenly finding two paws resting on his chest and a mouth full of sharp teeth close to his face, Ian let out a stream of curses that would have embarrassed a sailor.

Mortified, Nicole yelled for Sumo to get down, which he did, but not before dragging his tongue right up the side of Ian's face. "Oh, I'm so sorry. He doesn't usually do that to people. In fact, I don't remember him ever doing that to anyone."

"This beast is yours?"

"Yes, I'm afraid so." Sumo had returned to Nicole's side and she reached down to pat him on the head.

"And I assume he's here for dinner as well?"

Nicole flushed. "I'm sorry, I never thought to ask. It's just that he goes everywhere with me.

"Is he house trained?"

"Yes."

Sumo whined and looked from Nicole to Ian. Wagging the stub of almost non-existent tail, he looked at Ian as if knowing his fate lay in his hands. Nicole smiled. She knew what it was like to have the intensity of that gaze turned on her. She'd never seen a dog that could focus so intently, and if Ian liked animals at all, he didn't stand a chance.

It only took a second. Ian stared at Sumo measuringly while Sumo whined and wriggled his butt as if reassuring him that he'd behave himself. Ian laughed. "What the hell. Bring him in."

Instinctively knowing he'd won, Sumo rushed past Ian and into the cabin. Nicole made a move to follow, but realized that Ian was staring at her with that look in his eyes that drove her to distraction. Self-consciously, she walked up the stairs. Ian's gaze pinned her with an intensity of emotion that spoke to her inner instincts of passion and desire.

Her breath caught in her throat, and compelled beyond her control, she leaned closer. Without thought, she lifted her hand to his chest. Gently at first, she explored the hard contours, resting briefly on a few curly hairs that had crept out from his black silk shirt. All the while, her mind was yelling at her to stop; yet her hand ached to touch more.

Her gaze connected with his and an ancient sound of haunting sirens like those spouted about in Greek mythology filled her head. Leading her to destruction, no doubt. She couldn't stop, so she spread her hand on his chest and pressed closer. A predatory look of possessiveness filled Ian's gray eyes, causing Nicole to shudder. His gaze narrowed and shadows of the darkening sky reflected contrasts of dark and light upon his face. Nicole's gaze touched upon his forehead, wrinkled with lines of life, danced over his cheekbones, etched like finely-chiseled rock, then came to rest on his lips, quivering in anticipation, much like her own.

She was lost. She could no more keep her distance from this man than she could stop breathing. His hand gripped her arm, and in a move that brooked no argument, pulled her to him until their bodies formed one. A quick intake of breath was the only sound, followed by ragged breathing. Hers or his, Nicole wasn't sure, but it probably belonged to them both.

In heels, she was almost as tall as him, but he still had to lean over to reach her lips. The first kiss was not a gentle one of exploration. Instead, he possessed her with the single motion of taking her lips to his. Soft and hard, hot and cold, his lips pressed to hers, then with a smooth motion, forced them open to ravage her tongue with his.

Nicole quivered. It was all she could do to keep standing. So she did the only thing she could, she pressed her body closer to Ian's. Her breasts ached with the contact and she fought the urge to rub them against the warmth of Ian's hard body. A rush of warmth filled her groin and the evidence of Ian's arousal throbbed against her. Obviously not fighting the urge as Nicole had, he arched closer and rubbed his manhood against her. He cupped her butt in his hands and coerced her into motion with him. Nicole had no ability to function except on a primal level of lust. With that in mind, her hips rotated, melding with Ian's. She was lost.

"Dad, I think your water's boiling," Vanessa hollered from inside the cottage.

Nicole gasped, pushed Ian away from her and stood trembling. Tears formed in her eyes, but she was overwhelmed with too many emotions to know the cause. Ian's nostrils flared, and Nicole could see that he was trying to gain a semblance of control and reality.

He reached up to touch her cheek, and his hand trembled. "Nicole?"

"Hi." Vanessa stood in the door. "What are you two doing standing out here, anyway? I'm starving." Her face flushed. "Sorry. I'm not telling you what to do, Dad. You know, I can make dinner if you want. You don't have to."

"Don't be ridiculous. I said I'd make dinner, and I will. Maybe you could make a drink for Nicole while I go get things ready." His words were abrupt and his tone harsh, probably more from the residual passion than any kind of impatience with Vanessa. Nicole could see how his offhanded tone affected Vanessa, but he was too blind to see how she cringed as if slapped.

Ian stepped aside and motioned Nicole inside. Stepping past him was difficult, as soon as she passed by him the heat of his body engulfed her, and she fought the urge to wrap her arms around him and beg for more.

Beg. Was she insane? Probably, or she wouldn't have been making love to a virtual stranger with his daughter right inside the cabin.

Nicole felt his presence behind her, and then the gentle caress of his hand on her lower back, as he turned to the kitchen and left her and Vanessa in the living room.

"What would you like to drink, Nicole? You look a little pale. Maybe I should make you a double."

Nicole wriggled in the easy chair. She still felt the warm touch of Ian's hands on her rear, and it made her uncomfortable. "Not a double, just a regular dark rum and coke would be fine. If you've got it, that is."

Vanessa laughed and leaned behind the bar. When she stood up, she had a bottle of Captain Morgan's Original Dark Rum in her hand. "Dark rum and coke is Dad's favorite." Vanessa proceeded to pour a couple of drinks while rambling on about her afternoon shopping.

Nicole listened at the same time as she let her gaze roam over the beautiful ocean side cottage. Not bad for a home away from home, she thought. She ran her hand over the brocade of the loveseat, and appreciated the comfort of the blue tones of the room and its furniture. The walls had been painted to match the pale and darker blue tones of the outside, contrasted with some paintings of the sea and a couple of knick-knack shelves. The highlight of the room was the navy and cream, floral damask rug centered on the wooden floor. Simple in design, yet Nicole knew it was an expensive combination of silk and wool. It also happened to be the exact spot that Sumo had plopped himself down and was presently sleeping. Nicole smiled. Her dog had expensive tastes.

Vanessa stepped in front of her and offered a tall glass filled with coke, liquor, and ice. Her hand shook slightly and Nicole's heart went out to her. Not sure whether to offer words of comfort, she took the drink and gulped a mouthful, deciding she needed it after the way the evening had started.

Vanessa sat on the couch opposite and hastily sipped her drink. "I wonder if Dad needs any help in the kitchen. I feel guilty just sitting here."

"Vanessa, you don't have anything to feel guilty about. He offered to make dinner. Actually, he insisted on making dinner."

Vanessa frowned as if trying to comprehend such a thing. "I know."

Nicole reached over and gave Vanessa a pat on the arm. "Listen, I have an idea what you're going through, but Ian is not your husband. He doesn't have the same expectations, and he's not going to come out and slap you because you're sitting here enjoying yourself while he's in the kitchen."

Vanessa laughed nervously. "But, I'm supposed to be the one cooking."

No. You're not. Relax and enjoy the moment. How often has your dad ever cooked for you?" Nicole thought she'd try to get some conversation going to get Vanessa's mind off the kitchen.

"Hmmm...he did sometimes after my mother left."

"So he's qualified, and we won't get poisoned."

Vanessa laughed. "No, he can boil water and flip a pancake fairly well."

"Good, then we're fine. Relax."

Vanessa sighed and leaned back on the couch. "I suppose."

"How's your bruise?"

Vanessa brushed her hair back and posed for Nicole to see her upper cheek. "It's fading quite nicely, but the rib still hurts if I move too fast."

"Are you sure you won't go to a doctor?" Nicole questioned

as she finished the last of her drink. Already the alcohol was making her feel a little tipsy, but it had tasted too good to drink slowly.

"I don't need a doctor. I'm fine."

Vanessa hastily pulled her hair back over the bruise when Ian stepped into the room and spoke. "Dinner's almost ready. Vanessa, could you set the table, everything's in the hutch over there. Oh, and there are some red candles I bought, maybe you can put them on the table and light them as well. Nicole, can you help me in the kitchen for a minute?"

With knots in her stomach, Nicole followed Ian into the kitchen, while the sound of plates and cutlery rattled behind her. The kitchen door swung shut, muffling the sounds from the dining room. She was about to say that being alone wasn't such a good idea, when she found herself suddenly pinned against the wall by the hard, warm flesh of another human body. Instant heat raced through her body and she tried to speak, but couldn't. Instead, she wrapped her arms around Ian's neck and gave herself to the sensation of being fully aroused and thoroughly kissed. Her moan mingled with the growl that rose in Ian's throat. Her mind was barely able to function, but the thought intruded that they shouldn't be doing this. She pushed against his chest in a feeble attempt to stop him.

His response was to run both his hands through her hair and pull her into a deeper kiss. Nicole couldn't stand the sensations that electrified her body, not without completing what had begun. "Ian," she mumbled into his mouth. "We need to stop."

He growled.

"Really." She was able to push him far enough away to catch her breath. "Vanessa could walk in on us at any time."

A smirk tilted his mouth and he asked, "Is that the only reason you want to stop?"

"Well...I...you...damn it, don't be so arrogant. Even if she weren't here, I'd say the same thing. We don't even know each other, we've hardly spoken more than a few sentences, I'm not going to just jump into bed with you like I'm sure every other female you meet probably does."

"Good. I'm sick and tired of easy pickings."

Nicole gasped. "Easy pickings. Yes, I'm sure you've been inundated with available females, but you can be sure I won't be one of them. Now, or later." Nicole practically tore the door off its hinges as she careened out of the kitchen into the living room. Across the room, Vanessa had finished setting the table, and she jumped at Nicole's abrupt entrance.

"Nicole, are you okay? You look pale again." Blue eyes narrowed in consideration. "Did Dad make a pass at you? He just can't leave well enough alone. He always has to prove himself the macho guy." Vanessa looked ready to do battle with her father, but Nicole raised her hand to stop her.

"No, he didn't make a pass at me." She certainly wasn't going to admit that she'd literally thrown herself into his arms. "It was warm in the kitchen, and I need some fresh air."

To cover her story, she walked over and opened the sliding doors that led out to the beach. Fresh, salty air blustered in from the ocean and gave Nicole a sense of calm. The kiss had rattled her on more than a physical level. Her limbs felt like warm liquid, but the jumbled knot of emotions nesting in her stomach concerned her more. She'd never experienced anything quite so staggering. It had just been a kiss, but damn him for making her feel so much. Had he felt the same thing, or was she just another conquest for him? Could something so moving be one-sided?

Nicole wanted to believe not, yet she wasn't ready for the kind of relationship that such passion signified. Especially if she was just another notch on the bedpost.

Thoughts of the stalker intruded on her trail of thoughts, and she knew that was an even better reason to keep her distance from Ian. She needed to keep her distance, but she had to ask.

"Vanessa, what did you mean when you said that Ian always has to prove himself the macho man?" Her voice broke, and she wasn't sure if she wanted an answer, but she'd asked the question.

"Oh, you know, if there's a woman around, he's on the prowl. That was one of the reasons Mom left him. Their marriage had been in trouble for a while, but when the whole world heard about an affair he had with his co-star, Mom had to leave. Her pride wouldn't let her stay."

Of course he was a womanizer. She shouldn't be surprised, yet she'd seen more than just lust in Ian's shockingly blue eyes, hadn't she?

The kitchen door swung open, and Ian strode into the room with his hands full. The aroma of spaghetti sauce and garlic bread wafted in the air to mix with the salty breeze that blew in from outside. Nicole's taste buds tingled, and her mouth watered.

Ian placed the food on the table and remarked, "Vanessa, can't you see that Nicole's glass is empty. Get her a refill, while I get the rest of the food."

His abrupt tone cracked in the room like a whip. Vanessa's face crumbled and tears filled her eyes, but Ian had returned to the kitchen and didn't see. Nicole knew Ian was flustered from the kiss and was taking out his frustration on Vanessa, and if Vanessa were not in such a vulnerable state, it wouldn't matter. But his off-hand manner was insulting and hurtful. Nicole hastened to reassure her.

"Vanessa, I'm sure he doesn't realize how he sounds. I'd imagine he's under a lot of pressure from the film, and I understand they start shooting tomorrow."

"Don't worry about me. I stopped making excuses for his behavior a long time ago. Now, I just keep my distance, and I don't get hurt."

Nicole ached for her friend, but if she'd learned anything, it was that there was more than one side to a story. She gently reminded Vanessa of their conversation at lunch earlier.

"Vanessa, maybe you should talk to him, you know, fill him

in on some details you neglected to mention. You might find he's a very understanding person."

Vanessa had the grace to flush. "I know. I guess I haven't been fair, but..."

"No buts. Are you so sure he wouldn't care? He can't be that cold and uncaring. He needs to know the truth, so he can stop pushing all the wrong buttons and help you get through this."

The object of their conversation entered the room again, this time with a salad, and a tray of pickles and cheese. He glanced at Nicole's glass and saw it still empty, but before he could admonish Vanessa for slacking in her duties as hostess, Nicole spoke up.

"I don't want another drink now, thank you. And you don't need to worry about Vanessa's role as hostess, she's been treating me just fine."

Ian frowned, as if trying to figure out the cause of the hostility that laced Nicole's voice. "Okay, then. Let's eat dinner, I'm starving." As he spoke, his gaze drifted to Nicole and slowly wandered down the length of her body.

She flushed and hastened to sit down in the proffered chair.

Dinner passed with only a modicum of unease. Red candles flickered on the table, their gentle rose scent tickling Nicole's nose. Sumo lay beside the table and behaved himself better than at home, where he usually sat at attention drooling all over the floor in hopes of scraps. He seemed to follow the conversation as it bounced from one person to the other. Conversation was light and impersonal, everyone seemingly touchy about giving away too much information about themselves. Nicole knew what her and Vanessa's secrets were, but what were Ian's? Did she even want to know? Yes, actually. She did.

Whenever Ian and Vanessa weren't looking, Nicole snuck a peak at Ian. She was acutely aware of how the flickering candles threw shadows across his features, making him look alternately handsome and sinister. The candles lent a certain romance to the evening, yet Vanessa's presence quelled any thoughts in that direction. Ian was a witty conversationalist, but avoided anything personal, although he directed personal questions her direction.

"Where were you born?" His gaze pinned her with a forkful of spaghetti halfway to her mouth.

"A small town outside of Toronto, Ontario. I'm sure you wouldn't know the name." She shoveled the food into her mouth and chewed.

"I visited Toronto once. With Bob." Vanessa's voice trailed off as Ian frowned her direction.

"Speaking of Bob, have you called to let him know where you are?"

Fear flashed across Vanessa's face, but Ian was too busy dipping his garlic bread in spaghetti sauce to notice. Nicole noticed, and wondered how a father could be so blind to his own daughter. And she wondered at herself, that she could fall for such an arrogant so and so.

"No, I haven't."

Ian chewed his garlic bread and swallowed. "Well, I would think he'd be getting worried by now. You've been here a couple of days already. "

"I know how long I've been here, Dad."

"Fine. It's your marriage, but if I were Bob, I'd be getting pretty pissed off by now, having my wife gallivanting all over the country without a word." Unaware of the effect of his words, Ian continued talking as if it was a pleasant exchange over afternoon tea. "You know, I think you take him for granted. He's a good provider."

Nicole couldn't stand the look of defeat on Vanessa's face, and she worried that Ian's disregard for circumstances might send her scurrying back to an abusive husband. Memories of past humiliations, constant put-downs, and bruised cheeks, had Nicole shoves her plate away and directing the full fury of her gaze on the culprit who was dredging up things she didn't want to remember. Never strong enough to stand up for herself while Jeff was alive, Nicole let loose.

"What are you doing? Can't you see what's going on? Are

you a male chauvinist, or do you just not care? Sure, send the little woman back where she belongs, to the man who beats her and won't let her out of the house." With one sweep of her hand, Nicole brushed Vanessa's hair from her cheek and pointed to the now fading bruise.

"This is what Bob did to your daughter, along with a cracked rib or two, and it wasn't the first time. She had to climb out a window to escape from him. Are you really so blind?"

Nicole finished her tirade with a tiny sob of frustration, but she felt better. She had done for Vanessa what she had never been able to do for herself. Of course, she'd had no one to run to, not even an uncaring father. Silence pervaded the room. The only sound was the distant surf as it rolled gently onto the sandy shore. Vanessa sat stiffly, her eyes looking much like a deer caught in the headlights of a vehicle. Stunned, Ian sat and stared at the bruise on Vanessa's face.

Having unintentionally brought the situation to a head, Nicole decided that now would be a prudent time to leave. She tapped her leg for Sumo to follow and quietly made her way out the front door. A final look showed two people frozen in the moment as they faced each other across the food-littered table. Nicole closed the door and sent up a prayer for them to resolve at least some of their differences. She also prayed she hadn't made things worse by shooting off her big mouth. Oh, well, it was too late now. The wheels had been set in motion.

Chapter Nine

T he sound of the door slamming barely registered in Ian's consciousness. He stared into the face of the stranger who was his daughter. Had he really been so blind to his own daughter's dilemma that he ignored her need for help? Should he have heard her pleas even though they'd been hidden under the surface of polite conversation?

Still dazed, he looked deep into the blue eyes that so resembled his own. Vanessa, the daughter who'd grown up and away from him. How had it happened? Sure, he'd been busy with work and traveling around the world to exotic places, but it had been to provide for Vanessa and give her a home where she could be safe. The irony hit him then. He'd provided a home and material things, but he hadn't given enough of himself.

He had compounded his actions by confusing Michelle's actions with Vanessa's and handling the situation based on false assumptions. Michelle had been whining and clinging, while Vanessa endured pain and had always been independent.

A single tear fell from Vanessa's eye and trickled down her cheek, only briefly touching upon the discolored portion. Without thought, and for the first time in years, Ian stood and opened his arms. A second of uncertainty passed and then Vanessa stepped forward to be engulfed in his embrace.

Ian had no idea how long they stood like that with Vanessa crying before he gently took a step back and ran his hands through his thinning hair.

"I need a drink. How about you?"

She sniffled. "Sure, make it a double."

Ian smiled. "Me, too."

Liquid splashed, ice clinked, an owl hooted outside the window, but they spoke no words. Ian had no idea what to say. Instead, he handed her the drink and chugged his down in one gulp. Vanessa looked so vulnerable Ian knew he had to tread carefully to repair their relationship.

"Vanessa, why didn't you tell me?" That hurt him the most, the fact that she hadn't confided something of this magnitude.

She held out her glass for another. "I did. In so many ways. But you weren't listening. You kept talking about Mom and thinking I was just like her. I tried so hard not to be like her, to make you proud of me. I didn't want to admit my marriage was a failure.

With a moan, he sank down on the nearby couch. "Oh, man, not now." He meant that now was not the time for these kinds of inner revelations because he needed to focus on Vanessa's problem.

"Well, excuse me for intruding. I'm sorry I'm such an inconvenience."

Ian saw the hurt in Vanessa's eyes, but before he could explain, she twirled on her heel and stomped to her bedroom. He wouldn't ignore things this time. He strode to the door and without knocking, threw it open only to find Vanessa packing her suitcases. He picked up the closest one and dumped its contents on the bed.

"You aren't going anywhere. It didn't mean what it sounded like. I was thinking about something else."

Vanessa grabbed the discarded clothes and threw them back into the case, her face flinching as if in pain. "It's obvious I'm an intrusion on your life. I'll just go back to Bob. At least he wants me, even if he does beat me."

Ian was stunned. This woman before him was not the daughter he remembered. His Vanessa would never allow someone else to hit her. Placing his hands on her shoulders, he gently, but forcibly turned her to face him.

"What did he do to you?"

"Nothing. Let me go."

"No. Tell me how he hurt you, or I'll drag you to the hospital and let them strip you naked to find out."

Vanessa's eyes rounded in surprise. "You wouldn't dare."

"You're my daughter, I'll dare whatever I want."

"When did you suddenly start caring?"

"Damn it, Vanessa." He wanted her to tell him of her own free will. He had a feeling she'd grown too used to force.

Vanessa tugged her tee shirt from her jeans and lifted it to reveal bruises all up and down her right side. Her tears flowed freely. "I think he cracked a couple of my ribs."

Anger rose like bitter bile. "That bastard. It's a good thing he's not here now, or I'd kill him with my bare hands." Softly, slowly, he took her tee shirt and pulled it down to cover the bruises. "Come on. We're going to the hospital."

"No, I'm all right, really."

"Vanessa, please. For my own peace of mind."

Vanessa sighed. "Okay, if you insist." Quietly, she gathered her jacket and purse, stepped past Ian and out the front door to the car.

At least it was a start, but he knew there wouldn't be a finish until he'd healed his relationship with his daughter and dealt with the low-life scum she'd had the misfortune to marry.

***

He watched from the shadows of the pine trees and smiled morbidly when Nicole and her mutt left for an early morning walk along the cliffs. He needed to turn up the heat and let her know she hadn't been smart enough to fool him. He'd play with her, watch her squirm in fear, and when he grew tired of the game, he'd show himself to her.

By that time, she'd be willing to give up the whereabouts of the diamonds that she and her son of a bitch dead husband had stolen from him.

Once the bitch and the beast had disappeared down the

trail, the stalker stepped from the shadows and moved toward the lighthouse. Getting inside should have been easy through the open window, but he cut his hand on a loose piece of metal. Damn! He sucked on his finger and wiped blood on his clothes so as not to leave any behind.

His surprise would best be viewed on the wooden tabletop in the kitchen. He had the whole scene laid out in his mind, but nothing went right. First, he couldn't get the stupid doll into the position he wanted. He had to yank the arms off, which was okay because it made for a more morbid scene. Second, the marker he'd bought wouldn't write on the smooth surface of the well-polished table. He was lucky to find some old crayons in a drawer; they did the job nicely. Then, just as his mission was complete and he was about to leave, a knock sounded at the front door.

"Nicole, it's Jacob. Are you home?"

The sound of the front door opening sent him into a panic. He grabbed the first heavy object he could find, which was a cast iron frying pan, and hid behind the kitchen door. Footsteps approached from the front hall, and the visitor was mumbling to himself. Already frustrated, anger built until his heart beat fiercely, and he shook with the emotion. His hand throbbed, he was hot, and his stomach rumbled with hunger.

He whispered to the empty kitchen. "Goddamn bastard, interrupting my work. Just come in here and see what I've got waiting for you." He relished the thought of smashing the heavy pan on top of someone's head and hearing the satisfying crack.

Silently, carefully, he inched the kitchen door open to survey the living room. The guy was sitting at a small desk writing a note, presumably for the bitch. It looked as if he had brought her some kind of scarf or something because it sat on the table beside him. Stupid man, he was too old to be trying to make it with Nicole. He'd have to teach the old guy a lesson. Stepping closer, he raised the frying pan and got ready for the attack. His heart thumped so loudly he was surprised he couldn't hear him.

He stepped right behind the old guy and was about to bring the pan crashing down on his skull, when a wicked gust of wind blew through the living room and sent everything flying off the desk. Just as the frying pan arced downward, the old man grabbed for the flying notepaper, and instead of smashing his skull the pan only glanced off his head.

It was enough. The old man went down. Torn between finishing him off and escaping, he decided to run. In his haste to clamber out the kitchen window, he cut his other hand on the same piece of loose metal. Frantic, he tore off through the forest path. His only satisfaction was that he'd been able to leave a nice scene and an unconscious man to greet Nicole when she came home.

He smirked and wished he could be hiding in a closet or something, but that damn dog of hers would smell him immediately. It would be worth doing something about that dog. It would sure make access to the bitch easier for him. Yes, he'd go back. Now that he was away from the lighthouse, he rationalized the occurrences as a series of coincidental mishaps. He'd been a wimp to panic. Next time he wouldn't.

***

Nicole needed the early morning hike to clear her mind. She hadn't slept at all last night because her mind refused to stop thinking, and her body refused to settle down after the kiss she and Ian had shared.

"I said I wanted a sordid affair, didn't I, Sumo?" She scratched her dog on the head. "I just didn't know he was such a jerk, or that I'd lose control over my emotions so easily."

She thought about how he had treated his daughter and wondered how he had even found someone to marry him in the first place. But he was an actor, he'd probably put on a good show. Her thoughts of beginning a brief affair with Ian fell into the shadows of yesterday. He had too much on the go with the filming of the movie starting and handling Vanessa's problems. She didn't need to add to his full schedule. Oh, well, it had been a good idea, but they were probably better off avoiding each other.

As Nicole and Sumo meandered up the path from the cliffs near the lighthouse, Sumo perked his head and growled. His brown eyes focused on the lighthouse and his pace quickened until he ran to the front door and pawed. Without much persuasion, the door swung open, and the dog disappeared inside.

Butterflies fluttered in Nicole's stomach as she hurried to find out what was wrong. Sumo obviously hadn't found an intruder because he wasn't sounding the alarm, so it was safe for her to enter. With apprehension, she stepped into the dim interior from the afternoon sunlight and the sight that greeted her was not a good one. Jacob sat on the floor, with his head nestled in his hands and blood oozing through his fingers. Sumo sat beside him, his paw resting on Jacob's knee.

Nicole rushed to his side. "Jacob, what happened? Are you all right?" Gently pulling Jacob's hands aside, she parted his sparse hair and inspected the gash on his head. Jacob groaned in pain and tried to push her hands away, but Nicole was persistent.

"Let me look, Jacob." He gave up and let her have a look. "It doesn't look too bad, the blood makes it look worse. How did it happen? Did you fall?" Her eyes searched the room to see what he could have hit his head on.

"I didn't fall. Some slimy piece of fish-bait was inside when I got here. He snuck up behind and struck me." He pointed to the frying pan lying under the writing desk. "Looks like that's what he used."

Someone had been in the lighthouse, inside the building she had come to think of as home. She felt dizzy, but fought the feeling because Jacob needed her. With shaking hands, she helped him to his feet.

"Come on, I'm taking you to the doctor."

"Don't be silly, I'm fine," Jacob grumbled.

"Jacob."

"I said no, woman. Just get me something to clean up with and a good stiff drink to ease the pain. And quit fussin', I'm fine."

Jacob made his shaky way into the kitchen to sit down at the table. Sunlight filtered in to highlight the paleness of his wrinkled face. That same shaft of sunlight also illuminated the horrid display of twisted limbs and instruments of torture that lay so darkly artistic on the kitchen table.

Nicole gasped and felt the blood leave her face. She clutched Jacob's arm in an attempt to steer him back into the living room, but he had seen the mutilated doll and blotches of ketchup splattered against the starkness of the naked limbs. His face, white a moment ago, now filled with the redness of anger.

"Son of a bitch." Jacob shook Nicole's hand off his arm and hobbled to the display. He reached out and picked up a piece of paper tucked under the doll. He read the words aloud: *This will be you unless you give me what I want.*

In one swift movement of disgust, Jacob crumpled the paper and threw it into the sink. The sound of a leaky faucet dripping onto paper was the only sound as the two of them recovered from shock.

Nicole whispered. "He found me. He's sick. He's a killer, he's certifiably, disgustingly sick, and he found me." Lacking the strength to stand, Nicole sat on the floor and leaned against the wall. She wasn't going near the atrocity on the table. Sumo trotted over and lay down beside her, voicing his concern with a low, steady whine.

Jacob stood and stared at the scene, as his arthritic fingers briefly touched on the cold steel of a fish-gutting knife. Nicole recognized it as something she'd seen the fishermen on the docks use.

"You know who did this?" Jacob questioned, as he picked up a set of needle nose forceps, placed them back on the table and then ran his hand over a gaffing hook.

Nicole blanched at the thought of what instruments like that could do to a human body. Her body. She could almost feel the sharp prick of steel cutting into her skin and the sheer agony of it slicing her open bit by bit, just as the caricature of the doll suggested would happen. Fear overwhelmed her, and she frantically searched for a way to answer Jacob's question. She was spared when his knees sagged, and he clutched the counter for support.

Nicole jumped up and grabbed his arm. "Jacob, are you all right?"

"I'm fine, just feel a smidgen dizzy is all."

"We better get you to the hospital, come on."

"Quit worrying so much about me." He waved to the kitchen table. "We need to let the police know about this."

Nicole avoided looking at the table. She already knew she'd have nightmares and didn't need to reinforce her imagination any more. "We can let them know later, you're more important."

"You fuss too much, I'll be fine."

"You are so stubborn, Jacob. No wonder you live alone." Realizing how horrible she sounded, Nicole tried to apologize, but Jacob stopped her.

"Don't worry, you're right. I am cantankerous, that's why no one'll have me."

Sensing he was about to push for an answer to his question, Nicole asked, "Why are you here, anyway?"

"I brought you a present from *Wishes*. It's out on the desk."

Nicole moved to the living room and crossed to the table where she picked up the soft silken scarf and rubbed it against her cheek. "It's beautiful, Jacob. Thank you." The ugliness of the situation crept back into the lighthouse and Nicole remarked, "We better let the authorities know what happened, but first we need to get you to the hospital."

"I told you."

"I know what you told me, old man, now I'm telling you. You're going to the hospital." Without waiting for further argument, Nicole took Jacob's arm and propelled him out to her Wave, opened the door and set him in the passenger seat. He grumbled all the way, but went along nonetheless.

Nicole looked at Sumo's expectant face and shook her head. "You stay home this time, Sumo. I need you to guard the house. Okay, bud?"

He whined, but sat down as if to agree.

Climbing into the car, Nicole started the engine and drove as fast as safely possible down the trail to the road. As they reached the outskirts of town, Nicole said, "I'll drop you off at the hospital and then go get the police. I'm sure Corporal Moody'll want to talk to you, but I want you home and resting as soon as possible so he'll have to come to the hospital."

"Sure." Jacob had been uncommonly quiet, and Nicole assumed it was a result of his injury. She pulled into the emergency entrance of the small hospital in town and made sure he was processed and settled in an exam room before she took off.

As fate would have it, Corporal Moody was on lunch and perusing the books at *Wishes*. Driving through town, Nicole spotted him easily with his navy pants and yellow striped, dark blue patrol jacket. If the uniform hadn't been enough, the black gun belt complete with gun, flashlight, baton, and what looked to be pepper spray would have definitely have drawn her attention. When he spied Nicole approaching, he hastily put the book he'd been reading back onto the shelf.

"Hey, Miss Tyler." He tapped his two fingers to his cap. "Something I can do for you?"

Josephine had confided to Nicole that Corporal Moody's wife had taken off with a computer salesman who'd wandered into town one week and out the next. There wasn't a lot of call for computers in Solitary Cove, but the slick salesman hadn't left town empty-handed. Corporal Moody was a pleasant man, but slightly on the naive side. Fifteen years later, he still swore that his wife would come to her senses and return. Must be true love, Nicole figured. Either that, or Corporal Moody wasn't very intelligent, and Nicole pondered placing her trust in him.

"Miss Tyler?"

"Oh, sorry." Nicole lowered her voice in a natural instinct of secrecy, although she noticed Josephine standing nearby dusting shelves and ornaments. "Someone broke into the lighthouse while I wasn't there. Unfortunately, Jacob had stopped by to visit and the intruder knocked him out cold."

A startled gasp and the rattle of crystal wind chimes filled the shop. Josephine's face had turned pure white, and she stood in breathless shock. Quick to reassure them, Nicole added. "I think he's all right, just a bump on the head. He's over at the hospital right now. I told him I'd bring you over so he can go right home directly afterward."

"Good thinking. Let's go." Corporal Moody took her arm and ushered her out the shop and up the street to the hospital, but not so fast Nicole couldn't give Josephine a reassuring squeeze in passing.

"Don't worry, I'll tell him you'll be over to see him when the store closes."

Josephine nodded her head in agreement, tears of worry reflected in her eyes. Before Nicole and the Corporal had even left the store, Josephine was pulling down shades and counting cash. Nicole gave her about fifteen minutes to follow in their tracks. Funny, it was so obvious that the two cared for each other. Why wouldn't they admit it?

The doctor was in with Jacob when Nicole and Corporal Moody arrived, so they sat in the waiting room while he took what information Nicole had about the break-in, which wasn't very much. Within minutes, the door to the street opened, and Josephine breezed into the office to take a seat beside Nicole. They shared a tremulous smile.

"Are you all right?" Josephine asked.

"I'm fine. I was out walking. If only I'd been there, it might not have happened. Sumo would have stopped anyone before they got inside."

Josephine patted Nicole's arm. "It's not your fault. You had no way of knowing."

That was the thing, though. It was Nicole's fault. Some deep part of her knew the stalker would find her eventually. She had no doubt that it was him, that certainty burned until she felt like choking. If she hadn't befriended Jacob, he wouldn't have been at the lighthouse. Therefore, he wouldn't have been attacked. She should have stuck to her original plan to stay away from everyone and spend her time writing.

Just then, the doctor strode out of the examination room with clipboard in hand and a stethoscope hanging around his neck. He approached the trio and launched into a rundown of Jacob's condition.

"First of all, he'll be fine. He's a tough old codger. He has a slight concussion, but I don't see anything to worry about. He'll probably have a wicked headache for a few days. I'd also like him to stay overnight for observation. When he fell he must have fallen on his wrist, because it's broken, so I put a cast on." The doctor smiled. "He wasn't too happy about that."

Nicole and Josephine looked at each other and smiled as they imagined Jacob grumbling at the doctor for putting him in a cast.

"You can go in and see him now, but don't stay long, he needs to rest."

Nicole hung back. She'd learned her lesson. Having her life in danger was one thing, but putting the life of someone else in danger was quite another. If the stalker had found her here, it was time for her to move on. Somewhere, anywhere. "Why don't you go, Josephine, I have errands to run." Choking on the thought of leaving those she had come to care for, Nicole brushed tears away from her face and stumbled from her chair and out the door.

***

Josephine frowned as she watched Nicole's hasty retreat. She'd been right to worry about Nicole, and she fully intended to find out what was going on. Maybe Jacob could give her some answers.

At Corporal Moody's request, she waited a few more minutes while he questioned Jacob. When the officer finally came out, his face was a study of concentration lending more credence to Josephine's theory that the situation was serious. Taking a deep breath, she opened the door to Jacob's temporary room, and her gaze locked with his instantly.

He was the first to speak. "Woman, how did you find out so quickly?"

Corporal Moody was in my shop when Nicole came with the news, and thanks for the warm greeting." She stepped closer to the bed, taking in Jacob's pale face and the sight of a bruise already gathering color and peeking out from his hairline.

Jacob humphed. "I wouldn't be in this predicament if I hadn't been doing your bidding."

Guilt tugged at Josephine. "I know," she whispered. "I'm sorry." She felt the tears threaten and then spill from her eyes.

"Oh, willikers, woman. Don't start blubbering. It's not your fault. I'm just being my usual grumpy self. Anyway, I'm fine." He accented the comment with a weak groan as he attempted to sit up straighter.

Josephine rushed to his side. "Take it easy, you've just been bashed on the head."

"Don't I know it," he groaned. "How's Nicole?" He looked to the door. "And where is she? You'd have thought she could at least come in to make an old man feel better. After all, I was attacked in her house. Bastard tried to kill me. Almost did, too."

Josephine brushed a stray lock of hair from his forehead and smiled. "I'm glad you're okay." Jacob snorted and sighed deeply as the painkillers did their job, and he drifted off to sleep. Josephine sat back in her chair and wondered what was going on in Solitary Cove that respectable people were getting beat over the head for no reason. She also wondered just how much this had to do with Nicole, who was still a stranger in town. No matter how much Josephine liked her, she didn't know anything about her past, but she had a feeling that the unconscious man snoring away in bed knew more than he let on.

No worry, she'd find out all in good time. Picking up a book she'd brought with her, Josephine started to read. She was planning to stay for the night and settle Jacob in at home tomorrow before she went back to the store. He'd argue with her, but this was one time she wasn't giving in to him.

Chapter Ten

N icole left the hospital in a daze of fear. She hadn't said a word to the Corporal about her stalker, mainly because she'd decided to leave town. The stalker would follow her, and the people she cared about in Solitary Cove would be safe.

A commotion on the main street drew her attention. Lord, how had she missed the movie set earlier? Her only excuse was that her focus had been on getting Jacob to the hospital. Now, nothing looked familiar. New signs on the lampposts proclaimed the town to be Owls Head, Maine—The Pine Tree State. Large pots with freshly planted pine trees adorned the front of each store and the entrance to the park, while an abundance of bright flowers colored the garden in front of the post office.

Nicole barely recognized some of the stores, as they boasted either a new paint color, or false fronts with false names. Parked along the street were various vehicles with Maine license plates and magnetic signs advertising local Maine businesses. Off to the side of the commotion and new look, sat about three or four crane-like structures mounted with huge cameras.

"Amazing."

Just then, a flash of gray and the outline of an achingly familiar jaw line caught her attention. Taking a half step over and leaning around a bouncing teenager, Nicole was able to see Ian across the street. He was in deep conversation with someone who exuded the aura, if not the look, of authority. Nicole assumed the short, stocky man with dark, lanky hair was the director, as he was pointing here and there giving direction.

Ian nodded his head and added an opinion now and again.

Nicole enjoyed the brief, undisturbed moment of watching his stealth-like grace and a heavy urge to rely on his strength tugged at her. It would be wonderful to be able to share her problems with him and work things out together. But that would never happen, she was leaving town. Besides, her problem was the kind that got people killed, and there was no way she'd let anyone else die because of her.

With one last, longing look at Ian, Nicole practically ran back up the street to where she'd parked her car. She needed to pack and get out of town right away before she changed her mind and stayed.

***

"I'm telling you, woman, I'm not staying here overnight, I've got to get out to the lighthouse. I've already wasted half the day snoozing," Jacob stated while carefully pulling on his clothes.

Josephine didn't bother turning her back, and Jacob didn't seem to care that he had an audience. "Jacob, you're going against direct orders from the doctor."

"Don't matter." He slipped on his well-worn sneakers and stood, only to clasp the bed for support. He grumbled at the, *I told you so,* look on Josephine's face. "Just give me a minute, and I'll be fine."

"Sure you will. You could at least tell me why you're so damned determined to go see Nicole. You almost got yourself killed, for goodness sake." Josephine's voice cracked with emotion, and only then did Jacob take a close look at her face.

"Josie." He patted her hand reassuringly. "I'll be fine, I promise. It's Nicole I'm worried about."

"The police will send someone to keep an eye on her. What more can you do?"

"I'm not afraid of someone getting to her."

"Then what, Jacob? Talk to me."

"Fine. She knows who attacked me. Sounds to me as if she's running from him. I'm afraid she'll pack up and leave town to protect us, and in the process, set herself up for more danger. At least here people who care about her can keep an eye on her."

Josephine shook her head. "Jacob, you're not making any sense."

"Wouldn't be the first time. Josie, I need you to drive me out to the lighthouse. I feel a tad too lightheaded to be driving."

"I guess your brains didn't get all the sense rattled out of them. Come on, let's go."

Jacob grinned and followed a disgruntled Josephine out of the hospital, right under the nose of the protesting nurse.

***

"Don't worry, Sumo, we'll find another place just as nice, I promise." The woebegone look on Sumo's face attested that he was smart enough to know an empty promise when he heard it. Nicole didn't have time to convince him. She threw the last of her clothes into a suitcase and zipped the top shut in a final gesture. "There, I guess that's it, bud."

Heaving the suitcase off the bed to add to the small pile of personal items downstairs, Nicole jumped in fright when the zipper suddenly split wide open and her clothes spilled all over the bedroom rug.

"Damn." Crouched on the floor in the midst of picking up her strewn clothes, Nicole stopped and listened, but heard nothing. "Ridiculous. It's a good thing we're leaving, Sumo, I think I'm getting as fanciful as some of the locals here."

She'd done everything to cover her tracks, yet it hadn't been enough. Nicole recalled each step of her plans and wondered what she needed to do different this time. What small detail had she messed up that had almost caused Jacob's death?

Repacking complete, Nicole called Sumo and made her way down the winding staircase to the front door where she'd piled her other belongings. Damn, she'd forgotten the small television up in the bedroom. With shaking hands and pounding heart, she ran back upstairs to the bedroom, unplugged the television and carried it downstairs to the waiting car.

Sumo's sudden bark made Nicole jump. The sound of a car coming up the drive had instigated the alert, and Nicole recognized Josephine's red car as it broke from the dense forest foliage. Squinting against the sun reflecting off the windshield, Nicole could swear that Jacob sat in the passenger seat, but that didn't make sense. He should still be in the hospital. As the car came to a halting stop, Jacob stepped from the car and hobbled over to Nicole.

"Jacob, what are you doing here?" Nicole noted the bruise spreading around the curve of his hairline and the way he held his cast-clad arm tight against the side he'd banged on the table. It was her fault that this wonderful man had suffered— was still suffering. She needed to get rid of her visitors fast, get her car packed, and leave town before anyone else was injured.

"Sorry, Nicole," Josephine said. "I couldn't talk him out of coming. He won't tell me why, just that he had to come."

"I told you, it's not my place to tell you. Nicole here will do that." Jacob stared Nicole down until she blushed.

"Ah, sure, but not right now. I've got to run into town. I've made arrangements to meet someone." She moved toward her car as if she had been about to leave before they showed up.

Jacob stepped in front of her. "Don't you think you're forgetting something?"

Nicole panicked. He couldn't know what she was up to. Could he?

"Your purse. I don't see it anywhere," Jacob remarked rather smugly, while Josephine just stood there looking confused.

"I...oh, well...I."

Jacob took her arm and led her toward the lighthouse. "Here, I'll come with you. I need to use the bathroom anyway."

Nicole couldn't think of anything to say to keep him from opening the door and discovering all her belongings sitting in the front entranceway, which is exactly what happened.

Jacob stood in the open doorway, shaking his head. "I knew it. I knew you couldn't be trusted. You planned to leave town without a single word to any of us. Isn't that just fine and dandy," he grumbled.

A confused Josephine stood looking at the heap of boxes and suitcases. "Nicole, what is going on?"

With two people staring her down, Nicole didn't know what to say. She was leaving for their own good, so they didn't have the right to get mad at her. They should be glad to be getting rid of her. Of course, Josephine didn't know about the stalker, but Jacob had been sharp enough to figure out her strategy. Fine. All that meant was that she'd get to say good-bye to her two friends before she left.

Grabbing a suitcase, Nicole lugged it out to her car and threw it in the open trunk. "What's going on here is that I'm leaving. Smart of you to figure it out, Jacob." She slammed the trunk and trounced back for another suitcase.

Jacob grabbed her arm, flinching in pain at the same time. "You're not going anywhere, young lady. Not until we've talked."

Nicole carefully extracted her arm from Jacob's weak hold. "There's nothing to talk about. Please get out of my way," she pleaded as he stepped between her and the car.

"I'm not moving, and if you try to make me you might re-injure me."

"Don't tempt me, old man."

The two of them stared belligerently at each other until Josephine stepped between them and demanded, "Settle down, both of you." She raised her hands in the air in a gesture of frustration. "I have no idea what's going on." She took each of them by an arm. "But we're all going inside for a cup of tea, and I'm going to find out."

There was no arguing with Josephine once she'd made up her mind, and before Nicole or Jacob could warn her, she'd marched them into the kitchen. Jacob tried to shield the mutilated doll from view, but he wasn't quick enough. Josephine gasped. Wanting the hateful reminder of a sick mind removed, Nicole grabbed a garbage bag, swept everything from the table in one movement, and proceeded to wipe the table with disinfectant.

"That probably wasn't a smart thing to do," Jacob whispered.

"I don't care." Tears choked Nicole's voice. "I'm leaving, and even if I wasn't, the police wouldn't do anything but recite platitudes about how they'd like to help, but there's not much they can do."

No one seemed to know what to say. Nicole and Jacob faced each other across the kitchen table, while Josephine put the kettle on for tea and pulled out cups, milk, lemon, and sugar. No one spoke a word, and the tension in the room rose.

Once ready, Josephine poured the water into a teapot and sat down at the table. Looking from one to the other, she said, "Okay, Nicole, it's your story. Talk."

"There's nothing to tell."

"Oh, that's very obvious." She turned to Jacob. "Jacob?"

He shrugged.

"Well the story won't tell itself and none of us are leaving until I know the truth, no matter how long it takes." She sat back and folded her arms across her chest.

Now what? Nicole looked at her two friends and considered her options. She didn't have any. If she tried to leave, Jacob would try to stop her, even if it meant hurting himself more. She couldn't let that happen. Josephine was stubborn enough to sit here from now until eternity, so holding out wouldn't work either. She'd have to tell the truth. Once they realized that her leaving was the only way to keep them safe, they'd let her get in her car and go.

"Okay, I'll talk."

Jacob and Josephine gave an audible sigh. While Josephine poured the tea, Nicole related Jeff's death and the events since. Her two guests sat dumbfounded as the tale unfolded. As Nicole spoke, the memories came back to her with frightening reality and pain. The argument at the restaurant, how Jeff had stomped out to the limo he'd rented for the occasion of his first gallery opening. She'd tried to placate him.

***

"Jeff, I don't want the evening to end like this. You have so much to be proud of, and I'm sorry if I said or did anything to upset you. I promise I'll be more careful of what I say."

Jeff sighed deeply and shot her a resigned look. "It's okay. I suppose I'm more temperamental than usual tonight. Let's just forget your lapse and go back to the hotel." Jeff opened the limo door and waved her forward.

That moment changed her life.

A horrendous crack echoed in the city streets. Jeff yelled and shoved her into the limo. Face to the floor, Nicole couldn't see anything, but she heard another crack followed by a sickening thump. Recovering her balance, she scrambled from the limo, her heart beating a fierce staccato. So much blood. Jeff lay sprawled on gray cement, his face was white and blood seeped from a bullet wound in his chest to congeal in a dark pool beside him. With a sob, Nicole fell to his side and shook him. Strange faces surrounded her, gaping in fascination until she screamed for help.

Someone grabbed her arm, pulled her roughly from Jeff's body and into a nearby alley. Without the presence of streetlights, the darkness of night surrounded them while the smell of garbage and dampness made Nicole want to gag. She started to scream, but the assailant rammed something hard into her ribs. "That was supposed to be you, but your stupid husband got in the way."

Nicole couldn't shake the sight of Jeff's bloodied body. Nothing seemed real. She shook her head. "I don't understand. What?" Her words elicited a stream of curses.

"Your greedy husband. He has what's mine, and I want it back." He licked her ear with his tongue, an act that sent shivers through Nicole. "Give them back to me, or you'll be next."

Nicole struggled as comprehension dawned. This maniac had killed Jeff and now held the gun on her. Someone must have seen him drag her away. But she couldn't hear any shouts or sound of pursuit, just the distant sounds of sirens and jumbled conversations that slowly receded into a hazy fog as dizziness threatened.

"Don't you dare faint, or I'll shoot you as well." He shoved the gun harder into her side. "Tell me where they are."

"What? Where what are?"

"Come on, bitch, you know what I want. What your husband stole from me."

No longer so distant, the blare of sirens now sounded out a howling tempo, and Nicole prayed the police would be here before this lunatic killed her.

"Shit! I'm not done with you yet. I want what's mine, and I always get what I want."

With one final shove of the gun into her ribs to accentuate his statement, the killer thrust her from him and ran from the alley to melt into the gathering crowd. Sobbing with relief, Nicole ran over to Jeff and sank to the cold cement beside him. He was obviously dead. One side of his head was no more than a pulp of red gore. Nonetheless, Nicole gently eased it into her lap and cradled it until the police car screeched to a halt beside her, their sirens bathing the scene in macabre red.

Through the ordeal of the night, the whispered promise repeated itself in her mind like a vow of death.

I'm not done with you yet. I'm not done with you yet. I'm not done with you yet.

***

Her own sobbing brought her back to the present, and she found comfort in Josephine's arms as her friend rocked her gently. Wiping her face, she smiled at Josephine and continued the story.

"Shortly after, I started receiving threatening notes, each one demanding that I hand over what belonged to him, or he'd do horrible things to me." She shivered at the memory, and Josephine patted her shoulder reassuringly.

"What does he think you've got that belongs to him?"

"I have no idea." Nicole shrugged her shoulders. "Obviously he's a delusional murderer who's convinced that Jeff stole something from him. Whatever it is, he thinks I have it. After someone tried to break into my house one night, I packed up, changed my name, and left town."

"Changed your name?" Jacob frowned. "Who can you trust, if you can't trust your friends?"

The corner of Nicole's mouth twitched, but the circumstance was too serious for her to laugh at the woebegone look on Jacob's face, a look that matched Sumo's best *pity me* look. She laid her hand on top of his wrinkled one. "Jacob, I didn't know you very well. I couldn't tell you everything. Besides, I wasn't even sure if I'd be staying."

"So what is your real name?" Josephine asked.

"Oh, it's Nicole, but not Tyler. Nicole Warner is my real name."

Josephine extended her hand, a bright smile lighting her features. "Nice to meet you, Nicole Warner. And thank you for trusting us enough to tell me your story."

Nicole hesitated, then took the other woman's hand in hers. "Josephine, I'm so sorry I lied to you, I only did it because I thought it was the only way to stay safe. I'm glad I told you the truth before leaving, because I hate the thought of you not knowing why I left or thinking that I didn't care about you."

"Leaving? You're not leaving." Josephine sat up straighter in her chair and lifted her chin in defiance.

Jacob smiled and straightened his usually hunched shoulders. "I'm with you, Josie, she's not going anywhere."

Nicole was stunned. "Are you two crazy? Jacob, you almost got killed just coming to visit me. Josephine, if you're around me for any amount of time, you'll become a target as well. Don't you understand? This guy killed my husband, and he'll kill me unless I give him what he wants. Since I have no idea what he wants, my life is worth nothing as long as he knows where I am. I care about both of you too much to put you in danger. I have to leave." She rose from the table with an abrupt move of defiance.

Jacob and Josephine each grabbed an arm and yanked her back to her seat.

"You're not going anywhere."

"I have to. As long as I'm here, everyone is in danger." She looked from Josephine to Jacob, willing them to understand her logic.

"Oh, and we're just supposed to let you ride off into the sunset to get yourself killed? Says a lot for friendship, doesn't it." Jacob's voice snapped with anger.

Nicole couldn't help it. The tears came. Slowly at first, but the salty wet drops went from a drip to a deluge. As gruffly given as it had been, Jacob's words had been a vow of loyalty and friendship, and Nicole had no other way to respond except to cry. Josephine wiped a tear from her own eyes and leaned over to hug Nicole.

"I feel the same. Although I may have stated my feelings in a different way." She patted Jacob's arm to take the sting out of her words.

"Okay, okay, enough blubbering." Jacob's eyes held the suspicious glint of tears. "It's time to plan."

"Plan?" Nicole wiped her eyes and looked to Jacob for an explanation.

"Yes. You're not leaving town, but you're definitely not safe alone at the lighthouse."

Josephine poured more tea for everyone and suggested, "I think we should make Corporal Moody aware of the situation. That way he can keep an eye on strangers in town. Oh, no, that's going to be difficult, isn't it?"

The three of them looked at each other as the same thought

struck them. The movie. Strangers walked the streets in abundance and would for the next month or so.

"Well, he or his deputies at least need to keep a twenty-four hour watch on Nicole," Josephine stated.

"But that'll be next to impossible way out here." Nicole frowned.

Jacob had been relatively quiet while sipping his tea for the last couple of minutes. Now he spoke with steely determination. "There's no way you're staying here all by yourself, girl. Since your bags are packed, let's load the car and drive you into town. You can stay at the *Wyllow Wood Inn*."

Nicole contemplated her friends. Josephine's blue eyes beamed with concern and caring. Jacob's wrinkled, age-worn face bordered on sulky and stern. He expected her to argue with him, but she wouldn't. He was right. She didn't want to stay here, even with Sumo for protection. If the stalker would kill a human being, there was nothing preventing him from killing a dog, and Nicole would be devastated if anything happened to Sumo.

"You're right, Jacob. I can't stay here, but I can't afford the *Wyllow Wood* either. We'll have to find somewhere else for me to stay."

"It has to be the *Wyllow Wood* because I can see the main building from my boat. I won't feel right unless I can keep an eye on you, even if the R.C.M.P. are doing their job."

"Jacob is right. We'll figure a way around the money problem. Corporal Moody can claim it's some police emergency or something and get you a reduced rate. If not, we'll chip in to help financially. Besides, the rates are reasonable if you're getting a room and not one of the cabins."

A sudden, intense wave of love swept over Nicole. Since her mother had died a few years ago and she'd never known her father, she missed having someone care for her the way these two people had come to over the last few months. Tears ran down her cheeks and splashed on the kitchen table. Josephine gathered her into a warm embrace, while Jacob cleared his throat and left the kitchen, mumbling something about finishing loading the car.

Nicole's tears subsided, and she wiped her tears with a nearby paper towel. "Josephine, I'm sorry I wasn't honest with you, but I just wanted to leave my past in the past."

"It's okay, Nicole. I knew you were keeping a secret." her gaze strayed toward the door where Jacob had just left. "I just thought it was something else."

A blush crept up Josephine's face. Suddenly, Nicole knew. "Josephine, you're jealous."

"Pshaw, of course I'm not jealous. What is there to be jealous of?"

"Nothing."

Josephine stood and wandered over to the small kitchen window fashioned after a porthole. Her gaze settled out over the ocean, and she sighed. "You have to admit, there's more than nothing going on between you two."

Before Nicole could protest, Josephine turned to pin her with her stare. "I don't mean that in any sexual way, Nicole. But you two share a bond that comes easily. Josephine picked at the silken fabric of her mauve-colored caftan. "I suppose I am jealous. Jealous that I don't have such an easy relationship with him. But I know I'm being silly. Heck, I'm even jealous of his dead wife and the fact that he still visits her grave. He must have loved her so much."

Nicole rose and put her arm around Josephine's shoulders. "Josephine, I know for a fact that he cares about you. He puts flowers on her grave out of respect, not a misplaced love for a woman long dead." She chuckled. "And as for the ease of our relationship, don't tell him, but he reminds me of my grandfather, that's why I can look past his gruffness and find the softie beneath."

Josephine laughed and Nicole joined in with her until the tears fell easily between them. Jacob walked into the scene of emotional release.

"Willikers, what's going on now? A man can't even leave

well enough alone for five minutes without women getting all teary eyed and such. Come on, the car's loaded, let's go." He swung the kitchen door open wide and waved Josephine and Nicole through. Before Nicole got in her car, Jacob remarked, "We have one stop to make first, so just follow Josie and me, okay?"

"Sure, Jacob." Nicole opened the passenger door for Sumo and then climbed into her seat. Jacob's one stop was the police office. The sun had long ago made its descent over the horizon and darkness had crept over the ocean cliffs, so Nicole put on her headlights for the short trip. As they rounded the curve that led to the one main street in the small village, two things happened. She had to slam on her brakes to avoid ramming into the rear of Jacob's car, and she had to cover her eyes with her hand to prevent the brightness of the light from blinding her.

Brighter than day and as harsh and vivid as a dream, the light glared across the entire length of Solitary Cove's main street. The cause was obvious. Four cranes outfitted with humungous spotlights lit the hustle and bustle of the film crew and actors as they went about their business. Not a care in the world. Not a consideration given for nearby houses and their inhabitants. Although, Nicole had to admit that it looked as if the whole population of Solitary Cove was standing on the sidelines vicariously soaking up the taste of Hollywood and fame.

Having decided on an alternate route to their destination, Jacob wheeled his car into the grocery parking lot and cut across the back streets. Nicole followed, allowing herself a brief chuckle as she imagined the curse words sputtering from Jacob's mouth at that moment. He hadn't been too keen on the whole filming business right from the start.

By chance, they found Corporal Moody in the office, and Nicole found herself trying to explain to him why she hadn't told him about her stalker. Especially after having, not one, but two break-ins at the lighthouse.

"Jacob is lucky to be alive. For that matter, so are you, young lady," Corporal Moody snapped.

Young lady! Cripes, she didn't feel young. "Okay, I'm sorry. I didn't say anything at first because I figured there was no way he could have found me, and after Jacob got hurt, I planned to leave town, so I didn't see any reason to say anything. Once I left, the stalker would have followed me."

"Therefore placing yourself in danger. Smart." His tone implied he thought she'd been anything but smart. He shuffled papers around his already tidy desk and drummed his fingers on the desktop.

Nicole grew frustrated. She'd already dealt with the police in her hometown, and they'd been unable to help her. Now the entire process started all over again and the only reason she still sat in this confined office was for the sake of Jacob and Josephine. Since they had vowed to help her, she had a responsibility to them as well as herself, and if they thought this was the best thing to do, she'd go along. Up to a point.

"Ahem." Corporal Moody cleared his throat. "So, we need a plan. You're one of ours now, so we need to keep you safe."

Corporal Moody's declaration on top of Jacob and Josephine's vows of friendship was enough to cause tears to well up again. Nicole brushed them away.

"Unfortunately, we've never had to deal with a stalker before." His eyes widened. "I don't mean unfortunately. What I mean is..."

Jacob exploded. "I don't care what you mean, what are you going to do about him?" The squat sailer stood, placed his hands on the desk and leaned forward so the tip of his nose practically touched the tip of Corporal Moody. "If he hadn't of beaned my noggin, it might have been Nicole. Just find the bugger, lock him in jail, and throw away the key!"

Corporal Moody flushed. "Does anyone know what he looks like?"

Nicole, Jacob, and Josephine shared a look.

"Okay. Does anyone know where he might be staying?"

"No, of course not," Jacob snapped. "But we can't just wait for him to come after her again. What if he gets her next time?"

"Look. I don't have all the answers. What I think we should do is move you in from the lighthouse to a place in town to better keep an eye on you."

"Done. She'll be staying at *Wyllow Wood*," Jacob said. "Good. Next, we set up a stakeout so that we're ready to grab the guy when he makes his move."

Josephine had been silent until then, but her voice sliced the air like a sharp sword. "Let me get this straight—you want Nicole to be bait for a proven murderer?"

Jacob and Josephine stared the unfortunate Corporal into his chair.

"I thought the police would be able to come up with something a little more elaborate," Jacob grumbled.

"I'm sorry to disappoint, Jacob, but we just aren't equipped to deal with this kind of situation. We've never had to deal with more than local kids whooping it up on a Saturday night. No, sir. Bunch of drunks and maybe the odd purse snatcher."

"We're talking about a murderer, not some purse snatcher. Don't you understand?" Nicole's voice broke. "This is my life."

"I know. I know. Look, my forces are limited, but I promise you, I'll stay on twenty-four hour watch if that's what it takes. You will never be out of my sight, or one of my officers." Corporal Moody shuffled some papers on his desk, as if trying to organize his thoughts. "In the meantime, I need to know the name of the officer you dealt with back home. I can do some investigating of my own. You never know what may turn up."

"It won't do you any good. They didn't find anything." Nicole recited the names to him anyway. They'd been burned into her memory. "I'll be at the *Wyllow Wood*." Josephine and Jacob followed her as she stomped from the office.

Outside, Nicole inhaled a breath of briny ocean breeze. "I already went through this after Jeff was killed. They couldn't find any motive for his murder. They found no fingerprints or anything on any of the letters. There was nothing. So they could do nothing. After awhile, they stopped sending patrols past my house."

Josephine patted her arm. "It must have been hard dealing with your husband's death at the same time as worrying about a stalker."

Jacob opened the car door for Nicole. "We'll see you at the *Wyllow Wood*. May as well get you settled, then we can decide what to do. Between Corporal Moody and us, you'll have someone around all the time. You'll be safe." The slamming of the door accentuated his words.

The *Wyllow Wood Inn* was only two minutes away, but it gave Nicole enough time to consider making a run for it. Sumo and her belongings were in the car with her, so all she had to do was keep driving rather than turn into the driveway of the inn. She'd been frustrated with Corporal Moody, but at least he was going to help. Although, since he wasn't used to dealing with actual crime, she wasn't sure how much faith she put in his abilities. She felt so alone, just like before. Then she remembered Josephine and

Jacob's disgruntled, albeit sweet faces as they asked her to stay and trust in their friendship to help her, and Corporal Moody's declaration that she was one of them. She wasn't alone this time, and it was that realization that prompted her to turn into the drive of the *Wyllow Wood*.

Okay, a small voice niggled in the back of her mind, egging her into admitting there may be another reason for staying. Steely blue eyes, silver-gray hair, and a kiss that would melt stone. She shivered. Yes, there was definitely another reason to hang around, even with the danger that hovered on the outskirts of her life.

Chapter Eleven

Ian rubbed his stiff neck and sighed. His morning had started at the first light of color on the horizon and was only now ending after eight in the evening. A hell of a long day. Used to more action and quicker paced scripts, Ian found the adjustment tough, but enjoyable. He yawned. "Hey, Jeb, I'm out of here. I need a good night's sleep. My boss expects me up early, you know."

"Yeah. I hear he's a bastard to work for."

"Your words, not mine." He turned to leave, but Jeb stopped him.

"Ian. Some people had objections to you playing the lead in this movie. Not to take anything away from your other films, but they tend to lack a bit in the character development department. What you did here today, though, will cast away any doubt. You have a spark that ignites the passion on the screen, even if it is with Candace, and you have a natural sense of where to lead the script and how to play the emotions. I'm glad I pushed for you."

Jeb's unwarranted praise touched Ian. "Thanks, Jeb, I appreciate the encouragement. To be honest, I had doubts myself, but I decided I'm getting too old to play the James Bond type. Although I'll probably miss being the only spy in the world who knows the secret code to save the human race from eventual doom." He chuckled.

"Yeah, but now you're a rock star, you get all the chicks."

"I think I'm getting too old for that, too."

"Never, man, never." Jeb laughed and gave a half-hearted wave as he turned to yell at some crewmember struggling with a rather large, expensive looking light.

When Ian entered his cabin, the enticing aroma of food wafting from the kitchen made his stomach growl. He was looking forward to a relaxing evening with Vanessa, especially since they'd come to some understanding last night.

His ponderings came to an abrupt stop when a familiar scent tickled his nose. He didn't even have time to consider his options before someone clutched him from behind.

"Surprise." Candace pressed herself against him. "I made myself a drink."

Ian wrenched her hands from around his chest and spun around to face her. Angrily, he snapped, "What the hell are you doing here?"

"Don't worry, I told Vanessa that we wanted some alone time."

Bitter anger mixed with frustration. What nerve. What self-centered stupidity. Ian cringed at the scene that must have ensued between the two women. Especially since Vanessa believed his supposed affair with Candace had ended the marriage between him and her mother. He gripped Candace's arms.

"What did you say to her?" He didn't know if it was the threatening timbre of his voice, but a flicker of fear rippled the icy surface of Candace's gaze.

She recovered quickly. "Oh, you want it rough, do you?" She lowered her voice and promised, "I'll do it any way you want." She lifted a leg and wrapped it around Ian's waist. Clenching him tightly, she pressed her lips to his, her probing tongue seeking.

The audacity of the woman shocked Ian, although it shouldn't have been based on her past actions. While she tried her best to arouse him, Ian tried his best to pry her loose. Mentally, he compared this kiss to the one he'd shared with Nicole. There was no comparison and disgust welled up inside him for this auburn haired, blue-eyed bitch.

"Damn it, I thought maybe...but I see I was wrong." Vanessa's accusing voice broke the silent struggle.

Ian literally threw Candace off him and onto the nearby couch where she sprawled in an unladylike manner with her dress bunched up to expose black thong underwear. With a catlike smile she slowly sat up and patted her dress into a more respectable position.

Hate raged through Ian, and he came to an understanding of how someone could actually commit murder in a fit of passion or anger. Vanessa stood in the doorway of the cabin, tears streaming down her face. How could he explain this? He couldn't, but he had to try. "Vanessa, it's not what it looks like." Great, how original is that line? "I swear." He beseeched her with outstretched hands, but she wasn't going to give him a chance.

"Don't even bother. I don't care. I'll leave you two alone. I wouldn't want to be in the way—like Mom was."

The words cut into Ian, and he knew he'd lost any ground he'd gained.

Always known for her sense of timing, Candace took that moment to speak. "It's nice of you to be so mature about this, Vanessa."

Ian lunged for Candace with his fist raised and ready to smash into her self-satisfied face. At least that's what he wanted to do. From the very bottom of his heart, he wanted to inflict on this woman some of the suffering and pain she'd inflicted on others. But he couldn't. He didn't hit women. With an effort, he pulled his shaking fist back and down to his side. He had a moment of gratification seeing the fear race across Candace's features, but it didn't last.

A gasp cut through Ian's rage, and he turned to see Vanessa with her hand covering her mouth and her eyes wide with un-certainty. Jackass! Could he have made things any worse? Ian cursed silently, while Vanessa struggled with her emotions. He moved toward her, but she backed away.

"No. Leave me alone. I started to trust you, even thought that you cared, but you're no different than Bob. You're a liar."

Her eyes fell to his still clenched fist, then to his face. "And you're just like him." With those words, Vanessa turned and ran from the cabin, leaving Ian alone with the woman that had ruined his life. Again.

***

Nicole stumbled over a tree root and almost fell. Ouch! Maybe going out at night hadn't been a good idea. If she were honest, she'd admit it was a terrible idea. She should turn back. But her rebellious feet had their own agenda, and they kept her on a course toward Ian's cabin.

Josephine, Jacob, and Corporal Moody had helped settle her in a room close to the front desk for safety reasons. Corporal Moody had warned her about not opening her door to strangers, keeping her curtains drawn, and not going out alone. He wasn't such a bad guy after all, just in over his head. Jacob said he'd be up all night watching the inn from his boat; he swore he'd be able to see her room from the port side. Josephine casually mentioned she'd always wanted to try the breakfast spread at the *Wyllow Wood*, so she'd stop by in the morning. Corporal Moody declared he'd assigned one of his men to her for the night. With fussing complete and advice given, the well-meaning trio had finally left her and Sumo alone.

Not that Nicole didn't appreciate the help, but she was used to being alone, and it just felt strange. She needed to adjust to the circumstances. Only problem was that instead of thinking about her plight, her thoughts wandered to Ian.

Damn. Her mind was made up. For his safety she'd keep her distance from him. She also remembered she'd decided that he was a jerk. But that didn't stop a warm flush from spreading over her body as she remembered how his lips felt on hers. The fact that he was an insensitive, slightly self-centered, typical male didn't stop her from aching for the touch of his hands.

Cursing Ian for his effect on her and hoping the officer guarding her was on the ball enough to follow her, Nicole found herself foolishly wandering in the dark trying to locate Ian's cabin. She was sure this was the correct trail. Sumo thought so as well, he perked up in the way he did when he found a familiar place. His pace quickened and Nicole admired how his powerful body glided over the ground with a grace you wouldn't expect. The night was a dark one, with clouds allowing only the occasional sliver of moonlight to break onto the earth's surface. It was that quiet time when the creatures of the day had scurried to their beds, yet the creatures of the night hadn't made an appearance. Muffled silence was the mood of the moment.

Just then, Sumo stopped. A throaty growl gurgled in his throat and his hackles rose. Fear clenched Nicole into a frozen position. Coming out here had been stupid; there was a stalker after her for goodness sake. Maybe he was growling at the officer supposedly guarding her.

Crunching gravel and the sound of someone making haste up the pathway toward them echoed in the dark of the night. Sumo's nose rose to track a scent and he didn't seem to feel there was a threat. In fact, his stub of a tail started to wag. It must have been someone he knew.

Just to be on the safe side, Nicole sidled off to the side of the trail, dragging a reluctant Sumo with her. The night shadows of overhanging branches and leaves would hide them. Footsteps came closer, hurried and uneven, as if someone stumbled their way over the path. As the figure approached, Nicole swore she heard sniffling and raspy breathing as if the person were crying. When the shadowy figure rounded the gentle curve that led to the lake and Ian's cottage, a shaft of moonlight lit familiar features. Vanessa. Relief swept through Nicole, and she stepped onto the trail. "Vanessa," she whispered, afraid to break the moonlit mood of somberness.

Vanessa gasped and her hand flew to her heart. "Nicole? Is that you?" Her whispered voice floated over the silence.

Realizing how foolish they were to be whispering, Nicole cleared her throat and answered. "Yes. Are you all right? Are you lost? Your cottage is back that way." She pointed the direction Vanessa had just come from.

"No. Yes. I mean." Obviously frustrated, Vanessa stamped her moccasin-clad foot on the ground and swore. "Damn him. Damn him. Damn him."

A crack sounded from the depths of the forest, and an ocean breeze ruffled the leaves. Nicole's fear of being out in the dark with a stalker on the loose prickled her senses. She should have known better, even with Sumo as protection. She shivered. "Look, Vanessa, why don't we go back to my room and talk."

"I don't want to be a bother. I'm fine, I just need to pull myself together."

"Do it in my room." Nicole wasn't taking no for an answer, so she put her arm around Vanessa's shoulder and gently led her toward the inn. Sumo helped by nudging Vanessa's hand with his nose. He had built in radar when it came to people being upset, and Nicole knew he'd do his best to cheer Vanessa up.

Nicole flipped the switch in her room, and the blaze of light settled her jumpy nerves. She silently berated herself again for going out in the dark. It was all Ian's fault. If he hadn't kissed her, she wouldn't be feeling the lonesome, restless feeling that had driven her out from the safety of her hotel room into the dark of the night where a stalker laying in wait for her.

"Nicole?"

"Sorry, my mind wandered. It has a tendency to do that now and again."

"Oh. I said that I hadn't had dinner yet, and I'm starving. Can we order room service?"

"Of course. I've had a busy day myself and haven't eaten yet. What do you feel like eating?"

"Whatever you have'll be fine. Can I use your bathroom to freshen up?"

"Sure." Nicole watched Vanessa retreat and wondered what had her so upset. More than likely Ian's fault. Nicole decided, again, that it was a good idea to stay away from him. He reeked of havoc and heartache.

The food arrived and Vanessa mixed a double rye, which she gulped down in two mouthfuls declaring that she needed the fortification. Nicole drank hers over the course of the burger and fries. They didn't say much until they finished eating, placed the dirty dishes in the hallway and armed themselves with another drink.

"Your eyes aren't as red now." Nicole offered up an opening remark and sipped her drink.

"Thanks." Vanessa fiddled with the ice in her glass, the clinking sound the only one in the room. Finally, she said, "I'm sorry to intrude on you, but I have nowhere else to go." She sniffled. "I guess you could say I'm homeless."

Nicole didn't know what to say because she had no idea why Vanessa was so upset. "Vanessa, you're always welcome here."

Vanessa gazed around the room as if seeing her surroundings for the first time. Awareness dawned on her face, and she remarked, "Oh, my God, I can't believe I'm so self-involved. Why are you staying here?"

Oops. Nicole had to think quickly. "They're doing some renovations out at the lighthouse, so Sumo and I have moved in here temporarily."

"Oh." Vanessa seemed satisfied with the explanation. "Vanessa, talk to me. What's wrong?"

"My father, what else?" Vanessa snorted, then she stood and paced the room. "Men. None of them can be trusted, you know, and he's worse than all of them combined. That was made obvious tonight."

Nicole sighed. She didn't want to hear bad things about Ian —he was far too amazing of a kisser. But Vanessa was upset, so she'd hear her story and take everything with a grain of salt. After all, there was always more than one side to a story.

"You probably don't know, but my parent's marriage ended because Dad had an affair with his co-star. The same bitch who's starring in the movie with him now."

Nicole's heart dropped. She had seen Candace MacGregor, and the woman was gorgeous.

"Earlier this evening she waltzed into the cabin, sweet as you please, all decked out in a barely there, screw-me-till-I-drop, dress. I think she was surprised to see me, but she recovered quickly enough to say that she and Dad wanted to spend some quality time together. Alone."

Vanessa's voice softened. "Dad and I had started to relate to each other for the first time in a long time, thanks to your outburst last night. After you left, he drove me to the hospital. It was awkward trying to talk to each other at first, but he seemed to really care." Vanessa poured herself another drink. "I guess he had time for me as long as nothing else interfered."

Nicole had no idea what to say. She had a hard time focusing on Vanessa's emotions, when her own felt battered and beaten. Realizing that she hadn't been breathing, Nicole took a deep breath and released. Unfortunately, as she let the breath out, she felt a couple of tears slowly trickle down her face. Hastily, she brushed them aside, trying to cover the motion by gulping her drink.

"Nicole?" Vanessa frowned and then understanding dawned. "Oh, my. I knew it. He came on to you last night, didn't he? I thought you looked kind of ruffled when you guys came out of the kitchen." She leaned across the knotty pine kitchenette table and gave Nicole a commiserating pat on the arm. "I'm so sorry, but Dad is a natural born flirt. I guess I was so caught up in my own problems that I never thought about warning you to keep a safe distance from him."

Personally, Nicole thought that nowhere in the same town would qualify as a safe distance. She should have known better. Why would someone who could have anyone be interested in her? Ice blue eyes, auburn hair, and a voluptuous female body flashed in her mind. Especially when the woman looked like that. Mentally downplaying how deeply his kisses had affected her, Nicole took a deep, controlling breath and said,

"It's okay, Vanessa. I'm an adult. I can handle a little flirtation." Such simple words. Such wrenching pain.

"Well, at least now you've been warned. I don't know what he expects me to do while he's cavorting the night away. How can he not care about what I'm going through? My marriage is over. I have no job, no money, and no place to live, but does he care? No. He's too busy with his slut."

"I'm sure he cares." Nicole could think of nothing else to say. Truthfully, if he cared he wouldn't be smooching it up with Candace. Jealously twisted through Nicole just thinking about the two of them together. "But let's forget about them and focus on you. First things first, are you sure your marriage is over?"

Vanessa frowned. "Sure. I can't stay with someone who hits me, can I?"

"That's the thing. You have to be sure it's over, and you're the only one who can make that decision. Women stay with an abusive husband for different reasons, and you're the only one who can decide when it's time to leave." Tears fell freely from Vanessa's blue eyes; eyes that reminded Nicole so much of Ian's. A struggle of emotions was evident on her face, and Nicole could only hope that Vanessa would make the right choice. As far as she was concerned, there was only one right choice. No one deserved abuse, whether it be physical or emotional.

The truth of that statement shocked Nicole with its simplicity. Flashes of her own marriage and Jeff's constant battering of her self-confidence invaded her mind. She raised her hand to a cheek that still felt the sting of an open hand and emotions wrung with the debilitating effect of living in constant fear and uncertainty. Suddenly, the knowledge struck her that if Jeff hadn't been killed, she would have ended their marriage eventually. It may have taken a while, but Nicole knew she would have struggled out from the mire that had become her marriage. With the new-found awareness of her relationship came a small release of emotions and guilt. Guilt for her perceived responsibility in Jeff's death, and emotions that had festered within long before that fateful day.

Vanessa's shaky voice drew Nicole from her reverie. "I don't want to stay, but I'm not sure if I'm strong enough to leave. I have nothing. How can I get by in the world on my own?"

Anger welled up in Nicole. Anger at the arrogant ego of an abusive husband, and anger at the insensitive attitude of a father who couldn't see the hell his daughter was going through.

"Okay, Vanessa, since your dad is preoccupied and you're in no condition to think straight at the moment, I guess I'll have to help you. You want out of your marriage, right?" She looked to Vanessa for confirmation, because nothing else needed saying if Vanessa planned to return to Bob.

A steely gaze of determination quickly replaced the flicker of uncertainty. Vanessa straightened her shoulders and flared her nostrils. "Damn right I want out. Who the hell does he think he is, anyway?"

Nicole laughed with relief. "Great. Now we need to decide your next step in getting the jerk out of your life."

"Jerk. I like that, it suits him. But he's not going to make it easy. All the bank accounts are in his name, as well as the house and vehicles. My credit cards are already maxed out just paying for the car rental and new clothes. I doubt he'll let me back in the house for anything."

Vanessa's voice shook, and she wiped away a tear that ran down her cheek. "I don't even have any friends I can call to stay with because somewhere along the way all my friends disappeared only to be replaced by his friends." She shivered.

Nicole hugged her. "I know it won't be easy, but remember you're entitled to half of everything, whether it's in his name or not. All you need to do is hire a good lawyer, and he'll handle the details. Technically, you never have to see Bob again."

"Wouldn't that be nice? But I can't afford a lawyer because Bob has all the money, and I can't get any money without a lawyer."

"Vanessa, I'm sure your father will help."

"No! He had his chance, and he blew it, again. Tonight he showed me what was important, and it wasn't me."

Nicole frowned. She knew Ian may be insensitive, but she had seen the look in his eyes when he'd looked at Vanessa last night. She'd lay her bottom dollar on the fact that he cared about his daughter. "Vanessa, remember our conversation at lunch yesterday?"

"Most of it. Why?"

"The part about only knowing half the story and the mistake of making judgments based on that."

"Yes. I remember." She frowned.

"You said that Candace was surprised to see you tonight, right?"

"Yes."

"Why? I mean, if your dad had invited her, wouldn't he have told her that you were staying with him. If they wanted to be alone together, wouldn't they have arranged to meet in her room, instead of at your cabin?"

"I guess. I'm not sure what difference it makes."

"Think. You said Candace came to the cabin and told you they wanted time alone."

"Yes."

"Again, why? Why wouldn't your dad tell you something like that? He's not a stupid man, and I'm sure he's not that insensitive."

"Okay, maybe. I guess that is strange."

"Think back. What exactly did you walk in on?" Vanessa snorted. "They were kissing. She was wrapped all around him."

"Wrapped around him?" The image struck Nicole like a hammer.

"Yes. She had her leg wrapped around his waist, and they were sort of, well, you know."

"I get it."

"But, when they saw me, he threw her to the couch and looked ready to explode."

"I'll bet." Nicole snorted. "Maybe you weren't jumping to conclusions."

"No. At the time I thought he was pissed with me for interrupting, but looking back, I think he was angry with her. Come to think of it, his hands were on her arms. Like this." She grabbed Nicole's arms. "Almost as if he was pushing her away. Maybe I misunderstood what I saw."

"Maybe."

"I don't know what to think. If I give him another chance and he fails, I couldn't handle it. Not now."

"I know. But now that he knows the truth about your marriage, you have to give him the chance to help. Tell him you need money. Tell him why."

Nicole looked at the crystal clock on the fireplace mantle and was surprised at the time. Standing and stretching, she said, "Listen, I think we could both use some sleep, and since the bed is king size, why don't we share. Truth is, I'm leery of staying alone and could use some company for a while. You're welcome to stay with me as long as you want."

"Really? Oh, Nicole, I can't thank you enough." Vanessa stood up and hugged Nicole. "I'd love to stay here with you."

Nicole dug out an extra tee shirt for Vanessa to sleep in, and within no time the two of them had stretched out on fine cotton sheets under a hand-stitched quilt of lavender, pale pink, and blue. Vanessa fell asleep immediately, while Nicole watched a sliver of moonlight shine through the balcony window and across the floor. Punching her pillow and rolling over on her side, Nicole decided she'd visit Ian. For Vanessa's sake, of course. So, she could find out his intentions toward his daughter.

***

He swore and threw another chair across the room. The offending chair crashed into the lighthouse window and left a spider-web design across its width, before it fell to a noisy stop on the floor.

"Bitch," he snarled in anger and frustration. "Where is she?"

He'd come here tonight to finally confront her face to face and force her to tell her where the diamonds were. She knew. He knew she knew. He'd even come prepared for the devil-dog. The cattle prod in his hand would have been the perfect way to stun the dog before carving him into pieces in front of the bitch. She'd have told him about the diamonds, unless she wanted him to carve her up just like the mutt.

It had been a perfect plan.

Until he got here, and the place had been empty. No clothes, no dog, no bitch.

Now he had another gripe to hold against her, and he'd make sure she paid. Oh, yes, as soon as he found out where she'd disappeared.

Abating his anger by trashing the lighthouse, he turned to leave, but voices approaching from the ocean pathway stopped him. A hint of a smile curled his mouth as he slid into the hall closet to wait in anticipation.

Empty, just like the rest of the lighthouse, the closet gave him plenty of room to hide. He heard a knock on the front door. Hushed voices. The door slowly opened on squeaky hinges and then nothing. He held his breath. Did she know he was here? Was it even her? Of course not, she wouldn't knock on her own door, and he didn't hear that damn beast that was always with her.

There was a giggle and a feminine voice whispering. "I don't think anyone's here."

A masculine voice. "Looks that way."

He strained his ears to hear what was happening. It sounded like some kind of a minor scuffle or something. When someone moaned, he realized they were making out.

"Mm, that's nice." The masculine voice again.

"It's more than nice, it's wonderful. But I think we should stop." The female voice sounded young and uncertain. They both did.

"Come on, babe. You said you wanted to make it in the lighthouse. Now's the perfect time. There's no one here but us."

He tried to place a face with the voice. It made it easier to imagine plunging his hard cock into her wet and willing body. Or unwilling. He liked it when they fought him, because it usually made it easier for him to satisfy himself. Without thought, he fingered the sharp knife that sat in a leather sheath at his waist. Maybe tonight wouldn't be a waste. He had the element of surprise, so the guy should be easy to kill and that would leave him with the whole night to play with the female.

Before he could decide whether to take the chance, the girl screeched. "My, God. What happened? Should we call the police?"

No. He couldn't let them call the police. He'd have to act fast. But they were on the other side of the room, so he'd have to move quietly. With a care, he turned the knob of the closet and opened it a crack while the two intruders continued talking, oblivious to the fact that their lives were about to end. He loved the power of deciding who lived and died.

"No. We can't call the police. We're not supposed to be here. Besides, the person who lives here is probably just a messy housekeeper. It doesn't look much worse than my bedroom at home."

The girl giggled. "That's true. You are a bit of a slob."

"Good. Now come here and kiss me."

The slut giggled, but she didn't stop the guy from kissing her. They weren't calling the police. Good. He stepped back into the closet to listen. No telling when Nicole would return. Better not to get distracted, even with such easy targets. Instead, he decided to watch through a crack as the two rutted like animals on the living room floor. All the while, he pictured the bitch, Nicole, laid out on the bed in front of him. A sacrifice for his enjoyment. Begging for her life. He might tease her with the thought that he'd let her live if she did everything she was told. Of course, once she gave him the diamonds and fulfilled his every dark sexual fantasy, he'd kill her.

Chapter Twelve

I an forgot his line again. Candace smirked at him across the table that was a part of the dinner scene set. She was upset that he'd kicked her out on her butt last night and was deliberately trying to sabotage him. So far, she'd miscued him, improvised her own lines to confuse him, and made faces at him that no one else could see.

Before Ian could try his line again, Jeb called for a ten-minute break. The director strode over to Ian and Candace and proceeded to ream them both out for being unprofessional.

"Jeb, darling. I'm doing my best, but it's hard to work with someone who detests me as much as Ian does."

"Oh, for Christ's sake." Ian wanted to throw up at Candace's deliberate pout. She mimicked a look of sincere innocence and round-eyed surprise that someone could actually find her distasteful. He itched to slap that look from her features, but that thought brought Vanessa and her accusation to mind. *You're just like him.*

Ian didn't want to be just like him. What he wanted was to find his daughter. Instead, he was stuck on this movie set trying to portray an undying love for a woman he hated. A woman who had ruined his marriage and turned his daughter against him. Okay, he'd done the damage to both his marriage and relationship with his daughter. Candace had only been the final wreaking ball strike that had toppled the building.

Jeb finished yelling at them and then proceeded to yell at Candace for making faces at Ian. It seemed that Jeb had been sitting in a position high on the camera crane and seen everything. Ian smirked until Jeb turned his anger back to him. "And damn it, Ian, I thought you said you could deal with this."

"And you promised you'd keep her away from me." Ian stood and shoved his face close to Jeb's, although he had to lean down to accomplish the feat. Anger had taken over, and he pulled no punches clearing the air. "Do you have any idea what this woman did to me last night? Of course you don't, so I'll tell you."

He did. He told Jeb about Candace's underhanded lies and manipulations and Vanessa's subsequent disappearance. "Vanessa is going through a real tough time in her life now. She's shaky, both physically and emotionally, and I'm worried about her. Because of this *person*, he sneered at Candace, "My daughter thinks I don't give a damn about her, and I can't even find her to explain." Candace had the grace to look sheepish. "I didn't know Vanessa was having trouble, or I would have asked her if she wanted to talk woman to woman."

Ian raged. "You weren't even supposed to be in my cabin in the first place. When will you get it through that empty head of yours that I'm not interested."

"If you weren't interested, then why did you kiss me like you did in the love scene yesterday?"

"It's called acting. You do know what that is, don't you?" The muscles in Ian's neck bulged, and his heart beat fiercely with anger.

Jeb put his fingers in his mouth and whistled sharply, bringing them both to a dead silence. "Candace, you promised me you'd behave yourself if I let you do this role."

"I was. I am. I only went to Ian's cabin to congratulate him on a great job of acting, the scenes came together amazingly. He's blowing it all out of proportion." She flicked her tongue across her lips and formed them into a perfect pout.

"Out of proportion? Jeb, do you remember that nice little blue number Candace wore to the awards last month?"

Jeb whistled. "How could I forget. Half the country talked about how sexy she looked, and the other half called her a brazen hussy."

"Yeah, well, that's what she wore last night."

"Christ. That's a definite take-me-I'm-yours dress if I've ever seen one."

"My point exactly." Ian said. "I can't work with her without wanting to choke her, and I'm afraid that won't make for a great love story."

Ian frowned at Candace when she opened her mouth to speak. "Don't say a thing. I don't even want to look at your face right now. Listen, Jeb, since I don't see how Candace and I can work together, you have a decision to make. I'm taking the day off. Call me when you decide if I'm in or out."

Ian didn't wait for an answer. He was too pissed at Candace and blamed Jeb for hiring her knowing their past. He'd enjoyed the scenes they'd shot so far. This movie gave him the chance to explore deeper within himself and act in a movie that might have some literary meaning. With those thoughts racing through his mind, Ian crossed the street to *Wishes*. He had a feeling that the woman who ran the store knew everything that went on in town. It was a good place to start. Besides, there was the chance he'd run into Nicole there.

Ian kept his sunglasses on and baseball cap pulled low on his forehead. He wasn't in the mood for signing autographs or hearing about how someone's grandmother had watched all his movies and loved him. He needed to find Vanessa and assure her how important she was to him.

That she could trust him to help her.

Uh-oh. Approaching from across the street came a middle-aged, overweight woman dressed in sky blue polyester and waving a camera and notebook. From experience, Ian knew she'd insist on a lengthy bout of picture taking and reminiscing about her favorite movies starring him. Damn. Without breaking stride, he changed direction and entered the closest store. Waving away the over-anxious salesperson, he asked if there was a back door out.

"Oh, yes, right over there."

The young woman pointed to the back of the store, and

Ian suddenly realized the kind of store he had entered. Silky nighties, lace garters, thong underwear—you name it, this store carried it. Oh, Lord, if the tabloids could see me now. He could just imagine the headlines labeling him as a cross-dresser or buying lingerie for his secret wife, whom he kept locked in a trunk under his bed. He needed to get out of there. Mumbling an apology, he made tracks for the back door. Once out on the dock, it was easy to slip in the back door of *Wishes*.

Feeling guilty for the deception, he defended his actions by reminding himself that he spent a good part of his time in the public signing autographs and saying all the right things. Occasionally, he needed time to himself. A glance through the billowy yellow curtains showed no one following him. He breathed a sigh of relief at the same time someone tapped him on the shoulder.

"Excuse me, but are you all right?"

Ian spun around, praying it wasn't the fan he'd just ditched. Instead, he saw Josephine dressed in an orange gauzy dress and frowning at him. "Yes, I'm okay." Sheepishly he admitted, "I'm afraid I just disappointed a fan. She's probably still searching the lingerie store for me."

Josephine laughed. "You probably gave her the thrill of her life when she saw you go in there, so don't worry about it." She cleared her throat. "I've been waiting for you."

"Pardon me."

Josephine hooked her arm through his and gently led him to the small alcove where coffee and cappuccino were always available. "I knew you were coming, and I have a strong sense that the matter is rather urgent."

"Yes, but how did you know? Oh, Vanessa's been here, right?"

"Vanessa?" Josephine motioned Ian to sit, then pulled out a deck of funny looking cards and proceeded to lay them on the table one at a time. "Oh, yes, your daughter. No, I haven't seen her, but the cards told me you'd be here today."

Ian's mentally slapped his hand to his forehead. Lord, the

woman's crazy, and I don't have time for this. He attempted to stand, but Josephine reached over and grabbed his arm. Her grip was strong and insistent.

"You may not believe, but hear me out." She examined the cards on the round table while the coffee pot exuded the delicious scent of freshly brewed beans.

Ian's mouth watered and he leaned over to pour some coffee, all the while trying to figure a quick way out. Josephine's next words gave him pause, and he leaned back in the rickety wooden chair that creaked under his weight.

"You have lost someone dear to you." Her lavender eyes searched his face. "Your daughter, I assume."

"Well, she's not exactly lost."

"Emotionally, she is lost. Her physical body remains close to you, but unless you can provide what you have denied her all these years, she will be lost forever."

"What do you know about what I've provided or not? Has she been here talking to you?" Ian grew agitated. He didn't like having his personal life poked into, and he didn't like some wacko in an orange dress pointing out his shortcomings.

"I've never met your daughter. I only relay what the cards show. See." She pointed to a card titled the Fool and depicting a jester of sorts. "This card shows that you are on a spiritual journey, on the road to wholeness and courage. You are attempting to develop relationships and balance your life. Over here, The Knight of Wands depicts change on a deep core level. Because of the positions of the rest of the cards, I see a very strong sexual attraction, and a dark energy that has twice torn your life asunder. Also a very rocky road for your daughter."

"Look." Ian pushed himself from the table and stood. "I only came to see if you knew where my daughter is, but if you've never met her, I guess you can't help."

"Never assume anything. I know who she is with, and I know that danger lurks for all of you." Josephine stood and looked him directly in the eyes. "I know you think I'm crazy, heck, maybe I am, but danger prowls the streets of this town."

She closed her eyes and shivered while reciting what seemed to be a poem of sorts.

Danger takes the darkest form, not once, but twice
Creeping like a creature from the pits of hell
The darkness will enter your life and threaten those you love well
Beware and be honest, this to you is my heartfelt advice

Ian shivered. Josephine's hypnotizing voice ran over him like cold water. Strange, maybe, but the woman in orange seemed to have his life figured out. Of course, anyone who could read would have some insight to his life, even if it was an exaggerated version. Besides, most parents devoted more time to their jobs than their kids these days, so the words *'unless you can provide what you have denied her all these years, she will be lost forever'*, really could apply in broad terms to anyone's life. And wasn't everyone at a crossroads in their life at certain times? It was sheer coincidence that he was at one now, both professionally and personally.

Okay, then there was the sexual attraction—that would be Nicole, and then the dark force that had torn his life asunder twice? Candace's pouting lips and ice-cold blue eyes flashed in his mind. Maybe there was something to it after all. His gaze fell to the cards spread on the table. They were dotted with swirling colors, figures dressed in floating, ethereal clothing, and different signs of the zodiac. Suddenly, the full impact of Josephine's words hit Ian. Danger.

"The danger, tell me more about the danger."

Just then, Corporal Moody entered the store and waved for Josephine. She excused herself and the two of them held a whispered conference in the corner of the store. Some of the words were loud enough to reach Ian across the store.

"...lighthouse...demolished...good thing, Nicole..."

Fear stabbed him in a way he'd never experienced. He'd felt the fear of standing in front of a camera for the first time, uncertain whether his talent would satisfy or if he'd be ripped to shreds by a fickle audience. He'd been afraid when his daughter had been born, so afraid that he wouldn't be good enough to raise such an innocent creature born of love. As his marriage had slowly crumbled, he'd also felt the fear of being alone. None of them had ripped his insides to shreds as much as those few words.

Without a thought to propriety or convention, he strode over to Corporal Moody and grabbed him by the shoulders. "Nicole. Tell me about Nicole?"

The officer glared at him. "What is your interest in her?"

"Tell me what you know about her." Not caring he was an officer of the law, Ian grabbed his shoulder.

"Nicole's fine." Josephine pried his hand from Corporal Moody.

The words took a second to sink in, but they brought relief and quelled the fear. He didn't question his reaction. He accepted that his feelings for Nicole went beyond sexual attraction, and they were feelings that would need addressing in the near future. When he got Vanessa's life in order, he'd concentrate on his own.

Rubbing his shoulder and looking at Ian with a wary gaze, Corporal Moody said, "I went out to the lighthouse and found it had been ransacked. So it's a good thing that..."

Before he could finish his sentence, Josephine interrupted him. "Yes, it's a good thing that Nicole noticed some dry rot at the lighthouse and moved to the *Wyllow Wood Inn* for a couple of weeks so it could be fixed."

"Yes. That's it." Corporal Moody looked confused Josephine was lying, and Moody was covering. It was as obvious as the hot sun glaring through the back door. Her words about danger wormed their way back into his mind, and Ian wondered if this was part of her prediction coming true.

He was about to grill her for more information, but the tingle of the bell over the front door intervened. Kiernan entered the store and stood for a moment until his eyes adjusted to the change of light. Upon seeing Ian, he remarked, "Hey, I thought you were filming all day today."

"I was supposed to be. Let's just say Jeb needs to deal with a minor problem."

"Candace?"

Ian snorted. "Yeah. You don't sound surprised."

"I'm not. I figured she'd cause trouble."

"If only Jeb had half your intelligence, I wouldn't be in this mess."

Kiernan looked sheepish. "Candace is a great actress, and Jeb only wants what's best for the movie."

"Well, it's her or me, so brace yourself for some changes over the next day or two."

"If Jeb's smart he'll get rid of her," Kiernan offered in a hesitant voice. "You know, I've always admired you, that's one of the main reasons I agreed to do this movie." As if embarrassed at his confession, Kiernan said, "Time for lunch, guess I'll go eat."

Ian was flattered. He had no idea the young actor looked up to him, but he should have wondered before now why the newest rage in action films had agreed to act in a romance. Now he knew.

"It's a humbling responsibility, isn't it?" Josephine prodded gently. "Having such a major effect on people and the decisions they make in life."

It was, but Ian had never really looked at it like that before. He'd always just done his thing, never relating to how his actions affected others. Now, Kiernan was in Solitary Cove because of his admiration for Ian, and lives changed because of that decision.

"Yes, it is."

Josephine put her hand on his arm and said, "You don't need to feel bad for how you've lived your life. Your restlessness has colored your days and led you astray, but it has also fed your ambition and nourished your talent. Every emotion you've experienced, every decision you've made has led you to this day. Now is the time for you to take everything you've learned and use it to help others."

Ian gazed into the eyes of this woman who earlier, he'd mentally ridiculed, and felt a connection. Her words soothed and stimulated. How could a stranger know him so well? How could this woman in her flowing, gaudy dress, owner of an eclectic small town store, know how to set him on the right path? He cleared his throat. "Now, you said you knew where my daughter is?"

"She's with Nicole. I'm not sure exactly what happened, but the cards show you have some explaining to do. She won't want to listen to you, but you have to make her. You will perform an act of protection that will help bring her to your side."

An act of protection? Ian shook his head. "I have no idea what you mean, but I have a feeling I'll find out."

"Good." Josephine crossed to a shelf of delicate figurines and various displays of jewelry. "Here, I want you to take this and keep it close. It will help connect you to your guardian." She handed Ian an oval medallion embossed with the figure of a pixie and hanging on the end of a gold chain. The fey features twisted into a conspirator's wink, and he wore a jaunty cap on his head that gave him a sweet appeal.

Ian looped the chain over his head, and the medallion came to rest in the middle of his curling chest hair. At first, it felt cool, but it quickly warmed and gave Ian a strange feeling of comfort. He smiled at Josephine. "A connection to my guardian, you say."

"Yes. Whether you believe or not, everyone has at least one guardian. Or angel if you prefer. Yours is an impish little pixie with a penchant for causing mischief."

"You don't say." Ian smiled. "No wonder I've been called everything from a brat to a rascal to a rogue. It's the pixie's fault."

"Ha. He wouldn't be your guardian if you didn't have the characteristics that match his. Like energy draws like energy, they say."

"Oh. Who are they?"

"Whoever. Now, don't you have a daughter to find?"

"Yes. I also want to find out what the police turned up out at the lighthouse." Not forgetting Josephine's reaction to the news of the break in, he watched her face closely for a reaction. He wasn't disappointed. A veil of secrecy settled over her face.

"What aren't you telling me?"

"Nothing that's mine to tell."

She stuck her chin out in a stubborn manner and crossed her arms across her chest. Ian shook his head. He had a feeling there'd be no breaking through her defenses. Instead, he gave her a quick kiss on the cheek, thanked her and left the store. Stepping onto the walkway of the main street, he took a moment to decide his course of action. Concern for his daughter and Nicole ran through his veins. According to Josephine, they were together. The *Wyllow Wood Inn*. Keeping an eye out for prowling fans, he pulled his cap low, put on his sunglasses and hightailed it for the inn.

After much persuasion and some smooth talking, the front desk clerk finally gave out Nicole's room number. Grateful for such tight security, Ian was nevertheless frustrated by the time he knocked on Nicole's door. There was no answer. He knocked again. Still no answer. Damn, now what?

He was fast losing patience. His daughter thought he was a woman abusing bastard, he had no close relationship with a woman and hadn't for a long time, and the woman he'd begun to care about seemed to be in some kind of danger. He had money and he had fame. Big deal. He banged his fist against the offensive door that stood silent, which earned him a look of disgust from an elderly couple waiting for the elevator. Great, the papers the next day would probably detail how he'd had a drunken brawl in the hallway of the local inn.

His stomach roiled with a sour sense of frustration. Couldn't he even self-evaluate without having to worry about ending up in the papers? Obviously not, he thought, as the couple whispered to each while looking his direction. He threw a smile their way. They smiled back tentatively and then stepped onto the elevator as the steel doors slid open and waited to transport them.

Realizing he still had on his make-up and clothes from filming the scene, he decided the best thing to do would be go back to his cottage, get cleaned up, and then contact the police to see what they'd come up with at the lighthouse.

***

Nicole whistled for Sumo, who at that moment was bounding through the underbrush hot on the trail of a rabbit or something. He usually obeyed, but spending all night locked up in the hotel room with no exercise made him stubborn enough to ignore her command. As a result, Nicole stood alone on the pathway to Ian's cabin. She listened to the not too distant waves surging with a graceful power onto the rocky shore and the warbling of songbirds paying homage to the beauty of a summer day.

If her reason for coming here weren't such an emotional one, she would have enjoyed the peace and serenity of nature's bounty. As it was, butterflies fluttered in her stomach, and her mind raced. She wanted to confront Ian about his insensitivity to his Vanessa and ask him to help his daughter.

When the cabin came into view, Nicole still hadn't decided what approach she was going to use. She could take a gentle *'You know your daughter's hurting and needs help'* approach. That should guilt him into feeling some sort of responsibility, but if he didn't feel responsible for his daughter after twenty-seven years, he wasn't about to start now. What she really wanted to do was take him by the shoulders and shake until some common sense and compassion rattled itself loose inside.

She was afraid that when she'd knock on the door it would open to reveal the sultry Candace. Nicole's heart jumped in her chest. What did she care if Ian spent his night with his co-star? It didn't matter if he slept with half the women of Solitary

Cove while he was here, so it certainly didn't matter if he slept with Candace, even if she had made People's 100 Most Beautiful People list.

Damn him for kissing her and making her care.

With a snort of anger, she stomped up the front stairs of the cabin and knocked loudly on the door. If Candace answered the door, she'd simply say she had business with Ian. If Ian answered the door, well, she'd probably melt into a puddle on the front deck.

When the door finally swung open, neither Ian nor Candace stood before her. Instead, a man in an expensive looking, charcoal-colored business suit stood with one hand on the door and the other cradling a cell phone to his ear. He frowned and gestured her into the cabin while continuing his phone conversation.

Nicole hesitated. It was the right cabin, and there was no way Ian would have checked out and this man checked in since last night. Therefore, the stranger must be a friend of Ian's. If Ian wasn't here, this man might be able to tell her where he was. She stepped into the cabin and jumped when the man swung the door abruptly shut behind her.

"I don't care what it takes, make it happen today. I'll be there as soon as I take care of some personal business." He glanced toward Nicole and waved her over to the nearby couch.

She took a couple of hesitant steps forward, but a glimmer of a warning wound its way from the lower regions of her belly. The man yelled sporadically at the poor person on the other end of the phone, all the while pacing the carpeted floor and throwing an occasional glance Nicole's direction. She managed a slight smile while soaking in the details of the man's appearance. A word her mother used to use popped into her mind. *Smarmy.* Yep. This guy could have licked the snake of a belly, but would have to stretch up to reach. Expensive clothes, slicked back hair, perfectly shined shoes that reflected the diffused afternoon sun, he'd even buffed his nails to a shimmering opalescent sheen. He possessed almost handsome features, but somewhere over his lifetime, they'd developed into a sharp display of impatience, anger, and frustration. His mannerisms mirrored his face as his free hand fidgeted with his clothing in a vain attempt to make sure all was as it should be. When he found his tie slightly askew, he frowned and straightened the offensive article of clothing.

His energy was disjointed and expansive. It filled the room and overpowered Nicole.

She knew who this was. Without a doubt in her mind, he was exactly as she'd imagined when Vanessa had described him, only more suffocating in person. How had Vanessa put up with him for so long? Two minutes in the same room as him, and Nicole felt the need to make a hasty exit.

She didn't have the chance.

Before she could even turn to the door, Bob was snapping a good-bye to the unfortunate person on the other end of the phone. Somehow, unobtrusively, he had maneuvered himself between Nicole and the front door. When he spoke, his voice had calmed and taken on a charming, pleasant tone meant to garner trust.

"Hi. Sorry about the phone call, it's hard to find good help these days, you know." He laughed as if he'd created some new joke instead of an over-used cliché. He extended his hand to Nicole. "My name's Bob."

Nicole's parents had raised her to be polite, so she found herself raising her hand to shake the hand of a man she had vicariously come to detest. "I'm Nicole." She wanted to come straight to the point. "Is Ian here?"

Bob's gaze wandered the length of Nicole's body before answering. "No. Maybe I can help you with something."

Nicole couldn't believe it, he was flirting with her. His wife had run away from him, and he was no doubt looking for her, yet here he was flirting with the first female he could find. Bastard. Nicole kept her voice neutral and non-committal, she just wanted to get away.

"No, thank you. I need to speak with Ian. I'll come back

later. Nice meeting you." With ease born of experience, Bob easily countered her move to the door.

"Wait a minute." He gripped her arm tightly. "If I can't help you, maybe you can help me. I'm looking for my wife, Vanessa?"

His hawk-like gaze pinned Nicole, and it took her a second to control her features when he mentioned Vanessa's name. It was a second too long. He squeezed her arm.

"You do know where she is. Tell me," he demanded.

"I...I don't know where she is. I haven't seen her since the night before last when I was here for dinner."

Bob's eyes narrowed as if weighing the validity of her statement. Nicole's arm hurt where Bob still grasped, and she didn't know if she was more pissed or scared. The black hollow look in Bob's eyes pushed the fear a notch higher than her anger. She was alone in an isolated cabin with a man known to abuse women, and if she wasn't careful, she might become the latest patient at the hospital emergency. On the other hand, she swore she'd never let another man use her as an emotional or physical sounding board again.

Vanessa's bruised ribs and battered face raced across her mind, and Nicole's body tensed with anger. Her nostrils flared and eyes met obsidian black. Silently, stupidly, she challenged him. He recognized the challenge, and a sneer curved his mouth.

"I see my wife has been telling tales out of school." Another cliché. Could this man not come up with an original sentence? Probably not. Nicole imagined his brain to be no larger than a gumball. One that had been chewed and spit out on the sidewalk. She stifled a chuckle at the vivid image, but quickly realized her mistake when Bob jerked her close to him and snarled in her face.

"How dare you laugh at me?" He raised his hand and growled, "Tell me where to find my wife."

Instinctively, Nicole ducked and then realized she was assuming the familiar subservient role. Never again. Lifting her head and straightening her shoulders, she thrust her face close enough to Bob's to feel his breath on her cheek. Her insides quivered, and she could taste steely fear on her tongue, but she wasn't backing down. She would not allow this bully to browbeat her and undo all the self-confidence she had developed since Jeff's death.

Bob's face flushed with anger. His breathing increased in tempo. "I've traveled a hell of a long way to bring Vanessa home, so forgive me if I don't have patience for your games." He tightened his grip on Nicole's arm and brushed her ear with his lips. "I want my wife, and I want her now."

Nicole breathed deep, and imbuing her voice with confidence she didn't feel, spoke a single word of determination. "No."

Bob's reaction was an instantaneous act of retribution. Using the full force of his masculine strength, he threw her toward the couch. Nicole landed in a tangle of arms and legs. Her heart pounded in her chest. She ignored the throbbing hip that had banged against the decorative wooden arm of the couch and attempted to gain a better angle of defense against the attack she was certain would come. She tasted fear, but wouldn't give in. The bastard could beat her black and blue, and she'd still protect Vanessa. Clenching her fists, she angled herself to a sitting position and readied her foot to make contact if it became necessary. Bob advanced on her with the lust of hate and fury glaring in his eyes. Nicole was terrified. This man was insane, and she had just deliberately pushed his buttons. Maybe she was insane as well. Damn it, she didn't care. Adrenaline pumped through her veins. She was going to give this man the fight of his life or die trying.

***

Ian was weary. Making his way back to his cabin, he had time to think about past mistakes. Mentally, he laid his life bare with brutal honesty and found himself wanting in many ways.

He'd always been restless, and that had made him a bad father and husband. Meeting Michelle, falling in love, he'd relied on that relationship to steady the streak of wildness within. It hadn't worked. Instead, the responsibility for another person's happiness had weighed him down. A person who wasn't strong enough to stand on her own, let alone try to build a strong relationship with her husband.

He'd been faithful to Michelle in a physical manner. It hadn't taken long for him to let her down in other ways, though. His absences from home and his marriage had grown longer, until Michelle had no choice but to believe he was having an affair. She was stuck at home raising a baby without the benefit of a husband. In the manner of a male chauvinist, Ian refused to consider Michelle getting a job. He was the man of the house and would provide, while his wife stayed home and took care of their daughter. Ian realized now what an egotistical and selfish bastard he'd been. He hadn't been there for Michelle, yet he wouldn't allow her to have a life of her own. She'd gotten bored, and he'd been arrogant enough to blame the failure of their marriage on her, taking no blame for himself.

He came to the stone path that led to his cabin and paused to breathe the salty tang of the ocean air. He liked to think that years of life and experience eventually gave way to wisdom, and since he was fifty-four, he should have some wisdom stored somewhere. Damn, he'd been a bad father. Vanessa had expressed doubts about marrying Bob. And what had he done? Dismissed them. Said Bob would be a good provider. Heck, a husband needed to be more than that.

One last breath of fresh air, then he covered the last yards to his cabin with a purposeful stride of determination. As he stepped onto the front porch, he heard a commotion. Familiar voices filtered through the half-closed windows. Voices he felt he should know, but they'd been spoken in anger, and it took a moment for him to identify them. He lept up the steps two at a time. Flinging open the door, the scene confronting him woke the slumbering beast he usually kept subdued.

Hell, he hadn't had a good bar fight in about fifteen years, but the instincts had been bred into him from his father, a champion lightweight boxer. Nicole's pale face and defensive crouch on the couch and Bob leaning over her with fist raised, was enough to send Ian flying across the room with no thought to his own safety. His hand closed over Bob shoulder, and he spun him around to stand face to face.

Black eyes gazed back as an ancient ritual of masculine intimidation played itself out in body language. Each man tensed ready to do battle, fists slowly clenched in readiness. Ian shook with rage, and the power of his emotion must have communicated itself to Bob, because the younger man took a step back and raised his hands in surrender.

"Whoa, Ian, take it easy." His voice took on a wheedling tone. "Look, I wouldn't have done anything. I just lost it when she wouldn't tell me where Vanessa is. I've had a hard time these last few days, you know. Vanessa just took off without telling me anything, and I've worried myself sick over where she might be. I called the hospitals, the morgue, and all our friends. You understand, don't you?"

Ian's fists clenched and unclenched in an attempt to cool his anger. He imagined how good it would feel to smash in his snide looking face. A quick glance at Nicole, and he decided that she'd been through enough.

"Bob. I would suggest you get your ass out of this cabin and out of this town before you find yourself charged with assault."

Various expressions crossed Bob's face as he tried to decide what to do. He must have realized that he couldn't cajole Ian onto his side as he'd done in the past, so he changed his tactics. Striding to the door, he grabbed his briefcase and turned back to Ian and Nicole. Ian didn't recognize the man. Gone was the chummy, good ole' boy face Ian had gotten used to over the years, and in its place was a face of an evil man intent on having his way. Ian realized that it was the face that Vanessa had lived with, and he hated himself for being so blind.

Bob stabbed the air with his forefinger and snarled, "You may be a big time star, but you can't drive me out of town. I'm here to find Vanessa, and I'm not leaving until she's with me. She's my wife, and the law is on my side."

Bob made a hasty exit, as if afraid that Ian might change his mind and beat the crap out of him. A sniffle reached through Ian's sizzling anger, but when he made a move toward Nicole, she pulled away as if afraid of him. The action tore into Ian, and he swore silently wishing that he'd followed his instinct to smash Bob's face with his fist.

"Nicole, it's okay, he's gone." He inched closer, making sure to move slowly.

"I know. I know." Her voice was weak. "Just give me a minute." Nicole shifted on the couch and shaky hands smoothed out her wrinkled tee shirt. A shuddering breath wracked her body, and then Ian was amazed to see the glimmer of a smile touch her lips.

"Nicole?" He sat on the couch beside her, careful not to touch her no matter how he ached to pull her into his arms and comfort her. She turned to him. Her eyes shone the golden tint of amber and sparked with proud resolve. Ian touched her hand with his, and she responded by accepting his hesitant caress and grasping his hand in hers.

"I didn't let him beat me."

Tears flowed freely from her eyes, but to Ian they seemed to be tears of freedom and a sudden understanding of unknown strengths. Nicole sniffed and wiped the tears from her face with the back of her hand.

"He was nice at first, but when he asked where Vanessa was, and I refused to tell him, he changed. He threatened me and threw me onto the couch. I almost lost it, but I didn't. I was ready to fight him, and no matter what he did to me, I wasn't going to tell him where to find her."

Light glowed from Nicole's eyes, and Ian found himself forgetting the circumstances that had brought them to this moment. Their surroundings receded into a fog, and Ian leaned forward to capture Nicole's lips with his. The first touch of flesh upon flesh was exquisite, and Ian prodded Nicole's lips with the tip of his tongue. God, she tasted so sweet. Her lips opened willingly beneath his, and Ian felt the urgent need of his inner beast raging for release. Nicole moaned and met his tongue with full force and intent. A melding of souls and heating of bodies occurred, and Ian wanted to make love to this woman, oh, so badly. But the time wasn't right. Bob was on the loose, and Vanessa was out there, vulnerable. He pulled away ever so slowly, allowing them both to come to their senses.

"I'm sorry, Nicole." He brushed a stray hair from her face and kissed her nose. "You shouldn't have been subjected to him." His lips found their way to her forehead and lingered before moving back to her cheek and down to her lips. Whispering her name, he let his hands fall to her shoulders and drew her closer. She didn't resist. Her body melded to his, and Ian reveled in the wonderful feeling of sexual arousal that had been so scarce for him lately.

Thoughts of Bob and Vanessa became nothing but a whisper in the darkness of his mind, as he explored the soft yielding body that turned him on so much. He shifted to enable them to stretch out on the couch in a more comfortable manner. Nicole's body pressed against his and at that point there was no way she couldn't be feeling the evidence. Testing her reaction, he rotated his groin. Oh, God, she felt so good and he ached to bury himself inside her softness.

Suddenly, he realized that Nicole had stiffened and pushed lightly against his shoulders. Oh, no. Please don't stop. He groaned and tried to pull her closer, his earlier reasons for stopping disappearing in the mist of arousal. Nicole resisted, and he knew then that there'd be no release for him that day. With a quivering sigh of self-restraint, Ian let her go and sat up.

"Fine, I can take a hint," he murmured.

Nicole recoiled as if slapped, and Ian immediately regretted his tone, but it wasn't induced by anger toward Nicole. Rather, it was frustration with the circumstances and his lack of control. He opened his mouth to explain, but was cut short when Nicole stood to face him with her hands on her hips.

"Who do you think you are, anyway?" Tears reflected in the amber depths of her eyes. "Do you feel it necessary to man-handle every woman you come across, or are you just amusing yourself with me because Candace isn't around to satisfy your urges?"

Ian was stunned. He had thought Nicole would be upset by her confrontation with Bob, instead she was ranting about Candace. God, she was beautiful with her masses of wild hair that caught the rays of the sun and shone back shades of ma-hogany and coffee. Her eyes quivered between tones of gold, emerald. A gold and brown goddess, that's what she looked like.

Too busy admiring her looks and reveling in the feeling of wanting a woman and being able to back up the desire phys-ically, he didn't even pay attention to the words she spewed at him. He didn't care what she said, he only knew that he was going to claim her as his own.

"Damn you, do you even care about your daughter?"

Those words shook him from his fog. "What did you say about Vanessa?"

She threw her hands up in the air and exclaimed, "You haven't heard a word I said have you? No wonder she came to me for support. I mean besides the fact that you put Candace above her on your scale of what's important."

Ian flew from the couch and grabbed Nicole by the shoul-ders. "You don't know what you're talking about. And what is your obsession with Candace?"

Comprehension was slow in coming, but he realized what must have happened. "Oh, I see. Vanessa told you about last night. Damn, why is everything suddenly so complicated? Look, first things first okay, I need to know where Vanessa is so I can get to her before Bob finds her. It's a small enough town that it shouldn't take long if he starts asking questions."

"Yes, I suppose you're right. When I left to come here, she

was in my hotel room, so I would assume she's still there."

"I was just there, and no one answered the door when I knocked." He frowned and looked at Nicole. "Why did you come here anyway?"

"You weren't listening to me, where you? I told you already, I came here to tell you that Vanessa needs your help, and you should stop being so self-centered and selfish and spend some time helping her figure out what to do with her life, because she sure as hell isn't going back to the son of a bitch that I just met." Nicole had worked herself up with the short, impassioned speech, and her face flushed with the emotion.

Ian smiled and crossed his arms over his chest. "Self-centered and selfish, am I? Maybe I am, but you should know by now that there's always more than one side to a story. Vanessa only saw a snapshot of what went on last night."

"What happened last night is none of my business."

Those words of denial hit Ian hard, and his frustration rose to the surface. He really thought he had better control over his emotions, but this woman seemed to have the ability to push all the wrong buttons. "None of your business. I wouldn't exactly say that, unless the kisses we've shared mean nothing to you."

"Kisses, that's all they were. Anyway, you don't seem overly particular about who you share your kisses with. So, don't worry, I won't place any importance on the few you've deigned to give me."

Ian grabbed her arm and dragged her to the front door, muttering all the way. "There are things that need saying, but I'll only explain myself once, so we're going to find Vanessa, make sure she's safe, and then all three of us are going to talk."

Nicole tried to resist, but between last night's fiasco, Vanessa's messed up life, the fact that he was quite likely unemployed, Bob's abrupt and violent arrival, and the feelings of lust racing through Ian's blood, he ignored her feeble attempts to break free from his grasp. He knew his rough actions would need some explaining later, but what the heck, he was already in hot water. What was one more act to explain away?

Chapter Thirteen

J osephine put the closed for lunch sign on her shop window and locked the front door. Operating a small, specialized store like *Wishes*, didn't make enough money to pay for help, so she usually ended up brown bagging it for lunch and eating while she worked. Occasionally, she was lucky enough to have a friend stop by and offer to go pick her something up from the bakery or deli.

Today was different.

She crossed to the back of the store and firmly locked that door as well. Habit dictated a quick look over the docks to where Jacob kept his boat. The slip was empty, but her eyes recognized the squat, blue and white lines of his fishing boat on the horizon. He must have had a good morning to be returning so early in the day. She smiled and wished she had the luxury of wandering over when he docked and maybe suggesting they have lunch together, but two things stopped her from acting on her urge.

Jacob was the first thing. He embarrassed easily, and if she showed up unannounced, he would only grumble about what everyone would think. After all, his boat was his home as well as his place of business. As far as Jacob was concerned, her presence there would make a statement to the entire town, and it wasn't a statement he wanted to make. Josephine liked to think it wasn't a matter of not wanting, but more that he wasn't ready.

The second thing stopping her from marching down there and forcing the old codger to make some kind of declaration, was the restless energy that wouldn't leave her. She'd been restless all day, and the air tingled with sinister undertones that demanded attention. So she decided to close the shop for lunch, which she didn't usually like to do and take her tarot cards to the loft she lived in above the shop. It was time to do a reading.

Her hand drifted slowly over her decks of cards. She needed to choose the right deck for the occasion, and she trusted in her guardians to guide her hand. A brief tingle and flash of heat in the palm of her hand prompted her to pick up the fourth deck she passed over. Of course, she should have known. Her hand hovered over the Thoth deck, not always one of her favorites, but one of her most powerful.

Designed by Aleister Crowley and painted by Lady Frieda Harris, the Thoth deck garnered much gossip and speculation. Aleister Crowley had been a colorful character who embodied a hedonistic life of magic, philosophy, drugs, and literary pursuits during a period of history very unforgiving of such things.

Josephine fixed a cup of herbal tea in her small kitchen, but nothing to eat, because the roiling in her stomach was not especially conducive to food at that moment.

Her yellow living room curtains matched the store curtains exactly, but this was not the time for cheerful, so she crossed to her bedroom where the darker navy curtains would block out the sun more appropriately. With shaking hands, she lit a black candle for protection and a silver one for clairvoyance. Taking a deep breath, she held the match to a stick of cinnamon incense and inhaled the pungent smell that would help bring love from the higher realms.

She turned her attention to her cards, and drawing the first card from the deck, laid it upon the smooth dark surface of wood. Vivid colors of orange and yellow reflected, even in the dim light of the curtained room. Knight of Wands—interesting. But she wouldn't read anything into the cards until they all lay on the table. She drew another and another. The fourth card she lay on top of the first one, the fifth on top of the second, and the sixth on top of the third, so she ended up with six cards paired. Not quite done, she knew there was one more card to draw, but her fingers hesitated over top of the card. She knew which card taunted her from the top of the deck. A fleeting thought of not exposing it to the light of day teased her mind, but there really was no choice. With heavy hand and heart, she lifted the card and laid it onto the table.

Not even the sound of her gasp broke the silence that permeated the room. She shifted in her seat and kept panic at bay until she'd had a chance to study the spread of cards. She needed to read them as a whole.

She sensed that the first three cards represented people, which was not always the case. The Knight of Wands was obviously Ian on a journey of spiritual evolution. Josephine had seen that in him from the first. His perceptions of the world were being tested and changed. The card was alive with vivid orange and yellow —fire and fire. Ian would need the double strength to deal with the deep core changes occurring within.

The card that lay atop the knight card was The Fool.

Again representing Ian, but more the situation and outcome of his situation. One Who Walks Without Fear, the hero moving through life as he balances and develops relationships. Confronted with relationships that pushed and tested, Ian would need to find his courage in order to overcome his obstacles and develop emotional richness in his life. He was relentless and courageous, but held it buried within, therefore denying himself a full life.

Josephine smiled at the implications of the next card. The Princess of Wands to represent Nicole. Another card of orange and yellow with a hint of green swirling about the background. The orange and yellow represented the fire that burned her fears and set her free. As the Princess grasped the tiger by the tail, she was subduing the fear she had lived with for so long, and the green hinted at increased self-awareness as she succeeded in her task.

Laid upon the princess was The Hermit, again a testament

to Nicole's desire to be alone. A desire to put the past behind her, and a desire to be alone based on fear of her stalker. But it was a fear that she was in the process of conquering. Being the number nine card signified completion, therefore Josephine felt that Nicole had powerful energy supporting her in her battle.

The third card must have represented Vanessa. Although Josephine didn't know the woman well, she had sensed the energy surrounding her, and the fact that Ian had been searching for her in an agitated state, confirmed that the card was meant for her. Oddly enough, it was the Queen of Wands, the Knower of Self card. The person this represented was in the process of self-discovery and had a strong desire for self-knowledge and understanding. The Tower card that lay atop it warned that Vanessa was experiencing a major internal change, but her strong healing gift would stand her in good stead. As long as she stayed true to herself and those she loved, she would be fine.

The three complimented each other and together they would be strong. But God forbid, if something were to happen to make them doubt or turn against each other. Josephine shivered as her eyes fell on the seventh card. Taunting her, warning her, the black skeleton of death danced on the face of the card. The death card did not always mean death, sometimes it was merely an innocent card of transformation, but not this time. Josephine knew it represented the evil that lurked in the darkness of the night and the shadows of the day. This time it represented death. Someone was going to die.

Josephine stared at the cards and tried to re-interpret them, but they were what they were. Someone would die before events had unfolded, and Josephine could only pray it wasn't anyone she had come to care for. As the cards had shown, the outcome would rely on the true spirit of one man and the loving acceptance and understanding of all involved.

Although there were no other cards to read, an insistent urge tickled the back of her neck. Prompted by an unseen energy, Josephine reached for the deck and plucked a card off the top.

Just one more card. A card to ordain the future of her uncertain relationship with the crusty sailor, Jacob. At first, her eyes refused to believe the truth of the card she held between her fingers. The Lovers card. A card of balance and duality, it depicted opposites in male and female, dark and light, but an overall theme of drawing together and harmonizing. It made sense applied to her and Jacob, because there couldn't be two more opposite people on the planet. Josephine felt overwhelming relief and certainty that things would finally work out for them.

Gently, she placed the card back on the deck and gave a silent blessing to her guardians for helping her interpret the energy of the tarot cards. Realizing she'd been gone long enough, she packed her deck away and returned to the store knowing that thoughts of how best to protect the people she cared about would fill her afternoon.

Nicole should be safe at the inn with Sumo, Jacob, Josephine, and the local authorities keeping an eye on her. She also knew the pivotal person in all this, the one to prove his true spirit, was Ian. What she didn't know was the source of the danger against Vanessa and how events would unfold. And that worried her.

***

Nicole shaded her eyes against the invasive sun and focused her attention across the street where Ian stepped out of the bakery doorway. Before leaving the cabin, they'd decided to split up and look for Vanessa. For the moment, they'd put their differences aside. Their eyes locked and thoughts unspoken charged the humid afternoon air. Nicole's heart thumped so loudly, she was surprised the passing group of tourists didn't hear and comment. Candace's sculpted features and overly endowed body drifted through Nicole's mind, prompting her to break from Ian's hypnotizing gaze. Disappointment flashed on Ian's face before he shrugged his shoulders and stepped into the next store.

Nicole pushed open the door to *Fred's*, and took a quick look around the cheery, disorganized store. Acting as magazine store, smoke shop, grocery store, and drugstore, *Fred's* was a popular place for the locals to shop. Unfortunately, there was no Vanessa.

Strange, she mused as she wandered out onto the street, when Ian grabbed her at the cabin, she hadn't felt threatened. She should have, because Ian had been a man under extreme emotional duress, pushed to the limit. Vanessa had said he had threatened to hit Candace the night before, so he was obviously the kind to resort to physical punishment. Why hadn't she been afraid?

Was it because she had become immune to physical man-handling during her marriage? Not that Jeff struck her more than once or twice, but he had pushed her around a lot. Maybe an innate sense of trust in Ian's character stopped her from being afraid. Yeah, right. Don't try to glorify him, just because you find yourself physically attracted to him. And there was the rub, she admitted to herself. She was inordinately attracted to a man who could never want someone like her, a man who lived in a world so different from her own that it was insane to even think they could have any kind of relationship.

"I had no luck, what about you?" The deep voice rumbled close enough for hot breath to tickle her ear. Hot stabs of lust quivered low in her stomach and unwound their way to her throat. Damn him.

"No. Nothing. But she's got to be somewhere."

"I know." Ian placed his hand casually on her shoulder and gave a reassuring squeeze.

No. Nicole didn't want him touching her. She couldn't think straight. She should have shrugged her shoulder to throw his hand off, but she didn't. Instead, she reveled in the warmth his hand created. For a brief second, she felt herself sway toward the man that had become an enigma to her, wanting to feel safe and protected. For a second of fairytale belief and movie make-believe, she pretended they were a couple of people in love, sharing a holiday on the coast. Creating worlds of make belief was her specialty—she did it with her writing all the time, so why not with her life?

"There's only one place left. We haven't checked *Wishes*." Ian's voice put an abrupt end to Nicole's fantasy.

"Fine, let's go." She spoke more sharply than intended causing Ian to raise an eyebrow.

"What did I say now to tick you off?"

"Nothing. You're just being yourself."

"Oh, and that's a bad thing?"

"What do you think?"

"I think that you have a one-sided view of a situation, and you should reserve your judgment until you hear the whole story." His eyes pierced into her, demanding that she give him the benefit of the doubt.

Nicole's own words thrown back at her. Words that she'd spoken to Vanessa only yesterday at lunch. Was it fair for her to judge Ian without knowing the whole story? No, of course not. But did it even matter if he had an explanation? No, of course not. She couldn't let herself get close to anyone, not with her stalker on the loose. If she cared for Ian at all, and it was beginning to look that way, she needed to keep her distance from him.

"I don't have to do anything." She pulled her shoulder from beneath his suddenly offensive hand.

"Excuse me," he mumbled. "Women, more trouble than they're worth."

"Oh, sure, and men are so much better." Nicole stomped down the planked sidewalk and pushed open the door to *Wishes*, leaving Ian to follow.

"I didn't say we are, but I'm willing to get to know you before jumping to conclusions about your character." He followed her into the dim light of *Wishes* and looked for any signs of Vanessa.

"You don't know me well enough to even begin to make judgments about my character."

"My point exactly."

"Hey, you two, keep the shouting to a minimum please?" Josephine's voice broke into the melee.

Nicole and Ian stopped mid-sentence. Blessed silence fell into the store, broken only by the sound of softly blowing wind chimes. Blue eyes melded with gold, and harsh words spoken hovered like smoke. Emotions raged, passions flared.

Ian ran his hands through his hair. "Listen, I don't have time for this now, Vanessa may be in trouble."

"A lot you'd care even if I were." Vanessa's voice echoed from beyond the bookcase at the back of the store. She stepped into the aisle and stood with hands on hips.

"Damn it, Vanessa, do you have any idea how worried I've been about you?"

"Oh, you mean you had time to worry? I thought you'd be too busy screwing the woman who ended your marriage."

Ian covered the length of the store in three strides, grabbed Vanessa by the arms and lifted her to his eye level.

Nicole's heart thumped, and she wanted to say something to break the stand-off, but Josephine's hand on her arm quelled her words. "They need to work it out themselves," she whispered to Nicole.

But there was no time to work anything out, because the front door opened and in walked Bob. Strutting his stuff as if the world should acknowledge his superiority he walked toward Josephine, but he immediately spied Ian and Vanessa at the back of the store.

"Ahhh, there you are, Vanessa." His voice came across polite and smooth, as if the last few days had never happened. "I've been looking all over town for you."

Vanessa's face drained of color, and she shrugged Ian's hands off her arms to stand and face the husband she had left in another country. "What are you doing here?" Her whispered words shook with fear.

"You're my wife, and you left without a word, where else do you think I'd be? And I must say, it wasn't easy finding you."

Bob walked toward Vanessa, but before he could get within reach, Ian stepped between them. "I think you gave up any rights you had in regard to my daughter."

"Come on, Ian, you know how it is with women. We had a little misunderstanding, and Vanessa thought she'd teach me a lesson by running away." He reached out to Vanessa with palms up and pleaded. "Hon, we've been through tougher times than this, I know we can work it out. I'm sorry for yelling at you."

"Yeah, are you sorry for hitting her, too?" Ian snarled. Bob dropped his hands and managed to look sheepish.

"I admit I lost my temper and made a mistake, but I love you, Vanessa. Please, let's just work this out." His voice changed from conciliatory to accusatory. "You worried me, you know, running out like that without a word."

He waited for a response and when he got none, he must have decided he'd pushed as far as he could, at least with an audience. "Look, I have business that needs my personal attention, but you're more important." In one swift move, he pulled a cell phone from his pocket and punched in a number. "It's me. I can't make our meeting, something important has come up. Keep me informed."

With a triumphant glare of arrogance, he snapped his phone shut and said, "Now, I've got the next few days free, so we'll have plenty of time to talk, sweetheart." He waited for Vanessa's reply, but she stood silent. "Damn it, Vanessa, you could at least say something."

"I don't think she wants to talk to you, Bob." Ian draped his arm across Vanessa's shoulders.

"She will. I'm her husband, and she knows I love her, no matter what. I'm staying at the Sailor's Inn. Give me a call when you're ready to talk, Vanessa."

The slamming of the door left a store full of mute people.

Vanessa was the first one to find her voice. "That's the first time he ever cancelled business for me."

Ian's gaze narrowed, and he turned to scrutinize his daughter. "Vanessa, don't even think what I know you're thinking."

"How do you know what I'm thinking?"

Nicole whispered to Josephine. "Oh, no, here they go again."

"I know." Josephine patted her arm. "I should close the store and let them argue." She crossed quietly to snap the lock in place and turn the sign from Open to Closed.

Ian ignored Josephine's move. He was too busy ranting. "You're thinking that he's suddenly a changed man, but you'd be wrong. He's only doing what's expedient to get you to go back to him."

"Yes, I'm sure that's something you can relate to, isn't it?" Vanessa raised her trembling chin in defiance.

"How could you even think about going back to him? He supposedly abused you enough to send you climbing through the bedroom window to get away from him."

"Supposedly? You saw the bruises."

"Yes, and if he gave them to you, how could you even think about reconciling with him?" Ian's frustration grew.

"He sounded sorry and he said he loves me. Maybe." Vanessa's voice trailed off into an uncertain mumble.

"Oh, come on, Vanessa!" Ian's roar echoed in the store.

"Okay, that's enough from both of you." Nicole had heard enough. She gave Vanessa a quick hug. "No decisions need to be made now, so I suggest we go back to my room and order some dinner. Maybe a nice, hot bubble bath as well. What do you say?"

"Sounds fine to me." Vanessa's belligerent glare snapped at her father as she stomped to the front door where she stood waiting for Nicole.

"Good." Nicole turned to Ian, stabbed her finger into his chest, and whispered, "You need to relax and get a perspective on things. Someone should give you a lesson in how to deal with women."

Impatient, Vanessa called out from the front door. "I'm waiting outside, Nicole, I need some fresh air." There was the defiant sound of the lock turning and the door slamming.

Nicole was quick to follow her friend, but Ian was quicker as he stepped forward and blocked her path to the door. "Call me later, and let me know how things are going."

"Do you care?"

"Of course I care. About both of you." A look crossed his face that reminded Nicole of a vulnerable child wanting to please, and then it was gone in a blink. With a lopsided smile at Josephine, Ian turned and left by the back door.

Josephine clicked her tongue and remarked, "I must say, the sparks are flying in every direction today."

"It's his fault. He is so infuriating."

"Dear, I don't think it's anger that sparks between you two." Josephine teased with a twinkle in her eyes.

Nicole had the grace to blush, because the statement was not far from the truth. "Well, be that as it may, I think he's spoken for." She leaned forward to plant a quick kiss on Josephine's cheek. "I better go, Vanessa's waiting."

"Wait." Desperation laced Josephine's voice. "Have the police come up with any new information on the break-in?"

"No, there were no fingerprints on the doll or anywhere else, and since Jacob didn't see his face, there's not much they can do."

Josephine gasped, and her hand flew to her throat. "Oh, dear. You haven't heard, have you?"

"Heard what?"

"The lighthouse was broken into again. Corporal Moody was up there earlier today because a couple of teenagers stopped by the office and told him that they'd seen the door open and the place trashed. Supposedly, they weren't going to say anything, but the young girl convinced her boyfriend to report the break-in. Humph! Doesn't take much imagination to know what they were doing up there alone at night." She folded Nicole into a hearty hug. "Thank God, we got you out of there, dear."

Nicole was too busy trying to comprehend the fact that her stalker had struck again. He had probably been furious when he hadn't found her there, so he tore the place apart in a fit of anger. Her voice trembled. "Maybe I'd better check in with the police."

"Good idea." She pressed Nicole's hands in hers. "You'll be fine. You've got Vanessa and Sumo with you. Jacob, the police, and I are keeping an eye on you as well. I do think it would be a good idea not to go wandering anywhere alone, though."

"I agree. I better go. See you later, Josephine."

It only took a couple of minutes for Nicole and Vanessa to reach the police station. Nicole almost wished she'd not come when Corporal Moody grumbled it was about time she checked in, and that he'd been trying to get a hold of her for most of the day.

"I'm sorry, but I only now heard about the break-in."

"Have you found anything?"

"Well, it just so happens that we did find something, but I'm not sure it's suitable to relate to you." Corporal Moody blushed.

"I'm the one this maniac is after, you can't not tell me." Scrutinizing the two women as if trying to imagine their reaction, he finally spoke. "Well, since this is such high priority and not the first break-in, we did a thorough search. What we found was not encouraging."

Nicole snorted. "Not encouraging. This lunatic killed my husband, now he's trying to kill me, and you're not encouraged?"

Vanessa's gasp reminded Nicole of her presence, but it was too late, the cat was out of the bag, so to speak. She hadn't wanted Vanessa to come with her, but she'd never been any good at lying, and hadn't been able to dissuade Vanessa from accompanying her.

"Sorry. What I meant is not only is this guy a murderer, but a pervert as well."

"Please, just tell me what you found."

"Ahem. It seems that the perp performed a rather disgusting act in your front hall closet."

"A disgusting act?"

"He masturbated. We found his sperm. Oh, he tried to clean up after himself, but he didn't get it all." Corporal Moody voice rose in excitement. "We sent it for analysis and should have some results in a couple of days. If we can find the guy, we can match him up to the sperm and have proof it's him."

Nicole's skin crawled in disgust at the thought of that bastard jerking off in her closet. She sent a silent prayer to the heavens that she hadn't been there. "But you have to find him before he gets to me." The last words escaped in a whisper.

Corporal Moody looked abashed. "Yes, I'm afraid so. But this is the first evidence anyone has been able to come up with on this guy. That's a good thing." The phone on his desk rang, and he dismissed Nicole and Vanessa with a wave of his hand.

Warm sunlight beat down on Nicole, but the heat wasn't enough to stop the chills from racking her body. She shivered.

Vanessa laid a warm hand on her shoulder and squeezed. "Nicole, I had no idea. My, God. I don't even know what to say, except that I've been so selfish with my own problems when your life is in danger. Do you want to talk about it? What are you going to do?"

"It's okay, Vanessa." Feeling weak, she sat down on the cement steps of the police station, and Vanessa sat beside her. "There's not much I can do, except maybe pack up and leave town."

"No, don't do that." Vanessa hesitated as if not sure what to say. "I know we just met, but I consider you a friend. You helped me and stood up for me more than my own father ever has. I don't think I can handle losing you as a friend. Besides, a lot of people care about you and if you leave, you'll be alone. I don't think that's a good idea."

"I know. Besides, he found me once, he'll find me again." Breathing deeply, Nicole let her gaze wander down the street and tried to imagine running away again. It wasn't going to happen. "No, Vanessa, it's either him or me, but the showdown happens here."

Chapter Fourteen

Nicole recognized all the excuses. She'd used most of them herself. It's probably my fault. I pushed him too hard. He's under a lot of pressure. He promises not to do it again. Maybe I should give him another chance. He sounds sincere this time.

She poured them both another drink and sat on the couch beside Vanessa. The other woman clutched tissues in her hand while tears rolled down her face. They'd come back to Nicole's hotel room after the confrontation with Bob and indulged in a gripe session about men. Fathers, as well as husbands. The afternoon sun had fallen to dusk, and the last rays colored the hotel room in shades of muted blue and somber gray.

Nicole sighed and wished there was something she could say that would help Vanessa see that she deserved better than Bob. Vanessa had run the gamut of emotions from fear to anger, denial to indifference. Nicole had tried to remain diplomatic and supportive, but she felt a twinge of impatience at Vanessa's obvious refusal to open her eyes to circumstances. Had she ever been so blind to the faults in her own marriage? Probably, or she wouldn't have stayed married for so long. But the abuse in Vanessa's case was more blatant and physical, and Nicole had a hard time understanding how anyone could remain blind to the obvious.

Nicole rationed that it was probably just a matter of degrees, because her relationship had started out great, and then somewhere along the line she had realized things weren't what they had been. Small incidents occurred along the way, then the excuses came and you accepted them, but each acceptance of the unacceptable took you further down the road. It was all a matter of how much you'd accept before saying, Enough.

"Vanessa." Nicole's spoke quietly, gently. "You know you can't go back to him, don't you?" She brushed her hand lightly over Vanessa's cheek hoping somehow to give the comfort and strength so badly needed.

"If I don't, what will I do?" Vanessa fixed her teary blue eyes on Nicole, as if waiting for the answer to all her problems.

Nicole knew there was no easy answer. Damn, Ian. He was the one who Vanessa needed. He was the one who had contributed to her lack of self-confidence and her ingrained need to please. Choosing her words carefully, she tried her best to reassure.

"I don't know what you'll do, but you're a lot stronger than you give yourself credit for. You don't need him to be whole." She downed her drink in one gulp and without asking, took Vanessa's almost empty glass to pour them each another.

Vanessa giggled. "I think you're trying to get me drunk."

Nicole poured the amber liquid into crystal glasses, added ice cubes, but no mix, and said, "I am." She weaved her way back to the couch and plopped down, spilling only a drop or two of alcohol. "Oops." She licked her fingers and passed a glass to Vanessa. "I have a feeling that we'll both think better when we're drunk."

"That's a theory I've never heard before." Vanessa gazed deep into the swirling liquid rye and then with swift intent, downed the entire glass. The fiery liquid gave her voice a husky, harsh quality when she spoke. "I can't go back to him. I've come this far. I won't go back. I'm afraid, though. I've done nothing. I've been nobody for so long that I don't know who I am. I don't know how to find myself. I don't know what to do."

Nicole cried along with Vanessa, as they held each other in a drunken, comforting embrace. It seemed like forever, but Nicole knew by the anchor-shaped clock on the mantle that only a couple of minutes had passed when she felt Vanessa's shoulders relax and her breathing deepen. She smiled when a light snore escaped the other woman's mouth. Carefully, she lay Vanessa down and pulled the quilt from the bed over her.

She thought they'd made progress and that Bob was going to have a rude awakening if he tried to coerce Vanessa into going home with him. At least that's what Nicole hoped, but she knew it wasn't a certainty until it happened. Vanessa needed her father's support and understanding.

Nicole knew what she had to do. Crossing to the bedroom, she closed the door and picked up the phone. Sumo lay in the corner where he had retreated when the crying started, but now he raised his head as if wondering if there was a walk on the horizon.

"Take it easy, fella. I'm just making a phone call. But if you want out for a pee, I'll let you out." With unsteady hands, she pulled open the balcony door and let Sumo out.

He'd go down the stairs and do his thing, then come back. Nicole's hazy brain tried to work itself around her next step. She wanted to talk to Ian. Okay, she wanted to ream him out, but with the stalker on the loose, she couldn't walk to his cabin in the dark. She could yell at him on the phone just as easily. Clumsy fingers pushed what she hoped were the correct ones to dial through to Ian's cabin. She giggled when she had to start over again because she'd hit the wrong button. Her fingers seemed to have a mind of their own.

Success. She smiled when the phone rang at the other end, and her heart leapt in her throat when she heard Ian's deep voice. For a second, she sat stunned just trying to get her pulse to stop racing.

"Hello." Ian sounded impatient. "Look, I don't have time for games. Who is this?"

Nicole managed to choke out, "It's me."

Ian's impatience changed to smooth seduction. "Nicole."

How could a single word set such an array of emotions tearing through her insides? And why was it that only Ian had that ability?

"Hi." Good, she sounded relatively sober. "How's Vanessa?"

"Oh, you mean you care?" Her voice wobbled a little. She'd better be careful or he'd know she was drop down drunk.

"Of course I care. She's my daughter."

"Ha. Well, then maybe you had better start treating her like your daughter instead of a burden."

"Are you drunk?"

"What?"

"I said, are you drunk? I hear a definite slur in your words."

"I...I'm not exactly drunk."

The full richness of Ian's laugh oozed over the phone line and melted Nicole right where she sat. Thank God, he wasn't close by, because in her condition it wouldn't take much for him to have his way with her. And why was she thinking about sex when there was both a stalker and a wife abuser on the loose? It just went to show how drunk she really was.

"Nicole, I want to see you. Come to my cabin."

Nicole was tempted, oh so tempted. But she couldn't, even with Sumo for protection. She might be drunk, but her sense of survival ran strong. "No. I can't."

"Come on, I know you want to."

Soft, smooth, and oh, so sexy, his voice raised goose bumps on Nicole's arms. "I can't. I'm afraid of the dark."

"More likely you're afraid of me. Tell you what, how about I come there. We can meet in the restaurant, that way you'll feel safe."

Nicole considered his request. It was a reasonable alternative to hiking to his place in the dark, and then being alone with him. "Okay. I'll meet you there."

"I'll be five minutes."

"Okay." Nicole replaced the receiver and hung her head into her hands. Man, she was more than a little tipsy. Crossing to the bathroom, she looked at herself in the oval mirror above the marble sink. She groaned at the stark whiteness of her face, but blamed it on the fluorescent lighting. She splashed cold water on her face and rubbed vigorously with a towel until color appeared in a healthy red glow. Using her hands, she fluffed her hair, pleased with the amber and mahogany high-lights gleaming in the mirror.

"Idiot. This is for Vanessa, not you." In a gesture of censure, she stuck her tongue out at her reflection. Checking on Vanessa, who was in a deep sleep, Nicole quietly left the suite.

She barely made it to the restaurant. The elevator ride set her stomach to doing flip-flops and convinced her to take the stairs when she went back to her suite. The waitress seated her easily, as it was past dinner and the small restaurant was virtu-ally empty. She ordered herself a coffee just as Ian appeared at the balcony entrance to the restaurant. He filled the doorway, and with the luminescent glow of the half moon behind him, he appeared ethereal.

"Have another drink, why don't you," Nicole muttered to herself.

Even in the dim lighting, Ian found Nicole easily, and he strode across the room to the corner table where she sat. "I see you went for privacy." A wave of his hands encompassed the surrounding ferns that virtually hid the table virtually from view.

"Not me. The waitress."

Ian sat. His knee brushed against Nicole's, and she clenched her hands under the table. "I...uh, ordered a coffee, but I didn't know what you wanted."

"Coffee sounds fine." Blue eyes glinted in the soft glow of recessed lighting, and he reached his hand out to brush a strand of hair from her face. "I'd say you're more than halfway polluted."

Nicole's chin shot up defensively. "So what? Vanessa and I had some serious talking to do."

The waitress appeared with Nicole's coffee, and Ian ordered the same. Once she'd left, Ian asked, "I assume she's fine?"

"Not really, no. Her life has fallen apart around her, and the one person she needs more than anything doesn't give a damn because he's too busy gallivanting with..."

Nicole didn't have a chance to finish her sentence before Ian's fist slammed down on the table, an act that earned a wary frown from the approaching waitress. He didn't bother apologizing as she placed his coffee on the table and asked if they needed anything else.

"No, that's all for now." Ian waited for her to leave.

"Vanessa and I have always had a complicated relationship, and you have no right to make any judgments on something you know nothing about."

"Know nothing about? Ha. Vanessa spent the entire evening pouring her heart out to me, and don't forget the fact that I know what happened last night."

"You know nothing. You have one side of a very complicated story and what Vanessa thinks she saw last night."

"She was told by Candy or Candycane, whatever her name is, that the two of you wanted time alone. Then she walks in on the two of you in a very compromising situation. What more could there be? Your daughter's life is in a state of upheaval, and you're more concerned with satisfying your baser urges.

"Candace, her name is Candace, and she jumped me. I had no idea she'd be there when I got back to the cabin last night, and when I tried to be polite she threw herself at me. I was in the midst of trying to pry her off when Vanessa walked in. If she'd been ten seconds later, she would have witnessed me reaming the bitch out for daring to intrude on my life that way."

Nicole's fuzzy brain tried to understand what Ian was telling her. Could it be true? Heck, she'd become a firm believer that there was always more than one side to a story, so could she in all good conscience ignore Ian's words? She didn't have much chance to decide because a screech from the other side of the room interrupted them.

Without even turning to look, Ian groaned. "Don't tell me, it's a woman dressed in blue polyester, and she's got a camera and notebook ready for use."

"Well...yes, how did you know?"

"Intuition."

Even in her inebriated state, Nicole marveled at the care Ian took with the woman's feelings. Gone was the intense, demanding, achingly sexy man of a moment ago and in his place was a polite, easy-going character who seemed delighted to sign autographs and pose for photos.

Amidst vows of undying gratitude, Ian was finally able to send the woman on her way, much happier than when she came.

"Amazing," Nicole remarked.

Ian's raised his eyebrows and smiled. "Lots of women say that about me, but why are you saying it?"

"Because that woman was intruding on a very serious conversation, yet you didn't tell her to get lost. Instead, you put aside your troubles to make her day. I don't think I'd have the patience to do that."

"It becomes second nature. I figure that it may be my hundredth autograph of the day, but it's her first. Whether it's right or not, the way I treat a fan can either make or break their day. That woman will go home and recite the story to everyone she knows of how she met me. She'll wave my autograph around and preen over the photographs until her friends get sick of the whole thing. I suppose it's the responsibility that's goes along with fame."

"But not every famous person feels the same way. I've seen some of them be quite rude to their fans."

"That's understandable. It can be irritating at times, but I'd rather make people feel good about themselves than grind their feelings into the dust."

"Damn you. How can you be such a jerk and such a nice guy at the same time?"

Ian laughed. "I don't know, why don't you set me straight." His demeanor changed to serious and he leaned on the table, his face only inches from Nicole's. "Tell me what I need to do to make Vanessa end this marriage of hers."

"You don't do anything. It has to be her decision to leave,

or she'll end up right back with him again. What she needs from you is your support—emotionally, physically, and maybe even financially. I'm pretty sure she's not going back to him, so suddenly she has nowhere to live, no one to talk to, no job, no furniture, no clothes. Bob has all the bank accounts, the house, cars, and credit cards in his name. He's denied her access to everything."

Ian snorted. "He can't do that. She's entitled to half of everything by law."

"Sure, but in order to get half of everything, she needs a lawyer to get access. She has no money remember and can't get to it without Bob's okay. You can damn well bet that he's not going to give her money to hire a lawyer."

"How could she have let him put her in that position?"

"See. That's exactly what you can't do. Vanessa doesn't need her mistakes rammed in her face. She knows them, she's lived with them. Bob's had years to batter her self-confidence, and you haven't helped any either, pressuring her to make her marriage work."

"I never pressured her, I only pointed out that Bob was a good provider. She kept talking about being bored when all she had to do was go out and get a job or go back to school. It was her mother all over again."

"No. It wasn't. Bob wouldn't let her work or go to school. He cut her off from her friends and family and made her feel as if she couldn't do anything right without him. Vanessa is going to need to be strong to get through this, and you're going to have to be strong right along with her."

"How can he stop her from having friends or doing what she wants?"

"I already told you that he controlled the money, so that takes care of taking any courses or going to school without his okay. As to having friends, that's easy—he tells her that her closest friend has come on to him and maybe it would be a good idea if she stays away from someone who couldn't be trusted."

"Why would Vanessa believe something like that? She's smart enough to talk to her friend and find out the truth."

"You men can be so dense sometimes. The whole point is that if she talks to her friend and finds out that her husband has been lying, she'd have to do something about it. By believing him and ignoring the whole problem, her life stays the same. She remains in her comfort zone and doesn't have to make any major decisions."

"But that's not even logical. Vanessa's not a doormat. She's always had great self-confidence."

"Oh, really? And how much time have you spent with her over the years? Part of the whole abuse thing is that the spouse slowly chips away the self-confidence, leaving the person doubting everything they say or do."

Ian shook his head. "I just don't understand."

"You don't have to. You just have to offer Vanessa your support in any way possible."

Ian chewed his lower lip. Shaking his head, he spoke. "This is so far out in left field that I'm having a hard time comprehending any of it. Why didn't she talk to me?"

"She wanted to make you proud of her and figured that having a successful marriage would do that."

"But her happiness is more important. She should know that."

"Well, she didn't, but you can tell her that now. It's something she needs to hear." Nicole glanced at her watch and gasped. "Wow, look at the time. I should get back up to the room in case Vanessa wakes up."

"I'll come with you and talk to her." Ian pushed his coffee cup away and stood up.

Nicole stood and placed her hand on his chest. "No, I don't think she'll feel up to talking tonight. Why not come by tomorrow sometime."

Ian placed his hand on Nicole's. "Maybe you're right. Besides, you look like you're ready to pass out yourself."

He brushed his thumb over Nicole's lower lip, the intensity

of his gaze pierced her and created an aching need for fulfill-ment. Fulfillment only he could provide, damn him. Nicole felt the tremor start in the pit of her stomach, and slowly wind its way through her chest and into her throat until she felt like choking with tears of submission. Therein lay the trouble.

She'd never allow a man to have that kind of control over her again. Showing that kind of weakness allowed a man to take advantage, and Nicole had already traveled that road. Drawing on the inner strength she'd developed over the last months, she focused her mind on subduing the rising feelings of lust. Slowly, the tremors dissipated into nothingness, and she regained control of her emotions.

Ian must have noticed the change in her, because he narrowed his eyes and pulled back, both physically and emo-tionally. A bitter, cold sensation that she'd destroyed some-thing valuable replaced the sensuous feelings of lust that had warmed her.

"It looks like Vanessa isn't the only one who needs to admit a truth that's glaringly obvious." Without even a good-bye, he turned and left the same way he'd come.

Nicole shook her head, wishing that she didn't crave his kisses so fiercely. And who did he think he was to tell her what she needed to do? He knew nothing about her or her past. She wasn't about to throw caution to the wind and put her trust in someone like him. But that opened the question of what she was looking for in a relationship. How would she know when she could place her trust in someone? Would a bell ring? Would her toes tingle? She had no idea.

With a sigh of frustration, she left a tip, waved at the waitress, and returned to her room where she was glad to see that Vanessa was still asleep. She yawned, the stress of the day catching up with her as she sank gratefully into the soft bed. Hovering on the edge of sleep, she couldn't shake the niggling thought that she was forgetting something. But her tired brain wouldn't work, so she gave in to the blessed peace of slumber.

***

Ian couldn't sleep. He tossed and turned, thinking how his life was supposed to flash before his eyes when he died, not at midlife. He was supposed to have it all, so why did he feel as if he stood on a slippery slope that slowly eroded beneath his feet?

The hovering moon shone in the bedroom window and caught his eyes with its glow. He cursed, rolled over, and punched his pillow. The blankets wrapped around his naked form and aggravated him with their stifling embrace. He needed a drink. No, better yet, he needed a woman. He needed Nicole.

Giving in to restlessness, Ian rose and padded into the living room where he poured a generous amount of whiskey. He fired the amber liquid down his throat, bracing himself for the hot wave that would engulf his mind and body. While waiting for the languor to encompass him, he noticed the reflection of his naked body in the sliding door. His tanned skin gleamed in the moon's rays, and he took a second to feel pride in the firm, masculine lines of his body. No wonder women still found him attractive; it was only in his own mind that he found flaws within himself.

He felt good too, especially now that...well, now that his problem seemed to have been resolved. Running his hand over his groin, he moaned in anticipation of having Nicole spread naked and willing beneath him. Within an instant, his cock responded to his thoughts and the light pressure from his hand. Damn, if his life hadn't taken a turn for complicated, chances were that he'd have Nicole with him right now. He wanted her so badly, but he knew his needs had to take second place to his daughter. They never had before, but they would now.

He slammed the glass onto the bar top and felt better as the liquor numbed his senses. He didn't usually resort to alcohol as a crutch, but tonight was an exception, with its undertones of sexual frustration, Vanessa's marriage taxing their already troubled relationship, and Candace's antics that had probably lost him his role in the movie. He didn't care about the movie, if he never worked another day in his life, he wouldn't run out of money. What he did care about was finding common ground with Vanessa, and the sudden realization that he didn't want to be alone any more. He couldn't hide his loneliness with one-night stands and fair weather friends. He couldn't fill his days with false promises and empty actions any longer.

Suddenly, he needed more. Suddenly, he wanted a life.

A vision of hazel eyes glimmered in his mind. Rich brown eyes flecked with amber, gold, or green depending on her mood. Mahogany hair with soft tones of varying shades. A face of innocence that also held shadows of a hidden self—a secret part that Ian intended on exploring. Nicole was not all she seemed, she was much more, and her easy ability to help others attested to that. Ian's worry for Vanessa eased in light of the fact that Nicole had his daughter in her care.

Ian opened the sliding door to the back and gazed over the deck to the vast expanse of ocean that shimmered in creamy tones of moonlight. The liquor must have relaxed him enough to appreciate the powerful energy emitted by the combination of ocean and moon. Gently rolling in a dance of nature, the ocean was a constant giver of life enhanced by the cycles of the moon. Ian felt nature's power seep into his skin and race through his veins, giving him a certainty that had been lacking in his life. The time to set his life on course was here, now.

He remembered Nicole's earlier words. They had held truth within their drunken depths, so tomorrow Ian would take Nicole's advice and talk to Vanessa. He would give her whatever she needed to get her life in order. His heart ached with the knowledge that she had probably stayed in her marriage to please him, but it wasn't too late to make it right between them. She had come to him for help, something he couldn't remember her ever doing because she was always too busy trying to prove herself to him.

Then there was Nicole. Whether she wanted to admit it or not, she was a growing part of his life. He needed her, he wanted her, and he knew the feelings were mutual. It wasn't only sexual either, because she triggered a fulfillment of mind as well as body. He wasn't going to spend his life alone anymore, and he knew with a primordial knowledge, that Nicole was the one he wanted to share time with. Now, he just had to get past her shadows and convince her they belonged together.

Crack! The loud snapping sound came from the pathway leading to the ocean, startling Ian from his reverie. "Hello." His voice echoed in the stillness of the dark night, fading into a mere whisper as the single word drifted to the ocean and mingled with the rolling waves.

The only answer was the distant hoot of an owl and the crackling of underbrush, caused no doubt by some nocturnal creature foraging for food. Ian inhaled the pungent freshness of rotting leaves and tangy ocean air. His home in the city, even if it was by the ocean, seemed so far removed from that moment. Yearning for something unknown touched his soul, and Ian had to tap down the rising sense of restlessness.

***

He froze as the sound of a man's voice drifted to him over the sound of his own careful advancement through the bush. Damn. He'd tried to be quiet, but it was hard when he had to lug such a heavy load. Intent on his revenge and retribution, he hadn't noticed how close he'd come to one of the cabins on the grounds of the *Wyllow Wood Inn*.

He listened intently for sounds of pursuit, but heard only the fearful beat of his own heart. He glanced to the burlap sack on the ground beside him and frowned. He didn't have much time left before that stupid dog woke up. The tranquilizers had barely been enough, but since the drugstore was closed, he'd had to go with what he had.

His plan was to kill the beast in a way that would get

him out of the way, but leave the bitch wondering whether he was dead or alive. If there wasn't a body to confirm the dog's death, she wouldn't be able to grieve. She'd always be wondering. Much better to let her imagination take over and create all kinds of horrid scenes in her mind.

Finding her had been easy, as she wasn't exactly in hiding, but the fact that she wasn't isolated as she had been at the lighthouse would test his powers of manipulation. Getting rid of the dog was his first step and getting her alone would be the next.

A shifting of the sack alerted him to the fact that the dog was waking. He'd better hurry, or he wouldn't be able to complete his plan. The rocky shore lay just ahead. He could see the glimmer of the water through the thick shadows of trees. He'd grab some rocks to weigh the sack with and toss the bag, dog and all, into the ocean. With any luck, the stupid dog would wake up long enough to struggle and suffer as he drowned alone in his dark prison.

With a grunt, he settled the sack on the rocks of a small bluff just around the bend from the farthest cabin of the inn. The moon disappeared behind some passing clouds and impeded his search for rocks. His questing hands touched upon some about the right size, just enough to weigh the sack and drown the dog. Grasping them close to his chest, he dropped them beside the sack. The loud thud as they hit the ground must have jolted the dog from his drug-induced sleep, because the animal set up a sudden horrific howl that tore the night air like a knife.

"Shut up." The stalker kicked out at the writhing sack in an attempt to shut him up, but to no avail. His efforts only increased the tempo of the howling and incensed the dog who tried snapping at him through the sack. Thinking quickly, he found a nearby branch lying on the ground and he used that to prod the sack to the edge of the small cliff. It was like trying to direct water. Every time he pushed one way, the dog went another, but he was finally able to get the sack to the edge and with one last shove sent it flying over the rocky lip to the waters below.

He had a moment of uncertainty about whether the dog would drown without the rocks to weigh him down, but decided since the animal couldn't swim wrapped up as he was, he'd die eventually.

A fearful yelp punctuated his moment of triumph, as the dog hit the water and began his struggle against death. Yes, next it would be the bitch's turn.

***

Ian heard it again. It sounded like someone, or something in pain. He peered through the dim night and listened intently. There it was. A primal howl of pain and fear, and it was coming from the beach area just around the bend.

He shivered.

The mournful howl knifed into him and sent tingles up his spine. It was the sound of death, and Ian knew he had to do something to help the poor animal. He didn't think that wolves inhabited the area, so it must be a dog in trouble.

It took only a second to pull on jeans and a tee shirt. Not even bothering with shoes, he flew out the door and down the path toward the beach. The howling had stopped, which left Ian with no idea where to go once he reached the beach area. To his right was the sandy area that sunbathers and swimmers frequented the most, while to his left rose a rocky bluff that majestically merged to the distant cliffs upon which sat the lighthouse.

The moon took that moment to drift out from the clouds and throw its glow to the earth and water below. Ian's gaze instantly became aware of a foreign object floating in the water just beyond the rocks. Floating wasn't the right word, because the sack moved with a life of its own and an occasional whine broke the sounds of the waves.

"No way." Ian's heart thumped with anger and adrenaline.

It couldn't be what it looked like. He'd heard of people leaving unwanted animals on the side of the road in a garbage bag, but to throw one into the ocean to drown. Ian couldn't fathom such an act.

Moving faster than he ever imagined possible, Ian ran the twenty feet or so to the edge of the rocks and looked for the best way into the water. He had to hurry, the dog's struggles were decreasing, and Ian couldn't hear him whining anymore. Without conscious thought, he dove into the water and pumped his arms and legs with every fiber of his being until he came up beside the sack. Frenzied, he grabbed the sack and clutched it to his chest. The shape and feel of the body inside was definitely a dog, and tears of pity filled Ian's eyes and mingled with the salty water of the ocean.

One arm wrapped around the dog, and the other led them to shore. Ian swore all the way back. It was an arduous swim with the extra weight, and a good portion of the ocean found its way inside his mouth. Some son of a bitch would pay for this, especially if the dog was dead. Panting and exhausted, he realized that he couldn't feel any movement from the sack, so he sent a prayer to the heavens for the life of the abused animal.

Cutting his hands and knees on the sharp rocks, he was able to hoist the dead weight of the dog onto the rocks and then barely able to haul himself from the water. His limbs shook, and he coughed up a mouthful of salt water, but he didn't give himself time to recover. He had to see if the dog was alive. He ripped and tore at the sack with his bare hands until he found a weakness in the cloth and was able to tear a hole. From there, it was easy to rip the length of the cloth until the dog lay fully exposed to his probing gaze.

He knew this dog. Sumo.

What was going on? Frantically, Ian searched the dog for signs of life and relief washed over him when he felt a light heartbeat. He must have swallowed a pile of water, but what to do about it? Ian smacked his fist into his hand. He couldn't let

Sumo die.

"Shit. Can you give a dog mouth to mouth?" Even as he spoke, he rolled Sumo over on his back and pressed the palms of his hands where he thought the dog's diaphragm would be. Pumping in a rhythmic motion, he massaged the dog's chest and kept talking to him. Nothing happened, and Ian panicked.

"Damn it, Sumo. You can't die, because Nicole would never forgive me. She loves you, so you had better live you flea-bitten mutt. Come on. Live." He yelled as he continued to pump and massage the dog's chest and abdomen.

Something worked because Sumo coughed. A stream of water trickled out the side of his mouth, and he coughed again. Ian saw his eyes open and try to focus.

"Come on, boy. You can do it," Ian coaxed in a soothing voice.

Sumo's brown eyes fixed on him, and Ian knew the dog would be all right. Ian smiled and before he knew what hit him, Sumo's tongue traced a pathway from Ian's chin to his forehead. In the breath of a moment, he found himself pinned on the sharp rocks, as a hundred and more pounds of dog staggered up and awkwardly knocked Ian to the ground.

Ian didn't feel the pain from the sharp rocks digging into his back, and the fatigue he should have felt from the rescue faded with the warmth of a live dog atop him. Memories of playtime with Jasper tugged at his mind, and Ian hugged the dog with long forgotten affection. For a second he wondered why he hadn't bought himself another dog, and then he remembered the numbing pain he'd felt when his first canine friend had died. That was why. He hadn't wanted to feel that way again. By denying himself another dog, he also denied himself the undying loyalty and bond shared between dog and man.

"Okay, fella, I think it's time to let me up now." Ian pushed at Sumo and was surprised how easily he was able to dislodge the dog from his chest, but he frowned when he saw the dog stumble as his rear legs gave out from under him. "Hey, are you all right?" He sat up and ran his hands all over Sumo's body looking for an injury.

At that moment, Sumo's hackles rose, and he raised his muzzle to sniff the night air. Rising to unsteady paws, he made a few hesitant steps toward the pathway, growling all the way. His efforts were in vain, because he collapsed on the rocks and looked to Ian with eyes full of trust and uncertainty.

Ian knelt by his side and looked into his moonlit eyes. He saw no blood, Sumo hadn't winced when he ran his hands over his body, and there didn't appear to be any injury, so Ian concluded that the perpetrator of this horrible act must have drugged him. How else would someone get close enough to put him in a sack and drag him to the ocean? Yep. Dilated black pupils and an unfocused gaze confirmed Ian's suspicions. Ian considered his options, and then with a sigh, reached down to lift Sumo into his arms. The strain made Ian grunt, but it wasn't so much that he couldn't carry the dog to his cabin.

He talked softly to Sumo all the way, trying to make him feel safe, but even as the words of comfort left his mouth, Ian wondered who would do such a thing to a dog. Was it a random act of some teenager? Or was it a personal attack directed at Nicole? Did this have anything to do with the secret he knew she harbored? One thing was for certain, he thought as he re-directed another sloppy tongue licking, he'd find out.

Thank God, the cabin was in sight. His arms wouldn't hold out much longer, not to mention his legs and his back. The effort was worth it though, because Sumo's adoring gaze was payment in full.

Ian set him gently inside the front door on the plush carpeting. "Lay there, boy. I'm going to call the vet to come and see you." He gave him a reassuring pat on his head, and received a whine in response. "You'll be fine, I promise."

Anger seethed through Ian. The bastard who had done this to him was going to suffer immensely. He'd make sure of that.

Chapter Fifteen

Nicole woke with a headache and the sounds of dishes rattling in the living room. With a moan, she raised her head and surveyed her surroundings, only to find that sometime during the night she'd collapsed on the bed with all her clothes on. Rubbing her eyes and dragging herself from bed, she tried to remember what had happened the night before, and who was in the living area of her suite.

Oh, right. Vanessa. Their one-on-one bonding was the reason for her hangover. She needed coffee and aspirin. Trudging across the bedroom, she opened the doors to the living room and had to shield her eyes against the intruding sunlight. Slowly, her eyes adjusted, and she saw Vanessa pouring coffee from the room service cart, which miraculously also held food.

"Good morning. I didn't want to wake you, but I figured the smell of food would do that." Vanessa extended a cup of coffee to Nicole and smiled. "Here. I know my first cup tasted great."

"Oh, you're reading my mind." With one swift but shaking hand, Nicole grabbed the coffee cup and inhaled the aroma. Her mouth watered, and she took the first slow sip to judge temperature. Finding the liquid hot, but not overly so, she proceeded to pour the entire cup of coffee into her system. She welcomed the jolt as caffeine and heat hit her stomach.

Then she remembered Sumo. She'd let him out last night, gone down to the restaurant and had never let him back in when she returned to the room. Where was he? Worried, she ran to the balcony door, opened it, and called his name. Nothing. No answering whine.

"Does he usually stay out at night?" Vanessa asked.

"No. Never. I feel horrible. I was drunk and forgot all about him.

"Maybe we should go look for him."

"Let me call the front desk and see if anyone has seen him. They might know something."

Nicole made the call and the woman assured her that they'd look around and question some of the guests. She replaced the phone and frowned. "I'm not sure whether to worry or not."

"He's a smart dog, I wouldn't worry," Vanessa reassured.

"I know, but I can't stay here waiting. I'm going to go look for him."

"I'm with you."

Using the stairs because the elevator was too slow in coming, Nicole and Vanessa searched the front lobby for any sign of Sumo. Nothing. They went to the front desk to see if they had news.

"No, I'm sorry, no one has seen him."

"But he has to be somewhere." Nicole's voice rose, and the young man hastened to assure her. "We're doing everything we can. I'm sure he'll turn up. Someone may have taken him in for the night thinking he was a stray or something."

"Maybe. We're going to look for him, if you hear anything leave a message for Nicole Tyler, room 305."

"Oh, Miss Tyler, did you get your message?"

"What message?"

"It was that actor, you know, Ian. Ian Calder. He called and said that you were to call him as soon as you woke up. He said it was important, so I called your room and left a message, but you must have been on your way down already. Maybe he has news about your dog."

***

Ian looked at the silent phone willing it to ring, but nothing happened. Sumo rested his paw on Ian's lap and whined as

187

if asking what was wrong. "It's okay, I guess your mistress just didn't get my message."

He stood and mumbled, "Or she couldn't be bothered returning my call. I guess there's only one thing to do, and that's to take you back where you belong. Come on." He slapped his hand on his thigh and hoped that Sumo was well trained enough to follow him to the main building and not go wandering off.

This actually worked out better, because it gave him an excuse to see Vanessa, which was idiotic because he shouldn't need an excuse to see his own daughter. It was a short, relaxing walk to the inn and the freshness of the crisp morning air seemed to revive Sumo because he ran off the path to chase something every few feet. Ian's blood boiled as he recalled how close the dog had come to death.

When he'd called the police to report the incident, Corporal Moody hadn't seemed surprised. In fact, he'd been evasive enough to make Ian wonder if the police officer knew whatever secret Nicole kept so closely guarded.

Then he remembered that the lighthouse had been broken into. His blood ran cold at the thought that Nicole could easily have been alone and isolated when the intruder struck. What happened to Sumo could so easily have happened to her. One thing for sure, he wasn't going anywhere until he got answers.

Ian had just stepped into the front lobby of the inn when Nicole's voice carried across the room. "Sumo. Oh my God." Sumo responded with a round of excited barking.

Nicole knelt down and opened her arms wide. The force of his body almost knocked her across the shiny floor.

The reunion warmed Ian's heart. He didn't want to worry Nicole by telling her about Sumo's almost death, but she needed to know. Alight with joy and relief, Nicole's face tugged at the very center of Ian, and he had to clear his throat to keep the threatening tears from coming.

"You didn't answer my message, or you would have known he was all right." His voice held a hint of censure.

Nicole flushed. "I didn't get your message."

An awkward silence descended, broken only by Sumo's excited whine as he sucked up for attention from Nicole. Ian broke the silence.

"Good morning, Vanessa."

"Hi."

"I'd like to talk. Do you have some time now?" He kept his voice light. He didn't want to sound demanding or dictatorial.

Vanessa's hesitation lasted only a second, and then she nodded. "Sure, we can talk in the restaurant."

"Don't be ridiculous," Nicole remarked. "You need privacy, so why don't you use my room. I have a few errands to run anyway."

"Wait." Ian grabbed her arm. "We need to talk as well."

"Fine." Nicole frowned at his hand and her arm and tried to shake it off. "We can talk later."

"Oh, we will, you can bet on it. But right now, aren't you curious as to how I ended up with Sumo for the night?"

"I assume he followed you back to your cabin last night after we met in the restaurant."

Ian ran his hand through his hair, trying to figure out the best way to tell his story. There was no good way, so he just blurted it out. "When I got back to my cabin last night, I heard some strange sounds coming from the beach, so I went to investigate. What I found was your dog in a burlap sack, drugged and fighting a losing battle against the ocean."

Nicole and Vanessa gasped. Nicole's hand flew to her mouth, and her face paled so much that Ian was afraid she would faint. But she didn't. Instead, she leaned down and hugged Sumo. Rocking him gently, her eyes filled with tears that fell onto the dog she held so tightly.

Ian continued. "I swam out and pulled him to shore. It was close because he wasn't breathing by the time I ripped into the sack. I took him back to the cabin and called the vet who said Sumo'll be fine, but should take it easy for a day or two."

Nicole's eyes shimmered as she whispered, "You called the

vet."

"Of course I did."

"Thank you. Let me know how much he cost, and I'll pay you back."

"I don't give a damn about the money."

"Dad, keep your voice down."

Ian took a deep breath to control his emotions. "Sorry. I don't care about the money, what I care about is finding out what's going on. I know the lighthouse was broken into and now this." He waved his hand at Sumo. "I informed Corporal Moody what happened and he wasn't surprised."

He searched Nicole's face, but she didn't say a word. She only stared at Ian as if measuring him. Ian sensed a battle going on within her. A warring of emotion against logic, maybe, he didn't know, but he must have come up wanting, because she just shrugged.

"Nothing is going on. It's just a coincidence."

"Nicole, maybe you should tell him." Vanessa's remark earned a glare from Nicole.

"There's nothing to tell."

"Damn it, Nicole."

He didn't get any further with his questioning before getting interrupted by a gorgeous woman dressed in a short jean skirt, a white cotton shirt that clung to her well-endowed features, and high heels that emphasized her long and shapely legs.

"Excuse me." The woman set herself between Ian and Nicole as if Nicole didn't even exist. "I'm so sorry to interrupt, but I just love your movies and I'd be so very grateful if you would give me your autograph." She licked her lips and held a pen and notepad for his signature.

Not too long ago, Ian would have been attracted to the blatant display of sexuality and the promise of fulfillment that sparked her greedy eyes. Now, he was just impatient to get her out of his way. Didn't she realize he was busy? Without bothering to attempt conversation, he grabbed the pen, scribbled his name, and gave her a gentle, yet persuasive push away.

On some level, he noticed the surprised look on Vanessa's face and knew she had expected him to take the woman up on her unspoken offer. He was happy to disappoint her and hoped the act would help open the door to a better relationship between them. First, though, he needed to deal with Nicole, because she seemed to be in more immediate danger.

Suddenly he remembered Josephine's words about danger twice threatening those he loved. Vanessa was in danger from her husband, whether she wanted to admit it or not. Nicole was in danger from something, and he meant to find out what. Those he loved. Did that mean he was in love with Nicole? Could his life get any more complicated?

"Look, I need to know what's going on, and I'm not leaving until I do." Ian knew he sounded like a bad line from a B movie, but he didn't know what else to say.

Vanessa came to his rescue. "Nicole, the more people you have on your side, the better, but it's your place to tell him, not mine." Vanessa sent Nicole a smile of encouragement.

"Excuse me, Mr. Calder?"

"What?" Ian yelled at a geeky looking man whom he recognized as one of Jeb's lackeys. Baggy jeans, a horrid plaid shirt, running shoes, and glasses that sat low on his nose, the young man practically cringed when Ian yelled at him.

"Dad, use your inside voice," Vanessa said.

"My what...oh, yeah." He frowned at the latest intrusion and snapped in a quieter tone, "I'm busy. This better be important."

"I...I'm only doing what I'm told. Mr. Braxton needs to see you right away. He tried to reach you at your cabin, but when you didn't answer, he sent me looking for you."

"Oh, come on. What now?" Ian felt ready to explode, but if he wanted to build Vanessa's trust, he needed to stay calm and collected. He took a shuddering breath. "Go back and tell Jeb I'll see him later. I have some things I need to take care of first."

The man looked to be in mortal fear for his life, as he nervously pushed his glasses just before they were able to slip off his nose. "Oh, I couldn't do that. He told me not to come back without you for fear of my life being forfeited. Please."

At that point, Ian didn't give a damn about the movie, but he didn't want the young man to get in trouble because of him either. Vanessa took the decision out of his hands.

"Go ahead, Dad."

He turned to the nervously shifting gofer and said, "Okay, I'll come with you." His gaze fell to Vanessa, and he jabbed his finger at her. "But I'll take care of this and be back soon."

"I'll be waiting." Vanessa assured him.

Ian took her chin between his thumb and forefinger, his eyes pleading with her. "I'll be back. I promise we'll get things straightened out." Turning to Nicole, he said, "You may as well get used to the fact that I'm in your life, and I'm going to find out what's going on." With a quick pat on Sumo's head, Ian turned and strode from the hotel, the skinny young man running to keep up with the pace he set.

***

Ian walked with a self-confident swagger that demanded the attention of everyone in the room and elicited Nicole's envy. His comment about being in her life and finding out what's going on made her feel as if life were spiraling out of control. When he locked his gaze on her, the look brought to mind a phrase she'd heard once. Eyes of age. Face of time.

Trying to keep him out of her life would prove futile. The sheer power of his will battered any walls she may have built to protect herself or others. No wonder the man was a star, a common man he definitely wasn't.

"Earth to Nicole."

Vanessa's waving hand jolted Nicole from her reverie. "I'm sorry, I was thinking about something else."

Speculation filled Vanessa's eyes. "You look like one of the star-struck women Dad is always fighting off. Please don't tell me you've fallen for him."

Nicole flushed. "Of course I haven't." *Of course I have.*

"That's good, because I'm thinking he hasn't changed in the least. Here we both are in danger and he goes running off as soon as the director snaps his fingers."

"Hold on, Vanessa. First, he doesn't really know I'm in danger, he just suspects something's not right. Second, he promised he'd be back and you'd get things straightened out. Besides, you told him to go."

"I did, didn't I?" Vanessa sighed. "Maybe I'm being too hard on him, or maybe you're just a dyed in the wool optimist."

"Give him a chance."

Vanessa sighed and shrugged her shoulders. "Come on, let's walk down to the docks, I could use some fresh air."

As they made their way to the docks, the lonely sound of a ship's horn rumbled somewhere on the distant horizon. Nicole shielded her eyes with her hand and looked out over the shimmering sea, but was unable to see anything due to the reflection of sun on water. All along the dock, seagulls flitted and dived, screeching for handouts from anyone with food. Sumo lay at Nicole and Vanessa's feet, his head resting on his paws. He was probably worn out from last night Nicole thought, as she leaned over and stroked him affectionately.

"It's nice." Vanessa sighed. "The relationship the two of you have. You don't find such loyalty and devotion these days. Especially if you're looking for those qualities in a man." She smiled. "Maybe I should get a dog."

Nicole didn't reply. No words existed to lighten Vanessa's disillusionment. Only time and a relationship with a man who treated her right would work. Of course, some help on Ian's part wouldn't hurt either.

"Tell me about growing up with a famous father."

"It was interesting. But Dad's career made him very unreliable. Do you know he forgot to pick me up from camp one summer? I sat with my suitcases as all the other parents came to pick up their kids until I was the only one left. I remember the counselors arguing over who would be stuck staying with me until someone came. They didn't know I could hear them, but I could. Talk about a humbling and degrading experience."

Vanessa shifted on the wooden bench and wiped a tear from her cheek. "When they finally reached Mom, she flipped out. I heard her yelling over the phone, cursing Dad out and saying how she wasn't surprised he'd forgotten me because he'd never wanted me anyway."

"Oh, Vanessa, I'm so sorry. That must have been awful for you."

"It was. When Mom finally came for me the next day, I wanted to disappear into a hole in the ground. One of the counselors had to stay an extra night, and he wasn't too happy about that. On the way home in the car, I asked Mom about what she'd said on the phone, you know, about Dad never wanting me. I thought maybe I'd misunderstood, but I hadn't. She told me that Dad had yelled at her when he'd found out she was pregnant and said that he'd never accept the baby. It was the summer when I was eight. Ever since then, I've done for myself, never relying on him again."

Nicole frowned. "But not really."

"Not really, what?"

"You may have been independent and done things for yourself, but from what you've said, I would guess that everything you've done has been to impress him. From my uneducated, layman point of view I'd say that you've been trying to win his approval and love. As a result, you ended up in a bad marriage and stayed so you wouldn't disappoint your father. I don't know your father well, but I don't get the feeling at all that he's a cold-hearted bastard. He may be abrupt, and he may sometimes have a lot on his mind, but you should talk to him and find out what he's thinking and feeling."

Mentally, Nicole crossed her fingers, praying that her talk with Ian last night would prepare him to handle Vanessa with kid gloves and not in his usual manner.

Vanessa seemed to consider Nicole's words until a boat

horn sounded. This time closer. The familiar lines of Jacob's fishing boat chugged into the harbor. Weather bitten white with accents of apple red, the boat rode the swells with grace born of years on the water and Jacob's expert navigation. It was only early afternoon, and Nicole wondered what brought the crusty fisherman back so early in the day. If she looked hard enough, she could identify Jacob's wiry form as he prepared to dock the boat. She turned back to Vanessa.

"Promise me, you'll talk with your dad. I know he'll help you."

"Sure, I promise."

Nicole patted her arm. "Great. I think you two should have dinner together and talk, but you're still welcome to stay with me if you want."

Vanessa giggled. "Do you always plan other people's lives out so efficiently?"

"Only when it's someone I care about."

Tears filled Vanessa's blue eyes, and she pulled Nicole into a tight hug. "Thank you for being my friend. I need one now more than ever." Suddenly, she pushed Nicole away and held her at arm's length. "But what about you? You still have the stalker after you, I can't leave you alone."

"It's okay. I'll have Jacob and Josephine over for company. I'm working on getting them to spend more time together anyway."

"Really. That would be an interesting relationship."

"Tell me about it. It's so obvious that they're attracted to each other. I don't understand what's taking them so long to act on their feelings."

"Okay, Nicole, if you get Josephine and Jacob to spend the evening with you, I'll make arrangements with Dad for dinner. I won't feel so bad if I know you're not alone."

Nicole gave Sumo an affectionate pat on his rock-like head. "I'm never alone as long as this guy is with me. Thank God your dad found him in time. Losing him, especially like that, would have been devastating."

"Nicole, I am worried about you. Bob may be a bastard, but this guy after you is a murderer." Vanessa shivered and rubbed her arms.

"I know. This incident with Sumo makes me realize that I can't run my whole life, because this guy is crazy enough to never give up. He wants something from me, but the problem is that I don't know what it is, or I'd give it to him. Regardless, it has to end." Nicole chewed her lip in concentration, and then looked at Vanessa. "Listen, you have to promise me you won't tell your Dad about the stalker."

"But why? The more people who know the better, that way we can all keep an eye on you."

"Maybe, but I don't want him to know. Don't ask me why, just please promise me." She had no idea why she didn't want Ian to know, but figured it was probably because he'd insist on helping and end up getting hurt. Nicole couldn't stand it if someone she cared about got hurt again. And she did care about him. She couldn't deny how his face haunted her and his kisses enticed her. Wrong time. Wrong person. Wrong place. Wrong everything.

With a burst of sudden energy, Nicole jumped from the bench and grabbed Vanessa's arm to pull her along. "Come on, let's go see Jacob."

Jacob had just finished tying off his boat, *Crickety Cradle*, when Nicole and Vanessa approached. Nicole thought he looked tired, that the etched lines in his face seemed more prominent, and his tan not as dark as normal.

"Hey, Jacob." She waved.

"Hi." He acknowledged them with a two-finger salute to his temple. "What brings two beautiful women to see an old bugger like me?" He placed both hands on his lower back and stretched.

"I was kind of wondering if an old bugger like you would like to have dinner and maybe watch a movie with a young chick in her hotel room," Nicole offered.

"Ha, now wouldn't I be crazy to turn down an invite like

that."

"So you're free?"

"That's what I'm sayin'," Jacob leaned over and took off his rubber boots to replace them with a pair of worn deck shoes.

"Good. I'm just on my way to ask Josephine over as well." Nicole almost laughed at the hooded look that crossed Jacob's face.

"Now I'm not sure if you need to be botherin' Josie." Jacob fumbled with the buttons on his jacket.

"It won't be any bother. I happen to know she'd love to spend the evening with you.I mean us."

Jacob narrowed his eyes and muttered, "Don't you be gettin' any matchmaking ideas, young lady."

Nicole laughed. "Of course not. By the way, how come you're back so early?"

Jacob flushed and he stammered. "I decided to call it an early day, is all."

He was lying. Nicole knew it by the way he avoided looking her in the eyes and shuffled his feet in a sporadic manner. She was certain that his lie had something to do with her situation.

"Jacob, why are you back early? And don't try lying to me, I know you too well."

"Willickers, woman." Caught in his lie, Jacob suddenly went the other direction and lashed out in anger. "What the hell do you think would happen? This is a small town, everyone finds things out eventually. Corporal Moody told Josephine, who radioed me and told me about what happened to that beast of yours."

In an agile move that belied Jacob's age, he stomped down the gangplank and shoved his face close to Nicole's. "Ain't no way I'm stayin' out there," he thrust a finger toward the water, "while you're in trouble." Without wavering his gaze from Nicole's, he swore. "Christ almighty, that could have been you drugged and shoved in a sack. So here's the thing, I'm not leaving your side until this maniac is rotting in jail, or better yet, dead."

"I suppose, but..."

"Don't argue. I'm stuck to you like glue."

Nicole leaned over and kissed Jacob's weathered cheek. "I'm not arguing, you old codger. I'm grateful."

Vanessa wiped away a tear. "I don't know about you, but I wouldn't mind some lunch and then maybe some shopping."

"Shopping? I said I'd stay close, but shopping?" Jacob protested.

Vanessa and Nicole hooked an arm through each of Jacob's and led him off the docks. "Oh, yes, shopping can be such fun. We'll have to be sure to stop at *Wishes* and invite Josephine to the inn for dinner," Nicole teased.

"Of course, we wouldn't want to forget that little chore now, would we?" Jacob grumbled.

***

Ian found Jeb on the main street of town amidst the hustle and bustle of set changes. With a precise expertise that belied his rather disheveled appearance, the director waved a hand and barked an order that sent crew members scurrying to organize the set for a new scene. Like magic, the midday scene of busy confusion quickly transformed to a hushed evening mood of dim solitude.

Ian grumbled as he shuffled through hovering fans and crew busily rearranging the entire street for the next scene. It looked like the midnight stroll scene, but that didn't make sense. He was about to be fired, and it would take time to hire another actor who would then need to study the script. No, they couldn't shoot that particular scene for another few days at least.

Finally finding Jeb, Ian waited patiently for the busy director to notice him. He cleared his throat. Jeb glanced his way, and stared until the dazed look in his eyes cleared.

"Great, Brett found you."

"If Brett is your current gofer, then yes, he found me." Not wanting to waste time, Ian decided to just approach the subject and get it over with quickly and painlessly. "Jeb, I know why you want to see me, and don't feel bad, I really didn't think it was going to work out anyway."

"But..."

Ian raised his hand, palm forward. "No, it's okay. I'm sure whomever you find to replace me will do a better job anyway. Besides, I'm going through some personal stuff with my daughter and need to get that straightened out, so the timing couldn't be better."

"Ian."

"Look, Jeb. We both know Candace is a bitch, and I hate letting her screw my life up again, but I've come to realize there are more important things in life, so I'm not going to stress out about it." He reached out to shake Jeb's hand just as a loud crash sounded from across the street.

"Now what?" Jeb swore when he saw that the false front on one of the buildings had toppled and now leaned haphazardly against the veranda post. "No one looks hurt. Christ, good help is hard to find." Striding across the street, he yelled over his shoulder. "We're not through. Tonight. Seven. Your cabin. Be there."

"But." Ian didn't get to say anything else, because Jeb was already yelling and gesticulating in a crude manner to the hapless crew.

"Guess I've got company coming tonight." Ian muttered. Suddenly at odds with what to do with his time he perused the street looking for the best escape with the fewest hassles from his fans. It was then that he spied Nicole, Vanessa, and an older man, a local he had seen around town. The threesome stepped from the doorway of the Horizon Cafe and looked to be heading for *Wishes*.

Perfect. He'd arrange a time to talk to Vanessa and maybe ask her about Nicole's situation. He knew the danger in Vanessa's life, but had no idea what trouble Nicole was involved in. He'd damn sure find out, though.

***

Adjusting her vision from the brightness of outside to the subdued indoor light, Nicole made a quick visual sweep of the bookstore, a gesture of self-preservation that had become a common part of her life. Josephine had obviously been re-arranging and the store had taken on a purple theme. Purple crepe paper decorated the shelves, purple candles glowed gently in the dim light, purple books, purple crystals, purple everything.

"Hello." Josephine spoke to the three of them, but her eyes rested on Jacob. "You better be careful, Jacob, visiting my store could become a habit for you. This is the second time in as many days."

"I'm only here to keep an eye on her." He gestured his thumb toward Nicole.

Josephine's features turned to worry. "I heard about what happened to Sumo. You poor baby." She leaned over to hug Sumo, who responded with a whimper of self-pity and an ex-uberant wriggle of his rear end.

Jacob cleared his throat and spoke. "You can bet I'm going to make sure what happened to him doesn't happen to Nicole." His chin lifted in a gesture of stubborn will. "We'll make sure of that." Josephine remarked as she gave Vanessa a comforting pat on the arm, "Don't worry, we'll keep an eye on you as well."

Vanessa flushed. "Oh, it's okay, I'll be fine. My situation can't compare to Nicole's."

"Be that as it may, we take care of our own, and if you're a friend of Nicole's then you can consider yourself one of us."

Soft tears threatened to fall from Vanessa's blue eyes, and Nicole sensed her friend's whirling emotions. She could relate. A lifetime of struggling trying to win approval from those she cared for, those who should have loved and cared for her, yet here she was in some small town where no one knew her, but they accepted her. As simply and easily as breathing.

A shuddering breath of gratitude shook Vanessa's chest. "Thank you. Thank you all so much." She wiped her tears away with a tissue offered by Josephine. "I came here for help, which is what I'm getting, just not from where I thought I would. I can't believe you're being so kind to me and asking nothing in return. No one's ever given me so much for so little."

Nicole squeezed Vanessa's hand and smiled at her, while Jacob cleared his throat and shifted uncomfortably. He threw an uncomfortable look toward Josephine. Their eyes met and a spark of understanding jumped between them.

Silence and harmony hummed in the store broken only by the sound of chimes blowing gently in the window and the distant commotion of movie members shouting and shuffling on the street. Sumo whined and leaned on Nicole's leg, as he looked up at her with adoration in his brown eyes. Her heart filled with the love that flowed so freely from person to person to canine.

A moment of peace and caring.

"I hope I'm not interrupting anything." The intrusive voice shattered the moment.

***

No one's ever given me so much for so little. Vanessa's words cut into Ian like a dull chainsaw. Each word tore another piece of his heart into shreds. He'd entered the store only a moment or two after Nicole, Vanessa, and the old man, so he'd heard the whole conversation. Regret welled from deep within, and he ached for what was lost, maybe never to be. His daughter had come to him for help and he'd let her down, again. It seemed to be the story of his life. Damn it though, he wasn't the only one at fault; she'd never wanted his help.

Yeah, you idiot, but she wants it now, and you let her down. It wasn't too late. It couldn't be.

He stood on the threshold of the store, surrounded by whimsical faeries, colorful paintings of pixies and angels and books on subjects he refused to understand, and his daughter was only feet away from him, yet he stood alone. He didn't want this. He didn't want to watch the display of emotions unwinding in front of his very eyes. He couldn't stand the thought that his daughter didn't need him, because he suddenly realized that he needed her.

He felt dizzy with the overflow of emotion. Visions of Vanessa as a young girl raced through his mind, a cute blond haired child giggling as she wrestled under the Christmas tree with her new puppy. A solemn faced girl as she faced her first day of high school with uncertainty and fear. A young lady nervously twirling her hair while waiting for her first date— a pimple-faced, all arms and legs geek, if Ian remembered correctly. And he did. He also remembered her wedding day, the day he'd walked her down the aisle and handed her to the man who would abuse her.

He needed to set things right.

Clearing his throat, he stepped from the shadows and into the light. "I hope I'm not interrupting anything." His voice filled with anger at himself and frustration for a situation that never should have happened.

He startled the foursome as his voice carried across the store to intrude on a moment of sharing. Sumo's ears perked up and with an excited yelp, he ran across the floor and slid to a stop in front of Ian. Josephine winced as the dog's nails scraped the finely polished hardwood, but she just shook her head and smiled.

Ian reached down and scratched Sumo's ears, giving the dog just the kind of massage he loved. With one melting motion, Sumo plopped himself at Ian's feet, belly and all four paws extended to the ceiling. His antics helped break the awkward tension.

"I think you've found a friend." Josephine laughed.

"Yes, Sumo doesn't usually make friends quite so easily."

Nicole smiled at him and the unabated physical desire assaulting Ian shook him to the core. Fifty-four years on this planet, and he'd never felt such gut-wrenching desire. He couldn't decide if it was a good thing or a bad thing. "It probably has something to do with saving his life."

Awkwardly, Jacob pulled his hands from his pockets and took a couple of steps forward. "I heard what you did. Got to say I admire your gumption, and I'd be proud to say I shook your hand." He extended his hand.

Ian figured the man to be a softie, whatever he tried to portray with his crusty exterior. Reaching out, he took shook Jacob's hand and was not surprised by the calluses he felt, the calluses of a man used to physical labor. Ian had a lot of respect for any man who lived by the whims of nature, especially the fickle moods of the ocean. "I'm honored to meet you, sir."

Jacob's usual hunched posture suddenly became less noticeable as he stood just a little bit taller. "Well, you don't need to call me sir, Jacob'll do just fine."

An awkward silence followed with no one exactly sure what was a safe subject, until Ian decided to get to the point. "Vanessa." He looked at the faces of the surrounding people and realized they weren't going anywhere, so he'd have to beg in front of them. He ran his hands through his hair, and then thrust them imploringly out front, palms up.

"Look, Vanessa, we need to talk." Her unflinching stare burned into him, and he stared right back. This was harder than he thought, but he wasn't one for flowery words and had no idea what to say to convince her. But he tried. "I want us to work together to make things right."

Vanessa's glare wavered. She sighed. "I don't have plans tonight. I suppose we could have dinner together."

The pressure lifted from Ian's chest. Thank God, he had a chance. "Great. Why not come to the cabin so I can cook your favorite meal."

Vanessa frowned. "You don't know my favorite meal."

"Chicken and dumplings."

It started with one small tear in the corner of Vanessa's blue eyes followed by another and another, until she had a steady stream flowing down her face.

"What did I say?"

Between gulps, Vanessa was able to choke out, "You know my favorite food."

Ian could only stand and wonder that such a simple thing could cause such a reaction. How? Why? What had he done to his daughter over the years to bring her to this point? Maybe tonight they could find out together where their relationship had gone wrong.

"Come on, it's no big deal." Oops, the disapproving looks on the faces of Nicole, Jacob, and Josephine let him know he'd said the wrong thing.

Vanessa stopped crying and she took a step back. "Sure, how foolish of me to make it a big deal. What time did you want me tonight?"

Great, just when he was making headway, he had to go and stick his stupid foot in his mouth. "Anytime. I'll plan dinner for around six o'clock. We can have a drink or two before we eat." *And I'll probably have one or two before* that.

"Okay, I'll be there."

Ian had a feeling that the evening would be fraught with misunderstandings due to past hurts, but he held out hope that he and Vanessa could develop a new relationship based upon new understandings. Ian still felt like an outsider, but maybe not quite as much of an outsider as before he had entered the store. He hazarded a look at Nicole, almost afraid to see what she thought of the exchange between father and daughter. He was surprised to see the hint of tears shimmering in the gold and brown of her eyes.

A smile tugged the corners of his mouth as he thought of how he would enjoy straightening out their relationship, when the time was right, of course. Suddenly, he remembered his rescue of Sumo and the fact that Nicole was in the middle of a dangerous situation he knew nothing about.

"Wait a minute, if Vanessa's with me, that leaves you alone, and considering I don't know what's going on, I don't think leaving you alone is a good idea."

Josephine and Jacob exchanged glances with Nicole and Vanessa, and Ian knew that they knew, which left him firmly ensconced as the outsider again. Anger snapped inside him, and he slammed his fist into his hand. "Well, isn't that just great, everyone knows what's going on except me."

Before anyone even dared to hazard a reply to his remark, the front door opened and the object of Vanessa's problem sauntered in as if he didn't have a care in the world. With his city-slicker smooth way, Bob managed to look as out of place in *Wishes* as Jacob would look dining in a five star restaurant. Bob appeared to be oblivious to that fact. The smarmy smile pasted on his face only enhanced what Ian could now see was a weak character. He narrowed his eyes and waited for Bob to come closer to see what his son-in-law would do.

Cocky and self-assured, Bob ignored everyone except Vanessa. To her, he flashed a smile and bestowed a deceivingly loving gaze. "Sweetheart, I've been looking all over for you. You're not registered at any hotel, so you must be staying with your dad."

Ian seethed. The rat hadn't even acknowledged his presence, he was too busy trying to woo Vanessa. We'll see about that.

Vanessa was quick to answer, her eyes flashing. "I couldn't get a room at a hotel, because someone cancelled all my credit cards."

Bob stepped closer and spoke softly, as if not wanting anyone to hear his words. "I'm sorry. My only excuse is that I thought you'd be so angry with me that you'd spend to the limit just to get even. Not that I'd blame you, but then we'd have to pay them all off. I figured it was safer to cancel your cards. Come home with me, and I'll make sure you get your own card."

"You mean my own card in your name."

"Well, yes, we discussed this before, remember. I have a better credit rating, so we can get a higher limit and lower interest rate."

Bob's jaw tensed, and Ian could tell he was having a very hard time controlling his temper. He also knew that if there wasn't an audience, Bob wouldn't be retaining his precarious hold on his emotions. Ian saw fire in the depths of the man's eyes and wondered how he could have missed it before. Had he been so tied up in his own life that he hadn't noticed? Or had some part of him ignored it, because otherwise he'd have had to do something about it?

"Vanessa." Bob extended his hand. "Can we talk alone?" He acknowledged the presence of other people and his eyes flickered in fear when he saw that Nicole was restraining Sumo. His voice raised a notch. "Can we just go somewhere else? Now." He grabbed her arm and dragged her two steps toward the front door.

All hell broke loose. Sumo exploded in a growling frenzy of raised hackles at the same time as Ian lunged for Bob. Sumo's teeth latched onto Bob's pant leg while Ian's fist landed on Bob's face with a smacking crack that echoed to the ceiling. With an undignified tangle of arms and legs, Bob fell to the floor, while Nicole called Sumo off and Vanessa grasped Ian's arm. Jacob reached for Josephine and pulled her back from the disorganized fray.

"Godammit, I'm going to sue." Bob scrambled from the floor and tried to regain his dignity. "I'll sue you." He pointed to Josephine. "For allowing this creature in here." Sumo bared his teeth at the insult. "I'll sue you for owning such a dangerous animal." His red-rimmed eyes pinned on Nicole. "And I'll sue you for daring to lay your hands on me. I don't give a damn if you are a major movie star."

Bob ran his hands through his hair to flatten it back into its former greased down glory, then brushed his hands over his clothes to dislodge any dirt and straighten himself out. He turned to Vanessa. "This is it, Vanessa, you have until tomorrow to decide if you want our marriage to work. I'll be leaving to go home, and if you don't come with me, our marriage is over."

His gaze fixed on Vanessa and he whispered, "You've seen my lawyer at work in a courtroom, and I'm sure you don't want to be on the receiving end of his talent." With his threat thusly delivered, Bob stomped from the store looking a little less confident than when he had entered.

Vanessa looked stricken and if Bob had stayed a second longer, Ian would quite happily have torn him from limb to limb for putting that look on his daughter's face. He growled, and Vanessa turned to look at him. "I...I..." Vanessa's voice shook.

Nicole and Josephine each put an arm around her shoulders and turned a questioning gaze toward Ian. As if I have the answers. His head throbbed in a steady drum of tension, and his eyes hurt even in the dim light of the store. "Listen, Vanessa, he's all talk, bullies usually are. Don't worry about anything."

Vanessa shivered. "I don't know, maybe it would be easier for me to just go back home with him. You have no idea what his lawyer is capable of. I've even heard rumors that he has ties to the mob."

Ian swore silently and wished he'd hit Bob harder. "Vanessa, we'll work it out. I'm here for you. Promise me you won't do anything until we've talked."

When Vanessa didn't say anything, Ian snapped, "Promise."

"Okay, fine, I promise. There's no need to yell."

"Sorry. Look, I'm going to get some groceries, come over whenever you want. Okay."

"Sure, I'll be there soon." Vanessa smiled tremulously. Ian pointed a finger at Nicole. "Now, what about you?" Jacob spoke up. "Don't worry. Josie and I are spending the evening with Nicole, so she won't be alone." His eyes connected with Ian's and a moment of understanding passed between them. A silent message that gave Ian pause, because the old man's message reeked clearly of danger. Ian's heart leapt as Josephine's tarot card reading haunted his mind. *God, one thing at a time, please.*

"Thanks." With a longing look at Nicole, Ian left the store. He'd had a busy day and his evening was shaping up to be even more stressful.

Chapter Sixteen

T he mellow sound of dolphins and whales mingled with light harmonies of flute and piano to create a mood of relaxation. Aromatic scents of meaty chowder, scallops au gratin, and poached halibut wafted through the hotel room and onto the balcony. Nicole took her last spoonful of butterscotch custard pie and practically swooned.

"Lord, if I keep eating like this I'll gain twenty-five pounds in no time."

"Wouldn't hurt to put a few extra pounds on your skinny frame," Jacob chastised and earned a look of reprimand from Josephine. "What? I'm only telling the truth."

Josephine threw up her hands and exclaimed, "Men, they have no sense of diplomacy. Don't listen to him,

Nicole, you look amazing, and it's no wonder Ian can't keep from drooling over you."

"Josephine."

Jacob chuckled and put his empty plate down, yawned, poured himself a cup of coffee, and then poured one for Josephine. Fixing the brew with one sugar and two creams, he handed her the cup and sat back down. "Josie's right. The actor fella can't keep his eyes off you. In fact, I would wager that if you two were alone in a room, he'd not be able to keep his hands off you either, even if you are on the skinny side."

Red-face, Nicole launched her linen napkin at Jacob's head. "Enough out of you, old man, or I'll regret inviting you here for dinner."

"You didn't invite us, we forced ourselves on you. Right, Josie?"

Jacob's tone dropped to a lower level of intimacy whenever he spoke to Josephine. It was a gently spoken caress that still surprised Nicole every time she heard it coming out of the mouth of a crusty sailor like Jacob.

"I'd like to think we're welcome guests and not ones who've forced themselves on anyone," Josephine replied.

Nicole reassured. "Of course you're both welcome, always. I love having you here." She took the opportunity to do some of her own teasing. "Especially since I get to see a whole side of you I never knew existed, Jacob."

"What are you talking about?"

"Oh, you know, pulling out Josephine's chair, pouring her coffee, flirting with her."

"Nicole, I think you're exaggerating just a little. Besides, I doubt Jacob is interested in a flaky bookstore owner like myself."

"Humph! Don't be putting any words in my mouth. I'll say who I have an interest in." Jacob leaned back and folded his arms in a defiant motion. "It just so happens I do have an interest in you, Josie. Can't really see how you've been so blind to my feelings. With all these happenings lately, it makes a man sit up and take notice about the important things in life, you know."

Jacob's sudden and long awaited confession surprised both Nicole and Josephine, who sat in open-mouthed confusion. Nicole chuckled and watched her friends stare at each other in a heated embrace of silent words. If she were to guess, she'd say their feelings ranged from passion to confusion, lust to sentiment, and an awakening of other feelings that had lain dormant a very long time. She raised her wine glass with a flourish and declared, "I do believe this occasion calls for a toast. So, to the fisherman and the book lady, I wish you all the best. Especially you Josephine, having to deal with a cantankerous old buzzard like Jacob."

Josephine smiled and put her hand over Jacob's. "I can't think of anything better than having to deal with the cantankerous old buzzard." Affection blazed from her eyes, and a flush crept up Jacob's neck.

Nicole decided it was an opportune time to leave the two of them alone to iron out their newfound relationship. She snapped her fingers for Sumo, but he just looked at her and laid his head in his paws as if to say, *Yeah, right.*

Shrugging her shoulders, Nicole stepped out onto the balcony with an offhand excuse of needing fresh air to clear her wine-befuddled brain. Too busy staring at each other, Jacob and Josephine didn't even mumble a response.

Nicole took a deep breath, enjoying the crispness of the late summer evening and the glow of the almost full moon outlined on the horizon. Her balcony overlooked the outdoor cafe whose arbor led to extensive gardens and then down to the distant shore that sounded a constant rumble of seawater rolling upon sand and rock. Night sounds echoed in the muffled darkness, bringing a sense of peaceful energy. The power of the night reverberated in a different way than the day. More subdued, yet more powerful. Nicole relaxed and opened herself up to the moon's rays and whisper of the ocean. Raising her arms to the sky, she let the moon rays wash over her body, and she hummed with awareness of her surroundings.

Then she heard the cough.

It was close by. She could have sworn it came from the shadows of her balcony. Her skin prickled with instant fear and blood rushed to her head, causing her to experience a moment of dizziness. With the sound of her heart beating in her ears, Nicole turned to the darkened corner occupied by a fichus tree. Slowly, her eyes adjusted, and what she saw sent instant spikes of fear into her heart.

A pair of eyes gleamed at her through the leaves of the fichus. Knowing he'd been detected, the intruder stepped from behind the tree and took a threatening step toward Nicole. She froze. A scream caught in her throat. She stared into the blackest eyes that she'd ever seen. Eyes of death.

Strange how she hadn't noticed them the night of Jeff's

murder. Then again, the night had been dark, and she'd been facing down a gun. Adrenaline raced through her body, but she couldn't scream. Her throat gurgled as the intruder took another step forward.

Nicole saw his face clearly in the light thrown from the room. What she saw terrified her. Deep creases marked his cheeks and furrowed his brow, while black eyes flashed, and thin lips curved into a sneer of satisfaction. His dark hair fell across his forehead and almost touched his slightly crooked nose that twitched in the feral manner of sniffing out prey.

The rush of adrenaline prodded Nicole, forcing her to finally let loose with a scream. Once released, the scream couldn't be reined in. She screamed until her throat hurt, and her head felt ready to burst. Even as the startled stalker leapt over the railing to land with a thump on the ground two stories below, Nicole kept screaming. Even when Jacob, Josephine, and Sumo ran onto the balcony, she kept screaming. Bloody visions of Jeff lying dead in the street, and Sumo drugged and drowning in a burlap sack fed her hysteria until she collapsed in a heap on the cold cement.

Sumo licked her face and Josephine kept talking to her, but she'd receded to a place of safety. A place where she was barely aware of her surroundings. Somewhere in the back of her mind, she knew that Jacob ran down the stairs after the stalker. She tried to stop him, but even though the words rattled about in her mind, she couldn't get them to pass from her lips. She didn't want Jacob hurt, but she couldn't stop him. Stubborn old man.

Josephine disappeared briefly, and Nicole heard the distant hum of her voice. She returned a moment later with a shot of rye and handed the glass to Nicole. When Nicole was finally able to swallow it, the liquid burned her already raw throat and fired her blood. With a stammer of protest, she scrambled to her feet and scanned the darkness beyond the balcony railing. "Please tell me Jacob went for the police and not after the stalker." Nicole forced the words through her raw throat.

"Stubborn old fool went after the man himself. I called the police. They should be here any minute." Josephine's voice shook and Nicole patted her arm in reassurance and understanding.

"I thought there was supposed to be someone watching my room twenty-four hours a day. Where is he?"

"I don't know, but you can bet we'll ask Corporal Moody when he gets here. I just hope Jacob's okay."

"Jacob'll be fine. He's too crusty to die." Nicole reassured, but she worried Jacob's hasty pursuit could prove disastrous.

The two women practically jumped from the balcony when a knock on the door startled Sumo and set off a ferocious round of barking. Exchanging a worried glance with Josephine, Nicole hastened to the door and asked who was there. Recognizing Corporal Moody's voice, she let go of Sumo's collar and opened the door.

Corporal Moody looked more flustered than Nicole had ever seen. He'd buttoned his uniform haphazardly, and his hat perched crookedly on his head as if he'd shoved it on while on the run. His boots lacked their usual polished appeal.

"I was just getting off shift when your call came in. Is everyone all right?" Fervent energy replaced his usual habit of drawling repetition. His eyes darted about the room.

"No, everyone is not okay," Josephine snapped. "Nicole almost got killed on the balcony of her own hotel room, Jacob has taken off after the stalker, and where the hell was your man?" Josephine crossed her arms, and the steel in her gaze left no doubt that she held Corporal Moody responsible for the situation.

Corporal Moody cleared his throat. "An unexpected emergency came up with Officer Pasquale's family. I told him to leave, and I'd send someone to cover for him. He'd only been gone about ten minutes. I swear." He turned to Nicole. "Are you all right? Should you be at the hospital?"

"No, I'm fine. He didn't hurt me."

"Then you were able to fight him off."

"No, I didn't have to. As soon as I started screaming, he ran."

"But he was threatening you with physical harm, right?"

"He didn't really say anything; he just started moving toward me."

Corporal Moody removed his hat and held it in both hands, his fingers working the brim as if it were one of those stress-relief balls. "He didn't touch you. He didn't say anything threatening. Are you sure it was your stalker?"

"Oh, for God's sake, who else would it be? And I would thank you to stop trying to wriggle yourself out of the responsibility of your job." Josephine defended Nicole.

"I'm not trying to wriggle out of anything. Just checking to make sure it wasn't some teenager having a bit of fun peeking in hotel rooms."

"No. It was him." Nicole shivered. "There's no doubt."

"Unfortunately, we still don't know his identity. I sent the DNA sample taken at the lighthouse in for testing. If he's in the system, we'll know soon enough. Now, I better get after Jacob. You two lock the doors and windows and stay here."

Corporal Moody strode from the room, barking orders into his radio and leaving Nicole and Josephine standing alone in the room.

Josephine snorted, "I'm not waiting here. I'm going after Jacob." She thrust her feet into her loafers and shuffled around in her purse until she found what she was looking for. With a grunt of satisfaction, she pulled out a small but powerful flashlight.

"You're not going alone. Sumo and I are coming with you." Nicole pulled a sweatshirt over her head and patted her leg for Sumo to follow.

They started their search below Nicole's window where the stalker had jumped from the balcony. The hard cement patio slabs of the outdoor cafe's flooring showed traces of blood, as did one of the table edges.

"Oh, no. Could it be Jacob's blood?" Josephine whispered.

Nicole's mind raced with possibilities. "It has to be the stalker's. He would have been long gone by the time Jacob got down here, so there'd be no way they could have gotten into a confrontation. No, it's not Jacob's blood, it belongs to the stalker."

"Yes, I suppose you're right. Too bad he didn't hurt himself a little more, then we could have turned him over to the police."

"He went this way, let's go." Nicole pointed toward the lattice arbor sitting at the end of the cafe patio. With Sumo panting at their heels, Josephine and Nicole followed the trail of blood.

Josephine's flashlight was a blessing, as it was easy to follow the occasional red droplets on the white stone pathway of the garden. The stalker had been staggering, as his trail occasionally drifted off the path, leaving behind trampled flowers before returning. With heart pounding and worried about what they might find, Nicole made sure to keep Sumo close even though he kept whining and straining to run forward. Nicole and Josephine fervently searched the shadows of rustling trees lining the garden path and strained their eyes against the encompassing darkness. The farther they traveled from the comforting light thrown from the inn's windows, the darker the night, and even Josephine's flashlight beam provided merely a false veil of protection.

"I think I hear something," Nicole whispered. She gripped Sumo's collar tighter and fought the urge to return to her hotel room and lock the door. But Jacob was out here somewhere because of her, so in spite of her pounding heart and the thread of cowardly fear running through her system, Nicole knew she wouldn't turn back.

She took Josephine's arm and gently pulled. "I'm going to let Sumo go. He might lead us to Jacob." She released her hold on the straining dog, which immediately took off into the bush with a fervent round of barking. Nicole took a deep breath, smiled at Josephine, and then the two of them took the first steps off the pathway and into the swaying branches of the forest.

Following Sumo was easy, his barking was persistent and drifted back to them from the direction of the shore. Branches slapped her face, but Nicole didn't care, she pushed them aside impatiently and stumbled over fallen limbs and the occasional rock. They drew closer to Sumo's bark, and her heart rate escalated. Suddenly, there were no more branches impeding progress, and the darkness gave way to a moonlit small clearing.

What Nicole saw froze the blood in her veins.

The silhouette of a man and a dog were easily visible in the moonlight, but the man lay on the ground, while the dog anxiously licked his face. Oh, God. Not again. Cold fear shot through Nicole's blood and mingled with the hot ache of guilt. The flash of light flickered in the corner of her eye and then the sudden jolt of memory as Jeff threw her into the limo only to take the bullet into his own chest. Blood. Fear. The end of a life and the beginning of the fight for her own.

Now, Jacob lay on the leaf-strewn ground in the dark of the night because of her. Nicole rushed to his side and knelt on the ground. Josephine stumbled beside her, and the two of them shared a frantic look before pushing Sumo aside and reaching out to check for signs of life. Frantically, Nicole pressed her fingers to his neck searching for a pulse and was rewarded with the strong beat of life beneath her fingertips.

"Thank God, he's still alive." Though spoken in a mere whisper, her words spat through the night like a gunshot.

The sun had set hours ago, and the breeze wafting in from the ocean caused the ground to cool. Nicole worried that Jacob would be more susceptible to the night air because he was unconscious. Frantic with fear for his life as well as the fact that the stalker could be close by, she didn't know what to do. If they moved him, they could do more damage to an existing injury, but if they stayed, they were in another kind of danger. She looked to Josephine for an answer, but the other woman just shook her head.

"I don't know if we should move him."

Nicole glanced at the shadows of the forest, each one holding the possibility of a hiding place. She shivered. "I don't think we should stay here. We have to try to wake him up."

Josephine nodded and gave Jacob a gentle shake. "Jacob. Jacob, you have to wake up. Please." Her voice shook as tears wound down her cheeks. "Jacob, dammit, you stubborn old fool. For once, would you just do what you're told and wake up."

"Woman, if you keep insulting me, I may just change my mind about courtin' you."

Jacob's voice cracked, but his mumbled words gave hope, and when he shuffled his body so that he was able to sit, albeit stooped with head resting in his hands, Nicole wanted to let loose with a shout of relief.

Through tears of relief, Josephine retorted, "You're too ornery to change your mind, besides, you know a good thing when you see it."

"The good thing being you, I assume?" Jacob snorted as he leaned on Josephine and attempted to stand.

"Yes, of course. Be careful, Jacob. Are you sure you're able to stand?" Josephine helped him balance on shaky feet.

"I'm fine. I just banged my head. Again."

"Oh, Jacob," Nicole whispered. "I'm so sorry I got you into this. It's far too dangerous."

Hands on his lower back and stretching carefully, Jacob replied, "Don't worry yourself, it wasn't actually...well, he didn't...dammit, I tripped on my own big feet and fell head first onto that rock. The stalker was nowhere in sight. I don't know if I was anywhere close to him."

The beam of Josephine's flashlight accentuated the flush that spread across Jacob's face as he confessed to his own clumsiness. Nicole was relieved the stalker hadn't been the cause of Jacob's injury—at least, not directly. For all they knew, her nemesis was halfway to another province by now.

Sure, and hell froze over earlier that evening.

Nicole knew the killer hadn't left, just a surely as she had no idea what he wanted from her.

Shaky, but able to move on his own, Jacob put an arm around both Josephine and Nicole's shoulders and stated, "If you two ladies would assist me, I think I'd like a soft place to lay down. By the way, did Corporal Moody show up?"

"Yes, and he's out here somewhere looking for you," Nicole replied. "We'll call when we get back to the room and let him know you're okay."

A sudden, blinding flash of light accentuated her words. Within the dark of night, it suddenly became bright as day. All three shielded their eyes against the invasive light that reached into the shadows of the path and lit the distant inn as if it were the full light of day.

"Damn, I forgot. When I checked in, they told me the movie people would be shooting a day scene tonight." Nicole pointed to four cranes at each end of the *Wyllow Wood* garden. A huge spotlight outfitted each crane and all four cranes focused on the garden area of the inn.

"Not again. Can't those movie people film during the day?" Jacob rubbed his head and stared in awe at the creation of night into day.

The hustle and bustle of movie crew and cast impeded the way back. Security blocked the most direct pathway, so they took the long way around the garden to the lobby. The din of filming rose and fell with each take, and Nicole was thankful that her room was on the opposite side of the inn. She felt sorry for the people in rooms and nearby houses facing the unnatural light and rising noise.

Jacob was walking better by the time they reached the lobby. With a smile of thanks, he removed his arm from Nicole's shoulder, although she noticed he left his other one draped across Josephine.

Nicole was just glad that the two had finally admitted their feelings, but she worried that her trouble placed them in danger. Weaving their way through electrical cords and past rented vans full of equipment, Nicole wondered if Ian was part of the filming tonight. Probably not, or he wouldn't have arranged for dinner with Vanessa. Hopefully, the two of them had been able to come to some understanding. Nicole gave herself a mental shake. It didn't matter. It was none of her business. Her stalker waited out there somewhere, prowling, planning, assessing, watching. Stalking his prey for the right moment to move in for the kill.

Nicole had to make sure no one else was hurt because her past had followed her to Solitary Cove.

***

Ian had received many awards over his career, and as a result, was used to facing auditoriums full of people. His face graced the television screens of homes world wide, his name alone earned him millions per film. He'd hob-nobbed with some of the most famous and powerful people in the film industry, yet as he faced his daughter across the dinner table his mind turned to mush. She looked so much like her mother that Ian's gut twisted with bittersweet memories of young love and broken promises. He had failed her mother, he couldn't fail Vanessa.

"Dad, I had no idea you could cook like that." Vanessa put her fork down and leaned back with a satisfied sigh.

Her praise warmed Ian, but he played it cool. "It was nothing. There was a time when you were younger that money was scarce so we hardly ate out, and since we both know that your mother's all thumbs in the kitchen, I had to learn to cook."

"Funny, I know Mom can't cook, but until now I had forgotten the time you used to spend in the kitchen." She looked quizzically at him. "What else have I forgotten?"

Ian stood and started to clear the plates from the table, giving himself time to figure out how to handle Vanessa's question. She followed him into the kitchen, plates in hand. A waiting silence hummed as they stacked the dishwasher and put the leftovers in the fridge, both being very careful not to get in each other's way.

Back in the living room, Ian mixed a couple of drinks, handed one to Vanessa and settled onto the couch. It was time to face life, time to face his daughter's anger and misconceptions. He gulped down half his drink and began.

"I remember reading you stories before bed. At least, before I got so busy with work and didn't have the time anymore."

"I remember. You'd tuck me in and read me all the classic fairytales, while I'd lay in bed and imagine that I was the princess and you were my prince."

She looked at him with a puzzled expression, and Ian felt the sharp pang of regret mingle with the powerful force of absolute paternal love. He'd never imagined being anyone's prince. Usually, he was just the guy that saved the world.

Vanessa's eyes hardened, suddenly infused with memories not quite so pleasant. "I also remember crying because you stopped tucking me in, and I remember how I had trouble getting to sleep for the longest time. Mom used to get mad at me for bothering her when she was trying to entertain, but I couldn't help it, my prince was gone."

Ian frowned. "But your mother was supposed to read to you. She told me she would, and she never told me about you having trouble sleeping. I was busy with work at that time and doing a lot of traveling. I couldn't be there for you, I'm sorry."

Vanessa stood, smoothed her silk pants, and moved to the bar to fix another drink. "Do you want another one?" she offered.

"Sure." Ian handed her his glass at the same time the door-bell rang.

"Oh, damn. I forgot that Jeb was coming over."

"What!" Vanessa turned an accusing glare at Ian. "Figures, we can't even have a serious conversation without your work interrupting.

"He won't be long. He's here to fire me." Ian crossed to the door, throwing the words over his shoulder. Jeb's greeting was ebullient, probably spurred by the alcohol Ian smelled on his breath. He gestured for Jeb to sit, but the director had other ideas, as he crossed the floor and enveloped Vanessa in a hug.

"Vanessa. I knew you were around, but didn't think I'd be lucky enough to see you." He held her at arms length and leered comically at her. "You look mahvelous, dahling." They both laughed at the old Billy Crystal quip.

"Thanks, Jeb." Looking unsure what she should do, she asked, "Do you want me to leave you two alone?"

"God, no." Jeb waved his hands in front of his body and hiccupped. "Won't be here long. Just had to get something straightened with your dad." Swaying ever so slightly, he smacked his hand on his thigh. "Could really use a drink, though."

"Are you sure about that?" Vanessa raised an eyebrow.

"Yep. Sure as I'm standing here half-drunk. Rum and coke's my poison." Order placed, he wobbled across the living room and threw his arms around Ian. "You have no idea what I've gone through for you, old man."

"Whew." Ian waved a hand in front of his face. "Are you sure you're only half-drunk?"

Jeb giggled. Vanessa handed him his rum and coke and laughed at the unmanly sound.

Ian smiled. "Look, Jeb."

"No, man, you look." Jeb downed his drink in one noisy gulp, wiped his hand across his mouth, and put his hands on his hips. "You wouldn't give me a chance to say a word this afternoon—too busy trying to quit my film, he was. Said his daughter came first. But you didn't give me a chance to tell you the news." Jeb burst forth with his news. "I fired Candace."

Ian and Vanessa watched as Jeb danced a jig in the middle of the carpet.

"Look, Jeb, you can't fire Candace. You fired me, remember."

Jeb threw his arms in the air as if asking for patience from above. "No. That's my whole point. I didn't fire you; you assumed I was firing you. Hell, no one in his or her right mind would take Candace over you."

Jeb threw his arm around Ian's shoulder in a gesture of comradeship. "You rock in this film, you know. There's no way I'm letting you go." Drunkenly, he looked at Vanessa. "You don't expect your old man to give up one of the best roles of his life, do you?" He peered at her face, as if willing her to do his bidding.

"Well, I..." Vanessa stammered.

"It's my decision, and I told you I'm off the film."

"No way, man, it's not your decision." Jeb punctuated his remark with a finger to Ian's chest. "You have a contract, and I'm holding you to it." He looked flustered for a moment. "That is, if it's all right with you."

Ian stared at the drunken director who hadn't fired him. Jeb had said he rocked. Ian assumed that meant that Jeb liked his acting, and he had fired Candace, the last thing Ian would have expected. Who would have figured that an action hero turned romantic could have succeeded quite so easily? And it had been easy. He could slip into the role without thought, but found his acting abilities tested, and he enjoyed the flexing of his talent.

Doubt in his own acting ability had almost stopped him from taking on this role, and it had only been frustration with his life and lack of any solid foundation that had prompted him to take on a project that he would have shied away from another time. Pride formed a small bubble in his chest and rose only to escape in the sound of a snort. Ian slapped Jeb on the back, causing the poor guy to stagger.

"So, you fired Candace. I guess that means I have you over a barrel now, doesn't it."

Worry furrowed Jeb's brow, and he seemed to sober rather quickly. "Oh, well, I don't know if..."

Ian laughed at the hilarious expression on Jeb's face. "I'm only kidding, Jeb. You're right, we do have a contract." His gaze searched out Vanessa, who had been standing quietly assimilating the conversation. "But my daughter is in trouble."

"Dad." Vanessa's voice cut sharply into the room startling both men. "Didn't you hear what he said?" Her voice softened. "You rock. He fired Candace. *Candace.* America's sweetheart. And he did it for you. There's no way you're not finishing this film." She punctuated her words by placing her hands on her hips and staring Ian down.

His heart leapt with pure, unadulterated joy. Heck, he was secure enough in his manhood to admit that he wanted to leap around the room like some idiot in a commercial running through a meadow of wildflowers. At least, he'd admit it to himself, but what he did was give Jeb a masculine smack on the back, and say, "I guess you've got yourself a rock star."

He turned to Vanessa and shrugged. "I don't know what to say, except thanks. I know I haven't always been there for you."

Vanessa raised her hand and shook her head. "Dad, you don't have to thank me. It would be selfish of me to expect you to give up a role that could well be a turning point in your career. Besides, you do have a contract."

Jeb whooped with delight and danced another jig. "Great. So, Amanda should be here day after tomorrow, and since she's studying the script I sent her, we can start shooting then. That gives you tomorrow off, Ian, my man." He slapped Ian on the back, but grimaced in pain. Shaking his hand, he said, "Well, guess that's that, time for me to go." He staggered to the doorway and turned back with a frown. "Hey, Vanessa, babe, whatever the problem is, hope it goes away."

Jeb's rather exuberant presence left the cabin starkly silent. Ian and Vanessa looked at each other hesitantly. Ian's smile relieved the tension. "How about that drink you were getting for me before we were so vigorously interrupted."

"Sure."

Vanessa moved to the bar, while Ian sat down on the couch and contemplated his daughter. Jeb's interruption had only delayed what was to come. He also knew that the sooner they got things out of the way, the sooner they could get on with patching their rocky relationship. "So we were talking about how I traveled so much and was never home for you."

Vanessa stopped pouring, whiskey bottle frozen in mid-air, and her eyes took on a hard quality of self-preservation. Lips pursed, she finished pouring the drink and handed it to Ian with the accusation. "You also stopped coming to my school plays, ballet recitals, and pretty much avoided anything in my life that was important. But I suppose you were too busy traveling for all that as well." She sat and sent an occasional glare of anger toward Ian.

Ian was only slightly shocked at the bitter tone coloring Vanessa's accusations. "Yes, it's true that I didn't hang around for all the important events in your life, but..."

"But what?" Vanessa snapped, as she stared down at him. "You didn't have time for your own daughter."

Ian raised a hand to calm Vanessa. "I had time, or I could have made time, but I didn't think you needed me. In fact, you told me to go make movies because it made you so proud to see your daddy up on the big screen, so you could brag to all the other kids. I thought I was doing what you wanted, what made you proud of me. I had no other way of showing my love, because you were so damned independent and kept pushing me away. How could you even think I didn't want to be part of your life?"

Vanessa's blue eyes shimmered with unshed tears. "I could think you didn't want to be part of my life because you never wanted me to be born in the first place. Mom told me you wanted her to have an abortion." Defiantly, Vanessa stood in as if daring Ian to deny her words.

"What?" Ian stammered as his mind flooded with old arguments, bitter words, and deeply buried memories. When he spoke, his voice was barely a whisper. "That is not what happened. My God." Ian jumped from the couch, grabbed Vanessa's shoulders and forced her to look him directly in the eyes, "Is that what you've believed all these years, that I didn't want you?"

Vanessa pulled from Ian's grasp and backed up a step.

"That's what Mom told me, so why would I believe any different. Besides, you were always away, so I thought you didn't want to be around me."

Ian shook his head and thrust both hands through his thinning hair. "Jesus. Jesus. Jesus." His legs gave out, and he sank back on the couch, then motioned Vanessa to do the same. "I think it's time you hear my side of the story, a side I would have told you a long time ago if I'd known your mother had opened her big mouth."

Vanessa hesitated, and Ian snapped at her, "You brought it up, so you owe me the courtesy of hearing my side."

Vanessa sat.

"Your mother's and my marriage was rocky at the best of times, but I'm sure that was obvious even to a child. Oh, sure, at first things were fine, but then we drifted far apart. I'm not even sure how it happened, but it did. I came home after being away for about three months filming Wings of Honor, and your mother told me she was pregnant."

Ian couldn't sit still, he knew what he was about to say would cause immeasurable pain, but there was no way to deny the fact any longer. It was a time for truth and healing. "Vanessa, your mother was six weeks pregnant." He paused and let the words sink in, hoping that Vanessa would figure out the timing without him having to say any more. He watched her forehead wrinkle, and her eyes cloud with doubt.

"But, that can't be right." She licked her lips and pleaded with her eyes for him to take the words back. "You must be mistaken on the time. Maybe you came home for a weekend or something?"

"I didn't come home. I hadn't been home for over three months. Even before that, your mother and I hadn't slept together in about six months. There is no doubt. When I found out about the pregnancy, we argued ferociously. I demanded that she get an abortion, because I didn't want to raise someone else's child." As he said the words, he looked at Vanessa silently pleading for understanding and forgiveness, but she sat still and breathless.

He sighed and continued. "She refused. At that point, we talked about divorce, but your mother liked the life I provided, and I was off to shoot another film and didn't have time to argue. As the months passed, we settled into an amicable relationship, if not a close one."

He snuck a peak at Vanessa just to make sure she was following the story so far. Her pale face reminded Ian of an alabaster statue that sat on his mantle at home. Graceful and beautiful—yet lifeless. His heart breaking, he leaned over and attempted to take her hand in his, but she snatched it from him before he could. Not so lifeless after all. Her usually pale blue eyes arced with the darkness of midnight blue, and she defiantly sparked her gaze at him.

Swallowing the steely taste of fear rising in his throat, Ian finished his story. "When I got the call that your mother was in the hospital to give birth, I almost didn't go. It was only the thought of how the bad publicity would hurt my career if I didn't that made me." Vanessa's look of distaste prompted him to defend himself.

"Yes, I went for appearances sake, but I have to tell you, Vanessa, when I held you in my arms for the first time, my heart about broke in two. You were so small and achingly beautiful. As you wriggled around, I realized that your life had suddenly become my responsibility. Whether you were born of my blood or not, you were my child. From that point on, I tried to do everything I could to make you happy. Unfortunately, along the way, things screwed up. I couldn't stand coming home and seeing that look of stubborn independence on your face. I wanted to baby you, but you would have none of it. So, I respected your *Wishes*."

Vanessa frowned and gulped down the remainder of her drink. Thoughtfully, carefully, she placed her glass on the table in front of the couch and sat back hands folded in her lap. "When I was five, we did a Christmas play at school. Remember the one where I was an angel?" She looked to Ian for confirmation and continued when he nodded. "I wanted to be the best damn angel in the world. I wanted to show you that I was just like you. That I could act."

Ian's heart twisted sharply. He knew what was coming.

"Mom and I spent so much time on my costume because I wanted it to be perfect, for you. I was so excited standing up on that stage looking out over the audience to make sure you were there. You had said you'd be there." She turned the full force of her gaze on Ian. "You never showed up. I was so upset that night. Mom had a date, but she couldn't get me settled down to bed, and I wouldn't let her leave me with a babysitter. I held my breath and started screaming every time she tried to leave."

Ian smiled at the thought of a six-year-old child controlling Michelle, who hated not being in control herself. Leave it to his daughter to be the only one who could do that. The smile froze on his face when he saw that Vanessa was crying.

"Mom was so angry, and she started cursing me, you, the world in general. In a fit of frustration, she slapped me and told me that I shouldn't expect anything from you because you never wanted me in the first place."

A sob racked her shoulders, and she didn't push Ian away when he put his arm around her and pulled her close. Ian didn't know how long they sat like that, but they both needed the calm of silence to soothe the despair of the past.

Finally, he said, "I wanted you, Vanessa. And I loved you. I thought I was doing what you wanted when I let you live your own life." He brushed a stray hair from Vanessa's face and looked her straight in the eyes. "When you found Bob and fell in love, I was so relieved that you had someone else to love you. Someone you would let into your life and help you. I saw how you gave up your independence to him and thought that meant that you loved him in a way you could never love me. I was jealous of him, but happy for you."

Vanessa sat up and pushed herself away from Ian. "I gave up my independence because he didn't give me any choice. I didn't mind at first, because I'd been taking care of myself for so long that it felt nice to have someone take care of me. By the time I realized the stranglehold he had on every aspect of my life, it was too late. I convinced myself it was okay, that he really did love me, but somewhere along the way I knew I had to get away from him. He lied to me about my friends, and he wouldn't let me go to school. He wouldn't even let me take a correspondence course for God's sake. The bank accounts, business, house, everything, was in his name. I was stuck."

"But you could have come to me."

"No. No, I couldn't. That would have been admitting that I'd failed, and you were always telling me how lucky I was to be married to such a wonderful man. I was afraid that if I left him, I would have lost any respect you had for me whatsoever."

Ian choked. "I thought he was a wonderful man. I thought he was perfect for you. How could I have been so blind?"

"Dad." Vanessa fumbled with the couch fabric. "Did you mean what you said about the first time you held me?"

"Yes, of course I did. Never once in all these years have I ever considered you anyone's child but mine."

"We really screwed us up, didn't we?"

"Yeah. The question is, what do we do about it? And what do you want to do about your marriage?"

Vanessa stood and wandered over to the deck window to look out on the moonlit waves of the ocean. Sliding the door open, she inhaled the salty scent. "I can't stay with him. He hits me."

Ian pushed himself up from the couch, paced the floor, and went to stand by her. "That man needs a good beating himself. If I'd known he was hitting you, I would have come over to your house and dragged you out of there myself. After I'd given him a taste of his own medicine."

Vanessa turned from the open door and looked at Ian. "I should have trusted you with the truth." She paused and breathed deeply. "I'm trusting you now. I need your help, because I have no idea what to do from here."

Without thought, without hesitation, Ian opened his arms

for his daughter. In one swift movement across the floor, she came into his arms. Ian's body shook with long suppressed emotions, and he gave over to the feeling of giving the love he'd held back for so long.

"Oh, Daddy, I'm so scared." Vanessa sniffled in the circle of Ian's arms. "Without my marriage, I don't know who I am. I don't know what to do with my life." She gave a gentle, sobbing laugh. "I might find out that I'm good for nothing except being someone's wife."

Holding her at arm's length, Ian gave Vanessa a shake. "Don't be ridiculous. You're beautiful and intelligent. We'll get you out of this sham of a marriage and then concentrate on figuring out the rest of it. First, we need to hire a good lawyer, the best money can buy." He smiled. "I think I can afford it."

Vanessa stepped from the comfort of Ian's embrace and said, "I just want out, I don't care about how much money I get."

"You've spent the last nine years of your life waiting on that bastard hand and foot while he abused you, so you can bet I'm going to make damn sure you get your half of everything. You can't let him get away with how he's treated you."

Vanessa smiled and yawned. "Gee, I had no idea I was so tired." She looked at her watch. "I should probably head back to Nicole's room before she locks me out for the night."

"You could stay here."

"I know, but I don't want her to worry. Besides, I don't want to leave her alone."

Ian suddenly remembered that danger lurked in the shadows of Nicole's life as well. "You know what's going on, don't you?"

Vanessa fidgeted with the empty glass she'd picked up to place on the bar, and she couldn't meet his gaze. "I do, but I promised I wouldn't tell you."

"Why would you make a promise like that?"

She shrugged. "Nicole made me promise, I don't know why, but...it's bad. Far worse than my situation."

She studied him as if gauging his response to her words. "You care about her don't you?"

"Yes."

"And not just as another easy lay or one night stand?"

"Vanessa."

"Dad, I'm not stupid, and I can read. You're prowess with women is well documented."

Ian chuckled. "My prowess with women, you say." His chuckle grew into a deep belly laugh, and he was sure Vanessa must have thought him crazy, but he couldn't help himself. "Yes, Vanessa, I care about her more than my usual one night stands." Suddenly serious, he said, "If she's in danger, I need to know."

Hesitation colored Vanessa's words, but she remarked, "She's in danger, but she'll have to be the one to tell you about it. I promised her." Her eyes locked with his and asked for understanding.

"Fine, I'll ask her. You can tell her I'll talk to her in the morning."

"I'll tell her. Goodnight, Dad."

"Not so fast. I'm walking you back to the main building."

"I'll be fine."

"No buts. Come on." He took her arm and led her out the door. The walk was short and the night warm. Leaving Vanessa in the lobby with a kiss on the cheek, Ian strode back to his cabin. He closed the door and leaned against it with shaking legs barely able to hold him up. "Jeez, what a night." But it was okay, he'd finally been able to come to some kind of understanding with Vanessa. All in all, a darned good night.

***

His breath caught in his chest like the point of a sharp knife, and his forehead trickled with the sweat of fear. On a stabbingly painful ankle, he stumbled his way through the pitch black, the forest undergrowth obliterating any possible light from the moon above. Curses screamed in his mind as he chastised himself for letting arrogance overcome caution.

He should have checked that she was alone. He should have made sure that damn mutt had actually drowned. Instead, he'd made his way onto her balcony and had planned to end the whole thing. Instead, he'd found himself leaping off the damned balcony and landing sideways on his ankle, only to have to run from the stupid old man chasing him, and the threat of the dog finding him and ripping his throat to shreds. He should have beaten the animal to death when he had the chance.

He paused for breath, the night air seeping through the clothes dampened from his dash to safety. His ears pricked at the sounds of night—a distant ship's horn, the hoot of an owl, scurrying and scampering sounds hidden by the dark. What he didn't hear was any sound of pursuit. Thank God. No, forget that. No thanks to God, because he still didn't have his diamonds or his revenge.

Carefully, he slunk through the forest, looking for the pathway to the ocean and the cave he'd commandeered for his own. He sneered as he thought of Nicole. His fantasies of late had become dark and sinister, bloody and powerful. They screamed for satisfaction. Next time everything would go his way, he'd make sure of that. The bitch was his.

Chapter Seventeen

Nicole woke with a start and lay listening to the early morning sounds. She wasn't sure what had caused her to jolt from a sound sleep, but it hadn't disturbed Sumo because he still slept at the bottom of the bed—snoring. She chuckled and pushed the warm covers off her body wondering why Sumo's snoring didn't bother her, while Jeff's had driven her crazy. Maybe it had something to do with not loving Jeff. If she'd loved him like she did Sumo it might not have bothered her. Food for thought. Or maybe not. She was tired of trying to analyze a marriage that should never have happened and tired of missing a husband who wasn't worth missing.

With a sigh, she turned and gazed out the bedroom window. The angle of her room allowed a perfect view over the treetops to a red-toned sky as the sun rose above the ocean's distant horizon. Nicole loved this town, and the thought of having to leave made her heart heavy. She didn't want to leave, but after last night, she might have no choice. She didn't like placing her friends in danger, and she didn't want anyone else hurt because of her.

Sumo realized she was awake, because he raised his massive head and sent her a droopy-eyed look, as if to say, What are you doing up so early?

Nicole reached down to the end of the bed and gave him a vigorous rub on his head. "Come on, it's time to get up." She threw her legs over the bed and stood up with a prolonged stretch. "Besides, I want to see how Vanessa's dinner went with Ian."

She didn't have to admit to a dog that she was also interested in hearing anything and everything she could about Ian. That man had wound his way inside her, and she couldn't shake him off. And his kisses, dear Lord, they thrilled her to the bone.

"Woman." She slapped an open palm to her forehead. "Get a grip. He's just a man for God's sake." She said the words aloud, but they made no difference. And considering he could have any woman he wanted, Nicole knew she was opening herself up for major heartache.

"Hey, are you talking to yourself in there?" Vanessa hollered from the living room.

"No, of course not. I'm talking to Sumo." Nicole laughed.

"I don't know if that's better or not." Vanessa opened the door and peered in. "Are you decent?'

"Sure. Come on in. How did things go last night?"

"Pretty good. I think Dad and I are finally on the right track. And I owe it all to you, Nicole." Vanessa threw her arms Nicole and hugged her until they both became teary eyed.

"I'm so happy for you."

"By the way. He said he's coming over to see you this morning. And he wants answers.

"Oh." Nicole's heart flipped. "Everyone else knows what's going on, so I don't have much choice but to tell him as well. What are your plans?"

"I'm going to do some research and find a good lawyer. Dad's paying the bill."

"Great. Make sure you get a real shark. Bob deserves nothing less."

They laughed, and Vanessa left. Nicole quickly brushed her teeth and hair, washed her face, and threw on jeans and a tee shirt. Seemed she had a date this morning. She might as well look good.

She snapped her fingers for Sumo. "Come on, Sumo, let's get you outside for a pee and then get some breakfast." Over bacon, eggs, and coffee, Nicole thought about last night and she found herself wavering in her course of action. Dammit, she didn't want to leave, but last night could have ended worse than it had, and she couldn't leave her friends open to that kind of danger. The police, although well intended, hadn't been much help. She had to leave town whether she wanted to or not. The steady hum of conversation drew her attention across the dining room. Ian approached. On some level she was aware of heads turning and fingers pointing, but her most immediate sense was of longing. Her fingers ached to brush across his face, her lips craved the touch of his, and her heart pounded in the tempo of want and need.

Their eyes locked, and Nicole was sure that anyone close enough could hear the roar assaulting her ears. Rubbing her palms on her jeans, she prepared herself for the onslaught of rising emotion. Star quality. This man has it in spades.

Nicole didn't want to be another fawning fan who swooned with the slightest bit of attention from him, but she was afraid her hormones would give her no choice, as they already raged uncontrollably.

His journey across the restaurant seemed to take forever, but finally he stood beside her table, his blue eyes piercing holes in her defenses. He reached out his hand and brushed a stray strand of hair from her face, and Nicole fought the urge to turn her face into the gesture and kiss his palm. Shaking with the intense emotions raging within, she was barely aware of his words as he spoke.

"Morning. Mind if I sit?" He gestured to the empty chair beside her.

Feeling as if cotton balls filled her mouth, Nicole choked out a reply. "No, of course not. Although I think you'll disappoint every other female in this room." She was proud of herself; she had even managed to smile.

Ian pulled out the chair and sat, never once taking his eyes from her face. A flush crept up Nicole's neck and warmed her face.

"You're a very beautiful woman, Nicole."

Straight forward and matter of fact, but Nicole wished he'd

practice his lines on someone less vulnerable. She regained her composure when the waitress hurried over to take Ian's order. Nicole rolled her own eyes when the over-sixty woman batted her eyes and then wriggled her behind in an exaggerated motion as she walked away.

"Do you affect all women that way?"

"I don't know." His lips formed a slow, sinful smile, and he brushed his thumb across her trembling lips. "Do I affect you that way?"

It took every ounce of Nicole's self-control not to open her mouth and take his thumb between her teeth. She was sure that her body swayed in reaction to his touch, she was also sure that every person in the restaurant watched them. It was that thought that gave her the strength to lift her hand and push his away.

"No. You don't."

Laughter lit his eyes, and he sat back in his chair to pin her with his gaze. "Liar."

Nicole glared.

"Okay, I can see you're not in the mood to play." Ian became serious. "I'm here for answers."

Before Nicole could answer, Corporal Moody approached with his hat in hand and a sheepish look on his face. "Excuse me. I don't mean to interrupt but I have some information of interest to you, Miss Tyler." Corporal Moody nodded in acknowledgement at Ian as he sat.

"What?" Curiosity and a tiny flicker of hope sparked in Nicole.

"We received the results from the sperm sample. Seems the DNA matches a man who escaped from the Kingston Penitentiary. Gary Halverson. He'd been locked up for sexual assault.

"Kingston. That's where my husband lived when I met him."

"Husband." Ian's throat seemed to constrict. "You didn't tell me you were married."

"I'm not anymore." She turned her attention to Corporal

Moody. "If this Gary Halverson is an escaped felon, you should be able to help me now." Hope grew that the nightmare she'd lived with for so long might end soon.

"Yep. He's a wanted man, which means we'll get all the help we need from the Major Crime Unit. There are also outstanding warrants for aggravated assault, sexual assault, breaking and entering—a list long as my arm."

"Don't forget to add murder to that list." Nicole spoke flatly.

Ian clenched his fist. "Murder?"

"There's more." Moody clutched his hat and cleared his throat. "The police know that Gary pulled off a huge diamond theft with an accomplice. They never recovered the merchandise."

Nicole touched her fingertips to her temples to quell the throbbing that pulsed there. "So you think this has something to do with the diamonds this guy stole."

"I think it's a distinct possibility."

"I don't understand how that would involve my husband. You think Gary thinks Jeff has...had...the diamonds?"

"You said it yourself." The corporal shifted weight from one foot to the other. "Your husband lived in Kingston, so he and Gary probably pulled the theft together. When Gary got locked up on another charge, your husband would have been the one holding the diamonds until Gary's release. Obviously, Jeff didn't want to give them up when Gary escaped and came looking for his share."

"But I don't know where any diamonds are. If that's what he wants, I cant' help him. What happens now?"

"The Major Crimes Unit will be here within twelve hours. It's their show after that." He stood. "I need to get ready for them, but I'll keep in touch." He looked pointedly at Ian. "I would suggest that you don't let her out of your sight." Touching a finger to his hat, he spun on his heels and left.

Silence. Nicole lost in thought. Ian waiting for an explanation. He reached over and brushed a strand of hair from Nicole's cheek. "Start talking."

***

The story that unfolded stunned Ian. The woman beside him had been to hell and back. He didn't know whether to take her in his arms and comfort her or shake her for not telling him sooner. Looking into the depths of brown eyes flecked with amber and green, he understood that his life was changed forever. No more self-centered actions. He had Vanessa's situation to deal with, as well as falling in love with a woman he barely knew who was being stalked by the man who murdered her husband. Jeez, there had to be movie plot in there somewhere.

Nicole waited for his reaction.

Reaching out, he touched a finger to her cheek and traced a line to her chin and down her neck. She shivered. With deliberate intent he cupped her face in his hands and leaned over to place a gentle kiss on her lips. He felt her relax and lean into the kiss. Aware of their surroundings, he reluctantly ended the kiss before his roiling emotions prevented him from doing so.

Nicole sighed and shifted back into her chair.

"You should have told me sooner. I never would have had Vanessa come over last night and leave you alone."

"I wasn't alone. Josephine and Jacob were with me."

"Great. An old man and a loony tune."

"Ian."

"Sorry, I didn't mean it like that."

"I know. But you're right. They're only going to get hurt protecting me, and then I'd never forgive myself." A quiver of fear tinged her voice.

Now that he'd heard the whole story, Ian knew there was a reason to be afraid. "Come on." He took her hand. "I could use some fresh air."

Once out on the street, Ian inhaled deeply and turned to Nicole. "So, is he after the diamonds?"

"I have no idea, and that's what's so awful. If I knew

for sure, I'd find whatever it is and give it to him. But I swear I know nothing. Especially about any diamonds." Nicole sniffled. "Sorry. So much has happened, and I don't know how much more I can take. I'm frustrated and feel helpless."

Ian tried to imagine the courage it had taken for Nicole to change her name, sell off everything she owned, and leave her home. It would require gumption that Ian doubted he possessed. And the frustration of the law not being on his side would have driven him insane. He'd only had to deal with the local authorities for an hour or so over Vanessa's disappearance, and he'd been ready to explode.

"I'm sorry." His voice shook with varied emotions, as well as the threat of tears. "I admire what you've done, and I'm sorry for everything you've gone through."

"But it's not enough." Nicole's voice shook as well. "I'm going to have to give it all up again. The only way to keep everyone safe is to leave town." She pushed Ian away. "If I leave, he'll follow."

Ian's heart stopped dead in his chest. The thought of never seeing Nicole again and her facing her stalker alone froze him where he sat. He grabbed her shoulders and forced her to face him. "You have too many people who care about you, so there's no way you're facing this alone."

"When I moved here, the plan was to find somewhere secluded and to keep to myself. I thought Sumo would be all the company I'd need. I could write and send my work to my editor, shop in town once a week—pretty much just keep human contact to a minimum. That way no one could get close, and the stalker would never be able to find me."

She smiled. "It would have worked. It should have worked, but the people in this town are too nice. Jacob pushed me from the start, damn stubborn old man. And Josephine, well, she didn't have to say anything. She just became part of my life."

Ian melted. No doubt. He was a goner. The woman pouring out her heart to him was the person he'd waited for all his life. With a groan, he gathered her in his arms and held her tightly.

Damn, she felt good. He ran a hand over the silky hair that touched his face, and the scent of lavender tickled his nose. He couldn't hold her close enough. His body throbbed with need, and God help him, he was getting a hard on. He wanted to rejoice with the forgotten yet familiar feeling, but the somberness of the situation held him back. There was plenty of time later. With an effort he broke the embrace, but couldn't resist dropping a final kiss on her upturned nose.

Nicole moaned. "You know, when Vanessa and I met, we started talking as if we'd known each other forever. There was no awkwardness, no uncertainty. We just clicked. I don't want to lose the kind of friendship I've found here. It's too rare. And then I hadn't planned on." She blushed. "What I mean is, well, it doesn't matter."

Ian was sure she'd been about to confess her feelings for him. Needing to know the truth, he prompted her. "Finish what you were saying."

"No. It's nothing, really."

"I think it is something." Taking her chin between his thumb and forefinger, Ian turned her to face him. "Were you about to say that you hadn't planned on falling for me?" He saw the truth flash in her eyes and then it was gone, disguised by an expression of careful concealment. Why was she fighting what was so obviously happening between them?

"Nicole?"

"Don't worry, Ian, I understand. Let's just chalk it up to my shaky emotional state and forget whatever almost happened between us. I can control my emotions, so you don't have to worry that I'll embarrass you or say anything to Candace."

Ian couldn't wrap his mind around the meaning of Nicole's words. They didn't make sense. She cared for him, yet she wanted to forget what had happened between them. And what did Candace have to do with anything? Suddenly, it struck Ian that Nicole had no idea that Jeb had fired Candace. She was still under the impression that the two of them had some kind of relationship. Relief flooded his limbs and he managed a chuckle.

"Nicole."

Before he could explain his feelings to her, and the status of the Candace situation, a well-wishing fan stopped to ask for Ian's autograph.

Chapter Eighteen

Nicole's heart dropped to her knees when Ian chuckled. Oh, why had she opened her big mouth? Now, he probably thought she was some naive, star struck fan, and heaven knew he'd probably seen enough of them in his lifetime. She didn't want him to think of her that way. What she did want was a normal life, and life with Ian would definitely not be normal. Okay, what she wanted was a life with Ian, whatever that entailed. Unfortunately, he was rich and famous, could have any woman he wanted, and had obviously taken up with his co-star. Nicole supposed that kind of thing happened frequently, but she hated imagining the gorgeous Candace lounging in Ian's arms, enjoying his kisses and caresses.

Thank goodness a fan stepped up to ask for an autograph. It gave Nicole a chance to cover her embarrassment and put her emotions back in line before saying something she'd regret later.

Once they were alone again, Ian turned to Nicole. "Look, about Candace."

"Please, not now. I can't handle any more complications. Can we just focus on finding the stalker? Or the diamonds?"

He gave her an odd look, but acquiesced. "Sure. Whatever you want. Personally, I think we should look for the diamonds. It doesn't sound as dangerous as going after a murderer."

"Okay. But I honestly have no idea where they are. Or if that's even what Gary's looking for."

"It has to be. Nothing else makes sense. Gary stole the diamonds with an accomplice. Your husband and Jeff knew each other. Gary comes looking for something that he's willing to kill for. What else could it be?"

"You're right. But knowing it doesn't help because I don't know where the diamonds are."

"Maybe you know more than you realize. Why don't we grab a cappuccino at *Wishes* and try to figure it out?"

Josephine was busy with customers, so they grabbed a couple mugs of frothy, hot cappuccino. The creaking of old wood protested their weight as they sat in the chairs in the corner. A small cloud of dust puffed upward to glimmer in the sunlight shining through the back window. The hint of chocolate and cinnamon wafted from their mugs, and the ubiquitous books and faerie trinkets emitted a tranquil stillness that had Ian thinking how perfect this moment could be. Under different circumstances.

"Like I said." Nicole started the conversation. "I have no idea where the diamonds are. I didn't even know anything about them until Corporal Moody mentioned them earlier."

"We have to try and figure out where the diamonds might be. You may know about them without realizing that you do."

"How can I know about them, but not know about them?"

"Your husband might have said or done something you didn't think anything of at the time, but now you know about the diamonds, it may take on a new meaning. It could have been an unexpected trip out of town, dinner out with a stranger that you didn't meet, a safety deposit box he rented that you never saw. Anything that would have been out of character for him."

"I don't know. Jeff didn't have character." Nicole blushed. "I mean he didn't have any set characteristics. I'd never know from one day to the next what he would do or say. He had an unpredictable.volatile nature. I'm sure that he didn't have a safety deposit box or anything, because I handled all the bills. Besides, he never went to the bank, he did his banking online."

Ian shook his head. "As far as I'm concerned, unpredictable and volatile, means self-centered and hot-tempered."

Nicole frowned. "I guess I'd never thought of it that way. Maybe." Admitting her husband's abuse to herself was one thing, but she wasn't ready to say it out loud. Now was not the time to assess her marriage anyway, and Ian's touch on her arm brought her back to the urgency of their mission.

"Okay, then." Ian prompted. Do you still have any of his possessions we can dig through? Maybe we'll get lucky."

"I have most of his things—mainly art—at a storage facility in Ingonish, about thirty-five minutes from here. I didn't want it as a daily reminder, and I wasn't ready to go through everything and decide what to keep and what to throw away. When I started getting letters from the stalker and had to sell the gallery and got out of town fast, I brought Jeff's stuff and stored it to deal with later."

Ian chugged the last of his cappuccino and wiped the back of his hand across his mouth. "So, I guess we go to Ingonish." Without waiting for Nicole's answer, he stood and stretched.

"Yes," Nicole whispered. "I guess we go to Ingonish."

***

Ian handled Nicole's car on the winding Cabot Trail with ease born of confidence, enabling Nicole to focus on the chore ahead. Scattered thoughts and snatches of memories flitted in and out of her mind until guilt from her past shut her down. She gave up trying to figure out her dead husband and where he may have hidden the diamonds, they'd just have to search everything when they got to the storage facility.

The horizon glowed with vivid shades of twilight that flowed from the expanse of sky onto shimmering water. Both heaven and earth became one entity as they shared the beauty of nature's glory, and a tear escaped Nicole's eye. Whether the tear was one of appreciation for the beauty or prompted by churning emotions, she didn't know.

A brief flicker of movement drew her attention from the ocean to a motor home whose driver was obviously having trouble handling the hairpin turns that spun down and around the small mountain at a steep grade. Thank goodness she and Ian were headed the other direction, or they'd be stuck behind the lumbering, top-heavy vehicle that looked to be traveling a mere fraction of the posted speed.

Poor people, they probably have no idea what lies ahead for them on the Cabot Trail with a contraption like that. Feeling bad for what would likely be a harrowing experience for them, she sent a silent prayer their direction that they'd make it to the bottom in one piece.

A roadside sign declared two miles to their destination. Neither of them had said much during the thirty-five-minute drive north, and Nicole was relieved that neither of them felt the need for conversation, because she felt numb. She was aware of lush green valleys, rugged terrain, and the crystal sheen of the ocean, but she wasn't able to appreciate the beauty. Instead, she wound her fingers around her key chain and chewed her lip in nervous anticipation of having to open the storage door for the first time since she'd locked Jeff's belongings up months ago.

"Why did you store the stuff in Ingonish rather than Solitary Cove?"

Ian's deep voice startled Nicole and caused her to drop the keys. Shifting her butt back in the seat to enable herself a better angle to lean down, she retrieved the offensive key chain —a key chain that she almost wished she'd lose, thereby preventing her from having to open the storage locker. Feeling the cool metal of the key chain, she grasped it and sat up only to find Ian's eyes glued to a point just below her chin. Mortified, she realized that her tee shirt must have offered him a rather pointed view of her lacy black bra.

She blushed.

His eyes met hers for a brief, burning moment of desire before he turned his attention back to the precarious road. Nicole cleared her throat and tried to focus her mind on the question that she knew he had asked her. Oh, yeah.

"There was no storage facility in Solitary Cove. Besides, I couldn't stand the thought of touching any of it ever again, so I wanted it far away from me."

"Simple enough. Okay, so what made you move to Solitary Cove?"

"Oh." She blushed. "I threw a dart at a map." She waited for the sneer and condescending remark, much like what Jeff's reaction would have been. Instead, his bark of laughter surprised her.

"You've got to be kidding me. You actually moved somewhere based on the throw of a dart. Goddamn, I admire your nerve."

Emotion welled inside Nicole. He admired her. She didn't think anyone had ever admired her before.

Ian was obviously in the mood for asking questions. "Do you regret the move?"

"No. I love Solitary Cove. I fell in love the first time I drove through the downtown area."

"Downtown?" Ian laughed.

"Downtown...what?"

"I'm sorry, but only someone who lives in a small town could call the main street of Solitary Cove a downtown. Forgive me, continue."

Nicole was glad to see him relaxing and no longer clenching the steering wheel quite so tightly.

"Anyway, I drove around and found a small trail—barely even a road—leading to the lighthouse. When I drove from the forest into the clearing on the cliff top, the expanse of ocean and the majesty of the lighthouse rising up against the horizon mesmerized me. I was hooked. I knew I had found where I wanted to be."

"Look, we're here." The touch of Ian's hand on hers sent a shaft of burning heat through her body, and if she hadn't been sitting, she may have fallen. *Does this man have any idea what he makes me feel?*

Ingonish, a testament to the rugged glory of the eastern

coast, and a town alive with history and tales of battle and sacrifice. A cluster of small communities on the Cabot Trail, Ingonish lay snugly between Cape Breton Highlands National Park and the Atlantic Ocean. Lush green valleys, wild, rugged highlands and sandy beaches, it was a place of beauty and character.

Entering an area with some signs of civilization, they passed a small white building that housed the Royal Canadian Legion and the war memorial erected in memory of the soldiers who had fought in World War I and II. Farther on, a rough-hewn stone church sat nestled among a garden of wild-flowers. The small structure sat perched on the cliff's edge with the regal blue of the ocean highlighting its simple lines.

"There." Nicole pointed. "Make a left, the storage unit is only a few blocks away."

Smoothly, Ian slipped the car into the left lane and made the turn. Tension imbued the air with an uncomfortable silence, and Nicole was glad when the storage building came into sight even though her heart pounded in reckless abandon.

An abandoned fishery, the building had been renovated and put to use for storage. The rates were cheap and anyone renting a unit had access twenty-four hours a day, seven days a week. Nicole dangled the key chain from her finger and cautioned herself to remain calm. She'd be fine. She wasn't alone.

Ian pulled the car into a designated parking spot, turned off the car and looked at Nicole. The understanding look of support gave Nicole the edge needed to open her door and face the imposing building.

Fire engine red accented white window frames, and the clapboard structure rested on the edge of a sandy beach. A cedar shake roof gave refuge to a number of seagulls who, tired from spanning the ocean waves for lunch, had perched on the slanted peak. Three flagpoles dotted the grassy area of the side yard—a Canadian flag, an American flag, and a province of Nova Scotia flag, all wafting in the soft evening breeze.

Ian reached out to Nicole, who hesitated, then placed her

hand in his. He gave a gentle squeeze of assurance. Nicole took a deep breath of preparation and took her first step towards the past waiting in the shadows of the building.

***

Four hours later in the dimly lit and dust filled room, Nicole threw her hands up and plopped down on a partially empty box of clothes. "I give up. We don't have time to search everything." Her eyes helplessly searched the contents of the room. "I don't remember there being so many boxes, no wonder I kept putting it off."

Ian threw another box into the growing pile of items they'd searched, and stretched. "You're right. There's too much here, and the problem is that the diamonds wouldn't take up much space. They could be stitched in a jacket hem or hidden in any one of those books." He waved his hands the direction of a pile of boxes filled with books. Boxes they hadn't even touched yet. "They could even be laid flat and hidden in the back of any one of those paintings."

Nicole and Ian looked in dismay at the stacks of paintings leaning against the opposite wall, then over to the untouched boxes of personal items from Jeff's desk, closet, and private studio. Jeff had collected so much over the years there was no way the two of them could go through everything with the intense scrutiny that was necessary.

"Jesus." Ian paced the room and ran his hands over his head and down the back of his neck.

"I'm sorry. I just hired a moving company and had them move everything. I didn't bother going through any of his stuff. I figured that the day would come when I'd be able to, but I didn't realize it would be under such circumstances."

"No, no, I'm not swearing at you, Nicole. I'm pissed with the situation."

"I know." She put her head in her hands and moaned. "This is all my fault."

"Your fault. How can you say that?"

Ian stopped pacing and sat down on a box beside Nicole. "Heck, if you're taking the world on your shoulders, why don't you take the blame for world hunger and the state of the economy. I'm sure if you dig far enough and get creative, you can claim responsibility for more world calamities."

Nicole was stunned. Then a tiny giggle escaped. "I guess I was being a wee bit martyr-like, wasn't I?"

Ian put his arm around her shoulder and pulled her close. Uh-oh. A throb of passion threatened to overwhelm her. This small room forced them into a closeness that made it hard to keep her wits in line. Half of her wanted to lash out at him for kissing her the way he had during dinner that first night, and then turning around and kissing Candace just as passionately. That half of her wanted to anger him and build a wall between them, a wall high enough that no feelings could batter their way through.

She felt like she was succeeding until he turned his gray-blue eyes to her, and she melted. Damn him. She turned away from him and studied the boxes, as if deciding which one to rip open next. His fingers brushed her cheek and pressured her chin to turn her face his direction. His will drilled into her very soul, and Nicole hated the fact that she had no control over her emotions. Why was she so attracted to this man? He wasn't that handsome, yet the line of his jaw brought to mind gods of Greek mythology, the movement of his body mimicked a feline creature of the wilds, his eyes radiated warmth that wound into Nicole's limbs and left her weak with want and need.

"Nicole, the guilt you feel for your husband's death is unwarranted."

"I don't...I haven't. You have no idea what you're talking about."

"Fine. Look me in the eyes, and tell me you don't feel guilty."

Nicole tried. She stared directly into Ian's eyes and felt herself drowning. Oh, how she tried to say she felt no guilt, but blue eyes engulfed her, surrounded her with a wave of shimmering, stirring warmth that left her weak and powerless. She couldn't lie to him. Instead, she turned away, crossed her arms across her chest and rocked slowly in a motion of comfort.

"Nicole, he stole the diamonds, lied to you, ripped off his partner, and left you in the middle of everything." He grabbed her by the shoulders and shook gently. "You have nothing to feel guilty about."

Through a haze of self-recrimination, Nicole was only partially aware of Ian's words. They took a moment to sink into her sub-conscious, but word by word, her mind assimilated and assessed. Chiseling away at guilt forged over the course of the year since Jeff's death, Ian's words finally gave her the ability to climb out from under the burden. The ensuing rush of release left Nicole shaking with the effort of letting go. Panicked, she looked to Ian for guidance and found understanding in his eyes. Without hesitation, he opened his arms for her, and Nicole moved easily into them, as natural a motion as if she'd been doing it for years.

Guilt in the form of tears wound their way from her heart, out her eyes, and onto Ian's shirt, but he didn't seem to mind as Nicole poured out the past year of pain. He held her gently and caressed her hair, all the while murmuring words of comfort.

If her shaky emotions could have been trusted, she would have said that she felt loved at that moment. As tears slowed and the past receded to the past where it belonged, Nicole took the reins of her heart back in her hands and concluded that any such feelings of love were wishful and a mere product of an emotional moment.

"Are you okay?" Ian's deep voice whispered in her ear, his breath brushing gently across her face.

She sat up straight and wiped her face with the palms of her hands. "I'm fine. Thanks. I'm sorry I broke down like that, I guess you touched the right button at the wrong time, or vice-versa."

"Yes, well, I'm glad you're all right." Ian brushed his shirt as if to brush away the tears and then stood.

Tucking a stray hair behind her ear, Nicole slid off the box and onto the floor where she rummaged through familiar clothing, hoping that her movements covered her discomfiture. Risking a quick look at Ian, Nicole was surprised to see him staring at her.

"What?" She questioned, afraid of the answer.

"What? What do you mean, what?"

Nicole was confused. Had she missed something? She shrugged her shoulders, which only caused Ian to react by kicking a nearby box. Unfortunately, books filled the box and Nicole stifled a chuckle when the great movie star hopped around on one foot while grasping his injured one. The words crossing his lips would have made a sailor blush, but Nicole laughed. Vexed by her laughter, Ian planted both feet on the floor, slammed his hands to his hips, and confronted her with a belligerent stare.

Nicole craned her neck to look up at him as he towered over her. He did not look happy. She attempted an apology. "I'm sorry."

"Really. What are you sorry for?"

"For laughing at you."

"And?"

"And, I don't know what else."

In an effort to level the playing field, so to speak, Nicole stood. Unfortunately, she found herself cramped into a corner with Ian blocking her from making any move. Her eyes were level with where his shirt opened at chest level, and she stared at the curling gray hair peeking out from blue denim. Her stomach rose to her throat. She wanted to curl those hairs around her finger, then push her hand under his shirt and feel the firm, powerful lines of his chest. Suddenly afraid, she swallowed and took a step back against the wall. She felt a hand wind itself in her hair, another wrap around her back and slowly trace a pathway lower until its warmth settled just where her back curved into butt.

She shivered. Then she looked up.

Ian growled. "You really have no idea how you make me feel, do you?"

No. She didn't. But if he felt anything like what she was at that moment, they were in trouble. Someone had to retain control, and it wasn't going to be her.

"Nicole. Look at me." He used his finger to push her chin up until their eyes clashed.

Molten gold washed over her limbs, leaving her hot and weak. She swallowed, trying to get her stomach back where it belonged. It didn't work. She tried to speak, but couldn't. Instead, she watched her hand rise of its own accord and hesitantly touch Ian's cheek. He moaned, and she was lost. Rising onto her toes, she licked her lips and leaned forward, no longer caring if she was making a fool of herself, caring only that she feel his kiss one more time.

He didn't disappoint. The hand he had wound in her hair tightened, and he pulled her to him. In one craving motion of hunger and passion, his lips took hers and Nicole felt devoured. His lips were strong and his tongue darted into the warm recesses of her mouth. Oh, God, it felt so good. This time, Nicole moaned, although she didn't recognize the primal groan of sexual surrender and enticement. Like an animal, she wanted to rip the clothes from his body and use hers to explore what she knew lay beneath the offensive material.

In a daze of unbelievable heat, Nicole slowly became aware that Ian was pushing her away from him. Oh. My. God. It felt as if he'd thrown cold water on her, as she became instantly aware of the musty room and messy surroundings. A sob threatened to find its way from her, but Ian didn't give her a chance for recriminations.

"Nicole, we need to talk."

How did she regain her self-respect? She'd thrown herself at a man whose whole life revolved around beautiful women doing exactly that. Before today, she would have sworn she was above such idol worship.

"No, Ian, I understand. You don't have to worry because I won't embarrass you, or me, like that again. Let's just chalk it up to the emotion of my past unraveling before my eyes."

Praying that she'd saved a semblance of her self-respect, she peered at Ian to see his reaction. He looked stunned, and then he laughed. He was laughing at her, damn him. She slapped his shoulder and swore at him. He captured her hand and pressed his lips into her palm, which caused the butterflies in her stomach to flutter their wings.

"Nicole, I think I'm falling in love with you."

The words fell into the room and smacked Nicole like a wet dishrag. Not a great reaction when someone tells you he loves you—thinks he loves you.

"Nicole?" He sounded worried.

She looked around the room trying to find an escape. Anything rather than face the prospect of such a serious conversation while standing amidst the ruins of her last marriage, which had been a total sham. The confusion of half-empty boxes and clothes strewn on the floor only added to her state of mind.

"Ian, this is crazy. It's wrong."

His strong features molded into a mask of dejection and in the dim light of the small room, Nicole detected a flash of pain deep in his eyes.

"I know. I'm sorry. I shouldn't have said anything. Why would you be interested in an old man like me anyway? The story of my life, you know. Wrong time, wrong place."

"Old man. What are you talking about?"

"It's okay, Nicole. I know that the women who chase me don't give a damn about me. They're interested in the Hollywood illusion. I also know that you're not the kind of person who'd be impressed with fame and fortune. That's one of the things I love about you. I was only hoping that someone could love me for myself."

Ian ran his hand over the back of his neck and stepped back a couple of steps, allowing Nicole the ability to move that she'd wanted so badly a moment ago. Now, she felt cold and alone without the warmth of his body close to hers. And was he really saying what she thought, or was she placing her own meaning into his words? Before she could clarify anything, either in her mind, or verbally, Ian started talking.

"Funny, sometimes I'm not ever sure who I am, you know. I start to believe the stories I hear about my exploits, and suddenly I'm a stranger to myself. Taking the part in this movie and coming to a small town was my attempt to discover myself. It seems as if the fates are forcing me into a discovery of my own depths, throwing my mistakes in my face and presenting me with love for the first time."

"Ian, this is a stressful time for both of us. When you get back home, you'll see everything in a different light. You'll be glad that I didn't take you seriously."

"I suppose there's only one way to make you believe me."

Before the last word had left Ian's mouth, he clasped Nicole in an intense embrace and kissed her, completely, passionately, lovingly. She'd never experienced anything so invigorating, so shocking, so total. One by one, her doubts disappeared, and the wall she'd managed to build became only a memory. She couldn't get close enough and wriggled in a manner to meld their bodies closer. Ian moaned, and Nicole flared with intense need. When she felt the evidence of Ian's arousal pressing against her, she knew she was lost. She belonged to him and was willing to give herself completely to him, here on this hard, dusty, cold floor.

She could have screamed when he pushed her away, abruptly ending the embrace. Again! What was wrong with this man?

"Nicole."

At least his voice sounded shaky, so she must have had some effect on him.

"We have to find the diamonds."

Cold reality crashed into the new found relationship, giving Nicole another reason to curse the stalker. With a deep, shaky breath, she put a lid on her reeling senses and nodded.

"Yes, you're right." She rubbed the goose bumps on her arms and managed a quivering laugh. "Ian, I can't believe...I mean, you're...I'm..."

Ian laughed. "Nicole. I love you, okay. Let's leave it at that and analyze the why's and wherefore's later."

"Deal." She was in love with a man who loved her back. Wow. The lightness of love made her want to dance around the room, shout from the rooftops, and fly through the sky. This kind of commitment with another human being didn't bind, rather, it gave one a sense of freedom.

Hold it. A thought nudged Nicole. Something was trying to make itself heard. But what? What was different from a moment ago? She tried to remember what she'd just been thinking, and she must have looked perplexed because Ian stopped midway through unloading a pile of books.

"What? You look strange."

"I don't know, but there's something. I just need to think." She tapped her fingers against her cheek and paced the floor talking to herself. "Love, rooftops, sky. No, that's not it. Fly, freedom."

Yes.

"That's it. Ian I think I know."

She ran across the room and started flinging Jeff's paintings aside, looking for the one she remembered. Faces, animals, trees, and colors of all kinds flashed through her mind as she gave each painting a brief glance. Finally, she saw it. Grace and beauty, freedom and power, all combined in the one painting Jeff would never part with, no matter the price offered. A hawk in flight.

Her shaking hands held the painting and she tried to remember the words Jeff had said that day. "We used to get at least one offer a week for this painting when it hung in the gallery, but Jeff always said he'd never sell it. Finally, he put it back in his studio where he was the only one who could enjoy its beauty. He said that the hawk stood for freedom. I always thought he meant freedom as the hawk being a wild bird in flight, but what if he meant something else."

"Yes, it makes sense. Let me see the painting." Ian reached over and carefully took the hawk painting from Nicole. "Here, hold this flashlight closer." He handed her a flashlight they'd brought in from the car.

The beam of light flashed on wings brushed with brown, gold, and tawny paint, then reflected in eyes of amber that leapt from the canvas in a vivid portrayal of life. With red-tipped wings spread full, and hooded black eyes scouring the ground for food, the hawk was beautiful and predatory. He reminded her of Jeff.

"He was very talented." Ian remarked as he ran his hands over the ornate frame encasing the painting.

"Yes, he was."

Ian ceased his exploration of the frame and sent her a speculative glance. She couldn't look at him. Instead, she shuffled a dust bunny across the floor with the toe of her shoe.

Ian cleared his throat, continued searching the painting and frame, and nonchalantly questioned, "Do you miss him?"

Did she? Nicole had been so busy trying to elude the stalker that she hadn't had time to miss Jeff. Ian had stopped again, the intensity of his gaze pinning her, silently waiting for an answer.

She shrugged her shoulders. "I don't think I do. I don't think I ever really did." Her voice lowered to an uncertain whisper. "Does that make me a bad person?"

Gently, he caressed her hair and held her close. "No, it doesn't make you a bad person. Especially considering the circumstances." Ian's arms fell to his side and the thread of vulnerability shot across his features. "To be honest, I get the feeling that Jeff wasn't a very nice person. More to the point, I get the feeling that he didn't treat you the way you deserve to be treated."

Nicole was shocked. To have her innermost, heretofore unacknowledged thoughts, given life with words was almost more than she could bear. She clutched one hand to her chest, while the other supported her as she slowly sat on a nearby box.

"Oh. My."

"Nicole, are you okay." Ian knelt at her side and rubbed his hands vigorously up and down her arms.

"No, I'm not all right. It's just that getting rid of guilt over Jeff's guilt was a major relief and life-changing event, but now.now, I've realized that I never even loved him. We were married for seven years and all that time, I was married to a man that I didn't love." She stood and took a step back from Ian, who still knelt on the ground. "How could I not have known that? How can I trust my feelings again?"

Ian jumped from the floor and took her by the shoulders. With intent and determination, he captured her attention. "Don't trust what you think, trust what you feel."

He lowered his head and kissed her with infinite care and subdued passion. The knots in Nicole's stomach let go and languor crept through her limbs until she was standing only with the help of Ian's hands on her hips, pulling her closer. He kissed her as if nothing else mattered, as if the rest of the world didn't exist. Nothing had ever felt so complete, and Nicole craved more. Before she could wrap her arms around Ian and sink into the warmth of his embrace, he pulled away.

No, not again. "What is it with you?" She stamped her foot and made herself busy straightening her tee shirt.

"What did I do?"

Nicole sighed. "Nothing. Forget it."

"Well?"

"Well, what?"

"Well, I just finished kissing you, using my best stuff I might add."

Nicole smiled. "Oh, I see." And she did. Ian wanted to hear the words that she hadn't said. Before the kiss, she'd had doubts about her ability to trust her own feelings, but the kiss had trampled any doubt into the ground. She loved the man who stood before her, as surely as she hadn't loved Jeff. Within the course of the evening, she'd come to know herself better than she had in the last thirty-eight years of her life. How does such a thing happen? How can a person stumble around, virtually in the dark, for so many years and then in the blink of an eye have such certain insight into their feelings? Nicole was stunned, yet ecstatic. She'd committed her heart to Ian, yet she felt freer than ever before.

That must be what happens when two people who love each other and care enough to share and be honest. Ian had made her face up to the pain that lingered, cast aside the guilt she had felt, and then given his love freely, even though he had no idea whether she returned his feelings.

At that moment, he stood in the meager light reflected from a single light bulb. Shadows crossed his face, highlighting the intense concentration that formed his features. He waited for her to answer.

So she did.

"I love you, too. Now, do you think you can kiss me without pushing me away?"

Ian groaned and made a move toward Nicole, then stopped. "No. If I kiss you again, I won't be able to stop. And right now, we have diamonds to find."

Ian had picked up the painting and was examining every inch. Nicole knelt beside him with her hand resting on his shoulder. He smiled briefly at the contact and continued his search. Made of dark oak, the carved, antique frame shaped into an ornate leaf and vine pattern. Ian ran his fingers over the detailed pattern, feeling each crevice and testing each curl, he covered the length and width of the frame.

Thinking she'd been wrong, and they'd spend the rest of the night searching, Nicole was about to go back to the stack of books when Ian grunted. His actions became frantic as he pulled and twisted something. Nicole moved in for a better look.

"Have you found something?"

"Maybe. One of these leaves feels loose." His face strained as he pushed his thumb against the carved leaf. "It's moving."

Nicole's heart leapt, and her breathing quickened in time with Ian's. Suddenly, the leaf pivoted as if on a hinge and twisted up to the corner of the frame, leaving in its wake a hole about two finger widths in size.

"Oh, Ian, this has to be it. The diamonds have to be here."

"We'll see." He continued fumbling around the mouth of the hole with his finger. "Damn, my finger won't fit. It only goes in so far and then the hole gets narrower. Here, you try." He moved the frame over to Nicole's lap.

With a silent prayer, Nicole pushed her finger into the opening, and slowly, because she had no idea what she might touch, she edged further into the hollowed frame.

"I feel something. It feels like cloth."

"Can you pull it out?" Ian's breath ruffled across the back of Nicole's hair.

"I'm trying." She couldn't get a second finger in, so she had to jam the cloth against the frame with her finger and keep pressure on it as she tried to drag the cloth toward the opening. It seemed to be working, the cloth slid smoothly.

Nicole's pulse raced. "It's almost there.just.one.more." She pulled the cloth close enough to grasp an edge between her thumb and forefinger and yanked.

Revealed in the thin beam of the flashlight that Ian held was a small pouch of dark blue velvet. Carefully, Nicole pulled the length of material from the hole and held it in the palm of her hand. Afraid to hope or even breathe, she looked at Ian, who'd fixed his gaze on the mysterious cloth in her hand.

"Do you think?" Nicole swallowed and was too nervous to say more.

"Only one way to find out." He picked up the pouch and pulled at the knotted strings that held it shut. "Put your hand out."

She did. Ian's gaze locked with hers, and he placed his free hand palm up underneath hers. Heat from his hand infused into Nicole's, and she knew the gesture was one of sharing. Whatever happened, they were in it together.

"Here goes nothing." Ian tipped the small pouch, spilling the contents into Nicole's hand.

Stunned silence. Even in the dimness of the storage area, the brilliance of the diamonds shot sparks of light into the room. Nicole gasped, amazed at the coolness of the stones in her hand.

"They're gorgeous, and there's so many of them."

Ian ran a hesitant finger through the hard stones responsible for Nicole's husband's murder. "Yes, they are stunning, and they must be worth a fortune."

"Thank goodness we found them"

"Yes, I guess. Hopefully, when we give them to the stalker, he leaves you alone. I get the sense that he wants more from you. Come on, leave this mess, we should get back."

They went down the stairs into the night air. Nicole was relieved to get out of the stifling room filled with memories of her fraudulent marriage. They climbed into the car, and Nicole jumped when Ian slammed his door.

"Ian, what's wrong?"

"I'm just trying to decide if we should give the diamonds to the stalker or the police. They may be better equipped to handle this whole thing."

"But won't that just make him angry? He'll come after me for revenge."

"I thought that as well. The man is obviously crazy and possibly vengeful. If we don't give him the diamonds, he'll come after you out of some misguided notion of revenge. But if we don't give them to the police, they might charge you as some kind of accessory. We need a plan, and I'm not sure it should involve the police." His voice was a mere whisper in the darkened interior of the car.

Chapter Nineteen

I t was after dinner when they returned to Solitary Cove, and they were both exhausted. Ian cleared his throat. "I want you with me tonight."

"But what about Vanessa?"

"She'll be fine."

"I'd like to make sure. You know she was looking for a lawyer today."

"You're right. You can call her from my cabin."

At her nod of agreement, Ian wheeled into the drive of the inn. Nicole's heart pounded. He said he loved her, but did he mean it? Or would he spend the night with her and then move on with his life? Did she care? Of course she cared, but she also wanted to be with him. Share herself in a way she never had with Jeff. Not just physically, but emotionally. If all she had was this one night, she'd have to be satisfied with that.

Ian's gaze burned into her as he opened the cabin door and motioned her to the phone. "Don't talk long. My self-control is wearing thin."

Nicole blushed and dialed the front desk to have them connect her to her room.

"Hello."

"Hi, Vanessa. How goes the lawyer search?"

"You don't want to know. Jeesh, talk about expensive. Thank God, Dad's paying the bill because I sure couldn't afford it."

"You'll be able to when you get what you're entitled to from Bob."

"Yeah, well, good old Bob's got a fight on his hands, because

I retained one of the best. I was on the phone with him for half the afternoon. By the way, I'll pay your long distance phone bill."

"Don't worry. I'm just glad you're getting things moving." She hesitated. "No second thoughts?"

"No way. In fact, I'm about to call and tell him to go home and leave me alone. No way am I going back to him. Dad helped me see that."

"I'm so glad. Just don't let him talk you into changing your mind."

"I won't. I feel like I'm finally getting my life back to some semblance of normalcy, and I don't want to give up control to anyone again. What about you, will you be back soon?"

"About that. I'm spending the night out."

"Oh, no. Don't tell me you're with Dad."

"I'm with your dad." Nicole jumped as warm hands settled on her shoulders and slowly kneaded her knots away.

"Nicole! Please tell me you know what you're doing."

"I don't."

"Please don't take anything that happens eriously. Dad's famous for his short-term relationships. Oh. I forgot. Did you find the diamonds?"

"Yes. And they are gorgeous." Seeking hands slid down her back and cupped her butt. "Ah, Vanessa. I have to go. Can you maybe run over to Josephine's and pick Sumo up? I'd feel better if he was there with you."

"Sure. I'll go get Sumo and even give him a big hug for you. He'll miss you, though."

"Me, too. I'll see you tomorrow."

"No problem. By the way, this poor police officer has been outside all night. I don't think he realizes you're not in your room."

Nicole moaned. "I forgot all about him. I almost feel sorry for him, but I don't want the police to know we have the diamonds. Maybe you'll just have to keep up the pretense that I'm still there."

"Okay. Nicole, about my father."

"Vanessa. I'll be fine. Talk to you tomorrow." She hung up the phone gently and turned around to face Ian.

"She warned you about me, didn't she?" His lips ran a warm trail down her throat, and he unbuttoned her top button.

Nicole cleared her throat and tried to concentrate. She needed to clear something up before they went any further. "Yes." A shiver wound down to her groin, and her legs wobbled ever so slightly. Oh, yes, she remembered. Ian's tongue traced a pattern across the top of her breast and his finger dipped under the lace of her bra to rasp over her nipple. Nicole knew it was now or never. "Ian, what about Candace?"

Her words had enough effect to stop the action. Her heart pounded.

Please let him say the right thing.

"Nicole. I tried to tell you."

Uh, oh. That doesn't sound good.

"Candace and I have never had a relationship, except in her own mind. In fact, Jeb fired her today for that stupid stunt she pulled with me. I'm sure Vanessa told you all about how she cornered me. Practically raped me, she did."

"Raped you?"

The corner of Ian's mouth lifted in a half smile. "Yes. And I'll have you know that I put up quite a fight for my virtue."

Nicole couldn't help it. She laughed. "I see. Are you going to put up a fight for your virtue tonight or just surrender?"

"Oh, baby. To you, I'll surrender."

With one easy sweep, Ian placed his hands under Nicole's legs and lifted her in his arms. Both of them shaking with desire, Ian carried her into his bedroom and kicked the door shut behind them.

***

The stalker climbed carefully off the balcony. No one saw him. Swiftly making his way down the path toward the front of the inn, he looked to make sure no one was around before he threw a stone at one of the lights. The pop sounded loud to him, but drew no one's attention. Silence surrounded him.

Smug and excited, he was becoming aroused. He'd seen the curvy blond with the bitch more than once and had imagined all kinds of interesting scenarios. The actor's daughter. And she was on her way to pick up that mutt. She'd have to take the very path he now walked.

Another stone. Another light.

The sound of glass breaking cut into him like winter cold. Careful. He didn't want to get caught. Not when he was so close.

Nicole and the actor had the diamonds. He'd stood outside the balcony door and heard the one-sided conversation. Now he needed a bargaining tool. An extra bit of insurance. He crept closer to the edge of the garden, keeping the moonlit path in sight. Carefully, he peered through the branches, waiting for the woman. Finally, he saw her. Briefly silhouetted against the horizon and moon, she came close enough for him to confirm her identity.

She passed close, and he caught a whiff her perfume. He waited for the perfect moment, and then he leapt. He grabbed her in a headlock and choked her out in seconds. He hadn't lost his touch. Before she could react, she lay limp in his arms. It took him only a second to sling her over his shoulder and hasten back to the cave with his trophy.

***

Morning dawned bright and clear. Nicole stood on the deck basking in the blaze of sun that crested the ocean horizon. She was aware of Ian the moment he stepped onto the deck. The strength of his arms wrapping around her gave her an amazing sense of security and fulfillment.

"Unfortunately, I have to work for a few hours this morning."

His breath brushed across her cheek. She was so aware of every sense in a way she'd never been before. Is that what love did to a person?

"That's okay. I should go back to my room for a shower and change of clothes. Besides, I want to check on Vanessa. I know she said she was fine last night, but the light of day might tell a different story, and I don't want her having second thoughts about going back to Bob."

Ian briefly tightened his hold on her. "Thanks for caring enough about my daughter to worry about her. That means a lot to me."

"I don't mind. She deserves to have someone care about her." Nicole flushed. "I didn't mean...I meant because of Bob."

"I know. Don't worry. I wasn't the best father, but I plan to make up for it now. Damn, look at the time. I've got to go or Jeb'll have my cojones for breakfast, but I'll walk you to the hotel first."

The walk to the hotel was short, and Nicole hated to see it end. It would be hours before she saw Ian again. Oh, God, she'd only met him a few days ago, slept with him once, and now she couldn't stand the thought of separation. What was wrong with her? She was in love, that's what. She hugged herself, reveling in the wonderful feeling, suddenly not caring that she wouldn't see him for a while, because she would see him again, and that was all that counted. She wasn't one of his one-night stands. He loved her.

"We're here. And what are you looking so pleased about?"

"Nothing, just thinking to myself." She reached up to kiss his cheek, but he wasn't settling for that. His lips settled on hers in a kiss that melted Nicole's limbs.

Nicole took the elevator upstairs in a euphoric state and let herself into her room. "Vanessa, I'm back."

No answer.

"Vanessa?" Her voice echoed in the empty room. Shrugging her shoulders, Nicole disrobed, set the shower to the intense spraying power she wanted and stepped under the sluicing water.

**

A couple of hours later, after her shower and breakfast, Nicole decided to wander over to *Wishes*. Josephine would be waiting for news about yesterday's trip to Ingonish, and maybe she'd find Vanessa there.

"Nicole." Josephine greeted her as she entered the shop. "My, my, someone looks as if they had an interesting evening."

A blush spread across Nicole's face.

"It's okay, you don't have to say a word. Just tell me if you found the diamonds?"

Relieved at the change of subject, Nicole replied, "Yes. And they are so beautiful that it's almost a shame to have to give them up."

"Ha. You're best rid of them as far as I'm concerned. Things should work out now, all you have to do is give them to the stalker so he'll leave you alone."

"I hope so."

A customer wandered into the store, and Josephine excused herself. Nicole took the time to explore the bookstore in a way she hadn't before. There was so much to look at that it was a couple of hours and three cappuccino's later before she realized that Ian should be there soon. They'd arranged to meet once he was finished filming. No sooner had she thought of him then the door swung open, and he stepped into the store.

Their eyes connected.

The phone rang.

Chaos ensued.

"Nicole!" Josephine shrieked. "The phone. You need to come to the phone. Now."

Shooting a worried glance at Ian, she crossed to the counter and took the phone from a white-faced Josephine. Hesitantly, she put the cool plastic to her ear and swallowed. Something was not right. "Hello?"

Silence greeted her.

Clearing her throat, she tried again. "Hello."

"This had better be you, Nicole."

"It is." Nicole recognized the voice, and her throat clenched with fear. She moved the phone away from her ear enough for Ian to listen to the conversation. The warmth of his breath blowing on her cheek and the heat of his body brushing against her gave comfort.

"I think you know why I'm calling."

Nicole nodded, but realized he couldn't see the action through the phone, so she quickly added. "You want the diamonds."

A deep-throated chuckle drifted over the phone. "Oh, yes, the diamonds. And I know you have them, in spite of your protestations to the contrary. A little birdie told me."

She frowned and glanced at Ian, who shrugged his shoulders. "A little birdie? I'm not sure what you mean."

"No, you don't. But don't worry, I'm going to enlighten you. You see, I've made a new friend. And such a beautiful friend she is." The sound of lips smacking together drifted over the phone. "She's almost as beautiful as you."

Nicole couldn't make any sense of the stalker's taunts. "You still don't know what I'm talking about, do you?" His deep, smug laughter filtered through the phone and Nicole shivered.

"Think. Are you missing someone?"

Nicole's oblivious state ended in a split second of awareness. "Vanessa." She whispered and felt Ian stiffen beside her. Their gazes locked a look of fear.

"Yes. She was so easy to grab. Now she's mine."

Ian tensed and his knuckles turned white as he clenched the counter top. Nicole felt the force as tremors of anger shivered through his body. Terror for her friend pulsed through Nicole's veins, and she gripped the phone in an attempt to remain calm. Vanessa's life depended on clear thinking.

"Please don't hurt her. It's me you want, not her."

The stalker, Gary, laughed quietly. "I only want what belongs to me. Any other enjoyments I experience along the way are just a bonus."

Before Nicole could react, Ian jerked the phone from her. Fear for his daughter and rage at the stalker's threats pushed him close to the edge. Nicole worried that he would lose his temper and force the stalker to hurt Vanessa. She tried to grab the phone back, but his grip was like a vice, and her attempts to wrestle it from him were as effective as trying to fell a mighty oak with a nail file. His eyes glazed, and even though he looked at Nicole, she sensed that he didn't see her at all.

His voice shook and was so low that Nicole and Josephine leaned closer to hear him. "If you harm my daughter in any way, I will drain my bank accounts, call in every favor owed to me—I know some very powerful people—and I'll track you down to make sure you pay in kind for everything you do to her."

"Ian Calder, I presume. The great actor. I love your movies. I'm mortified that Vanessa is your daughter, but I'm sure you understand. She was in the right place at the right time, and she knows the wrong people. Or person, I should say."

Nicole watched the play of emotion on Ian's face and the ever-present guilt rose in her stomach. Vanessa was in danger. How many times would people close to her get hurt? Even now, Ian's gaze pinned her in silent accusation. She backed up from the phone, instinct urging that she run, as fast and far as possible.

The reassuring pat of Josephine's hand on her shoulder steadied Nicole and halted her flight. "It'll be fine, Nicole, I've seen it in the cards."

Nicole didn't get to reply, because Ian shoved the phone at her. "He wants to talk to you."

The knowing glance he sent her let Nicole know that he'd been aware of her moment of guilt that almost led to flight. She wouldn't have left, but Ian didn't know that. First, she gets his daughter involved with a murdering madman, then he sees her about to run out the door. He must have been ready to murder her himself. No time to explain that she'd only been temporarily brain-fuddled. She took the phone. "Hello?"

Ian leaned close enough to listen to the conversation. "Time for fooling around is over. I want what belongs to me."

"The diamonds." Nicole barely managed to whisper. "Yes, the diamonds that you tried to keep for yourself."

His voice turned nasty with barely controlled fury. "Give me the diamonds, and I'll let your friend live. I might even let you live, bitch."

She trembled as the stalker's words battered her mind. Her brain refused to function and Ian tore the phone from her hand, effectively putting an end to anything she was about to say. He barked out the words, "We'll get them for you, just give us twenty-four hours."

He waited while Gary made some remark.

"It'll take twenty-four hours, because that's how long it'll take to go get them. If you want your diamonds, you'll wait."

Gary must have made another threat because a flicker of fear reflected in Ian's eyes, but he held it together long enough to finish the call. "Same time, same place, tomorrow."

He set the phone back in its cradle, and his shoulders sagged. Nicole's heart went out to him, but she had no idea how to comfort him, especially since Vanessa was in trouble because of her. She was probably the last person Ian wanted to talk to. With a ragged breath, he straightened his shoulders and looked at his watch. "We have until three tomorrow."

"But why don't we just give them to him now?"

Deep blue eyes swirling with fathomless emotions burned into her. "Because I don't trust a word the man says. You heard him, he said he'd let Vanessa live, and he might let you live. He wants you to deliver the diamonds."

"Me."

"Yes. And that's not going to happen because he'll kill you. I know it. We've twenty-four hours to find Vanessa on our own. He'll think we're going to get the diamonds from somewhere, but we'll be looking for Vanessa."

"Dear God. What have I got you and Vanessa into?"

"Nicole, this is not your fault. And don't you even think about running this time. He has Vanessa and if you run, he'll follow, but he'll kill her first."

"I know. I wasn't going to run. Believe me."

His gaze bore into her. "I know. I trust you."

"Has anyone wondered how he knew to call here?" Josephine questioned.

Nobody spoke. The implication was clear. He must be watching them from close by.

"Maybe we should call the police," Josephine suggested.

"No. He said no police." Ian tore his gaze from Nicole and pinned Josephine with the same intensity. "If you had caller display, we could have found out where he was calling from."

His accusation raised the tension in the room. In the distance, a foghorn sounded its lonely echo across the ocean, while boats gently rocking against the wooden docks drifted their sounds into the tense atmosphere.

Tears filled Josephine's eyes. "I'm sorry."

Nicole felt sorry for her friend. She placed a comforting hand on Josephine's shoulder and glared at Ian. "There's no need to get mad at Josephine, all she did was answer the phone."

Ian thrust out his hands, palms up and vented his anger. "Well, what do you expect? Everyone has caller display these days. What kind of a hick town is this where someone still has a rotary phone, for God's sake?" He pinned the offensive phone with the full force of his enraged glare, as if willing it to change from a dial phone to a more updated push button with caller display.

Nicole knew he was redirecting his frustration, and her heart went out to him, but she didn't know how to comfort him.

"I can find out where he was calling from." Josephine's words cracked like a cannon and had as much effect as a cannon shot. Ian stopped mid-pace and strode across the floor to grab Josephine by the arms and shake her.

"What did you say?"

"Ian, let her go. You're hurting her."

Nicole worried for her friend. Ian had shaken Josephine's braid loose and her face had become an unflattering shade of white.

Ian released her. "Sorry."

"It's all right." Josephine rubbed the circulation into her arms as she backed up a step from Ian's towering presence. "My sister works for the phone company in Ingonish. She can look at the records and see where the call came from."

Nicole reasoned. "It's probably the first thing the guys from the Major Crime Unit will do."

"My goodness, how did they get involved?"

"Oh, that's right, you don't know. It seems that the sperm sample they found at the lighthouse matched the DNA of an escaped felon, so the Major Crime Unit is automatically called in to the investigation."

"But that's great news, isn't it? I mean, at least they know who he is."

Ian stared at Josephine. "You knew about Nicole's stalker?"

"Yes."

Ian snorted and shrugged his shoulders. "Isn't that nice, everyone knew before me.

"Ian."

Nicole started to protest, but Josephine interrupted her. "You two can settle this later. We need to find Vanessa and get her out of the clutches of that madman. You saw him the other night, what did he look like?"

Nicole tried to recall the face peering out from behind her fichus. She shivered. "All I can remember are his eyes. I remember how the light from the room reflected in his eyes, but they had no reflection, they were so dark. Black. That's the only thing I remember about him, is how black his eyes were."

"Black eyes." Josephine frowned. "Black eyes." Suddenly she

smacked a palm to her forehead. "Of course, now I know. Ian, remember your first day in my store when you bought the red candles?"

"Yes, but what do candles have to do with anything?"

"Not the candles, but the strange man that bolted out of the store."

Understanding lit Ian's face. "Yes, I remember him. But why do you think he's the guy we're after?"

"I know because I looked into his eyes—they were black. The toneless depth of them sent shivers down my spine, and I was relieved to see him go."

Nicole broke in excitedly. "Yes, that's exactly how I felt when I looked into his eyes. It could be the same man."

"Great, we know what he looks like, but we still have to find him. Josephine, get your sister on the phone and find out where the call came from. Nicole, you and I need to hit the local inns, hotels, motels, B&B's, or anywhere else he may be staying."

"I don't like leaving Josephine alone," Nicole said. "He called here because he knows she's a friend. What if he tries something? You know, to make a point or something."

"I'll call Jacob. Once he knows what's going on, nothing will keep him away. And you're forgetting Sumo." Ian gestured to the corner where the Rottweiler lay watching the proceedings.

Nicole nodded. "Okay, where do we start?"

Chapter Twenty

Ian shielded his eyes against the sun and searched the street, hoping against hope that the man they were looking for would somehow materialize from thin air. No such luck. They'd checked out every place that rented rooms and were no further ahead than when they'd started two hours ago. The afternoon sun shifted across the sky and would soon touch the horizon and give way to night. Ian feared that today would give way to tomorrow, and they'd be no closer to finding Vanessa.

"Ian, maybe we should go back to *Wishes* and see if Josephine has any news."

Ian nodded, feeling fear eating its way through his stomach. He turned to Nicole, but no words would come, so he shrugged his shoulders and made his way across the street. He didn't want Nicole to see the tears that threatened to fall. Damn, he felt useless.

Josephine and Jacob must have been watching for them, because they greeted Ian and Nicole at the door with expressions of worry and anxiety, while Sumo ran over to give his usual effusive greeting.

"We've been waiting. Hurry, come inside." Josephine waved them in and gave a cursory glance up and down the street as if making sure no one was watching.

"You found something out, didn't you?" Nicole breathed as she gave Sumo a hug.

"Yes. Once I explained to my sister what was going on, she made this her top priority. You'll never guess where the call came from. Oh, I'm so sorry, I don't mean to make you guess,

I'm just so excited."

"Come on, woman, spill the beans," Jacob growled anxiously.

"Okay. The call came from the lighthouse," Josephine declared and then folded her arms in triumph.

"The lighthouse. My God, do you think that's where he's holding Vanessa?" Nicole couldn't believe the solution would be so easy.

"No. No, that would be too dangerous." Ian paced and considered the possibilities. "But I'd guess he's probably staying near the lighthouse. Are there any inns or hotels around there that we missed?"

"None that I know of." Nicole answered.

"No, there's nothing up that way," Josephine confirmed.

"Damn, damn, damn." Ian swore and banged his fist into his hand.

Josephine spoke, her voice breaking the tension. "Jacob, you've lived here your entire life. You should know the area well enough to have an idea."

He squinted, a frown creasing his forehead. Then his eyes lit with certain knowledge.

"The caves."

"Caves. What caves?" Nicole asked the question that was on the tip of Ian's tongue.

"About a quarter mile down the coast, just north of the trail that leads from the lighthouse to the beach, there are some caves. No one goes there because there's not anything much of interest, but that would make it the perfect hiding place."

Excited, Josephine's voice rose a pitch. "Nicole, you and Ian didn't find anyone matching the stalker's description at any place in town. If he were staying out of town, he'd have a long drive to get here, and I doubt he'd want to be that far away. I have a feeling he'd want to keep a close eye on you."

"Yes, I suppose that makes sense," Nicole agreed. "Well, it makes sense that he's staying in one of the caves."

Jacob nodded his head in agreement. "But even if he is, we

can't just go barreling in with pistols flashing."

"What are you thinking, Jacob?" Ian figured the old guy was smarter than he let on, so if he had a comment to make, they'd better listen.

"If he's in a cave, he's well positioned for a stand-off. He'd hear us coming and kill Vanessa before we could get to her." He shot an apologetic look at Ian. "Sorry, but that's how I see the situation."

"All right, so what do we do?" Ian asked.

"Instead of checking more hotels, we check out the restaurants, grocery stores, and variety stores. Any place he could have bought food. We can see if he's been in recently, or said anything to anyone that might give us a clue."

"Yes. If we know where he buys supplies, we can watch for him and check out the caves while the bastard is in town," Josephine suggested.

"Josephine?" Jacob looked shocked. "You swore."

"If we don't find this guy you'll hear me doing a lot more of it. So, everyone agrees, we check out the local eateries and grocery stores?"

Ian tapped his fingers against his temple, concentration furrowing his brow. "I think that's a good idea. I don't know what else to do." Resignation threaded his voice.

Tears filled Nicole's eyes. "I'm so sorry."

Ian felt for her, but there was no time to give comfort. "Nicole, we have less than a day to find Vanessa. We have to focus on that. Let's split up. Jacob and Josephine you take the east end of town, Nicole and I'll take the west."

"This might seem like a stupid question, but why don't we call the police?" Jacob asked.

"The stalker said he'd kill Vanessa if we did." Ian's voice cracked. "The son of a bitch said he'd kill my daughter." He wrenched his hands and took a deep breath. Now was not the time to lose control.

His words induced a deep silence. Wiping his hand across his face, Ian asked, "I don't suppose anyone has a cell phone, do they?" He shook his head at the across the board denial. "How do you people survive around here? Whatever. Just call me at this number if you find out anything." He wrote his cell phone number on a piece of paper and handed it to Jacob.

With subdued *Wishes* of good luck, the foursome left the store.

***

Water dripped a constant staccato in the far recesses of the dim cave. Gary traversed the terrain with an ease of familiarity as he reached for the lantern inside the entrance. Striking a match, he lit the lantern and used it to light his way to where a winding tunnel opened into a natural cavern of irregular proportions. The hiss of the lantern echoed in the small closed area of the place he had called home for the last while. The meager light glowed against the damp walls and caused shadows to dance in a macabre display.

A sound from the back of the cave reached Gary`s ears and he grinned in anticipation. The woman moaned and struggled against her bonds. It was futile. Much like the moth beating itself against the beckoning light. The bitch would continue to struggle—until her death. And her death was a forgone conclusion, though he was the only one aware of that fact.

Gary gave free rein to his rising laughter, and it bounced off the cave walls. He was powerful. Soon he would be rich. He'd have his diamonds, and if all went according to plan, he'd have two women to slake his passions on before killing them both. His only problem was how to kill them. Possibilities abounded. He could make them watch while he raped them one after the other and then peel their skin with his knife—oh, how he loved his knife.

Subconsciously, he caressed the bone handle of the hunting knife he wore tucked in the waist of his jeans, its presence hidden by his shirt. His fingers carefully slid over the sharp edges of the blade, the feel of steel cutting into flesh arousing him. He smiled and lifted his finger to his mouth to suck blood from the fresh wound.

He could let them starve while he watched them slowly die, all the while satisfying his needs on their bodies. But no, that would take too long. Once he had the diamonds, he needed to disappear. He'd have to kill them quickly after he'd satisfied himself.

Stepping across the uneven rocks, Gary lifted the light to expose the prone body of his prisoner. After knocking her out last night, he'd carried her here and thrown her onto the floor of the cave. After tying her up, he'd cut her clothes from her body so she lay nude before him. She was beautiful with her full breasts and rounded hips, and he'd let his hands roam her body until she'd moaned and shifted. When she woke, her eyes had filled with confusion, and he'd done nothing to enlighten her. Instead, he'd run his finger across her lips, down to her breasts and to the most secret part of her that throbbed with warmth. Thrusting his finger into her, he laughed at her struggles and warned her to lay still or much worse would follow.

Eyes wide with terror, she'd obeyed him and lay still while he explored her body. But nothing else. No, he wanted to wait until he had both women and the diamonds in his possession. Then he could let loose with his imagination.

Presently, she stared at him as if waiting for him to debase her further, but he wasn't in the mood. He was hungry, and the food he'd brought from the local deli weighed heavy in his hand, the aroma of roast beef making his mouth water. Smiling, he sat down beside the woman, unwrapped the sandwich, and sank his teeth into the crusty bread. Her eyes followed the sandwich from wrapper to mouth, and he heard her stomach growl. He reveled in the absolute power of life and death, but even headier was controlling a person's every waking emotion and sense. He reached out and pinched a nipple for the reaction. When she squealed and squirmed, the stalker took another bite of his sandwich and thanked God for allowing him such a fulfilling life.

Finishing his sandwich, Gary brushed his hands on his pants and stood. Noticing the tears that filled the eyes of the woman, he snorted and kicked her. "You don't actually think I'd waste food on you. Why bother, you'll be dead tomorrow anyway. Along with your friend."

Eyes wide with fright, the woman struggled. He laughed at the futile effort and went to lie down on his sleeping bag where he drifted off to sleep envisioning the fulfillment of his dreams. Tomorrow couldn't come soon enough.

***

Jacob was talking to Ollie the butcher while Josephine inhaled the scents of roast beef, bacon, mustard, pickles, and fresh baked bread that filled the store. Jacob's voice rose and fell while Ollie's usual cheery face curved into a frown of concentration. With a handshake between them, Jacob walked over to Josephine.

"Well, what did you find out?"

"It seems our stalker has formed quite a liking for Jessie's sandwiches. He's been here every day for lunch."

"That's great news. We wait for him to show up tomorrow and keep an eye on him while Ian and Nicole search the caves"

"Maybe." Jacob took her arm and led her outside. "But what if he doesn't show up tomorrow?"

"He has to eat."

"Yes, but he may plan on grabbing the diamonds and running. Food'll be the last thing on his mind."

"I guess."

Jacob put his arm around her shoulder and gave an awkward but comforting hug. "If it's all we've got, then come tomorrow, we'll be waitin' right here for him."

"And if he doesn't come?"

"We'll figure something out. We've got until three o'clock tomorrow."

"Maybe Nicole and Ian had better luck. We've done all we

can for now."

Sighing, she looked at Jacob and noticed how the stress was wearing him down. His eyes lacked their usual sparkle, the corners of his mouth turned down with weary resignation, and he held his jaw clenched tight. She'd never seen him do that before, but then, they'd never been in this kind of situation.

She touched his arm. "Jacob, there's nothing we can do. We need to touch base with Nicole and Ian and get some dinner."

"Damn! I feel so useless."

"I know. Let's go to the store. We'll call Ian's cell phone."

Ian answered on the first ring. "Hello?"

"Ian, it's Jacob. We found out where the scum buys his lunch."

Josephine fiddled with some books while she listened to the one-sided conversation.

"Yep. Every day. No sense in us looking elsewhere. Any luck on your end? What else can we do to help?"

"Dad-blast, that's too bad. Okay, first thing in the morning."

He hung up the phone. "They've got a couple more places to check out. Seems the stalker picked up some items at the hardware store. Flashlight, rope, and the likes."

"That would confirm that he's in the caves."

"Maybe. Ian and Nicole are going to take a look, but as soon as it's dark they'll have to stop looking."

"But why? We know that's where he is, why can't we look all night if need be?"

"No sense. It'll just put Vanessa in danger. We'd need flashlights, so we'd stand out like fireflies in the dark."

"But."

"No. It's time to eat and get some sleep. Tomorrow's a busy day." He laid his hand on her arm, and his face reflected feelings of care and love. "Josie, I know this is not the time, but the present situation kinda makes a person take stock of things." He cleared his throat. "You know I care about you, don't you?"

"Yes, Jacob. I know." She smiled at him and before she knew

it, Jacob leaned over and planted a kiss on her lips. She was stunned—at first—then the effect of the kiss worked its way into her limbs and befuddled her brain so she couldn't think of anything but how wonderful it felt.

Jacob ended the kiss as suddenly as he had initiated it. "There. Now let's get something to eat. I'm starving."

"Me too, Jacob." She spoke her thoughts before she lost her nerve. "I don't want to be alone tonight." There, she'd said it. The rest was up to Jacob. Please, God, I hope I didn't just make a fool of myself.

"Me neither."

Josephine's mind ran the gamut from whether or not she had enough food in the house to whether or not her bed sheets were clean. Then she realized that none of it mattered, they'd make do as long as they had each other.

***

Ian paced the floor of his cabin restlessly. "Damn. I can't just sit here and do nothing."

Nicole placed a ham sandwich and a glass of milk on the dining room table. "Listen Ian, we already decided there's nothing we can do for now. We can't see in the dark, and we'd only make ourselves a target by wandering around with flashlights. We know where he buys lunch, so Josephine and Jacob can stake that out tomorrow while we search the caves."

"Yeah, I know. They'll call if they see him, or there's any kind of news." He sighed and bit into the sandwich. "But all I can think about is Vanessa in the clutches of that maniac." He gulped some of the milk.

"I'm sorry. I know you say it's not my fault, but it is. If I hadn't come to Solitary Cove, the stalker wouldn't have either, and Vanessa would be safe." Tears welled in her eyes. "And if we hadn't left her alone."

"Nicole." He rested his hands on her shoulders. "You have to stop blaming yourself. It's not your fault. In fact, you amaze me. The anguish you must have felt losing your husband under such circumstances and then moving halfway across the country to a strange town. Taking control of your life with such strength of character, that I feel shame for the way I've lived my life."

"You give me too much credit. I only did what I had to." She yawned. "But thanks."

"Come on, let's get you to bed. You're exhausted."

"What about you?"

"I don't think I can sleep. I'm too worried."

"I'm not going to sleep without you."

"Oh." He measured her determined look and then shrugged his shoulders. "I have an idea."

He led her onto the deck, stretched out onto one of the lounge chairs and pulled her into his lap. Nicole adjusted her body to fit with his and relaxed as his warmth mingled with hers. She fell asleep while Ian stayed awake cradling her in his arms. He cried silent tears for his daughter, hoping she was warm and comfortable, praying they found her before it was too late.

Chapter Twenty-One

Bang. Bang. Bang. The sound pounded in Josephine's head, and she drew her pillow up to smother the noise. It didn't help. Slowly waking up, she realized that something was different. An unusual weight stretched across her stomach and in one blinding flash last night's memories rushed back.

Bang. Bang. Bang. Again with the banging. Now that she was fully awake, she realized that someone was knocking on her shop door downstairs.

Not quite awake, but obviously disturbed by the sound, Jacob mumbled, "Make them go away." He then covered his head with a pillow and proceeded to snore.

Josephine smiled as she reached for the robe. Making sure she was presentable, she went downstairs, turning on lights as she went. It was early enough in the morning that the sun hadn't risen over the horizon. She prayed it wasn't bad news as opened the door to Ian and Nicole.

"Nicole. Ian. Come in. Help yourself to cappuccino." She waved them to the machine that automatically produced the elixir each morning. Her guests did.

"Oh, that tastes so good." Nicole proceeded to down half the cup of foamy liquid.

The sound of someone clomping down the stairs interrupted any conversation. Josephine had forgotten about Jacob. She blushed. "I guess a lot has happened since yesterday."

Nicole quietly remarked, "It's about time."

Jacob only cleared his throat in embarrassment as Josephine offered him some cappuccino.

"Sure, but I'll get my own, so why don't you sit yourself down and let me bring you a cup." He gave her shoulder a light push, forcing her to sit in the wingback chair. Shuffling his feet, he mumbled to himself about how he wasn't an old man and could take care of himself as well as those he cared about.

Josephine didn't realize she was crying until Nicole waved a tissue in front of her face. Embarrassed, but grateful, she quickly took the tissue, wiped her tears, and then tucked it away where Jacob couldn't see it. After all, she didn't want him to see her cry, because then he'd think she was some silly woman who couldn't control her emotions. She smiled at him as he handed her a cappuccino and then sat on the arm of her chair, his own arm draped across the back.

"So, is the plan the same?" Jacob asked.

Ian replied. "I guess. Unless you've thought of anything since last night."

"Afraid not. I wish I had. This plan is shaky at best," Jacob confessed.

"I know." Ian frowned. "There are too many variables. What if he doesn't show up for food? What if he does show up, but doesn't stay long enough for you to call the police? What if he calls us before three and wants the diamonds? We need a better plan, dammit!"

"Maybe we need help." Nicole suggested.

Ian narrowed his eyes and scrutinized her. "What do you mean?"

Intertwining her fingers and rubbing her hands around each other, Nicole lowered her voice and said, "Maybe we should tell the police we found the diamonds and let them help."

"No. I understand what you're saying, but we can't take that chance. We only call the police if he shows up at the deli for lunch. Other than that, we're on our own.

"But, what if you show up at the caves, and he's still there? He'd have Vanessa at his mercy," Josephine said. "I hate playing devil's advocate, but you should be prepared for every eventuality."

"Josephine has a point. He's in control if he's holed up in one of the caves when we find him," Nicole reasoned.

Ian frowned. "But that doesn't stop us from searching for signs that he's even in the area. You said he called from the lighthouse." He asked Josephine, who nodded in affirmation. "Then we start our search there. We'll have a better chance of finding Vanessa when he leaves—if he leaves—to come to the deli."

Nicole agreed. "Yes. And since most of the trails from the caves lead back up to the main one by the lighthouse, we can hide in the lighthouse and see which direction he comes from."

Ian gave her a quick hug. "That's a good idea. Nicole and I will be at the lighthouse, while you two are at the deli. You'll have to call us from the phone at the deli if he shows up. If Nicole and I see what direction he comes from we'll know the general area to search. If we somehow miss him, you two call and let us know he's there. At least we'll know it's safe to search, even if we didn't see the direction he came from. That'll just mean that we have a larger area to search and less time to do it in."

Nicole spoke hesitantly. "What if..."

Ian raised his hand. "I know. What if he doesn't show up? Then we have to get back here by three for his phone call and play the game his way."

Ian struggled with the matter of fact words, and Josephine could only imagine the struggle he had controlling his emotions under such circumstances.

A knock at the door put an abrupt end to any further planning. Perplexed, because it was nowhere near time to open, Josephine moved to the front door. Pulling her robe tighter and smoothing her not yet brushed hair, she opened to door.

"Josephine, I'm sorry to disturb you so early." Corporal Moody tipped his hat and turned to a man standing beside him. "I'd like to introduce Inspector Patrick from the Major Crimes Unit."

Dressed in a gray suit with a perfectly matched tie, polished shoes, and neatly trimmed hair, the man inclined his head. Josephine extended her hand and found it enfolded in a grip of strength. She winced. No concession given for being a woman. She didn't know if that was a good thing or not.

"What can I do for you two?"

"We're looking for Nicole and that actor fella."

"His name is Ian."

"Yes, him."

Corporal Moody was about to say something, but was abruptly cut off by Inspector Patrick, who asked, "Have you seen them?"

"Why, yes. They're here."

The inspector's eyes narrowed speculatively. "I'd like to speak with them, please."

Josephine hesitated long enough for Inspector Patrick to notice. He clenched his jaw and stepped into the store. Ian, Nicole, and Jacob stood to face the two lawmen.

"What can we do for you?" Ian asked as his arm came to rest on Nicole's shoulder.

Inspector Patrick noticed that gesture as well. Josephine decided that not much got past him, and they had better be careful, or he'd put a wrench into their plans.

"I'd like to know what's going on."

Ian shrugged. "I have no idea what you mean, Inspector."

With a sigh of exasperation, Inspector Patrick said, "Let me spell it out clearly, I'm here to do a job, and I can do that job much easier if I don't have civilians getting in my way."

Ian kept his cool. "Oh, I see. And how exactly have we been getting in your way?" His blue eyes had taken on a calculating hue, and Josephine could have sworn he was enjoying the confrontation.

"My men started questioning some of the locals this morning and, guess what? It seems you've beaten us to it already."

"Sure, we asked a few questions around town yesterday."

"Well, stop. Stay out of our way. We're here to find Gary and recover the diamonds. It's our job."

Ian's jaw clenched, and Josephine worried that he was going to pop the guy or something.

"I know your intentions are in the right place, but you're just going to mess things up. Please, leave the professionals to handle the situation."

"But..." Josephine sputtered, afraid that their involvement would threaten Vanessa's life. Ian jabbed his elbow into her ribs. "You're right. We'll stay out of it from now on," he conceded.

"Good. I'm glad to see that you can cooperate. We'll be mounting our own investigation into the whereabouts of the convict and the diamonds. Hopefully, we'll have things wrapped up and be out of here without a lot of hassle. In the meantime, Miss Warner, you should stay in your room at the inn, and I'll post one of my men at your door for safety."

Oh, no. That would put a glitch in their plans. Josephine panicked trying to think of a way around the problem, but Corporal Moody was the one who offered the solution.

"No worries there, Inspector, I'll be watching her personally to make sure she's safe. That way your men are free to do what they do best." His tone was slightly sarcastic. Fortunately, no one but Josephine and maybe Jacob heard it. They'd known the officer long enough to sense the tension in his usually calm composure.

"Good idea, Moody. Fine. Now I've got work to do. I'll let you know when we've got it all wrapped up."

No one bothered informing him that they already had the diamonds, or that they had a very good idea where Gary was holed up. Inspector Patrick left and silence filled the room. Corporal Moody cleared his throat and glared at Josephine. She squirmed. Damn, he knew her well enough to know she couldn't lie. She shot a desperate look at the others, hoping someone would say something.

"Josephine, and you too, Jacob. I may not be a big city inspector, but I do know the people of my town well enough to know when I'm being lied to. What's going on?"

No one spoke.

"I'm waiting." He crossed his arms and leaned on the counter.

"Nothing's going on here, Officer." Ian stepped to within a foot of Corporal Moody and fixed his gaze. "Just some friends getting together for morning coffee."

"I see. Josephine, is that true?"

It wasn't her place to say. Vanessa's life was on the line and that was the only thing that enabled Josephine to look Corporal Moody right in the eyes and lie.

"He's telling the truth."

Narrowing his eyes, Corporal Moody looked at each of them as if measuring their sincerity. Then he smiled. "Well, since I'm official bodyguard for a day or two, I suppose I'll be having that cup of coffee with you."

The group held a collective breath, but Ian saved the situation with his quick thinking.

"Great. I feel so much better with you keeping an eye on Nicole. Not that your other officers haven't been doing a great job." Ian took hold of Nicole's arm and led her to the door. "Why don't you have that cup of coffee with Jacob and Josephine. Nicole and I just have a couple of things to pick up, and then I'll take her right back to her room. You can meet her over there after your coffee, and I can go to work knowing she's in safe hands."

Not waiting for Corporal Moody's reaction, they left. As the door closed behind them, Jacob snickered. Josephine shot him a warning look and laid her hand on Corporal Moody's arm before he could follow Nicole and Ian.

"Would you like coffee or cappuccino, Corporal?"

Chapter Twenty-Two

T he morning sun arched above the waves of the ocean and began its ascent. Nicole turned her face up to feel its warmth. Her back ached, and her emotions felt taut like the string of a bow at full draw. They'd searched the cliffs and trails in the immediate area of the lighthouse with no luck. But they weren't giving up, because as far as Nicole was concerned the stalker must have left some clue behind.

Shielding her eyes with her hand, she scanned the trail for Ian. When they'd split up, he had warned her to be quiet and careful. The point wasn't to find the cave, just any sign giving a clue to the direction the stalker may have gone. It was important to keep their distance, as long as there was a chance the stalker was in the cave with Vanessa. They couldn't warn him of their presence.

They'd separated, each one heading a different direction.

That had been three hours ago.

Now it was almost noon, and since Nicole hadn't heard differently, she assumed Ian had found nothing. She swiped at a buzzing in her ear, cursing all mosquitoes. The little bugger wouldn't give up, he kept coming back for blood, and it was in the middle of her gyrations to smack the pesky bug that she saw something.

A mere shadow of a trail where there should be nothing and a broken stem of a Nova Scotia wild rose bush adorned with vivid pink blooms. To make sure, she stepped closer and gently brushed aside the broken branch. Yes! Very faint on the ground, was the outline of a trail winding through the bush and down to the shore below. It would be a dangerous trail to follow, its main advantage being how well hidden it was.

Joy leapt in Nicole's heart, and she hoped they were one step closer to finding Vanessa. Maybe everything would be all right. She prayed so. They had to find Vanessa, and they had to find her alive. Brushing a stray leaf from her hair, Nicole mentally marked the area and quickly stumbled her way back to the main trail and up to the lighthouse. She had to find Ian.

***

Ian slapped another branch from his face and cursed the forest. They were no closer to finding Vanessa. Lunchtime was approaching, which meant time was running out. If they didn't see Gary going to town or get some clue to what direction they should be searching, Vanessa was lost.

Worry and fear tore at Ian, making him lose concentration long enough to step on a wobbly rock, lose his balance, and almost topple over the cliff top. He slid over sharp rock and rough terrain, his hands grasping for any handhold that would stop his precarious fall to the rocks below. Finally, his fingers brushed on the branch of a fallen tree. Clasping frantically, he was able to stop his descent and find a foothold in the crumbling edge of the cliff. So intent was he on pulling himself to safety that he wasn't immediately aware of the sound of someone coming up the trail.

Shit. What if it was Gary? Hastily, with supreme effort, he pulled himself up and sunk behind the nearest tree. Peering out between the branches, he searched the lower trail. A flash of blue jeans and a tee shirt flickered among the trees, and Ian realized it was Nicole. He decided to wait for her so they could plan what to do next. Obviously, they weren't going to find anything here.

Just then, another flash caught his attention through the trees. Nicole was halfway between him and the shore. The flash that caught his eye was at the line where shore met forest —and was headed their direction. Oh, dear, God. It had to be

Gary, right on the same trail as Nicole. He had to get to her first.

As quietly as possible, but with urgent speed, Ian raced down the overgrown trail. His track shoes slid on pebbles and twigs, while he grabbed at trees and branches to keep his balance. His descent brought him closer to shore, and he hoped that the roar of the waves would cover any sounds he made. Careening around a bend and bursting into a small clearing, he came face to face with Nicole, whose face registered shock at the abrupt entrance. Before she could speak, Ian put his hand over her mouth and dragged her into the densest area of the forest.

Although her eyes registered reproach at his high-handed methods, Nicole remained quiet. Ian's breath rasped raggedly from his instinctive flight, and he tried to calm his breathing. His heart beat against Nicole's back as he held her cradled between his knees on the ground. The softness of her body prompted him to wrap his arms around her and pull her closer.

Minutes passed and the urgency of the situation fizzled until Ian thought that maybe he'd overreacted. Risking the sound, he whispered in Nicole's ear.

"I saw a man at the bottom of the trail just below you, but he should have passed here by now." He hesitated, not sure what to do. He didn't want to jump the gun and give away their presence.

"I don't think he'll come this way."

"What do you mean?"

Nicole shifted her rear to kneel on the ground facing Ian. "I found a trail, and even though it was faint, it's been used lately. It leads from the shore, but veers off past the lighthouse rather than up this way. If you saw Gary, I bet that's the way he went."

"Show me." Ian didn't waste time on words or explanations. He followed Nicole as she backtracked and headed into the woods where she showed him the faint trail.

He fingered the broken shrubbery and examined the pathway. "You're right, it has been used recently. Probably by our stalker. I don't think I would have seen the path, as out of the way as it is, so I'm glad your eyes are sharp."

"Thank a mosquito. I never would have found the path on my own."

"Sounds interesting. You can tell me the story later, but now I need to think." Vanessa's life was in his hands, he couldn't fail her again. Damn it, he was no hero, he wasn't even a good person, who did he think he was trying to save his daughter? He should have let the police know what was going on.

He didn't realize he'd spoken out loud until Nicole's voice cut into his meandering.

"Ian. You haven't failed Vanessa. You may not have been the best father, you're only human, but the important thing is that you love her, and you want what's best for her.

And as for not being a good person, if I had to put up with what you do, I'd have gone crazy by now. You have no privacy, every move you make, every word you speak, is twisted into something else and then printed in some tabloid. You treat your fans with respect and consideration, which is more than I can say for how they treat you. You are a good man, an honest man, and a man who loves his daughter. We'll save her, I promise."

Nicole stood with hands on hips and the light of indignation glowed amber in her eyes. A lump lodged in Ian's chest, threatening to explode in an unmanly display of emotion, but he needed to hold it together. He smiled. "No one's ever stood up for me before. I think I like having my own personal hero."

"Oh, Ian, even with all your money and fame, I have a feeling that your life has been sorely lacking."

Ian shrugged. His voice lowered to a husky rasp. "Let's get back to Vanessa. We can only assume the man I saw was the stalker and that he took this trail into town. If we're wrong though."

"I know."

"Do you think we should wait to hear from Jacob and Josephine? You know, just to make sure it was Gary on his way to town."

Ian considered the time they had left as well as their options. "No. I think we have to assume, at least hope, it was him, and go search the caves."

"Okay, let's do it, but maybe you should call Jacob and Josephine to let them know we think he's on his way. They can call us if he shows up."

"Good idea." Ian made the call, letting them know Gary should be there in about ten minutes, if it was him, and to give them a call if he showed up.

"They said to be careful. Come on, let's go." Ian took Nicole's hand. The two of them practically ran down the rest of the trail and came quickly to the ocean's shore. A set of footprints in the sand between the intermittent rocks, drew Ian's attention.

"Look, there."

Nicole's gaze followed the direction he pointed. "They have to be his."

"Let's hope so. Come on, but keep quiet in case we're wrong, and he's still here."

The footprints led them away from the path, and the opposite direction of the lighthouse perched upon the cliff they'd left behind. Ian silently thanked the powers above for making such an obvious trail and began to hope for a swift and easy resolution. But as fate was wont to do, his hopes were dashed and stomped into the hard, smooth rock that suddenly comprised the ground they walked on. Hard rock that gave away no secrets and no footprints.

"Shit!" Ian frantically searched the surrounding area for another sign. Stretching the length of the beach, as far as he could see, were nooks and crannies cut into the rocky cliffs, any one of them could be the entrance to a cave. Small, large, oblong, round, tall, short, there were so many that Ian's brain whirled in confusion.

"Oh, Ian. We can't search them all."

"I know," he snapped. "Sorry, but I know." He softened his tone, tried to regain some perspective on the matter. "You know, the other night at dinner, Vanessa and I straightened out a lot of misunderstandings. She told me she trusted me, Nicole." His legs were shaking, and he was afraid of falling apart, but Nicole stepped in close and wrapped her arms around him, giving him strength.

"It's okay. Come on, let's get started. We don't have much time." They started with the nearest cave, figuring the stalker would have chosen one close to the trail. They searched three caves, and Ian's heart pounded harder with each failure. The fourth cave revealed itself to them as a shadowed indentation that became a gaping hole under the cliffs.

"Let's hope this is the one," Ian prayed. Nicole's ragged breathing sounded in his ear, and he reached out for her hand. Together they took their first steps into the cave, praying against hope that they'd find Vanessa.

"Look." Nicole pointed.

They were just inside the entrance, and it was already getting too dark to see much. Ian squinted the direction that Nicole was pointing.

"I don't believe it. It's a flashlight." Ian stepped over to the natural outcrop on the cave wall that had formed into a shelf. He reached up, grabbed the flashlight, and turned it on. The beam was strong and lit up the cave enough for them to see.

"Ian, I think I heard something."

"Yeah, me too. I think it's water, you know, dripping from the top of the cave. Christ, I hope this is the right place. That would explain the flashlight." Ian didn't know if he was trying to convince himself, or trying to make it a reality by saying the words. It didn't matter, he and Nicole quickly and carefully made their way deeper into the subterranean cave, stumbling over rocks and slipping in the odd puddle of water dripping from above.

Ian's shoulders brushed against the walls, and his chest felt as if a weight was crushing inward. His breath came in short spurts and butterflies of panic fluttered in his stomach. What if there was nothing here? What if they were wasting valuable time?

"Ian, shine the light up ahead."

He did. The narrow passage funneled into a small cavern, and the light from the flashlight that had beamed so brightly in the small tunnel, suddenly became insufficient to cover the area. Frustrated, Ian ran the beam over the walls and around the oblong shaped cavern.

"It's beautiful." Nicole's voice dragged him from his self-recrimination.

She was right. Dim as it was, the flashlight revealed the beauty capable of blooming even in the darkest caverns of the underground. As the light swept over the roof and onto the floor, it highlighted an extraordinary vista.

Just then, a scuffling sound echoed from the back of the cavern causing Nicole to let out a small scream. Ian automatically gave her a reassuring hug and shined the light deeper into the cave where the sound had come from. Nothing. He slowly scanned the back cave wall with the flashlight, making sure to touch upon each crevice and indentation. His search was rewarded when the light touched upon a pale object lying awkwardly on the cold cavern floor.

"Vanessa," he whispered. Relief flooded him, quickly followed by cold fury as he realized her naked condition. With no thought except the safety of his daughter, he stumbled into the depths of the cave.

Chapter Twenty-Three

S omething wasn't right. Gary paused at the crest of the cliff, close to where the path opened to the lighthouse clearing. He listened for the ever-present singing of birds and the occasional crunch as some other animal moved through the underbrush. He heard nothing but the surging of the sea rolling into shore. The eerie silence bothered him, giving him pause as to whether his gurgling stomach was worth a trip into town. He should be fine though. No one knew what he looked like, and since he'd seen them asking questions at the local hotel yesterday, he doubted anyone had even thought of the caves as a hiding place.

Hesitantly, but driven by hunger, Gary continued. Not wanting anyone to see him, he avoided the lighthouse clearing and circled around making sure to stay in the forest cover. His moves were slow and deliberate as he turned over in his mind what he had planned for the afternoon. He would demand that the bitch deliver the diamonds to him in person—without her dog. He'd tell her to go to the lighthouse, and everyone would expect the exchange to happen there, but he would leave a note for her to go somewhere else. Since he'd cut the phone cord, she wouldn't be able to call anyone about a change in plans. He'd be waiting on the main trail to seize her, and while anyone following would continue on the main trail, he'd use his alternate route to get her to the caves. No one would be the wiser.

Then the fun would begin.

Just about to duck under a tree limb and step onto the path that led directly to town, a flash of light struck him out of the corner of his eye. He immediately froze into a low stance and swept his gaze over the surrounding area. The sun had reflected off something, and he wasn't moving until he knew what that something was. At first, there was nothing to see except the usual foliage, dirt, and rock, but then the flash blinded him again. This time he knew exactly where it came from. Shifting position, he focused his eyes to the forest just beyond the lighthouse and was able to make out the shape of a car hidden in the trees.

Shit! Shit! Shit!

It was the bitch's car. Why would she hide it in the trees? Something wasn't right, he felt it deep in his bones. He had to get back to the caves. He had to get back fast.

***

Nicole's heart thudded dully in her chest, and she thought she could almost hear the echo of it beat upon the cave walls. Ian's ravaged face was a pitiful sight in the dimness of the flashlight, but not nearly as pitiable as the sight of Vanessa lying naked and tied on the cold floor of the cave.

As soon as the light had touched upon Vanessa, Ian moved like a man possessed. He raced across the cave and knelt down to check for signs of life. Realizing that she was standing in a state of shock, Nicole quickly ran to Ian's side. When she saw Vanessa up close, she had to suppress the urge to throw up. The poor woman's face was bruised and swollen, her hands and feet bled from the severity of the ropes, and her body had taken on a hue of deathly pallor. Maybe it was just the reflection of the light making her look dead.

While Ian fumbled for a pulse, Nicole tore off her denim shirt to cover Vanessa and then began to rub her limbs vigorously. She wasn't waiting for Ian to stipulate whether Vanessa was dead or alive, for as far as Nicole concerned, Vanessa was alive. She had to be alive. Because if she were dead...Nicole couldn't bear to think about being responsible for her death.

Ian's hand shook as he pressed his fingers to Vanessa's

neck. He couldn't find a pulse, but Nicole kept rubbing. Was it her imagination or had she felt a quiver of limbs beneath her hands? Silently she prayed, and silently she vowed to do anything God asked, if only He let Vanessa live.

Ian's hoarse voice cracked in the ominous stillness of the underground cavern. "I feel a pulse. Oh, God, I think she's alive."

Just then, the ringing of Ian's cell phone jangled through the cave, making them both jump. Nicole's nerves, already stretched taut, strained to the point of breaking.

"Grab the phone in my back pocket," Ian instructed. "It's got to be Jacob and Josephine."

With shaking hands, Nicole was able to grab the phone, flip the top open, and answer with a feeble, "Hello?" She had to clear her throat and try again. "Hello." This time her voice was audible.

***

Josephine listened to Jacob's frantic voice.

"He didn't show up. Do you understand? The stalker never made it to the deli!"

Jacob hung up the deli phone. "Dad-blast. His phone kept crackling out. Now I know why I don't own one."

"Who answered the phone?"

"Nicole."

"Did she hear what you were saying at least?"

"I don't know. I just don't know."

"Did she say anything?"

"Just hello. I have no idea where they are, or if they've found Vanessa. Goddamn, I feel so helpless. That bastard hasn't shown up. In my book, that means he could show up at the cave any time."

Josephine's mind slammed into overdrive. Nicole and Ian were most likely in trouble, but she and Jacob had only a general idea of where they were. Suddenly a thought struck her.

"Jacob, let's go." She grabbed his arm and dragged him from the deli, explaining as they went. "Sumo. Sumo will find Nicole. He can find her faster than anyone."

"By Jesus, woman, now I know why I love you." Josephine's heart soared at the words, but there was no time for consideration, not when people she cared about were in danger. Quicker than either one of them had moved in a long time, Josephine and Jacob tore across the street and up the stairs of *Wishes*.

"Wait." Jacob stopped her just before she was about to open the apartment door. "We'll never keep up with him. He needs to be on a leash."

"Yes. Good point." Josephine thought for a moment and then remembered the binding she used to tie parcels she sent through the mail. Within no time, they'd cut a piece of rope and tied it through Sumo's collar. The dog wasn't used to such restriction, but he must have sensed their urgency because he sat and whined while Jacob tied the knot.

"Come on, Sumo, you need to find Nicole," Josephine coerced. "Nicole. Find Nicole."

The canine cocked his head and perked his ears at the familiar name. Whining and pulling on the rope, he led them down the stairs and onto the front walkway. Before they were able to set a course for the paths by the caves, a voice interrupted them.

"Hi, I came by earlier, but you were closed." Corporal Moody beckoned from the street.

"Damn, just what we don't need," Jacob cursed.

"Don't worry, we don't have time for him, and I'll make that perfectly clear." Josephine took a deep breath and turned to Corporal Moody. "Corporal, what can we do for you?"

"What do I want? I want to know what's going on. Nicole never came back to her room, and I've looked all over town for her."

Josephine struggled to come up with some lie that would get them away fast.

"Josie. We need to tell him. There's no time for anything else. Besides, he may be able to help."

Josephine nodded.

"Ian, Nicole, and Vanessa are in danger. Gary kidnapped Vanessa and wants the diamonds in exchange for her. We're pretty sure he's keeping her in one of the caves on the coast. Ian and Nicole went to look for her, but we think the stalker knows they're there. We think he was on his way to town, but he never showed up. We're setting Sumo on Nicole's scent, hoping he can lead us to them."

"Why didn't you tell me this sooner?"

"The stalker said he'd kill Vanessa if we told the police. Are you with us or not?" Jacob prodded.

"We should tell Inspector Patrick."

"No time. Either you're with us or not. But it sure would be good to have an officer of the law with us when we confront this guy."

Josephine prayed that Corporal Moody's desire to help would outweigh his fear of going against a superior officer. His features mirrored conflicting thoughts and emotions, but Josephine could have wept with joy when she saw the light of determination shine in his eyes.

"I won't ask how you know all this." He gave his sidearm a pat, and straightened his shoulders. "But I'm with you. Let's go."

Chapter Twenty-Four

Vanessa's body jerked, knocking Nicole backwards onto her butt. Scrambling to her knees, she crawled forward to help Ian untie the rope that bound Vanessa's hands and feet. Now that they knew she was alive, it was imperative to get her out of the cave and to the hospital for medical treatment.

Without words they untied her and wrapped her in Nicole's shirt, while Ian lifted her gently into his arms. He looked at his daughter's face with unshed tears shimmering in his eyes. So much love shone from Ian's face, and so much regret. Nicole placed her hand on his arm to get his attention.

"Ian, we need to go. Now."

"You're right." He shook his head in an attempt to pull his emotions under check, and then stumbled the direction they had come from.

Nicole had the flashlight and did her best to light the way so Ian wouldn't trip on a jutting rock or the uneven surface. It was awkward for Ian to get through the narrowest part of the passage with Vanessa in his arms. He moved slowly so as not to scratch or bang her needlessly. Finally, Nicole saw an oval of daylight just ahead and knew they were almost at the mouth of the cave.

When they broke into the warmth of the sun the relief was palpable, and Nicole sent a thankful prayer skyward. But she'd sent her prayer too soon. At the edge of the forest, making his way onto the rocks, was Gary. He hadn't seen them yet, but it would only be a matter of seconds.

Nicole looked at Ian and a battered Vanessa. Guilt sent the

hot flush of acid into her stomach. It was her fault they were in this situation, so she had to make things right.

Without thought, without regret, she sent one last longing look to Ian.

Even as she moved, she spoke what was in her heart. "I love you, Ian." Urgency gave speed to her flight as she ran over the rocks directly toward the stalker. Behind her, she heard Ian call out her name, but still she ran.

She knew the instant that Gary became aware of her. A bellow of anger tore across the shore, giving the waves a tumultuous contest of sound. Driven by her desire to keep Ian and Vanessa safe, aware of wearing nothing but a bra and pants, she ran forward. She came close enough to see the black fury of Gary's eyes pinned on her. Shivering under the intent of madness, she veered into the forest just out of his reach. Her reasoning was that he'd follow her and leave Ian and Vanessa free to find their way to safety.

At first, she didn't hear any sounds of pursuit, so she stopped, hoping against hope that her plan had worked. Then the faint sounds of someone crashing through the brush reached her, and she ran again. Terror mounted as whipcord-like branches thrashed her face and impeded her flight from the shadowy figure that chased her into the unknown. The mugginess of the summer day faded in the shade of the forest, and within the creeping shadows, Nicole could smell the scent of decomposing wood and decaying leaves.

She stopped for a breath, but the sound of pursuit ravaged her senses. Her ragged breath would give away her position, so she had to keep moving. Her legs ached, and her side felt as if someone had stuck a knife in and twisted. The figure that stalked her would do worse should he catch her.

The thick forest made it hard to run and her progress resembled a stumbling parody of awkwardness. Then, suddenly, she was in the clear. The forest broke open to the brightness of the afternoon sky and the pathway winding its way around the rocky cliff beckoned her like a ribbon of safety.

If she could make it to the lighthouse, she could lock herself in and use the phone to call for help. She ran for the beacon of safety that had guided so many ships ashore. But before she could reach her destination, Gary broke from the dense forest and grasped her arm in a steely grip of inhuman strength. In slow motion, she watched him raise his gun above his head and bring it down directly at her. Pain exploded in her head as she struggled to remain conscious. She fought a losing battle.

***

"Did you hear a scream?" Jacob peered into the forest trying to pinpoint the direction of the scream.

"Yes," Josephine and Corporal Moody both answered while a suddenly frantic Sumo strained and twisted at his leash in an attempt to gain freedom.

"Let him go." Jacob motioned toward Sumo. "Nicole might need him."

Josephine unknotted the rope. As soon as he had his freedom, Sumo leapt forward and streaked through the forest. Josephine knew that Rottweiler's had intense focus and a fierce bond of protection for their owners. Of course, they were only guessing it had been Nicole screaming, but if it had been, Sumo would give his life to save her, and the three of them would be following closely behind.

***

Ian gave no thought to the branches scratching his face, or the stitch of pain stabbing his side. His mind raced between cursing Nicole for putting her life in danger and pride for the woman he loved risking her life to save those she cared about. Damn, he hated leaving her, but he had no choice. Vanessa needed medical help.

He'd get to the car and use his cell phone to call for help, but he didn't know what to do from there. Should he leave Nicole to her own devices and take Vanessa to the hospital? Or should he settle Vanessa into the car and go looking for Nicole? A glance at Vanessa's face showed some color returning, and her breathing seemed to be deepening. Thank God.

His arms ached, and he stumbled over nothing. He wasn't as young as he used to be, and even though he was in great shape, the stress of the situation as well as the strain of carrying Vanessa uphill on rocky terrain, was wearing him down.

Please, let us be there soon.

For once, God answered his prayers almost instantly. Within no time, they came to the clearing close to the lighthouse.

The sight that met him sent ice racing through his veins. He almost dropped Vanessa on the spot, but recovered quickly enough to set her down gently. Choices no longer remained. Gary stood about twenty feet away with Nicole on the ground at his feet.

Fury shaped Gary's face into an ugly mask, and even from a distance, Ian felt the man's wrath. If evil walked the earth, it had appeared in Solitary Cove, and Nicole was its next victim. Ian's heart raced and his feet had a mind of their own as he tore across the rocks toward the man who had abused his daughter and now threatened Nicole.

Hardly aware of anything except the scene before him, he barely acknowledged the streak of black and tan that tore across the cliff top headed directly for Nicole and her attacker.

Sumo.

The stalker was in for a holy taste of hell now.

Ian felt a sordid sense of satisfaction and ran faster. Sounds of savagery reached him as Sumo ripped into the stalker. His primal self wished it could be him tearing into the flesh of the man and somewhere deep inside he became one with Sumo as the dog defended his master with all the loyalty and fierceness that was inherent within his breed.

Ian ran to the stalker who screamed as Sumo's teeth tore him. Just then, Ian saw the flash of a gun. Time and motion slowed as Gary raised the gun and aimed directly at Ian. A gunshot rang through the air and a resounding thud hit Ian's shoulder. Pain exploded throughout his entire body and blackness threatened to engulf him.

God, I've been shot.

His mind flashed regrets for a life not yet lived. His soul raged at the injustice. Knocked to his knees by the bullet, he wavered between consciousness and unconsciousness. But Vanessa and Nicole were in danger. He had no idea how he managed, but he stumbled to his feet and threw himself into the raging melee of man and dog. His fingers found Gary`s throat and he squeezed, while Sumo's growls tore through his consciousness.

The he blacked out.

He had no idea how long he was unconscious, but when awareness returned, it hurt to move. Ian lifted his hand to his shoulder, and it came away covered with blood. Just then, Jacob, Josephine, and Corporal Moody approached from the direction of the lighthouse.

Through a haze, Ian saw Sumo laying on the ground by Nicole. Corporal Moody pointed his gun at Gary, who lay torn and bloody. Ian realized he was still clutching the man's throat, so he let go and heard the man immediately began screaming that he was going to sue. Good luck.

Ian leaned over to see Nicole. Fire ignited in his shoulder, and pain throbbed its way through his limbs as he knelt by her side and spoke her name. Blood streamed from her forehead. Shit. Head wounds were notorious for being unpredictable. Nicole moaned at the same time as a warm tongue licked Ian's ear. Sumo whined, rested his paw on Ian's arm, and turned trusting, chocolate brown eyes toward him.

"I know, fella, I love her, too. We'll make sure she's okay. I promise."

Jacob and Josephine knelt by Nicole. "How is she? What can we do?"

"I don't know. I just don't know. And Vanessa." Ian choked. He had no idea what to do. Who to take care of. His own consciousness slipped precariously.

Corporal Moody was the only one calm enough to take action. He radioed for an ambulance and back up, ran to his cruiser parked on the other side of the lighthouse, and returned a minute later with a first aid kit in hand.

"I have to get Vanessa. Keep an eye on Nicole for me." Ian directed this to no one in particular, knowing Jacob, Josephine, and Sumo would take care of her. It just felt good to have others to share the burden. Limbs aching and shoulder on fire with pain, he ran over to Vanessa and gingerly took her into his arms. Carefully, he placed her on the ground beside Nicole and then sat back to wait for the ambulance.

He felt the others looking at him with pity in their gaze, but ignored them. He was too busy watching over the two women he loved. Half naked, each one looked worse than the other. Not usually religious, Ian prayed.

Chapter Twenty-Five

S ure, it was a trite thought, but Nicole felt as if a Mac Truck had run her over. She tried to move, but couldn't. She tried to remember what had happened, but couldn't. She tried to open her eyes and was barely able to accomplish even that small feat.

She moaned. At least she thought it had been her, the sound seemed to have come from the end of a long tunnel. Another sound came to her from the end of that same tunnel. A familiar sound. A comforting sound.

Then she remembered. In a blast of fear and pain, her memory rushed into her mind full force, and she gasped at the intensity. That same familiar, comforting sound came again, and this time she realized it was a voice. It was Ian's voice, and he was telling her to relax.

With half-open eyes, she turned her head the direction of the voice, but the pain that shot through her neck prevented her from moving.

"Nicole, don't try and move. You've got a bad concussion."

She couldn't move, so she tried to speak. "Thir...sty." Within a split second, Ian spooned some ice chips into her mouth, and she felt the awesome chill wend its way down her throat. Blessed relief.

With her parched throat partially relieved, her sense of awareness slowly returned. She managed another question. "Tell me." Ian squeezed her hand and leaned close enough for her to make out the features of his face.

"Don't worry. Vanessa's fine, and Gary is in custody. Actually, Vanessa is in the room next door, and she's been waiting for you to regain consciousness.

"How long?" Thank God Ian could understand her half sentences, because she didn't think she could form an entire one if her life depended on it.

"You've been unconscious for three days."

Three days. So much time gone. Lost. It seemed like only a moment ago that the stalker had smashed his gun onto her skull. From then on, things were murky. She remembered a horrible sound as she hit the ground. She should recognize the sound, but it flitted just beyond her grasp. She strained to the point of physical pain.

"Sumo saved your life. He saw the stalker knock you out and tore into the guy."

Sumo. Yes, that was what she'd heard. Growling, snapping, snarling, and the sound of flesh tearing. She shivered. There had been another sound. The sound of gunfire. Panic filled her. Josephine and Jacob were still unaccounted for. Reaching to the depths for strength to speak, she whispered, "Jacob...Josephine?"

"It's okay, sweetheart. They're fine. Sumo's fine, too. In fact, he's a hero. He saved your life. Relief poured into Nicole, giving her a wonderful drugged feeling, or maybe it was whatever was dripping from the bag attached to her arm. Licking her lips, she uttered one last question. "I heard...gunshot."

Ian frowned, but answered her by unbuttoning his shirt to reveal a display of multi-colored bruises seeping out from under a white bandage on his shoulder. She gasped.

"Ian."

He rubbed her arm gently and reassured. "It's okay. I'm fine. I don't remember much except when I passed out, I had my hands wrapped around the stalker's throat."

"You saved my life."

"I guess Sumo and I both did."

Ian's words receded into a tunnel, and Nicole drifted away. This time she slept a peaceful sleep rather than the dream-scattered state of unconsciousness she'd suffered before.

The next week passed in a haze of uncertain memories. Nicole didn't trust herself to tell dreams from reality, but eventually she regained her health, her strength, and her mind. Ian had left for the day to finish some filming on the movie. Earlier that week, he had wanted to quit and spend all day, every day with Nicole, but she'd garnered her strength together and demanded that he fulfill his obligation. She'd reasoned that she'd be asleep most of the time anyway, so he shouldn't waste time sitting by her bed when he should be doing his job. People were counting on him.

Reluctantly, he'd agreed. Today would probably be the last day of filming in Solitary Cove. Of course, they still had a lot to do back at the studio, but the on-location stuff was finished. Which meant that Ian had no reason to stay anymore.

Which meant he'd be leaving her.

Oh, hell, what had she expected? He was a famous actor who lived a life so far removed from hers that it was ridiculous. She'd at least attempt to retain her pride and say good-bye with dignity.

"Hi, sweetheart."

There was only one voice that sounded so mellow, yet strong—so deep, yet soft. Nicole smiled and turned to look at the man she loved. "Hi."

"Are you feeling up to some company?"

"Sure. Come on in."

"I didn't mean me."

Ian smiled and stood aside to reveal the company he'd been referring to. Sumo sat at his side, bright eyes shining and rear end wriggling in an attempt to remain calm.

"Sumo!" Nicole cried out and lifted her arms to welcome him. Not needing any more encouragement, Sumo ran into the room, jammed his front paws on the edge of the bed, and proceeded to lick Nicole's face. Weak but ecstatic to see him, she leaned forward to hug him.

"Hey, bud, it looks like Josephine is taking good care of you."

"Actually, he's staying with me, not Josephine."

"Oh, I'm sorry. Was Josephine not able to take him?"

"Don't be sorry, and yes she could have taken him in, but I thought it a good idea that he get used to being around me."

Butterflies did a fluttery dance in Nicole's stomach, but she wasn't jumping to any conclusions. "Oh? And why would you think that?"

Ian sauntered closer and sat on the edge of the bed. He scratched Sumo's ears and the traitorous animal reveled in the attention. Whining and whimpering, he cocked his head to give Ian a better angle to scratch. The brief glimmer of a smile touched Ian's lips and an ache rose in Nicole, trapping her breath in her chest.

She wanted this man. She loved this man.

The gaze of ice blue eyes touched her, but they weren't cold. Rather, they burned hot and intense. Ian reached out to brush a stray strand of hair from her cheek, and his touch sent heat racing through her.

"Come on, Nicole, you know how things are." Gentle and prodding, his voice prompted an answer from her.

"I know how I'd like things to be."

"Ah, a woman who knows her own mind."

Damn him, she was too weak to play games with him. She'd risked her life to save him and Vanessa, he owed her at least the benefit of a firm answer. Of course, it had been her fault they'd been in danger in the first place, but that didn't matter, she still deserved to know what he had in mind. Having lived in the shadow of danger and fear for so long, Nicole had come to realize the important things in life. Love was at the top of her list. And it was time to know where she stood in the scheme of things.

"Look, Ian, I know it's been a strange couple of weeks."

"You could say that."

"I did. Now please let me finish talking before I lose my nerve."

"Yes, dear."

Nicole frowned at his teasing use of an endearment. "The

thing is...well...what I need to know."

"Nicole, let me make things easier for you."

Ian leaned down and gently touched his lips to hers. Slowly, he prodded her lips open with his tongue. Heat raced to Nicole's groin, as his tongue explored the inside of her mouth and flicked across her lower lip before he pulled away from her. Left shaking and very excited, Nicole stared at the man who had claimed her for himself. No words needed to be spoken, the bond was understood.

"By the way, I bought the lighthouse."

"You what?" Nicole was stunned and could only lay in silence waiting for him to continue, which he did.

He took Nicole's hand and squeezed gently, his eyes full of love. "I was out there with Corporal Moody, you know, going over the crime scene. I looked out over the water, and a mist rose from the ocean and drifted toward the lighthouse. I could hear the waves rolling into shore and the distant sound of birds in the forest. I was mesmerized. And I know that you've made friends here—so have I for that matter. So I figured we'd need somewhere to stay when we came back to Solitary Cove. I won't be working all the time, you know. And that brings me to my next point. You're allowed visitors as of today, so you have a waiting room full of people waiting to see you."

Nicole was stunned. Ian made it sound as if they had a future together. "What exactly are you saying, Ian?"

"I said you've got visitors." He frowned. "Is your head bothering you, sweetheart?"

"No. That part was clear, the rest of it wasn't."

"Oh. I was kind of busy proposing to you."

"You were...what?"

"Proposing. Didn't I get around to that?"

"Not really."

With a devilish glint in his blue eyes, Ian took her hand in his. "I love you, will you marry me?"

Speechless, Nicole could only nod. Thanks to this man, she'd gotten rid of any guilt over Jeff's death, and she felt alive and loved for the first time in her life.

"I hoped you'd say yes."

Reaching under Sumo's neck, Ian fiddled with the dog's collar and finally grunted in satisfaction. Nicole worried for a moment that Ian had lost his mind.

"I had Sumo hold onto this for me." Extending his hand toward Nicole, Ian slowly opened his fist to reveal an exquisite diamond solitaire.

Nicole gasped and reached out to touch the ring. It was gorgeous. Carved in a gold pattern of delicate filigree, a diamond sparkled in the overhead fluorescent hospital lights. It didn't matter, the beauty of the ring and the sentiment given with it made up for the surroundings.

"Well?" Ian prompted.

"Oh, Ian, if you don't know my answer, then you're not half the man I gave you credit for." The smile that lit her face softened her words and gave an answer all on its own.

Before either of them could speak more, the door flew open and a familiar voice complained. "What's taking you so long? You've kept us waiting out here long enough. Did she say yes? Has she seen the ring?" Jacob shot out one question after another.

Nicole laughed and turned to greet her visitors: Josephine, Jacob, and Vanessa. They all looked great, even Vanessa, whose bruises had faded to a shade of their former glory.

"Of course she said yes. She'd be crazy to turn down a famous movie star. In fact, you're just in time." With those words, Ian took Nicole's hand in his and placed the ring on her finger.

Nicole cried tears of joy and relief. She was happy to be with the people she loved, and she was lucky to be alive. Today was a new beginning, not only the beginning of a life free from fear, but a new Nicole. A woman sure of herself and what she wanted out of life. She touched the ring reverently and looked at the man who had given it to her.

"You might be famous, but you're so much more than that, Ian. You're the man who saved not only your daughter, but me as well. I love you."

Her words brought tears to the eyes of everyone in the room, but she didn't care, she was busy being thoroughly and soundly kissed by Ian. An occurrence she planned to take advantage of over the years.

About The Author

Cathy Walker

Thanks so much for purchasing and reading my book. If you enjoyed it, won't you please take the time to leave a review. I would very much appreciate your time and effort. ABOUT ME An avid reader since childhood, I used to wake up early in the morning to read before going to school. The books that first fired my imagination were the Black Stallion books by Walter Farley. My daydreams leaned toward finding myself stranded on a desert island with a black stallion only I could ride. Those daydreams helped me make it through, what I considered, the drudgery of school. Who wouldn't rather be romping in the freedom of the outdoors taming a wild stallion? As I matured, so did my taste in books along with my daydreams. Escaping into the pages of a book captured my attention and pumped my senses like nothing else. Unfortunately, I was always of the mind that I could never actually write a book. You had to be a writer to do something like that. Eventually, I came to my senses. As my fortieth birthday approached, I decided to write a book. I had no idea how to write, what to write about, or even how to begin, but, imbued with Capricorn stubborness, I wrote anyway. Currently, I am living my lifelong dream on 50 acre farm in Ontario, Canada. This move to the country has proven to be time consuming, especially since a friend gave me two baby goats as a farm-warming gift. I have added goats to the herd, as well as a Welsh pony, mini horse, various dogs and cats.

Books By This Author

A Witch's Lament

A Witch's Legacy

Crystal Of Light

Sword Across Time

Find Me Online:

Facebook
https://www.facebook.com/cathywalker.author/
https://www.facebook.com/qualitybookcovers/

Website:
https://writesbooks.wix.com/cathywalker
https://www.cathyscovers.wix.com/books

Twitter:
https://twitter.com/merlinsmuse1

Manufactured by Amazon.ca
Bolton, ON